Edward Pusey, John Keble

The Church of England a Portion of Christs one Holy Catholic Church and a Means of Restoring visible Unity

SALZWASSER VERLAG

Edward Pusey, John Keble

The Church of England a Portion of Christs one Holy Catholic Church and a Means of Restoring visible Unity

Reprint of the original, first published in 1865.

1st Edition 2022 | ISBN: 978-3-75259-071-5

Verlag (Publisher): Salzwasser Verlag GmbH, Zeilweg 44, 60439 Frankfurt, Deutschland
Vertretungsberechtigt (Authorized to represent): E. Roepke, Zeilweg 44, 60439 Frankfurt, Deutschland
Druck (Print): Books on Demand GmbH, In de Tarpen 42, 22848 Norderstedt, Deutschland

THE CHURCH OF ENGLAND A PORTION OF CHRIST'S

ONE HOLY CATHOLIC CHURCH,

AND A MEANS OF RESTORING VISIBLE UNITY.

AN EIRENICON,

In a Letter

TO

THE AUTHOR OF "THE CHRISTIAN YEAR."

BY

E. B. PUSEY, D.D.

REGIUS PROFESSOR OF HEBREW, AND CANON

OF CHRIST CHURCH, OXFORD.

SOLD BY

LONDON, OXFORD, AND CAMBRIDGE.

1865.

CONTENTS.

POSTSCRIPT.

A

LETTER,

&c.

My dearest Friend,

You think that, Dr. Manning's last letter having been addressed to myself, it is desirable that I should in some way reply to it. It would cost me much, not to undertake any task which you might wish me to essay. You know how long it has been my wish to part with all controversy, and to consecrate the evening of my life to the unfolding of some of the deep truths of God's Holy Word, as God might enable me, by aid of those whom He has taught in times past. This employment, and practical duties which God has brought to me, were my ideal of the employments of the closing years of a laborious life. The inroad made upon the Gospel by unbelievers, or half-believers, compelled me in part to modify this my hope. Still, since there is a common foe, pressing alike upon all who believe in Jesus, I the more hoped, at least, to be freed from any necessity of controversy with any who hold the Catholic faith. The recent personal appeal of Dr. Manning to myself seems, as you and other friends think, to call for an exception to this too; yet, since "the night cometh when no man can work," I trust that I shall not be thought to shrink from duty, if, hereafter, I should maintain silence, in order to give myself to that which seems to me more especially my calling.

Ordinarily, it would be of very little moment what is said of any individual. Yet since, in this juncture of the conflict with unbelief, I have felt it my duty to seek for hearty co-operation with those who have often felt it their duty to oppose me, and Dr. Manning calls this "a drifting back from old moorings [1]," it seems to me a duty both to them and to those with whom I have more commonly acted, to explain that it is not.

Ever since I knew them (which was not in my earliest years) I have loved those who are called "Evangelicals." I loved them, because they loved our Lord. I loved them, for their zeal for souls. I often thought them narrow; yet I was often drawn to individuals among them more than to others who held truths in common with myself, which the Evangelicals did not hold, at least explicitly. I believed them to be "of the truth." I have

[1] Dr. Manning's Letter, p. 36.

ever believed and believe, that their faith was and is, on some points of doctrine, much truer than their words. I believed and believe, that they are often withheld from the clear and full sight of the truth by an inveterate prejudice, that that truth, as held by us, is united with error, or with indistinct acknowledgment of other truths which they themselves hold sacred. Whilst, then, I lived in society, I ever sought them out, both out of love for themselves, and because I believed that nothing (with God's help) so dispels untrue prejudice as personal intercourse, heart to heart, with those against whom that prejudice is entertained. I sought to point out to them our common basis of faith. I never met with any who held the Lutheran doctrine of justification, that "justifying faith is that whereby a person believes himself to be justified." To others, who were not Calvinists, I used to say, "I believe all which you believe; we only part, where you deny." I formed some lasting friendships with some among them who have finished their course, and with others who still remain. When occasion came, as in some of our struggles at Oxford, we acted together.

What, then, I ventured on one occasion to remark to Archdeacon Manning, was *not*, that he "used to *join with those* with whom I could not [2]," but that he joined them *in a way* at which I was

[2] Dr. Manning, p. 36.

surprised. In plain words, he remained a member of, I think, two religious societies, some of whose principles I thought that we both held to be faulty. I have united with the Evangelicals now, as I did before, whenever they would join with me in defence of our common faith; I have not united with them in any of those things which were not in accordance with my own principles. It was not any thing new, then, when, in high places, fundamental truths had been denied, I sought to unite with those, some of whom had often spoken against me, but against whom I had never spoken. It was the pent-up longing of years. I had long felt that common zeal for faith could alone bring together those who were opposed; I hoped that, through that common zeal and love, inveterate prejudices which hindered the reception of truth would be dispelled. This, however, was a bright vista which lay beyond. The immediate object was to resist unitedly an inroad upon our common faith. This I had done before, upon occasions less urgent.

But while, on the one hand, I profess plainly that love for the Evangelicals which I ever had, I may be, perhaps, the more bound to say, that, in no matter of faith, nor in my thankfulness to God for my faith, have I changed. This was understood on both sides. We united to oppose unbelief, holding, each, what each believed that God had taught him. And this, perhaps, may be an occasion to mention what relates to a very sacred season of my life, when, sixteen years ago, amid increasing fever and decreasing strength and apparent inefficiency of remedies, death seemed, day by day, nearer. Then, had it so pleased God that I should then die, I should have worded the confession of my faith in words like these: "I believe *explicitly* all which I know God to have revealed to His Church; and *implicitly* (implicitè) any thing, if He has revealed it, which I know not." In simple words, "I believe all which the Church believes." This is my habit of mind now. This I confess when I say to God, "I believe one Catholic and Apostolic Church."

It is somewhat hard that when I, who ought to know myself best, have denied that I have "shifted my ground," the statement that I have should be reiterated. It is sowing mutual mistrust. This, however, is but personal. The real point of Dr. Manning's letter is to assert the contradictory of the statement, "that the Church of England is in God's hands the great bulwark against infidelity in this land." This saying was not mine, but that of one of the deepest thinkers and observers in the Roman Communion. I see that I did not say this distinctly. My words were: "While[3] I know that a very earnest body of Roman Catholics rejoice in all the workings of God the Holy Ghost in the

[3] Legal force of the judgments of the Privy Council, pp. 3, 4.

Church of England (whatever they think of her), and are saddened by what weakens her who is, in God's Hands, the great bulwark against infidelity in this land, others seemed to be in an ecstasy of triumph at this victory of Satan." In this last category, I would say at once, that I did not include Cardinal Wiseman or Dr. Manning. They "wrote gravely [4]," as I said, although I certainly thought Dr. Manning's letter dry, hard, unsympathizing.. He seemed to me so intent on proving his point against the Church of England, for the sake of those whom he wished to detach from it, that all sorrow for the triumph of Satan was dried up. I said nothing of this. But I imagined that he identified the glory of God with the gaining fresh converts to the Roman Church; and so he seemed to me to forget, that each blow which he thought ought to help to detach us from the English communion, was destructive to souls and a dishonour to God.

The saying itself, that "the Church of England *is*, in God's hands, the great bulwark against infidelity in this land," relates plainly only to a present fact. It does not aver, that the Church of England is the best possible bulwark; but only, as a matter of fact, that it *is* at this moment in God's Providence a

[4] Ib. p. 5. My statement about Cardinal Wiseman and Dr. Manning, was, "they wrote gravely, yet both of them (it now appears) were mistaken (as I was myself also), as to the legal effects of that judgment."

real and chief bulwark against it. Of course, any Roman Catholic must think that the Roman Communion, if it were of the same extent in this land as the English Church is now, would be a much stronger bulwark. But this is not the question. The battle has to be fought now. Dr. Manning speaks of the evils resulting from "seventeen or eighteen thousand men [the English Clergy] educated with all the advantages of the English Schools and Universities, and distributed all over England, who maintain a perpetual protest, not only against the [Roman] Catholic Church, but against the belief that there is any divine voice immutably and infallibly guiding the Church at this hour in the declaration of the Christian revelation to mankind [5]." On this last hereafter. But then, these 18,000 clergy have, to say the least, the same advantages for *that*, which they are vowed to do, viz., to "banish and drive away all erroneous and strange doctrines contrary to God's Word," which Dr. Manning attributes to us for *that*, which we have no thought of doing, and which he must suppose us to do by virtue of our position, not by any word of most of us, since we are thinking of nothing less. Faith is, of course, the gift of God; but, whatever advantages our intellectual training can give to any of us for what we have no intention of doing, *that* it must with God's blessing give to us, for that end to

[5] Letter, p. 35.

which our lives are consecrated, the maintenance of God's truth, as far as in man lies, and the teaching it to the salvation of souls for whom Christ died. But the teaching of the Clergy is only a small portion of the efficacy of the Church in repelling unbelief. *They* act but as individuals, subordinate to the Church in which they are God's ministers; the Church is a whole. And since we are more acted upon by what we do, than by what we hear, the Church, by putting into the mouths of all her members the ancient Creeds and Prayers which embody the faith, is, yet more, a continual unchanging teacher of the truth which Christ revealed and delivered to her at the first. She, through our mothers whom God had taught by her, taught us our faith at our mother's knee; she, through her Prayers and Creeds, has taught us all our life long; and our faith which we professed and uttered became, by God's gift of faith, part of ourselves. Our bodies could be severed from our souls, but our faith could not, without our will, be severed from our hearts.

We, of course, believe, that God the Holy Ghost, the "One Spirit" who animates and informs the "One Body" of Christ, teaches truth in her in a way different from that in which He, the Author of all Faith and Grace, is present with all Truth, wherever it is taught, and accompanies it by His Grace.

As individuals, we, too, thankfully acknowledge that whoever teaches any true faith in Jesus is, so far, one of God's instruments against unbelief. Nay, such is the power of Divine faith, that every child, who has it, is such. "Out of the mouths of babes and sucklings Thou hast perfected praise." When our Lord came in His great humility, the faith of children rebuked the unbelief of the Scribes and Pharisees. The simple faith of a child now has power against unbelief, because it is the gift of God. The faith of dissenters, although often a very naked and fragmentary faith, must in its degree be a power of God against unbelief. I rather implied that there were other bulwarks against unbelief, when I spoke of the Church of England as "*the great* bulwark." But I think that Dr. Manning has overlooked the fact, that the dissenters among us are indebted for very much of their faith to the Church from which they dissent. The dissenters, in the main, correspond to the Protestant bodies abroad. When then one compares the general condition of the English dissenters with that of the like bodies abroad, the unbelief in Holland, the rationalism in Germany, the Socinianism of Geneva, the Arianism or Semi-Arianism prevalent among the French Calvinists, or the Universalism which is desolating the United States, and (with the exception of one body) the almost entire neglect of baptism there among those who are the descendants of the English dissenters,—one cannot but think that the degree of faith surviving among them here is very much owing, under the mercy of God, to the

English Church, which enfolds them all around, even while they are hostile to it.

My own duties have not brought me into contact with dissenters; so nothing which I say can have a personal character. But I have understood that many of the more devout among the older denominations have acknowledged, that now there is more "life" in the Church of England than among them. I fear that those bodies which have most admitted among them the character of political dissent, have lost, as bodies, much of the life which they originally carried with them from the Church, and which God the Holy Ghost has preserved in individuals among them. The body, which apparently has most life in it, is (according to the universal rule) that which last and very slowly parted from the Church, the Wesleyan.

Individual portents, such as those which Dr. Manning points to, Dr. Colenso and the writers in the Essays and Reviews, prove nothing as to a large system. Rather the temporary notoriousness which they gained shows the more their anomalousness. The attraction about them was, a curiosity to see what men in the position of Dr. Colenso (then a Bishop, although under no jurisdiction in England) and of the clerical writers of the Essays and Reviews would venture to say. The curiosity was an evidence to the unnaturalness and strangeness of the facts. People are curious, not about the indigenous productions of a country, but about exotics.

Any thing more superficial than Dr. Colenso's first volume I never saw: the authors of the Essays and Reviews paid the tribute to the faith of the Church and people, that they did not speak out, for the most part, the unbelief or misbelief which they suggested. They were mostly unsystematic, disjointed, unreasoning. Any one who should wish to see what grounds were alleged for their statements, would have to go to the rationalist works of Germany, or to the infidel or Socinian press in England. Not any intrinsic demerits on their parts above other writings of their class gained them this unenviable repute; but the miserable fact, that persons who had pledged themselves to the defence of the faith had become its assailants. Dr. Davidson's work on the Old Testament, gathered mostly from the German rationalist works against it, which he largely translated, although more systematic and argumentative, excited no surprise, because he did not belong to the Church of England. The anomaly of such books as Dr. Colenso's and the Essayists did surprise people in England. Pious minds among the Protestants in Germany (and, I have heard, in France also), who correspond to pious English dissenters, were surprised, not at the attacks, which among them are every-day things to which they were inured, but at the strong feeling which those attacks called forth. The union of 11,000 or 12,000 Clergy, on occasion of the judgment of the Judicial Committee, to restate the doctrines which had been impugned (representing, as they did, other thousands of the same faith, who, on different grounds, did not join in that protest), showed how little that misbelief had penetrated among the Clergy of England. Mr. Wilson, on his trial, when he affirmed the everlastingness of future punishment, and denied that he had taught more than what is a modification of the Roman doctrine of purgatory [6], bore witness to the faith of the Church, in that he shrank from denying before his judges the truth which, in the simple meaning of words, our formularies affirm and he had denied.

But Dr. Manning goes further. He not only denies that the Church of England is "in God's Hands the great bulwark against infidelity in this land," but he maintains the paradox, that it is "the cause and spring of the existence" of that unbelief; and this, (1) by its denials of truths which, he says, it has rejected; (2) by "detaching the truths which it has received from the divine voice of the Church;" (3) by "denying the perpetual and ever-present assistance of the Holy Spirit, whereby the Church, in every age, is not only preserved from error, but enabled to declare the truth."

Happy world, if infidelity were the product of one time or clime, or of one set of causes only! It is one form only of man's rebellion against God.

[6] See Legal force of Judgment, &c., pp. 9, 10.

Any one who knows but a little of this side of human nature, knows that tendencies to unbelief, as well as a capacity for faith, lie deep in man's heart; he knows too, what variety of causes, dispositions, circumstances, what want of balance of intellectual or moral qualities or culture, what neglects of grace or spiritual defects predispose men to forfeit the gift of faith. It would then plainly be unphilosophical and untrue to charge upon any special cause alone, a spiritual disease, which is part of man's unsubmission to his God. Unbelief may be a strange epidemic at particular times or among particular nations. Now, among us, every thing comes to the surface. But the same causes were in operation when Julian apostatised, or he who became St. Augustine fell, before his conversion, among the Manichees. The same spiritual defects hindered the conversion of philosophers, to whom the Cross of Christ or the resurrection of the flesh appeared foolishness, which now destroy the faith of half-believers. A very thoughtful writer in the Roman Communion has said, "I prefer the open infidelity of the nineteenth century to the hidden infidelity of the middle ages; for we know now what we have to meet." The English Reformation cannot have been the cause of the infidelity of the middle ages, or of that which our countrymen found on their first renewed intercourse with Italy. It was not the cause of the unbelief, which absorbed successively the young Italians who went up to the capital under the late *régime* in Naples. For the causes of that unbelief are well known. Nor did it originate the worship of the Goddess of Reason in the first French revolution, since Catholic bishops and priests apostatized. Since it did not occasion the apostacy of Renan, why should it be charged with the heathenism of Colenso? The middle classes in France, I have been told by well-informed French Catholics, are well nigh lost to the faith. I remember the time when processions in France and Catholic Germany were attended only by a few women and children. It is said that, when the Churches were reopened in Paris after the first revolution, there were only fifty communicants at Easter. There has been, blessed be God, a great restoration of faith there, as among ourselves also. It is sad to point out a common misery, the destroyer of souls here and there. Yet so much is clear, that it is wrong to charge upon the English Church a terrible evil, under which every other part of the Catholic Church has suffered. It is more to our purpose to consider those grounds which Dr. Manning alleges for his assertion.

(1) That it "[7] rejects *much* of Christian truth." What we believe, Dr. Manning states thus: "[7] The Church of England has also preserved other doctrines" (besides those of the existence of a super-

[7] Dr. Manning's letter, p. 22.

natural world, the revelation of Christianity, the inspiration of Holy Scripture) "*with more or less of exactness*, such as the doctrine of the Holy Trinity, the Incarnation, Baptism, and the like. I will not," he adds, "enter into the question as to what other doctrines are retained by it, because a few more or a few less would make little difference in the final estimate a Catholic would make of it[8]."

Fourteen years must have strangely dulled the memory of that faith which Dr. Manning had before he entered the Roman Church, and it is strange to contrast his niggard concessions with the large-hearted statements of Roman Catholics of other days. "We are not in most things," says Du Pin to Archbishop Wake, "so far removed from one another that we may not be mutually reconciled. And would that all Christians were one fold[9]!" "This union," said Dr. Doyle, "is not so difficult as appears to many. It is not difficult; for, in the discussions which were held, and the correspondence which occurred on this subject, as well that in which Archbishop Wake was engaged, as the others which were carried on between Bossuet and Leibnitz, it appears that the points of agreement between the Churches were numerous, those on which the parties hesitated few, and apparently not the most important. The effort which was then made was not attended with

[8] Letter, p. 20.

[9] Letter in App. to Mosheim, t. vi. p. 770.

success; but its failure was owing more to princes than priests; more to state-policy than a difference of belief[1]." We have been wont to dwell with pleasure on the amount of faith which we confess in common with the Roman Church. In the three Creeds we confess together the whole doctrine as to the Holy Trinity and the Incarnation of our Blessed Lord; not, "with more or less of exactness," but in the self-same words, the only words in which the Church has ever embodied it. We teach alike the one end of man, the resurrection of the dead, and of the flesh specifically, the judgment to come according to our works, and the life everlasting, or the everlasting fire. We have the self-same doctrine of original sin[2] and its transmission; the same prayer against "deadly sin;" the same belief in the "full, perfect, and sufficient Sacrifice, oblation, and satisfaction" made by our Dear Lord, "by His one oblation of Himself once

[1] Catholic Miscellany, 1824, p. 234, sqq., quoted by Palmer on the Church, ii. 232. The learned Rev. J. Berington said to me in my early youth, "there is not much difference between us" (the Churches).

[2] The Council of Trent says, "This concupiscence, which the Apostle sometimes calls 'sin,' the sacred synod declares that the Catholic Church never understood to be so called sin, as though it were in the regenerate *truly and properly sin*, but because it is *from* sin and inclines to sin." Conc. T. p. 29. The words of our Article, "that it hath *the nature of sin*," involve the statement that it is not "*truly* and *properly* sin," as the Roman denial, that it is not *properly* sin, implies that it hath something of the nature of sin about it.

offered for the sins of the whole world." We both alike acknowledge our own unworthiness, that His merits alone can stand between us and our sins; both alike believe in the efficacy of "His most precious Blood," wherewith He cleanseth us; both, in His perpetual Intercession for us at the Right Hand of God. We use the self-same prayers in Baptism, and thank God, in the same words, that He has been pleased to regenerate our children therein. We both confess "one Baptism for the remission of sins." After confession, the Church directs the self-same words to be used in absolving from sin. I believe that we have the same doctrine of grace and of justification [3]. There is not one statement in the elaborate chapters on Justification in the Council of Trent which any of us could fail of receiving; nor is there one of their anathemas on the subject, which in the least rejects any statement of the Church of England. As to all the heresies which distracted the early Church, whether in regard to the Person of our Lord or His kingdom, or the Person and Office of God the Holy Ghost (those of Arius and his followers, Macedonius, Nestorius, Eutyches, Marcellus), or again, the practical heresies in the West (of Nova-

[3] I endeavoured to point out many years ago, that if people, on different sides, dwelt on their real agreement instead of their differences in wording their belief as to justification, this would be the result. "Justification," Univ. Sermon. To show this, is the object of Le Blanc, Theses Theologicæ.

tian, Pelagius, Donatus), we reject alike the same errors.

Even on other points, in the spirit of that prayer in which we all unite, that God would "inspire continually the universal Church with the spirit of truth, unity, and concord," and that He would "grant that all they who confess" His "Holy Name may agree, in the truth of" His "holy word, and live in unity and godly love[4]," we used ever to be glad to point out (as those whom we reverenced had done before us) how much there was in common even where there was divergence.

ii. Dr. Manning says, "If it" (the Church of England) "sustains a belief in two sacraments, it formally propagates unbelief in the other five[5]." We have pointed out again and again, how the Church of England, while teaching (as the fathers often do) that Baptism and the Holy Eucharist have a special dignity, symbolized by the Water and the Blood which flowed from our Redeemer's side[6], is careful not to exclude other appointments of God from being in some way sacraments, as channels of grace, or (in the old definition of sacraments), "visible signs of an invisible grace." This is indeed inseparable from the idea of Confirmation, Orders, Absolution, Marriage.

[4] Prayer for the Church Militant.

[5] Letter, p. 33.

[6] See Scriptural Doctrine of Holy Baptism ("Tracts for the Times," No. 67), pp. 294—298.

Marriage is, we know, directly called a "Sacrament" in the Homilies[7]. Of "Ordination" it is said, that neither[8] be it *nor any other sacrament else*, *such* sacraments as Baptism and the Communion are. "Absolution," it says, "has the promise of forgiveness of sins." "Our Articles," I said long ago[9], "do not introduce words at random. It has then some meaning when our Articles say, they 'are not to be counted for *Sacraments of the Gospel*,' that they 'have not *like* nature of Sacraments;' or the Homilies, 'that in the *exact signification of a Sacrament* there be but two,' or that 'Absolution is *no such Sacrament* as Baptism and the Lord's Supper are,' or that 'neither it *nor any other Sacrament* else be *such* Sacraments as Baptism and the Communion are,' or that 'the ancient writers in giving the name not only to these five, but also to divers other ceremonies, did not mean to repute them as Sacraments *in the same signification* as the two;' or that 'S. Augustine, in the *exact meaning* of the word, makes mention expressly of two.' And with this coincides the definition of our Catechism, that there are 'two only, generally (*i. e.* universally) necessary to salvation,' the others so entitled not

[7] Sermon on Swearing, P. 1.

[8] On Common Prayer and Sacraments, p. 1.

[9] Letter to Dr. Jelf, 1841, pp. 34, 35. The statement had been made in substance in the Letter to the Bishop of Oxford, 1839. It was repeated in my letter to the Bishop of London, 1851, pp. 5—22.

being of universal obligation, but relating to certain conditions and circumstances of life only. Certainly persons, who denied these rites to be in any way Sacraments, (according to those larger definitions of S. Augustine, 'a sacred sign [10]' or 'a sign [1] applied to things of God,' or of the Schoolmen [2] 'a sign of a sacred thing,') would have said so at once, and not have so uniformly and guardedly said on each occasion, that they were not such, in the '*exact*' or 'the *same* signification,' the '*exact* meaning,' '*such*,' 'of the *like* nature;' nor, of one which they regarded as in no sense a Sacrament, would they have said 'neither *it*, nor any other Sacrament else.'"

Even as to Extreme Unction, it only objects to the later abuse before the Council of Trent, when it was customarily administered to those only, of whom there was a moral certainty that they could not recover; and, if they should recover, it was a question whether it should be again administered to them when they should again be sick. This is manifestly the meaning of the words, "the corrupt following of the Apostles," Art. XXV., viz. that the unction of the sick, which the Apostle's words implies was to be given with the view or hope of their recovering, was given when, but for some special

[10] De Civ. Dei, x. 33.

[1] De Doctr. Christ. iii. 6, quoted by Bp. Jewel, Answer to Hard., p. 82.

[2] P. Lombard, l. iv. dist. 1, ib.

interposition of God, they could not recover. The Council of Trent, too, we used to point out, not only makes a distinction between the dignity of the Sacraments which it acknowledges, but pronounces an Anathema on those who deny it.

iii. Dr. Manning proceeds. "If it" (the Church of England) "recognizes an undefined Presence of Christ in the Sacrament, it formally imposes on its people a disbelief in Transubstantiation and the Sacrifice of the Altar." Those before us have pointed out, how the Church of England taught, not an "undefined," but "a Real Objective Presence of Christ's Blessed Body and Blood." Take, *e. g.* the statement framed word by word on our Formularies, in a work [3] which received the sanction of two of our then Archbishops, to whom it was, with permission, inscribed, and which used to be recommended to Candidates for Holy Orders.

"Taking as her immutable foundation the words of Jesus Christ—'This is My Body—This is My Blood of the New Covenant, and, Whoso eateth My Flesh and drinketh My Blood, hath Eternal Life,' she believes that the Body or Flesh, and the Blood of Jesus Christ, the Creator and Redeemer of the world, both God and Man, united indivisibly in one Person, are verily and indeed given to, taken, eaten, and received by the faithful in the Lord's Supper, under the outward sign or form of Bread and

[3] Palmer on the Church, i. 526.

Wine, which is on this account the 'Partaking or Communion of the Body and Blood of Christ.' She believes, that the Eucharist is not the sign of an absent Body, and that those who partake of it receive not merely the figure, or shadow, or sign of Christ's Body, but the reality itself. And as Christ's Divine and Human Natures are inseparably united, so she believes that we receive in the Eucharist, not only the Flesh and Blood of Christ, but Christ Himself, both God and Man."

With regard to the term "Transubstantiation," there must be a real difference between the meaning which it had in the minds of the Schoolmen, and that which it must now have since the Catechism of the Council of Trent. For it is there taught with authority, that "the Eucharist has been called bread, because it has the appearance, and still *retains* the quality, *natural* to bread, of supporting and nourishing;" but the Schoolmen thought, that with the "change of substance" that power of nourishing ceased. Yet this being granted, I know not what can be included in our term "substance," which the English Church affirms to remain, which is not also included in the Roman term "accidents," which they also affirm to remain. Clearly the doctrine which the Church of England rejects under the term "Transubstantiation, or the change of the *substance* of bread and wine," is only one which "overthroweth the nature of a sacrament," in that the sign and the thing signified became the same. This was so, according to the doctrine of the Schoolmen, in which "substance" was equivalent to "matter." The meaning of the word "substance" being changed, the Roman doctrine must be so far changed too. Archbishop Plato, in the Greek Church, admits the term μετουσίωσις in a sense which, if proposed to it, the English Church must accept. "The Eastern and Greek-Russian Church admits the word 'Transubstantiation,' in Greek μετουσίωσις, *not that physical and carnal transubstantiation, but the sacramental and mystical*, and receives that word Transubstantiation in the same sense in which the oldest fathers of the Greek Church received the words μεταλλαγὴ, μετάθεσις, μεταστοιχείωσις[4]." A sacramental or a hyperphysical change no English churchman, who believes the Real Presence as his Church teaches, could hesitate to accept.

The doctrine of the Eucharistic sacrifice depends upon the doctrine of the real objective Presence. Where there is the Apostolic succession and a consecration in our Lord's words, there, it is held by Roman authorities too, is the Eucharistic sacrifice. The very strength of the expressions used of "the sacrifices of masses," that "they were blasphemous fables and dangerous deceits," the use of the plural, and the clause "in the which it was commonly said," show that what the Article speaks of is not

[4] In Dutens, Œuvres Mêlées, Part ii. p. 171, in Palmer, i. 211, 2.

"the sacrifice of the Mass[5]," but the habit (which, as one hears from time to time, still remains) of trusting to the purchase of Masses when dying, to the neglect of a holy life, or repentance, and the grace of God and His mercy in Christ Jesus, while in health. I have been obliged to speak negatively, in order to explain what it is which is denied. But the Church of England, acknowledging the belief of the fathers whose teaching we are required to follow[6], and the doctrine of the Councils, which

[5] The Council of Trent was obliged to enact that "the ordinary Bishops of each place should give diligent care and be bound to prohibit and remove all those things which have been brought in by avarice, idolatry (Eph. v. 5), or irreverence, which can scarcely be separated from impiety, or by superstition, the false imitatress of true piety. And to comprise much in few words, let them prohibit altogether, in regard to avarice, all bargaining of all sorts or pay, or whatever is given for celebrating masses, and those importuning and illiberal exactions rather than requests for alms, and all else of this sort, which are not far removed from the stain of simony or certainly from filthy lucre." Sess. xxii. de Sacrificio Missæ. The Council of Trent also desired, as we do, that, whenever the Holy Eucharist should be celebrated, there should be those who should communicate, in which case private masses would have ceased. "The holy synod would wish, that at each mass the faithful present would communicate not only by spiritual affusion, but also by sacramental reception of the Eucharist, that so they might have fuller benefit from this most holy sacrifice." Ib. c. 6.

[6] "They [preachers] shall in the first place be careful never to teach any thing from the pulpit to be religiously held and believed by the people, but what is agreeable to the doctrine of the Old and New Testament, and collected out of that very doctrine by the Catholic fathers and ancient Bishops." Con-

it recognizes as "received by all men," receives what they taught. One thing alone she is jealous of, that nothing should seem to overshadow, or interfere with, or supplement the meritoriousness of the One Sacrifice of our dear Lord upon the Cross. This is what she every where guards: "The offering of Christ once made is that perfect redemption, propitiation, and satisfaction, for all the sins of the world, original and actual, and there is none other satisfaction for sin but this alone. *Wherefore* the sacrifices of Masses, &c." Plainly then, by the force of the word *wherefore*, she rejects no sacrifice which does not interfere with this. In celebrating the Holy Eucharist she pleads to "God, Who, of" His "tender mercy, did give" His "only Son Jesus Christ to suffer death upon the Cross for our redemption, Who made there, by His one oblation of Himself once offered, a full, perfect, and sufficient sacrifice, oblation, and satisfaction for the sins of the whole world." But that sacrifice, once made, lives on in Heaven. There our Lord, who shall come down to judge, as He went into Heaven, still bears the marks of the wounds which for us and our salvation He received, effulgent with the glory of His Godhead, irradiant with His Divine love. There He pleads that all-Atoning Sacrifice; there, for these 1800 years, has He lived to make intercession for us, generation after

vocation of A.D. 1571 (the same Convocation which enforced subscription to the Articles).

generation, yea, for each one of our sinful race. But since His perpetual intercession for us (which is an article of faith contained in plainest words of Holy Scripture) does not interfere with that One Atonement made upon the Cross, neither does any pleading of that One Meritorious Sacrifice which was finished there, in that to the *Merits* of that One Oblation our dear Lord Himself adds nothing. It sufficed for the sins of the whole world. That One Sacrifice we plead in every "through Jesus Christ our Lord," with which we end each prayer. Our Lord, as we confess to God, "did institute, and in His Holy Gospel command us to continue, a perpetual memory of that His precious Death until His Coming again," that we might plead to the Father that same Sacrifice. In the Holy Eucharist we do in act what in our prayers we do in words. I am persuaded that, on this point, the two Churches might be reconciled by explanation of the terms used. The Council of Trent, in laying down the doctrine of the sacrifice of the Mass, claims nothing for the Holy Eucharist but an *application* of the One meritorious sacrifice of the Cross. An *application* of that sacrifice the Church of England believes also. Many years have flowed away since we have taught this, and have noticed[7] how the words, "sacrifice," "proper," or "propitiatory sacrifice," have been alternately accepted or rejected, according as they

[7] Tracts for the Times, No. 81, p. 52.

were supposed to mean that the Eucharistic sacrifice acquired something propitiatory *in itself*, or only *applied* what was merited once and for ever by the One sacrifice of our Lord upon the Cross. "If you say," said even the Lutheran Pfaff[8], "that the Eucharist *applies* to the faithful the propitiation made by the sacrifice on the Cross, *no Protestant will dispute this.* But if you believe that the devotion of the Eucharist *acquires and obtains* propitiation, you may be saying what is perhaps at variance from the opinion of the Roman Church. For the Council of Trent[9] says that, 'our Lord, in order that He might leave to His Church a visible sacrifice, whereby that bloody Sacrifice, which was to be once accomplished on the Cross, might be *represented*, and its *memory* abide to the end of the world, and its *salutary efficacy be applied* to the remission of our daily sins, declaring Himself a Priest for ever after the order of Melchizedek, offered to God the Father His Body and Blood under the forms of bread and wine[1].'"

It is an Ultra-montanist Bishop, a Penitentiary of Pope John XXII., who, in the 14th century, in his work "On the moaning of the Church," said, "Our Church is full and over-full of altars, masses,

[8] Diss. de Oblat. Euch. Irenæi Fragm. Anecdot. subj., p. 211, quoted ibid.

[9] Sess. 22, c. 4.

[1] See Homilies, end of Book i., as vindicated in Pusey's "The Real Presence the Doctrine of the English Church."

and sacrifices, and therewith is, in the sacrifices, full of homicides, sacrileges, uncleannesses, and simonies and other wickednesses, excommunications and irregularities to the very utmost.—For at this day so many masses are said for gain, or custom, or complaisance, or to cover wickednesses, or for their own justification, that both among priests and people the holy Body of the Lord is now held cheap.—Whence also S. Francis willed that the brothers every where should be content with one mass, foreseeing that the brothers would wish to justify themselves by masses, and reduce them to a matter of gain as we see done at this day. And now through custom or rather corruption it has indurated, that a mass, priced at three or four denars or one shilling, is bought and sold by a blind people and by wicked simoniacal priests [2]."

This is but the echo of a part of what was said over and over again twenty-six years ago; and our dear friend's tract [3] has done good and lasting service, by breaking off a mass of unauthorized traditional glosses, which had encrusted over the Thirty-nine Articles. The interpretation which he then put forth, and which in him was blamed, was at the time vindicated by others without blame [4]. The

[2] Alvarus Pelagius de Planctu Eccl. ii. 5, quoted by Gieseler, K. G. ii. 36.

[3] Tracts for the Times, No. 90.

[4] No blame was attached either to my own vindication of the principles of Tract 90, or to that of the Rev. W. B.

blame was occasioned by two circumstances, owing to which Tract 90 was thought to intend to admit much more than our friend meant. 1) There was, in regard to Art. XXII., a purposed vagueness in the first edition, occasioned by his own diffidence in that he did not wish to suggest how much of any practice, disused but not forbidden by the Church of England, might be resumed by individuals in her. 2) It was misinterpreted in an extreme Roman sense by Mr. Ward. But the *principle* of Tract 90, viz. that we are not to bring into the Articles, out of any popular system, any meanings which are not contained in their words, rightly and accurately understood, was not and could not be condemned. Sound teaching has been condemned, not when it was put forth distinctly, but while there was any indefiniteness about it. Dr. Manning alludes to the censure of our friend, Bishop Forbes, by the Scotch Bishops. But when he explained himself elaborately in his defence, he was censured no more. The doctrines which he taught have been vindicated in the Church of Scotland, with the whole breadth and depth of Patristic teaching [5], and the paper, which censured his teaching before he was heard, is admitted to be only the private opinion of those who signed it.

Heathcote. I vindicated it in my letter to Dr. Jelf, as the natural grammatical interpretation of the Articles; Mr. Heathcote, as their only admissible interpretation.

[5] Theological Defence for the Bp. of Brechin, &c., 1860.

iv. Dr. Manning says, "The Church of England, in the Articles, affirms, that all Churches have erred, that General Councils may err." In saying that "General Councils *may* err," she affirms less than Bellarmine, and indeed all Roman Divines, who affirm that General Councils *have* erred. For they speak of "General Councils which have been disapproved," and of "General Councils which have been partly approved, partly disapproved." The Gallican Church held, as our Homilies also imply, that reception by the Church constitutes the true validity of a General Council. The language of the Homilies[6], "those six Councils *which were allowed and received* of all men," agrees with that of Bossuet, "*that* is a lawful Council, with which, while acting as Œcumenical, the whole Church communicates, and, the matter being dijudicated, *holds it to be adhered to*, so that the authority of the Council rests on the authority *and consent* of the universal Church, nay, is the very authority of the Catholic Church[7]."

But then Dr. Manning gathers up Article XIX. into the formula "All Churches have erred." True, in one sense; there has been error every where. Satan has sown his seed every where. But not all

In like way I preached in 1853, much more definitely and distinctly, the self-same doctrine of the Real Objective Presence, which was implied in my practical sermon of 1843 (which was condemned for reasons never published), and no one objected to it.

[6] Homily against Peril of Idolatry, p. 2.

[7] Projet de Réunion, iv. 3. Œuvres, T. xxv. p. 455.

at once, nor collectively, nor in any formal decision, so that the whole Church should agree in sanctioning what is untrue, which seems to be contrary to our Lord's promise, "The gates of hell shall not prevail against her." The Article says nothing about formal errors or decrees. This Article was a puzzle to me when young. Having received the then traditional interpretation, that the Article meant certain errors contained in decrees of the Church of Rome, I inquired what were the erroneous decrees of "the Churches of Jerusalem, Alexandria, and Antioch," in the corresponding clause. I could obtain no information, and thought it was my own ignorance. The two clauses, being put antithetically, must correspond. "*Since*," I argued, "they were decrees in the one case, they must have been decrees in the other." When upon fuller information I found that there were no canons of "Jerusalem, Alexandria, and Antioch," which were intended, then it followed, on the same principle of the correspondence of the two clauses, that neither were canons of the Church of Rome spoken of. The Article, moreover, does not say that "the Church of Rome *is* in error" in the present, but, "*hath* erred," in time past, just as it says of the other Patriarchates, that they "*have* erred," *i. e.* in time past. But whether its object is to state that corruptions had crept in in the Roman Church also, as a ground of the need of a Reformation, or whether it was meant as a protest against the infallibility of that Church by itself, in neither case does it militate against the inerrancy of the whole Church collectively. The fact that practical corruptions had crept in, was virtually owned by the Roman Church too, by the reforms which it instituted.

But neither is "Papal Infallibility" an article of faith any where. The Eastern Church, in its whole length and breadth, agrees, of course, with us. But in the West, too, the Gallican Church, also, which holds the consent of the Universal Church to be essential to infallibility, could not hold the infallibility of the Pope, by himself, without such an Œcumenical Council. You remember, how Bossuet [8] not only adduces instances in which questions remained open after the Bishop of Rome had expressed his decided opinion, (as the question of rebaptizing heretics was settled by the Council of Arles [9], or that of the keeping of Easter by the Council of Nice [1],) or how questions were decided by the joint authority of a Bishop of Rome and another Patriarch, (as when the Origenists were condemned, first by Theophilus, and, through his influence, by Anastasius [2],) such judgment being accepted by the universal Church; or how the judgment of the

[8] Defensio Declarat. Conv. Cleri Gall. 1682, L. 9. Œuvres, T. 33.

[9] The Council of Arles is intended by S. Augustine under the term "plenary universal Council." See Pusey's "Councils of the Church," &c., p. 98.

[1] Ib. p. 108.

[2] Bossuet, l. c. c. 12.

Bishop of Rome was confirmed by a subsequent Council; or appeal from him was, in principle, allowed by S. Augustine [3],—and not only this, but you will recollect how Bossuet even presses the case, in which Popes pronounced wrongly in matters of faith too. He urges the terrible and utter fall of Liberius (who not only subscribed a heretical creed and condemned S. Athanasius, but owned all the worst Arians, whence S. Hilary pronounced Anathema on him [4]), or how Zosimus, himself orthodox, approved the Pelagian confession of Cœlestius [5]; or Hormisdas, without enunciating wrong doctrine, yet, when appealed to in common with other Bishops, censured those who taught the right faith, as was afterwards owned by all [6].

He insisted also on the case of Honorius, who was anathematized by the sixth General Council, in that, when formally consulted by three Patriarchs, he approved of the heretical letter of Sergius, and condemned the orthodox letter of Sophronius, and the true doctrine equally with the false [7]. Bossuet showed

[3] "Suppose we think all those Bishops who judged at Rome were not good judges, there yet remained a plenary Council of the Universal Church, in which the cause might have been tried with the judges themselves, so that if they had judged amiss, their sentence might have been annulled." S. Aug. Ep. 43, ad Glor., &c., c. 7, n. 19, in Bossuet, c. 10.

[4] Pusey's "Councils," &c., pp. 169—172.

[5] Bossuet, c. 30.

[6] Ib. c. 16—18.

[7] Bossuet, Gall. Orthod. Præv. Diss. c. 54—57. Œuvres, T. 31, pp. 123—128. Def. Decl. Cler. Gall. L. 7, c. 21—23. T. 32, pp. 485—497.

too how Gregory II. and Stephen II., and Celestine III., formally gave wrong responses on questions touching marriage, and sanctioned what was in fact adultery[8]; how Stephen II. and Nicolas I. gave wrong answers as to the Sacrament of Baptism—Stephen as to its form, Nicolas as to its words[9]. In the long Franciscan controversy about poverty, Bossuet shows[1] that Nicolas III. praised that, as conformable to the example of Our Lord, which John XXII. subsequently declared it to be erroneous and heretical to ascribe to Him; and that he alleged that Our Lord did *that*, taking on Himself the "person of the weak," which was just and right. Lastly, John XXII. preached *that* publicly, and caused it (it is thought) to be preached at Paris, and defended it to the French king; the contrary of which, he, when convinced by the French Theologians sent to him, confessed, "together with the Catholic Church," to be true[2].

Bossuet[3] himself held the distinction between "the see" and "him who sat thereon," maintaining that what Roman Bishops "taught, believed, declared, was not as yet (the teaching, belief, declaration) of the Roman Church and of the Apostolic See, until, being promulgated by the Roman Pontiff, and *received by the whole Church*, it obtained; and that this was the Roman faith, the faith of

[8] Boss. Def. Decl. L. 9, c. 37. 40.

[9] Ib. c. 37.

[1] Ib. c. 41—45.

[2] Ib. c. 46.

[3] Ib. fin.

Peter, and of the Apostolic See, which could not fail." It is apparent that Bossuet and our Articles are, in this, speaking of different things, since Bossuet affirms *that* only to be *de fide*, which is *received* and sanctioned *by the whole Church*, our Article speaks of that which is *not* so received, since it compares the Roman Church with the Churches of Jerusalem, Alexandria, Antioch, as distinct from them. But the Church of England, equally with Bossuet, maintains *that* which has been received by the whole Church to be certainly true.

v. And this is, in fact, an answer to Dr. Manning's statement, that "the Church of England weakens the hold of the truths which it teaches, by detaching them from the Divine voice of the Church." The statement in the Articles, "The Church hath authority in controversies of faith," in itself implies a Divine authority; for none but a Divine authority can have any power to decide in matters of faith. It also implies a necessary preservation of the Church, as a whole, from error, (according to our Lord's true promise, "The gates of hell shall not prevail against her," "Lo, I am with you alway, even to the end of the world,") because it would be sinful to say, that the Church has authority to declare what is untrue. The Athanasian Creed, of course, implies the same. "Whosoever will be saved, before all things, it is necessary that he hold the Catholic faith." "We are forbidden by the Catholic religion to say." "This is the Catholic faith, which, except a man believe faithfully, he cannot be saved." For the "Catholic faith" can plainly mean nothing else than the faith held by the Catholic Church, which in our creeds we equally confess. It is a body of faith set before us on authority; confessed by us now, as it was centuries ago; immutable; which we own that they who have received would incur the loss of their souls by wilfully casting it away, and, in it, rejecting God Who gave it. There is no room left for inquiry here. And so again, when, in the exhortation to godparents in the Baptismal Service, they are bidden to provide that "the child may learn the Creed, the Lord's Prayer, and the Ten Commandments, in the vulgar tongue, and all other things which *a Christian ought* to know *and believe* to his soul's health," the Church of England plainly teaches, that there is a body of faith, beyond the Apostles' Creed, which to "know and believe" is essential to the well-being of all Christians. When asserting also the sufficiency of the Holy Scriptures for salvation, it defines on the one side the power of the Church, but it recognizes the power which it defines. "Holy Scripture containeth all things necessary to salvation, so that whatsoever is *not* read therein, *nor* may be proved thereby, *is not to be required* of any man, *that it should be believed* as an article of the faith, or be thought requisite or necessary to salvation." The Church of England would not have said, that certain things are "*not* to be required of any man that they should be believed," unless it held that other things, which *are* read in Holy Scripture, and which *may* be proved thereby, *may be* so *required.* So that the Article which sets forth the sufficiency of Holy Scripture, agrees with that which declares, that "the Church hath authority in matters of faith." It implies the authority of the Church, while it lays down certain limits to it.

Nor is this limitation other than what the old Catholic fathers, to whom in the homilies she so often appeals, have from the first so often and emphatically said. There was no contrast between Tradition and Holy Scripture. "We willingly acknowledge," says Bp. Usher too, "that the word of God, which by some of the Apostles was set down in writing, was both by themselves and others of their fellow-labourers delivered by word of mouth; and that the Church in succeeding ages was bound, not only to preserve those Sacred Writings committed to her trust, but also to deliver unto her children *viva voce* the form of wholesome words contained therein. Traditions, therefore, of this nature come not within the compass of our controversy, the question being *de ipsa doctrina tradita*, not *de tradendi modo*, 'touching the substance of the doctrine delivered, not of the manner of delivering it.' Again, it must be remembered, that here we speak of the doctrine delivered, as 'the Word of God,' that is, of points of religion revealed unto the Prophets and Apostles, for the perpetual information of God's people; not of rites and ceremonies and other ordinances, which are left to the disposition of the Church, and consequently be not of Divine, but of positive and human right. Traditions, therefore, of this kind likewise are not properly brought within the circuit of this question [4]."

The authority of the Church was given to her by her Divine Lord within certain limits. "Teach them," He said, "whatever I command you." All must admit then, that she could not command any thing which should be really contrary to Holy Scripture. Nor must she contradict herself. The Fathers of the later General Councils began their office by expressing their assent to the earlier, and considered their own work as only expanding what was contained in the earlier, with a view to meet the new heresy which had emerged. So neither is it any undue limitation of the authority of the Church to lay down another limit, that the Church may not require "as necessary to salvation" what is not read in Holy Scripture, or may be proved by it. This only implies the historical fact, that the same body of saving truths which the Apostles first preached orally, they afterwards, under the inspiration of God the Holy Ghost, wrote in Holy Scripture, God ordering in His Providence that, in the unsystematic teaching of

[4] Letter to a Jesuit, c. i. pp. 31, 32.

Holy Scripture, all should be embodied which is essential to establish the faith. This is said over and over again by the Fathers [5]. This limitation of the power of the Church does not set individuals free to criticize, on their private judgments, what the whole Church has decided. It is an axiom, "God cannot contradict Himself;" yet this does not set Rationalists free to deny any truth in Holy Scripture, because, in their private misjudgments, they think it at variance with some other favourite truth. And yet nothing is more common. "How apt are we," says Bp. Hall [6], "if Thou dost never so little vary from our apprehensions, to misknow Thee, and to wrong ourselves by our misopinions!" "God is love;" but we may not argue thence, that He did not create Hell. Rather, Hell itself is a portion of His love to those who *will* be brought to love Him. None will be shut out from the love of God, who do not formally reject God. But the Day of Judgment will alone reveal how many millions will love Him for ever, who would never have loved Him, unless the fear of Hell had first scared them to seek Him, and so to know Him and to love Him. Nay, since fear is here almost inseparable from love, it alone will declare how many exalted spirits there will have been quickened in their higher degrees of love by the awe lest they should endlessly lose Him. The truth

[5] See Note A. at the end.
[6] Cont., The Resurrection.

does not justify its abuse, "nor does the abuse take away the use." As the truth, "God cannot contradict Himself," does not set men free to criticize any portion of His revelation, so neither does the truth, "His Church may not lay down as necessary to salvation what God has not revealed in His Word," set men free to criticize what He has taught His whole Church to declare and to receive as saving truth, any more than that other maxim (which also limits the power of the Church, but which all receive), "His Church may not contradict His Word."

The statement that the three Creeds "ought thoroughly to be received and believed; for they may be proved by most certain warrants of Holy Scripture," is, in fact, only an application of that principle. The Athanasian Creed, indeed, was received tacitly, not formally, by the Church, embodying, as it does, the faith authoritatively set forth in the four first General Councils. But the General Councils themselves acknowledge the principle. The words, "according to the Scriptures," in the Nicene Creed, involve it. The Council of Ephesus says, "[7] The Holy Synod approved the letter written to him (Nestorius) by the most holy Bishop of Alexandria, Cyril, as written rightly and unexceptionably, and in no wise unharmonizing with the inspired Scriptures, or with the faith set

[7] Conc. T. iii. p. 1190, ed. Col.

forth at Nice." The Council of Chalcedon [8] "ratifies the doctrine on the Substance of the Holy Spirit delivered by the 150 holy Fathers met at Constantinople; which they made known to all, not as if they added any thing which was deficient in that before them, but making clear *by testimonies of Scripture* their thought of the Holy Spirit against those who essayed to annul His dominion." S. Athanasius mentions this, as a principle of the fathers at Nicæa, in answer to the Arians who tried to shake the Creed of Nicæa. "[9] Vainly do they (the Arians) run about with the pretext that they have demanded councils for the faith's sake. *For Divine Scripture is sufficient above all things.* But if a council be needed on the matter, there are the proceedings of the Fathers. For the Nicene Bishops did not neglect this matter, but stated the doctrine so exactly, that persons reading their words honestly, cannot but be reminded by them of the religion towards Christ *announced in Divine Scripture.*" "If [1] the expressions are not in so many words in the Scriptures, yet, as we said before, they contain the sense of the Scriptures, and, expressing it, they convey it to those who have their hearing unimpaired for religious doctrine." So that Constantine expressed a truth

[8] Ib. T. iv. p. 1458.

[9] Conc. Arim. et Seleuc. n. 6, in S. Ath. ag. Arians, T. i. p. 81, Oxf. Tr.

[1] Nic. Def. § 21. Ib. pp. 36, 37.

which he had been taught, when he exhorted the assembled Fathers to unity[2], "having the written teaching of the All-Holy Spirit. For the books of the Gospels and Apostles, and the oracles of the ancient Prophets instruct us clearly what we ought to think of the Divinity." S. Leo expressed his surprise that "some calumniators spoke of his letter, which was approved by the whole world" (being received by the Council of Chalcedon), "as obscure, since its doctrine was so plain and solid as to admit of *no novelty*. either in substance or language, *because whatever* he *had written* is shown to have been taken from the teaching of Apostles and Gospels[3]." S. Leo in the Epistle itself[4] ascribes the heresy of Eutyches to his ignorance of Holy Scripture; his own wonderful statement of doctrine is full of it.

vi. Lastly, Dr. Manning says, "If the Church of England teaches that there is a Church upon earth, it formally denies *a*) its indissoluble unity, *b*) its visible Head, and *c*) its perpetual Divine voice."

vi. *a*. How the Church of England can be said "*formally* to deny the indissoluble unity of the Church," I know not, seeing that we cannot approach the Holy Communion without confessing, "I believe *one* Ca-

[2] In Theod. H. E. i. 7.

[3] Ep. 152, ad Julian. "Which the consonant patterns of our forefathers attest to agree in all things with the doctrine of the Apostles." Ep. 131 ad Julian.

[4] Ep. 28, ad Flavian. n. 1.

tholic and Apostolic Church." In our Litany, we pray for "the Holy Church Universal," and not for our Bishops only, but for "*all* Bishops," all, accordingly, throughout the whole world, east and west. In our Ember Weeks, we pray "Our Heavenly Father, Who hast purchased to Thyself an Universal Church by the precious Blood of Thy Dear Son, mercifully look upon the same, and at this time so guide and govern the minds of Thy servants, the Bishops and Pastors of Thy flock." We pray accordingly for God's special guidance of the Bishops of the Universal Church. At Holy Communion we pray God to "inspire continually the Universal Church with the spirit of truth, unity, and concord," and for "all Bishops," not our own only. Certainly, since prayer is the voice of the soul to God, we express not our inmost belief only, but a loving belief, that the Church is one.

How it is one, the Church nowhere defines; but the faith is kept alive by prayer more than by definitions. Yet, whatever duties may follow upon the Unity of the Church, it is plain that no harmony of men's wills can constitute a supernatural and Divine Unity.

Unity, in part, is the direct gift of God; in part, it is the fruit of that gift in the mutual love of the members of the Church. In part, it is a spiritual oneness wrought by God the Holy Ghost; in part, it is a grace, to be exercised by man, a consequence and fruit of that gift. In one way, it is organic unity derived from Christ, and binding all to Christ, descending from the Head to the Body, and uniting the Body to the Head; in another, it consists in acts of love from the members one to another. Christ our Lord, God and Man, binds us to Him by the indwelling of His Spirit, by the gift of His Sacraments, administered by those to whom He gave the commission so to do, by the right faith in Himself. We are bound to one another, in that we are members of Him, and by the love which He sheds abroad in our hearts through the Spirit which He giveth us, and by common acts of worship and intercommunion.

Of these, the highest and chief is that which binds us to Christ Himself. Our highest union with one another is an organic union with one another through union with Him. It is not chiefly an union of will, or of mind, or of love, although these ought to be the fruits of it in its most perfect state, but an union through His indwelling Spirit. It is an union, in a degree, corresponding with the union of the Father and the Son. "As Thou, Father, art in Me, and I in Thee, that they also may be one in Us." It was the perverseness of the Arians to say, that the oneness of the Father and the Son was no other than that of Their creatures with Them, that either we too are of the Father's own substance, or the Son is not so. The words do not express identity, nor equality [5]. Else it

[5] S. Ath. c. Arian. iii. 22, p. 431, Oxf. Tr.

might be said, that "to be perfect as the Father is perfect," implied that the creature would become such as the Creator; or, that to be "harmless as doves," implies that we should have the harmlessness of irrational animals, not that which is inwrought through the Holy Spirit of God. The words do express a certain relation and analogy, an actual, real oneness, not in ourselves, but with God. As we are called "sons by adoption and grace," as being members of the Son, and are even called "gods," says S. Athanasius, through the indwelling of God the Holy Ghost; so we become one in Them, in that the Father is in the Son, and the Son cometh to be in us. "Since Thou," our Lord saith (it is S. Athanasius's paraphrase of His words), "art in Me, because I am Thy Word, and I in them, because of the body, and for Thee the salvation of man is perfected in Me, according to its perfection, I ask that they too may become perfect, having oneness *with* It, and having become one *in* It, that all, carried as it were by Me, may become one body and one Spirit, and may grow up into a perfect man." This oneness, then, is an actual mystical oneness, inwrought by Christ our Head, uniting the whole Church together in one with Himself in His Body; an actual oneness produced by grace, corresponding to the Oneness of the Father and the Son by nature. S. Cyril points out more distinctly the way of this union: 1st, with our nature, through the Incarnation, and then, with us, through

His indwelling, by the Sacrament of His Body and Blood, and by His Spirit. S. Cyril speaks first of imitation, next of indwelling. "Above," he says[6], "we have said, that the union of believers through likeness of mind and soul ought to imitate the manner of the Divine Unity, and the essential identity of the Holy Trinity. But on these words we will essay to show that the oneness, according to which we are bound to one another and all to God, is, in a manner, one of nature, and, may be, not lacking in a bodily oneness with one another, although our bodies are different from one another, and each has his own personal being. There being confessedly a natural oneness of Father, Son, and Holy Ghost (for One Godhead in the Holy Trinity is believed and glorified), let us consider in what way we too are found one, both bodily and spiritually, both towards each other and towards God. The Only-Begotten, having shone upon us from the very Essence of God the Father, and having in His own Nature all which the Father is, became Flesh according to the Scriptures, having, as it were, mingled Himself with our nature, through the ineffable concurrence and union with this body which is from the earth. Thus He, by nature God, was truly called and became a Heavenly Man (not 'bearing God,' as some say who do not accurately understand the depth of the

[6] S. Cyril Al. on St. John xvii. 21. L. xi. c. 11, pp. 997—1000.

mystery, but) being, in one, God and Man, that having, in a manner, co-united in Himself what by nature was far apart and alien from all sameness of nature, He might make man to communicate in and partake of the Divine Nature. For the communication and abiding of the Spirit passed through to us also, having taken its beginning through Christ and in Christ first, being, as Man, anointed and sanctified, although, as He was by Nature God (as He appeared from the Father), He Himself with His own Spirit hallowing His own temple and the whole creation made by Him, and whatsoever admits of being hallowed. The mystery of Christ, then, was made a sort of beginning and way whereby we too might partake of the Holy Spirit, and of oneness with God. For in Christ are we all hallowed in the way afore spoken. In order, then, that we ourselves too, although differing both in souls and bodies through that which is personal to each, might come together and be commingled into an unity with God and one another, the Only-Begotten contrived a way, devised through the wisdom befitting Him, and through the counsel of the Father. For by One Body, His own, blessing through the mystical communion those who believe in Him, He makes us incorporate with Himself and with one another. For who should separate and remove from a natural oneness with one another, those who through the One Holy Body are bound up into oneness with Christ? For if we all 'partake of the One Bread,' we are all made 'one Body.' For Christ cannot be divided. Wherefore the Church is called also 'the body of Christ,' and we too 'are members in particular,' according to the mind of Paul. For we all, being united by One Christ through the Holy Body, in that we have received in our own bodies Him the One and Indivisible, owe our members more to Him than to ourselves.—But that, by partaking of the Holy Flesh, we obtain that union with Christ which is in a manner bodily, Paul will testify, speaking of 'the mystery of godliness which in other ages was not made known unto the sons of men, but is now revealed unto His holy Apostles and Prophets by the Spirit, that the Gentiles should be co-heirs, and concorporate and co-partakers of His promise in Christ[7].' But if we are all concorporate with one another in Christ, and not only with one another, but with Himself, in that He is in us through His own Flesh, how are we not all clearly one both with each other and with Christ? For Christ is the Bond of oneness, being, in One, God and Man.

"But as to the Oneness in Spirit, we all, having received One and the same Holy Spirit, are in a manner mingled with each other and with God. For although in us, being many, Christ giveth the Father's and His own Spirit to dwell in each of us, yet is He One and Indivisible, holding together in

[7] Eph. iii. 3—5.

oneness through Himself the spirits which, in their several existences, are severed from oneness, and making all to appear as one in Himself. For as the power of the Holy Flesh maketh those concorporate, in whom It is, in like way, I deem, the One Indivisible Spirit of God, dwelling in all, bringeth all together to the spiritual unity. For since One Spirit dwelleth in us, God the One Father of all will be in us, through the Son, holding in oneness, both to one another and to Himself, whatsoever partaketh of the Spirit."

S. Hilary is even at pains to show, against the Arians, that the unity spoken of is not an unity of will, but an unity of nature; and so he overthrows the more their sophism that the Unity of the Father and the Son was an unity of will only. "I[8] ask those who thrust upon us an unity of will between the Father and the Son, whether Christ is at this day in us by truth of nature, or by harmony of will? For if the Word is truly made Flesh, and we truly receive the Word, being Flesh, in the Food of the Lord, how must He not be thought to abide by nature in us, Who, being born Man, took the nature of our flesh inseparably to Himself, and under the Sacrament of the Flesh to be communicated to us, blended the nature of His Flesh with the Divine Nature?"

And as to the other Sacrament, S. Hilary[9] says,

[8] De Trin. viii. 13. [9] Ib. § 8.

"The Apostle teacheth, from the nature of Sacraments, that this is the unity of the faithful. 'As many as have been baptized unto Christ, have put on Christ. There is neither Jew nor Greek, there is neither bond nor free, there is neither male nor female; for ye are all one in Christ Jesus[1].' But that in so great variety of nations, conditions, sexes, they are one, is this from consent of the will or from the unity of the Sacrament, in that they both have one Baptism and all have put on One Christ? What has concord of minds to do here, seeing they are thereby one, that, by the nature of One Baptism, they are clothed with One Christ?"

The first then and very chiefest character of Unity is not any thing which comes forth from us; it is infused into us by God. But this it is man's part to receive, and he receives it by faith. "There is One Body and One Spirit;" "One Body," as held together by the "One" Holy "Spirit;" "One Body," of all which are and have been and shall be, all too who before Christ's Coming believed in Him and pleased Him. "For to this end," says S. Chrysostom[2], "was the Spirit given, that He might unite those who are separated by race and by different manners; for old and young, rich and poor, child, youth, and man, male and female, and every soul become, in a manner, one, and more entirely so than if there were one body."

S. Paul also, following our Lord, places the

[1] Gal. iii. 27, 28. [2] Ad loc. Hom., 9 p. 207, Oxf. Tr.

origin of unity in God. God maketh us one body, by giving to us One Spirit, ingrafting us into One Christ through One Baptism, regenerating us to "one hope of our calling," freely giving to us, sonship, heaven, infusing into us One Faith; for "faith," he says, "is the gift of God."

But from this also S. Hilary [3] argues, that our union is an union of nature, not of will. "They who were of one heart and of one soul, I ask, were they one through the Faith of God? Yes; through faith was the heart and soul of all one. And the faith was it one or more? One certainly, since the Apostle himself sets forth 'One Faith' as 'One Lord,' and 'One Baptism,' and 'One Hope,' and 'One God.' If then through faith, *i. e.* by the nature of one faith, all were one, why is there not an unity by nature in those who are one by the nature of One Faith?"

But it is of man to retain the faith which he has received. *They* have not the same Lord, who do not believe the same truth as to Him. The heretics of old who did not believe that the Son was Consubstantial, Co-Eternal, and Co-Equal with the Father, or that, when Incarnate, He had a human soul, or true flesh truly taken of the Virgin Mary, or that the Blessed Virgin bare Him Who was God, or who held that God dwelt only in the Man Christ Jesus, or contrariwise, that the Manhood was absorbed into God, or that our Lord had no human

[3] l. c. § 7.

will—these and whatsoever else there was of ancient heresy on the Holy Trinity and the Incarnation, believed not the same Lord; as neither did the Pelagians believe in what He wrought for us, and the Donatists denied the existence of that mystical body, whereof He was the Head.

The Faith, S. Paul says, is one, one unchangeable faith, admitting neither of enlargement, nor diminution, so that either what the Apostles believed and taught the whole Church as faith, should cease to be faith, or that any thing should become faith which they, full of the Holy Ghost, knew not and taught not as the faith. But since the faith is one, one whole, then whosoever parteth with, or altereth any portion of the one faith, in fact changes the whole, so that it is not the same faith, whence the stress in the Athanasian Creed on "keeping the faith whole and undefiled."

This unity, derived from Our Blessed Lord as Head of the Church, is imparted primarily through the Sacraments. S. Paul says, that "all, baptized into Christ, have put on Christ," and, having put Him on, are one in Christ. And of the Holy Eucharist, "We, being many, are one bread and one body: for we are all partakers of that one Bread[4]." By Baptism we are ingrafted into the mystical Body of Christ; by partaking of His Body, we continue to be members of His Body. But as Christ Himself

[4] 1 Cor. x. 17.

worketh all things in all, He baptizeth invisibly, He consecrateth, He strengtheneth those who stand, He restoreth those who fall; yet to signify to us that He doeth it, He useth the outward ministry of men, appointed in succession, from the day when He breathed on the Apostles and said, "Receive ye the Holy Ghost; whose soever sins ye remit, they are remitted unto them; and whose soever sins ye retain, they are retained[5]." Such an organization, as essential to the transmission of grace from Christ our Head, seems to lie in the words of S. Paul, "holding the Head, from which all the body by joints and bands having nourishment ministered, and knit together[6]," "according to the effectual working in the measure of every part, increaseth with the increase of God[7]." The "joints and bands" are, in the image of the body, naturally those ministers by which the whole body is held together in one, and through which spiritual nourishment is ministered to the growth of the whole. Certainly, the Apostolic ministry was to continue to the end of the world. "Apostles, prophets, evangelists, pastors, and teachers," or those in their stead, He set in the Church, "for the edifying of the Body of Christ, till we all come, in the unity of the faith and of the knowledge of the Son of God, unto a perfect man, unto the measure of the stature of the fulness of Christ."

[5] S. John xx. 22, 23.
[6] Col. ii. 19.
[7] Eph. iv. 16.

Thus, then, we have from Holy Scripture, as means and conditions of the unity of the Church, One All-Perfect Author, the "One God and Father of all;" one end to which all tends, the "one hope of our calling;" "One Head," the Head of the Church, our "One Lord;" "One Spirit," giving life to every living member; the same Sacraments, "One Baptism," and "One Bread," by which we are all ingrafted into or maintained in the One Body of our One Head; one Apostolic descent of the Bishops and Pastors of the flock, coming down from One; "One" common "Faith," that which was given once for all, with the anathema that we hold no doctrine at variance with it, although an Angel from Heaven were to preach it. Of these we are receivers only.

These if any wilfully reject, they reject Christ. They sever themselves, not only from the Body of Christ, but directly from the Head, loosing the band which binds them unto Him. These while Christian bodies retain, they are, so long, like the river which "went out of Eden to water the garden; and from thence it was parted and became into four heads." They come from the Fountain of blessedness; they flow down to the Ocean of the Eternal Love of God; they water the parched land; they cool and refresh the weary and the thirsty in the places which God has appointed for them with the one stream coming down from Him. They are one in their One Original, from which they continually and unchangeably derive their being. They adore God, the Father, Son, and Holy Ghost, with the same new song of the Gospel; they confess Him in the same words of Apostolic Faith; they offer to Him the same incense of praise, and the same Holy Offering whereof Malachi foretold, "from the rising of the sun to the going down of the same," pleading on earth to the Eternal Father that One Sacrifice, as presented in Heaven; they receive the same "Bread which came down from Heaven to give life to the world." Unknown in face, in place separate, different in language, opposed, alas! in some things to one another, still before the Throne of God they are One Holy Catholic Apostolic Church; each several portion praying for itself and for the rest, united in the prayers and oblation which it offers for all, by the One Bread and the One Spirit which dwelleth in all. "In which mystery" (the Holy Eucharist), says S. Cyprian, "our people are shown to be united, so that, as many grains collected and ground and mingled together make one bread, so in Christ, Who is the Heavenly Bread, we may know that there is one Body wherewith our whole number is conjoined and united[8]."

But is then the whole unity of the Church from God and to God alone, so that it involves duties to God only, and none from man to man? Of the

[8] Ep. 63, ad Cæcil. § 10, p. 191, Oxf. Tr.

early Christians, the Holy Ghost bears witness that they were at first "of one heart and of one soul." The intensest conception of human affection, which the range of heathen poetry could imagine as having been once realized, that they were "twain in body, one in soul," was brought into being by the Day of Pentecost, not in two, but in thousands. For there was, what no imagination could conceive, not one soul in all, but One Holy Spirit, dwelling indivisibly in each, One and the Same filling each soul, the very Same in each, binding them together by the virtue of the Holy and Consubstantial Trinity, melting all into a perfect oneness of will by the fire of love which God is. Well might the heathen say then, "God is among them of a truth." For the glory which Christ gave them was greater than that of miracles; it was the greatest of all miracles, when souls purified, by His indwelling, from passion and envy and all unlove, presented no longer let or hindrance to His all-pervading warmth, but through the love of Christ were one, He says, "as We are One," Whose Oneness is indivisible.

The Divine gift of Unity requires, as a corresponding duty, mutual love, as the exercise of that "love of God which is shed abroad in our hearts through the Holy Ghost which is given to us." This has been called "subjective" unity, or "unison of wills," and of this, intercommunion is the natural expression. But is all unity forfeited, where the unity of intercommunion is suspended? No one, in the face of Church-history, can or does maintain that all interruptions of intercommunion destroy unity. For Church-history records too many such interruptions, which (although never probably without fault, on the one side or on both) yet did not exclude either side from the body of Christ. Unlove began its work even in Apostles' times. At Corinth, already, our Lord's words, "By this shall all men know that ye are My disciples, if ye have love one to another," were in a degree eclipsed. Divisions began within the single Church. In the next century, was that first wider rent in the Christian body, when the Bishop of Rome, against the remonstrance of many Bishops, renounced the communion of the Asiatic Churches, because they followed, as to the keeping of Easter, a tradition different from that of Rome and of the other Churches. "The East," says S. Epiphanius[1], "differing from the West, they received not from each other tokens of peace." The strife ceased not until the Council of Nice. Again, in the next century, was the temporary severance between Rome and both Asiatic and African Churches, through the Bishop of Rome, of whom one, now counted a saint, said[2], "While thinking that all may be excommunicated by him, he excommunicated himself alone from all." This

[1] Hær. 70, n. 9, p. 821.

[2] S. Firmil. in S. Cyprian, Ep. 75, § 25, p. 284, Oxf. Tr.

was allayed seemingly by a subsequent peace-loving Bishop of Rome, but the question on which they disagreed was settled by the large Council of Arles, not by the Bishop of Rome.

Lucifer, once an exile for the faith, and ready to suffer death for it, created a schism between Catholics. Paulinus, whom he hastily[3] consecrated against S. Meletius, was recognized at Alexandria and Rome; S. Meletius remained in the communion of the Easterns. S. Basil toiled in vain to heal the schism[4], and blamed the Westerns for their "pride, haughtiness, precipitancy[5]." S. Meletius, out of communion with Rome, presided (as it were, marked out by God) at the Second General Council. On his death, the fathers of the Council, with the people of Antioch, filled up his place, maintaining the rights of the Eastern Church, and after fifty-six years the schism was healed, a successor in the line of S. Meletius bringing back all into one flock. S. Meletius, when departed, was owned to be a saint by those who, in his lifetime, owned him not as a bishop. Lucifer, who created the schism, himself closed a life of labour for the faith by forming a small schismatic body in Sardinia; yet, for his faith's sake, is called by S. Jerome, who wrote against his sect, "the blessed Lucifer[6]."

What, when in the troubles as to S. Chry-

[3] Præproperus, Ruf. H. E. i. 27.

[4] See Pusey's "Councils," pp. 243—252.

[5] Ib. p. 252.

[6] Adv. Lucif. c. 20, Opp. ii. 193.

sostom, saints were on opposite sides, and, in the cessation of intercourse between Rome and Alexandria, the African Bishops had to exhort the Bishop of Rome, that "each[7] Church should keep towards the other the peace which the Lord commanded?"

The Fifth General Council, overruled by God to good, yet assembled by a heretical emperor, at the instigation of a heretic, was (in part through the vacillation, the alternate assent and dissent, of Vigilius) the occasion of a schism which rent the West, Africa, Upper Italy from east to west, and even Ireland, nor was the schism wholly healed for 150 years[8].

Our own heathen ancestors, in our S. Augustine's time, were in great measure converted by those who were not in communion with Rome, yet God blessed the zeal of both for His glory.

More miserable was that great breach, prepared perhaps for centuries, and which has lasted until now, between the East and West. Miserable in its origin and its issue. A quarrel begun by two Christian Patriarchs about authority over a province newly recovered to the Christian Faith[9], strengthened subsequently by offensive answers

[7] Conc. Afr. c. 68. Conc. T. ii. p. 1334, Col.

[8] See Hefele, Concilien-Gesch. ii. 899.

[9] Bulgaria. The province had originally belonged to the Patriarchate of Constantinople. When Arian emperors expelled the orthodox bishops and put Arians into the see, it put itself under the Patriarchate of Rome. The inhabitants

to an offensive writing, and anathema answered by anathema; involving a people which was acknowledged to be orthodox; embittered, in later times, by the mixture of this world's politics, the capture of Constantinople under the banner of the Cross, amid excesses from which even the Saracens abstained; the establishment of Latin Emperors of Constantinople and multiplication of Latin Patriarchs and Bishops, sometimes scandalous in their lives, oppressive to the Greeks, whom they ejected, banished, or at times destroyed. "The Latins," says Fleuri [10], "defeated the very end they had in view. The conquest of Constantinople drew after it the loss of the Holy Land, and made the schism of the Greeks irremediable." The conditions of reconciliation were, absolute submission to an authority which had grown up since the separation. They were to purchase help against heathen or Mohammedan invaders by the surrender of the Patriarchal system which they had from the times of General Councils [11], which had the sanction of the Universal Church, and was bound up with all their memories of all the victories of the Faith over heresy. Or lands were offered to princes to

were driven out by the heathen Bulgarians, who were converted from Constantinople. Rome claimed them, and pronounced anathemas to S. Ignatius as well as to Photius on this ground, as indeed the dispute was first with S. Ignatius.

[10] Disc. 6, sur l'Hist. Eccl. T. 18, § 5.

[11] Conc. Const. i. can. 2. Chalc. can. 28.

whom they did not belong, on the condition that they would renounce obedience where it was due, and transfer it where it was not due. If we may judge of the sentiments of the Greeks from one of their able and moderate writers, Elias Meniates, Bishop of Zerniza, towards the end of the 17th century, says, "I hold the dispute about the supreme power of the Pope to be the principal cause of our divisions. This is the wall of division between the two Churches. The chief controversy I hold to be about the sovereignty of the Pope. For this is at this time the great wall of separation which divides the two Churches. If all Christians were agreed on this chief point, viz. how the Church was to be governed, whether by aristocratical rule as we think, or monarchical as the Latins think, there would be very little trouble in agreeing about the rest[2]."

And can we think that the whole guilt of this miserable rent has fallen upon one side only, that, when both East and West confess the same Mysteries of the Faith, the East is no part of the Church of Christ, because it does not subject itself to the West under which God did not place it? Moses and Aaron pleaded with God, "Shall one man sin, and wilt Thou be wroth with all the congregation[3]?" And are we to assume, whatever were the original wrong tempers of two Greek Patriarchs, that their

[2] Lapis Offensionis, L. 2, c. 1 init., quoted by M. Trevern, Discuss. Amicale, T. i. p. 231.

[3] Numb. xvi. 22.

sin either then involved the innocent, or now lives on so fatally, after so many centuries, when terms are imposed, so different from those in the first quarrel? And that, when the great Russian Empire, converted to the faith by the preaching of Monks and Missionary Bishops since the separation of the East and West [4], is a witness to the Greek Church, that she is a true member of the One Church! "Rome cannot show, since she has been divided from the East, a conversion on so large a scale, so complete, so permanent [5]." And now too, the Russian Church has been and is, through Apostolic Bishops, winning tens of thousands beyond the bounds of the Russian Empire to the faith of Christ.

In the great schism of the Western Church, in which the Churches of the West were for forty years nearly equally divided, each party was by the other regarded as schismatic, yet we cannot doubt that each belonged to the true Church of Christ.

"After domination in temporals and spirituals was multiplied in the Church," says Gerson, "men began intrusions and schisms in the Roman Church, for the sake of which dominations and powers, there were continually hatreds and rancours between the

[4] See the Archimandrite Macarius' History of Christianity in Russia, p. 394, in Allies' Church of England cleared from charge of Schism, pp. 498, 499, supplied by Rev. W. Palmer.

[5] Allies, ib. p. 500.

Supreme Pontiffs, the Roman Emperors, and temporal Lords [6]."

There is then no ground to assume that suspensions of inter-communion (sad and mournful as they are) in themselves hinder either body from being a portion of the Body of Christ. The Donatists were not merely separated from the Catholic Church throughout the world, but denied its existence, and claimed to be the whole Church. The body was formed on a heresy, rejected by the English Church [7]. Probably real schism is always united with heresy, whether as springing from it or degenerating into it. There may be schismatic acts, which have not the deadliness of the sin of schism, as there may be degrees of unlove in an individual, which do not cast the Spirit of God out of his soul. We believe the Church to be universal, although there are large tracts of the world which it has not reached, or from which it has been driven out; we believe the Church to be holy, notwithstanding that the evil is more on the surface than the good; we believe the prophecy to have been fulfilled, "neither shall men learn war any more," although peace has been in these last days the exception among Christians; we believe our Lord's words that love is the test of His disciples, and that thereby shall they be known among men, although unlove and jealousy and self-interest and anger are far more visible.

[6] Status Ecclesiæ in V. et N. T. Opp. T. ii. p. 155.
[7] Art. XXVI.

Well then may we believe that the several Churches, owning the same Lord, united to Him by the same Sacraments, confessing the same Faith, however their prayers may be hindered, are still one in His sight, Whom all desire to receive; Whom all confess; Whose Passion all plead before the Father; in Whom Alone all alike hope. And so as to ourselves, our divines maintained (under appeal to a free general Council of the whole East and West, while there was yet hope, and God's Arm is not shortened, that He should not yet turn the hearts of the fathers to the children, and the children to the fathers), that we have done nothing to forfeit the Communion of the rest of Christendom.

vi. *b*. But Dr. Manning says, that we have denied the "visible head" of the Church, i. e. we do not, any more than the Eastern Church, own the monarchy of the Bishop of Rome. In the time of Henry VIII. the English Church submitted to the abolition of appeals to Rome; and what it then submitted to, it has since concurred in. But, if any thing is clear in Christian antiquity, it is, that such appeals are not of Divine right. Africa was converted from Italy. Yet England is not at this moment more independent of any authority of the Bishop of Rome, than Africa was in the time of S. Augustine. There are only three conceivable ways in which the Bishop of one Church could interfere in the internal regulations of another. They are, the Confirmation of its Bishops, or of its Canons or Ecclesiastical laws, or the reviewing of the judicial sentences of its Bishops. These would control its legislative or its judicial functions in detail, or the selection of those in whom the legislative and judicial functions are vested. Of these three, it is confessed by Roman Catholic writers too, that the confirmation of Bishops lay with the Primate, as in other countries with the Metropolitan, and that the Pallium was never sent to Africa. The African Canons stood on their own authority, as did those of all other Churches; the Greek, the Spanish, the Gallican, the British. The case of Apiarius evinces on both sides an entire unconsciousness of any inherent right in the see of Rome to receive appeals. The Bishops of Rome rested their right, not upon any inherent claim, but upon a Canon of the Council of Sardica, which they, by mistake, thought to be a Canon of the Council of Nice. The African Bishops, and among them S. Augustine, declared their willingness to obey any Nicene Canon, but stated that they had no such Canon as that alleged by the Bishop of Rome, in their collection of Nicene Canons which they received through him. The words of S. Augustine are still preserved. "We profess that we will observe this rule too [as to the appeals of priests or deacons], saving a more diligent enquiry as to the Council of Nice[a]." On this the question was put to the Synod, and the whole

[a] Cod. Eccl. Afr. G. in Bruns, i. 159.

Council said, "All things which were enacted in the Council of Nice, we all approve." St. Augustine also signed the synodal letter to Boniface from the 217 Bishops present from all Africa, in which they deprecated any "haughtiness" [typhus] on the part of the Bishop of Rome, and professed that they "will comply with what had been alleged on his part about the appeals of Bishops to the Bishop of the Roman Church, and about terminating the causes of clerks by the Bishops of their Provinces, *until ascertaining*, whether there was such a Canon of Nice, since they had none such in any Greek or Latin copy of the Canons [9]." They sent accordingly to the East and received copies of the Canons from S. Cyril of Alexandria, and Atticus, Bishop of Constantinople. After these had been sent to Boniface, another Council from all Africa was held, in which Bishop Faustinus urged that the unhappy Apiarius, having been received to communion by Celestine, should be received by the Church of Africa also. A three-days' hearing of Apiarius was ended by his own confession of all the horrible scandals of which he had been accused. Whereupon the Bishops of the African Council wrote thus to Celestine [1]: "We earnestly beg that henceforth you will not readily admit to your hearing those who come from hence, nor be willing to receive to communion those excommunicated by

[9] Cod. Afr. c. 134, Bruns, i. 197.

[1] See their letter in Bruns, p. 199.

us, because you will readily see that this is ruled by the Council of Nice. For although it may seem as if provision were there made as to the inferior clergy or laymen, how much more would it have this observed as to Bishops, that, being suspended from communion in their own province, they should not seem to be restored to communion by your Holiness hastily or over-hurriedly or unduly. Let your Holiness repel also, as beseems you, the shameless applications of presbyters and clergy below them, because by no statute of the fathers has this been derogated from the African Church, and the Nicene Canons have most plainly committed both the inferior Clergy and the Bishops themselves to their Metropolitans. For most prudently and justly have they provided, that all matters should be terminated in the places where they arose; nor will the grace of the Holy Spirit be wanting to each province, whereby the Bishops of Christ may both prudently see and constantly maintain equity; especially, since it is allowed to each, if he is dissatisfied with the judgment of those who took cognizance of his case, to appeal to the Council of his Province or of all Africa. Unless any one think that our God can inspire with justice a single individual, and refuse it to innumerable Bishops, assembled in Council. Or how should the judgment beyond seas itself stand, seeing that persons needed as witnesses cannot be brought there, for infirmity of sex or age or many other hindrances. For that any should be sent, as it were from the side of your Holiness, we find ordained by no synod of the fathers. For as to that which you sent by our fellow-Bishop Faustinus, as if from the Nicene Council, we could find nothing of the sort in more accurate copies, which we have received from the holy Cyril, our fellow-Bishop of the Alexandrian Church, and the venerable Atticus, Bishop of Constantinople, taken from the original, which we transmitted to Bishop Boniface of venerable memory. Moreover, whoever may ask you, do not send any of your Clergy to execute your orders; allow it not; lest we should seem to bring the fumes of secular pride into the Church of Christ, which holds out to those who desire to see God, the light of simplicity and the clear day of humility. For, now that the unhappy Apiarius has for his shocking wickednesses been removed from the Church of Christ, we are sure that through the probity and moderation of your Holiness, Africa, without violating brotherly charity, will not have further to endure our brother Faustinus."

This long process, which was carried on so perseveringly by four successive Bishops of Rome, is most remarkable for the principles which appear in the course of it, and the persons who enunciated those principles. For St. Augustine, forbearing, as he did, to the utmost, so long as there was even a bare possibility that the Council of Nice should have given a contrary decision, clearly showed by his short speech, that he knew of no other authority to which the Church of Africa should defer. He is further responsible for the Synodal Epistle to Boniface, which he signed, next after Aurelius the Primate. The bishops, and he among them, or rather chief of them, say, "We took care to convey last year by our letters to the same Bishop Zosimus, of venerable memory, that we would allow those [canons] to be observed without any detriment to him, *for a little while until the enquiry into* the canons of the Council of Nice. And now we ask of your Holiness, that you would cause those things which they brought in their instructions, [viz. the two Sardican canons,] to be observed as they were done or constituted by the fathers at Nice, by us, and among yourselves in Italy. These canons are inserted in the Acts until the arrival of the most authentic copies of the Nicene Council; which, if they are contained there (as they stood in the instructions which our brethren sent from the Apostolic See alleged to us), and if they are kept even among you in Italy, we shall not be constrained to endure what for the present we are unwilling to speak of; but we believe that, by the help of the mercy of our Lord God, while your Holiness presides over the Roman Church we shall not have to endure their arrogance, and *that* will be observed towards us which ought to be observed with brotherly charity, even without any suggestion of ours, which, according to the wisdom and justice which the Most High has given you, you yourself perceive ought to be observed, if perchance the canons of the Council of Nice prove otherwise."

But indeed the Canons of Sardica (had they been even generally received) involve the same principle. St. Athanasius insists on the distinction between matters of faith and positive enactment, as treated in the Council of Nice. "The faith they declared, 'Thus believes the Catholic Church,' in order to show that their own sentiments were not novel, but Apostolical[2];" but in matter of positive enactments, "They wrote concerning the Easter, 'It seemed good as follows,' for it did then seem good that there should be a general compliance." Now this is exactly the form of the Sardican Canon, "If it seem good, let us honour the memory of the holy Apostle Peter." The Bishops were providing against the recurrence of injustice to the orthodox Bishops of the East, such as S. Athanasius had undergone from a packed council of Arian Bishops, and, as in many other canons, so in this, they legislated to meet an emergency. "This form is very strong to show," says Tillemont[3], "that it was a right which the Pope had not had hitherto." "The words of the Canon," says de Marca[4], "prove that the institution of this law is

[2] Conc. Arim. et Seleuc. n. 5. Treatises ag. Arians, i. 80, Oxf. Tr.

[3] S. Athanas. Art. 50, T. 8, p. 110.

[4] Conc. Sac. vii. 3. 8.

new. 'If it seems good to you,' says Hosius," &c. The mention of Julius, Bishop of Rome, by name, "if to Julius, Bishop of Rome, should seem good," seems again to imply a temporary purpose, such as was protection against the Arians. Nor was the power given an appeal to Rome strictly. It only empowered the Bishop of Rome to have the cause reheard, if he judged right, by the Bishops of the neighbouring province, together with a presbyter to represent himself[5]. What was granted was the revision of a cause, not strictly an appeal[6].

What was not of Divine right cannot *become* such. A state of things may be matter of order, or of human law; it cannot *become* part of the Law Divine. That only is Divine Law which was given by God. Heretics, indeed, or bad men, excommunicated in their own country, betook themselves to Rome, where they were not known, as contrariwise, Pelagius, condemned in the West, betook himself to the East. a) Marcion, excommunicated by his father, a Bishop in Pontus, for seduction, received the worthy answer from the Roman presbyters in the vacancy of the see: "We cannot do this [receive him to communion] without the injunction of your honoured father. For there is one faith and one harmony of mind, and we cannot go against the excellent fellow-minister, thy father[7]." b) The Montanists did not apparently

[5] Conc. Sard. c. 7. [6] See de Marca l. c., c. 6 and 7.

[7] S. Epiph. Hær. 42, n. 2, p. 303.

appeal at all; but having been rejected in the East, they settled at Rome. They had been disallowed by the predecessors of Victor[8], whom they would have imposed upon, but for Praxeas. Tillemont conjectures[9], that they may have had the more hope from Victor on account of his quarrel with the Churches of Asia Minor, which had rejected them. c) Praxeas, at one time, signed a retractation of his heresy, which retractation was in the hands of the Catholics[10]. At that time there was neither appeal nor condemnation. When detected, he retracted. He acquiesced outwardly, without giving up his unbelief. Then it burst out again. d) Fortunatus was an anti-bishop[1], consecrated in opposition to S. Cyprian, who sought to get recognized at Rome, whither he sent letters, as Novatian[2], consecrated against S. Cornelius, sought to be recognized in Africa. Neither was an appeal. a) The case of Basilides and Martialis is more interesting. Both, besides other sins, had denied

[8] "This same [Praxeas] constrained the then Bishop of Rome, when on the point of acknowledging the prophecies of Montanus, Prisca, Maximilla, and by that recognition carrying peace to the Churches of Asia and Phrygia, to recall the letters of peace which were already issued, and to give up his purpose of accepting their spiritual gifts, by asserting falsehoods as to the prophets and their churches, and maintaining the authorities of his [Victor's] predecessors." Tert. adv. Prax. c. i.

[9] Les Montanistes, Art. 4, T. ii. p. 425, Note 4, p. 669.

[10] Tert. c. Prax. c. i.

[1] S. Cyprian Ep. 59, ad n. 10. 22. Corn. Oxf. Tr.

[2] Id. Ep. 44, ad Corn. O. T.

Christ in persecution. The Spanish bishops deposed them, and consecrated Felix and Sabinus in their stead. "Basilides, canvassing to be unjustly restored to the Episcopate from which he had been justly deposed, went to Rome, and deceived Stephen our colleague," says S. Cyprian[3], "residing at a distance, and ignorant of what had been done and of the real truth." The clergy and people of Astorga, Merida, and Leon appealed to S. Cyprian, through their newly-consecrated bishops. S. Cyprian, assembling thirty-seven other bishops, in a synodical letter, judged that the deposition of Basilides and Martialis was right, the election of Felix and Sabinus, of which an account had been sent, was canonical, and that the effect of "Basilides deceiving Stephen was not to efface but to swell the crimes of Basilides, in that to his former sins is added the guilt of deceit and circumvention." Conceive Spanish bishops now, having been consecrated in place of deposed bishops who had appealed to Rome, deputed by Spanish clergy and people to the Archbishop of Paris, and that he, with a Provincial Synod, should reply that the former bishops had been rightly deposed, that these had been canonically elected, and that the appealing bishop had only aggravated his crimes by "deceiving Pio Nono, our colleague," but excusing Pio Nono, in that "[3]he is not so much to be blamed,

[3] Ep. 69 (Synod.) ad Felic., &c. n. 5.

who through negligence was imposed upon." If the appeals of bad men were a precedent, the rest of the history is equally a precedent, showing that the relations in the times nearest the Apostles were very different from those which the Church of England laid aside. The English Church in the fifteenth century acquiesced in, or consented to, the suppression of appeals to Rome; the African Church in the fifth century not only forbade them, but excommunicated throughout Africa any one who should so appeal[3]. It was not a mere abstract question. About the same time, A.D. 1438, the Council of Basle complained of "[4] the very many

[3] "If presbyters, deacons, or other inferior Clergy, shall, in any cause which they may have, complain of the judgments of their own Bishops, let the neighbouring Bishops hear them, and determine any matter between them, being called in by them with the consent of their own Bishops. But if they think that they should appeal from them too, let them not appeal to Courts beyond seas, but either to the Primates of their provinces, or to a general Council [of Africa], as has been often enacted about Bishops also. But if any one choose to appeal to the parts beyond seas, let him be received to communion by no one within Africa." Cod. Can. Eccl. Afr. 28. In Can. 125 it is, "let them only appeal to African Councils or to the Primates of their provinces," without the words "as has often been enacted about Bishops also." The clause excommunicating those who appeal is repeated. In the Council of Carthage, A.D. 525, a canon is rehearsed from the 11th Council, "Whoso communicates not [i.e. is excommunicate] in Africa, if he should venture to communicate beyond seas, let him be condemned;" as also Can. 125 from the 16th Council, and "Let no one dare to appeal to the parts beyond seas," from the 20th. Conc. iii. 780. Col.

[4] Sess. 31, Decr. i. Conc. xvii. 371. Col.

abuses of intolerable vexations" consequent on appeals, especially from "remote parts," the "ease with which pettifoggers oppressed the poor, ecclesiastical benefices were obtained through the cavils of litigations, for the most part unjustly," &c. The Council prohibited, as far as in it lay, appeals from more distant parts, with certain exceptions. Louis, Archbishop of Arles, Cardinal, and President of the Council (of whom Æneas Sylvius, Pius II., speaks in high terms), asked in the Council, "What[5] at this day were bishops, but a sort of shadow? What had they left, but a staff and mitre? Could they be called shepherds, without sheep, when they could do nothing towards those under them? For whereas in the Primitive Church the chief powers were with bishops, now they have come to this, that in dress only and revenue they surpass presbyters. But we have restored them to their former condition. We [the Council] have made those bishops who were no longer bishops." "A General Council, representing the Universal Church," says Gerson[6], "if it aim to see complete union, to repress and put an end to schisms, to exalt the Church, must, before all things, after the manner of the holy fathers before us, limit and bound the coactive and

[5] In Æneas Sylv. de Gest. Bas. Conc. L. I. in Brown, Fasc. rer. exp. i. p. 23.

[6] De modis uniendi ac reform. Eccl. per Conc. Opp. ii. pp. 173, 174.

usurped power of the Pope[7]." "Which coactive power many supreme Pontiffs, at successive times, obtained to themselves, contrary to God and justice, depriving inferior bishops of the powers and authorities given them by God and the Church, who in the Primitive Church were of equal power with the Pope, when there was no sale of indulgences[8]," &c. "At length in the course of time (the avarice of the clergy, and the simony, cupidity, and ambition of the Pope increasing), the power and authority of the bishops and inferior prelates seem as though dried up and utterly overthrown, so that they seem now in the Church to be but painted images, to no end. For now the Pope of Rome has reserved all ecclesiastical benefices; now has he called all causes into his own court; now has he willed that a penitentiary should be held there; now he wills that the holy ordination of any person indiscriminately should take place in his own court; and they, who cannot obtain ordination in their own country, easily obtain ordination

[7] Gerson adds here, "The aforesaid Lord Alexander V. was altogether inclined to this before he was Pope, when it was in agitation that the said Council should be held at Pisa. He not only said this, but with many arguments from theology, philosophy, and jurisprudence, laboured at the limitation which was to follow. When created Pope, he had no care to publish them."

[8] The whole passage is, "when there were no Papal reservations of benefices, no inhibitions of Episcopal cases, no sales of indulgences, no commendams of cardinals, and distributions of benefices, of priories, and monasteries."

in that court." Nicolas V. plainly owned, "[9] The Roman Pontiffs, it seems to me, extended their skirts too far, in that they left no jurisdiction to the other bishops. Those of Basle abridged too

[9] In Baluz. Miscell. vii. 555, in Gieseler K. G. § 133. Nicolas of Cusa (A.D. 1448) still taught that "Peter did not receive any more power than the other Apostles; that nothing was said to him which was not said to the others; that all the Apostles were equal to Peter; that in the beginning of the Church there was only one general episcopate, without distinction of dioceses, throughout the world; that all bishops are of one power and dignity; that those above others, Archiepiscopal, Patriarchal, Papal, are administrations.—All bishops have the Apostolic command to govern themselves and their flocks in which the Holy Ghost has placed them to rule the Church, and therefore is the synodal judgment entrusted to them, because they are chiefs and rulers of the Church. If thou sayest that the Pope looses and binds those under the bishops, I say the same as to others, when there is the consent of their own bishops. For an act, null in itself, becomes valid through the consent or permission of one's own bishop in this matter.—Since, then, this has been introduced by common custom, and the consent is elicited from the custom, it is plain that its efficacy is derived from custom.—It is not read then that the Roman Bishops in old times intermeddled in these things, or granted such confessionals and the like; and perhaps it would not have been allowed. *Since then the Council of Africa, which S. Augustine subscribed, did not allow of an appeal from a Council to a Pope*, because it was not found in the Canons that this was allowed, but it was defined in the Council of Nice that the cause ought to be terminated by the Synod, where it arose: *how could they have admitted these things, and the irregular things done at this day?* But because consent has now from long custom introduced this, those things are valid as to the salvation of souls, *as long as they allow them, but they can be taken away by a Council*, and reformation requires this." De Conc. Eccl. ii. 13, pp. 726—729, quoted Gies. K. G. § 136, pp. 215, 216.

much the power of the Apostolic See. But so it happens. Whoso doth things unworthy, must endure things unjust. Those who would set erect a tree inclined on one side, draw it on the other. Our mind is, not to despoil of their rights the bishops who are called to a part of our charge. For so we hope to preserve our own jurisdiction, if we do not usurp what belongs to others." But things went on as before.

And if, after the Pope had not only excommunicated King Henry VIII., but had deposed him, deprived his future children, given away his dominions, laid the kingdom under an interdict, absolved his subjects from allegiance, and stirred up other princes against them if they rebelled not, given them to be slaves to their captors, and their property to be a spoil, the Church of England reformed by herself, it was always allowed to a Provincial Council to make decrees in matters of faith, subject to the ultimate authority of the Universal Church. Successive Councils, Pisa, Constance, Basle, had met and failed. Men's hearts despaired. Constance had been chosen to avoid Italian influence; at Basle it had been defeated, but the Council was therefore closed. "I can scarcely believe," said a Carthusian, A.D. 1449, "that the general Church can be reformed unless the Roman court be reformed first, which yet how difficult it is, the course of the present times shows. For no nation of believers so resists the universal reformation of the Church, as the Italian and others who praise them, bound by hope of promotion or gain or temporal benefit, or fear of losing dignities. They tremble at the very sound of a General Council, knowing by experience that General Councils speak not smooth things, but correct and amend without respect of persons[7]." "There will be no reformation," said a Bishop in 1519, "save in some general, free, and candid Council, where room shall be given, not to a malicious, but to the Holy Spirit to breathe. Alas! I conjecture with alarm, that our age is not worthy of the gathering of a lawful Council, wherein, virtues being promoted and vices censured, the Church shall be reformed; so deceived are we by the workings of error.. The Councils we need are rarely and sluggishly held; they are conducted at Rome or elsewhere before the powerful, where there is no freedom of speech to the humble and the faithful, so that in them what concerns the worship of God, the Christian religion and reformation, is slowly corrected[8]." And yet these three last Councils had borne witness to the need of reformation "in the head and the members;" and worse was feared if it was not hastened. "It is strongly to be anticipated with foresight and fear," says that same Bishop[9], "that the ruin of the Latin

[7] Jacob de Paradiso: de Virtutibus Eccl. in Brown ii. 106.
[8] John Chemensis, Onus Eccl. c. 19, § 16.
[9] Ib. § 14.

Church as to Ecclesiastical dignity is near at hand, since weakness in the foundations brings a fall."

"Unless," said a Cardinal, in the preface to a paper presented to the Council of Constance [1], "the Church be reformed speedily, I venture to say, that, albeit great are the things which we see, we shall soon see incomparably greater, and, after thunderings so aweful, we shall very shortly hear others yet more aweful. Wherefore we must watch with the utmost diligence for the Reformation of the Church." And Cardinal Julian, appealing to the Pope against the dissolution of the Council of Basle, "What will the whole world say, when it shall hear this? Will it not judge that the Clergy are incorrigible, and will for ever to remain in the defilements of their deformities? So many Councils have been held in our days, from which no reformation followed. The people looked that some fruit should come of this. If it be dissolved, it will be said that we mock God and man [2]." The Council was after a time removed to Italy, and reformation was no more spoken of.

vi. *c.* The last charge which Dr. Manning brings against the Church of England is, that "it formally denies" the "perpetual Divine voice [3]" of the Church. In this statement the stress, I conceive, lies upon the word "perpetual." Dr. Manning understands "the Divine authority of the Church"

[1] Peter de Alliaco, A. 1415, Browne i. 407.
[2] Epist. Julian. Card. ad Eug. iv., in Browne i. 57.
[3] Letter, pp. 34, 5.

to involve, not only what we confess,—that the whole Catholic Church has not collectively sanctioned error; and so, that what it *has* collectively pronounced is certain truth,—but also an ever-present power to declare new truth. "The perpetual and ever-present assistance of the Holy Spirit, whereby the Church in every age is not only preserved from error, but enabled at all times to declare the truth; that is, the infallibility of the Church at this hour—that it is, that the Anglican Church in terms denies. For three hundred years the Anglican Clergy have been trained, ordained, and bound to deny not only many Christian truths, but the Divine authority of the ἡ ἀεὶ ἐκκλησία, the living Church of every age." Conscious that we had never done any thing of the kind, nay that, in the Articles, we subscribe the contrary[4], I asked myself, What can this mean? For we are here concerned with an abstract proposition, not with a matter of fact, such as is that of the extent of the visible Church, viz., whether it comprises the Oriental and Anglican Churches, or whether it consists only of the Churches in communion with Rome. Dr. Manning has, naturally, identified the two questions; and assumes, in fact, that, in denying the infallibility of the Roman Church by itself, we are "denying the infallibility of the living Church at this hour;" because, on his hypothesis,

[4] See above, pp. 37—44.

the Roman Church is, alone, the living Church, to the exclusion of the Eastern Church and of ourselves. This, I understand, is a favourite formula with Dr. Manning,—"By whom does God the Holy Ghost speak? By the Roman Church? or by the Eastern? or by the Anglican?" I have been wont to say, "by all concurrently, in so far as they teach the same faith which was from the beginning[5], which is the great body of all their teaching; and, if need required, they could at this day declare concurrently any truth, if it should appear that it had not, as yet, been sufficiently defined, against some fresh heresy which should emerge."

But I see not, what this question as to the present ability of the Church to meet fresh errors which may emerge, has to do with the question as to the infallible certainty of the truths which the whole Church in common has received.

The office of our Divine Lord, as a Teacher, was, to be the perfect Revealer of the whole truth as to God, which God willed to disclose to His creatures here. This same office God the Holy Ghost undertook after the Resurrection, teaching invisibly to the Apostles that same divine truth. Our Lord said to His Apostles, "He shall teach you the whole truth (πᾶσαν τὴν ἀλήθειαν), and bring all things to your remembrance, whatever I have said unto you[6]." The whole revelation then was completed

[5] See above, ib. and pp. 53, 54.

[6] S. John xiv. 26; xvi. 13.

at the first. He, "the Spirit of Truth," was to teach the Apostles *the whole truth*. It was a personal promise to the Apostles, and fulfilled in them. The Church of this day cannot know more than St. John, else the promise would not have been fulfilled to him, that God, the Holy Ghost, should teach him *the whole truth*. Whatever the Apostles received, *that* they were enjoined to teach[7]. And that whole truth the Apostles taught, orally and in writing, committing it as the deposit (παρακαταθήκη) to the Bishops whom they left in their place[8], and, under inspiration of God the Holy Ghost, embodying it in Holy Scripture. At least we know from the testimony of those who followed, that they taught it orally in all its great outlines; and St. Paul himself says, "I have not shunned to declare to you the whole counsel of God." It does not indeed absolutely follow, that they *so* taught in detail all which is contained in Holy Scripture. How much, e. g., is taught in the Epistles incidentally, in answer to doubts which had arisen, whether this were so or no, even as to Apostolic teaching, or in correction of nascent heresies! But there is this difference between the teaching of the Apostles and that of the Church after them, that what the Apostles taught as the original and Fountain-head, *that* the Church only transmitted.

[7] St. Matt. x. 27. xxviii. 20. [8] 2 Tim. ii. 2, &c.

This I conceive to be the meaning of the Council of Trent too, that, when our Lord became Man, He completed His revelation to man. For the Council of Trent, at its outset, recognized as the sources of our knowledge, only Holy Scripture, and those "traditions, whether as to faith or morals, which had been dictated orally by Christ or by the Holy Ghost, and had been preserved by continual succession in the Catholic Church [8]." According to the Council of Trent, then, as well as ourselves, the revelation was finished in and through the Apostles. In Ravignan's words, "Achevé, sanctionné par Jésus Christ, il s'arrête, et Dieu ne revèle plus, ne doit plus révéler après la rédemption operée; car elle est le terme des promesses, le sommet de l'édifice et des conseils divins. La pierre fondamentale est posée, l'édifice couronné, et nul n'en peut bâtir un autre, comme s'exprimait S. Paul."

The office, then, which God the Holy Ghost vouchsafes to take for us, became different after the time of the Apostles. For they were the chosen instruments whom our Blessed Lord selected to be the primary authoritative teachers of His truth. And, in conformity with this choice, God the Holy Ghost dwelt fully in them, inspiring them and making them infallible teachers, and completing His revelation through them.

Thenceforth, then, it was the office of the Church, under the guidance of God the Holy Ghost, to

[8] Sess. iv.

transmit, guard, defend that truth, which our Divine Lord, and God the Holy Ghost, teaching the Apostles what, during our Lord's Bodily Presence, they had not been able to receive, gave to the Church once for all.

Again, within the post-Apostolic Church, God the Holy Ghost has been pleased to operate, in a twofold way, for the preservation of that truth, which He first gave, ordinary and extraordinary. Ordinarily He upholds and maintains that body of faith, once declared, which, without His continual presence and inspiration, would be lost. He operates also in sacraments; He ordains the succession of pastors, doctors, bishops, through whom He continually propagates the truth; He converts the Jews and heathen; He reclaims heretics, and those too who have done despite to His grace; He extends the bounds of the Church; He operates towards, or in every soul of Christians; He teaches in all true teachers. "The Holy Church throughout all the world doth acknowledge Thee." Through His continued operation and inspiration the Church every where, in East and West, North and South, confesseth, maintaineth, teacheth, propagateth the one faith,—that "which was once for all delivered to the saints."

Extraordinary operations of this same teaching of God the Holy Ghost have been on those occasions, when the Church has had to state, explicitly and formally, in correction of emerging heresies, the truth which God the Holy Ghost ever taught by her. I call these "extraordinary," because such occasions have been comparatively rare in the history of the Church. The form of "General Councils," to which our thoughts naturally are first directed, are rarer still. When there was a good hope that the East and West might be again united, the Western Church was willing to ignore all the Councils which it had held subsequently to the separation, and to count the existing Council from the last which East and West had held together. They virtually acknowledged the intervening Councils to have been, not in their fullest sense General Councils, but to have been Western Councils only.

Yet the same object of ascertaining the mind of the Church might be, and was, attained in another way. In the three first centuries a General Council was obviously impossible. It would only have marked out Christian bishops for martyrdom, on the supposition that they were engaged in a conspiracy against the State; yet emergent heresies were condemned, and the mind of the whole Church was ascertained as clearly without them as with them. St. Augustine says of the Pelagian heresy, "What need was there of gathering a Synod, to condemn a manifest mischief? As though no heresy had ever been condemned, except by the gathering of a Synod! Whereas, contrariwise, they were very few heresies, to condemn which there was any such need; and incomparably many more heresies have been rejected and condemned where they arose; and thence they could be made known through the rest of the world as things to be avoided[9]." Yet during all that time the assent of the whole Church would be obtained without any meeting. It is said of the Pelagian heresy, "the whole world embraced the enactment of the 214 [African] Bishops against the enemies of the grace of God[1]." "The Synodal decrees of the Council of 214 Bishops at Carthage were transmitted to Pope Zosimus; which, being approved, the Pelagian heresy was condemned through the whole world[2]." The doctrines of grace were thus established as part of the faith, as fully as if they had been formally received by a General Council. Mr. Palmer counted "more than ninety heresies, which were suppressed before the Council of Nice by the arguments and authorities of the Bishops and Provincial Synods[3]." In like way St. Jerome relates, "how the Bishops of Rome, Alexandria, Milan, Aquileia, *and the whole Synod of Catholics*, both of East and West, with a like sentence, because their mind is alike, denounce Origen to the people as a heretic[4]." We have no detailed account of the

[9] Cont. 2 Epp. Pelag. end.
[1] Prosper resp. ad Obj. Gall. 8.
[2] Id. Chron. A. 418. [3] On the Church, ii. 134.
[4] Cont. Ruff. ii. 22.

Synods to which St. Jerome refers, except that Origen was condemned first at Alexandria, then at Rome, at the instigation of Theophilus, Bishop of Alexandria, and then by other Synods. But the result St. Augustine sums up: "him, not undeservedly, *the Church hath rejected*[5]," on account of the heresy of Universalism, "and for some other things." He speaks of the doctrine as one which the Church *had* not been able to endure[6]. "The Catholic Church wholly rejects this, when it neither accuses him falsely, nor can be deceived by his defenders. For what Catholic Christian, learned or unlearned, would not be exceedingly horrified[7]" thereat?

Of these two ways of ascertaining the mind of the Church, neither have been adopted on any fixed rule. The Second General Council was originally only an Eastern Council, which became general through its reception by the West, which was not represented in it. The Church had to wait many years for the Council of Constantinople, which completed the Nicene Creed, until the accession of the Orthodox Emperor Theodosius gave scope for it. She had again to await the accession of the Emperor Marcian, before the robber-Council of Ephesus could be displaced by the Fourth General Council at Chalcedon. The Fifth General Council was assembled by a heretical Emperor,

[5] De Civ. D. xxi. 17. [6] Ib. c. 23.
[7] De Hær. c. 43.

instigated by heretics, yet was preserved by God's Providence and by His Spirit, under which it was *not* convened.

Nor is there any promise that the Church shall be guided, when and how to hold Councils, although it is promised that the whole Church should not be led into error. Centuries elapsed before the attempt to solve the great schism of the East and West by a Council.

Nor is it essential, according to the Church of Rome itself, that the Church should at once define even a matter of faith which is disputed. The controversies about the Immaculate Conception are older than the Reformation, but have only just been decided. It has now been ruled that that doctrine was always matter of faith; yet it has only been formally received in the Roman Church, when it had tacitly made its way, and its once powerful opponents had ceased. The object of the decision was understood to be, *not* to settle controversies which had long expired, but to obtain the favour of the Blessed Virgin towards the Church of Rome by doing honour to her. During the disputes between the Gallican and Ultramontane Divines about the supremacy of the Pope, each party held the opposite statements to be heretical; but the Church did not interpose. No doubt, wisely. Ultramontanism has been fostered by the tyranny of the State, driving people to take refuge in an authority external to the State.

Should Gallicanism be extinguished hereafter, it would be according to the analogy of the course as to the doctrine of the Immaculate Conception, that Ultramontanism, which is now the favoured opinion, should be declared to be matter of faith. But any how, it is clear from the old controversies as to the Immaculate Conception, that, according to the Roman Church too, what is subsequently ruled to be *de fide* may be allowed, for a long time, to remain matter of vehement dispute.

Nor, although it is promised that the whole Church should not fall into error, is it promised that they should in all things act wisely. The Roman Church long refused to accept those Canons of the Second and the Fourth General Councils which settled the rank of the Patriarchate of Constantinople, although it ultimately acceded to them. The fifth General Council, although marvellously preserved from error, and a maintainer of truth, gave rise to a lamentable schism among the orthodox as to "The Three Chapters," very chiefly through the vacillations of Pope Vigilius. The Latin Church has tacitly acknowledged that the Council of Florence acted unwisely in trying to force upon the Greeks the Latin formula as to the Procession of God the Holy Ghost, contrary to their uniform tradition, even while it granted that the formula of the Greek fathers, διὰ τοῦ Υἱοῦ, expressed the same truth as the Latin "Filioque." On this and other grounds the Council failed of its object, and the opportunity was lost of effacing the inveterate prejudice of the Greeks, that the Latin formula had an heretical meaning, viz. that there are two Ἀρχαί in the Divine nature. The Latin Church has tacitly allowed that it was a mistake to insist that the Greeks should adopt our Western expression, by allowing the Greeks, who have submitted to its authority, to say the Creed, as the Council of Constantinople left it.

It is, then, no essential part of the office of God the Holy Ghost in the Church to direct it, how, when, and for what to assemble General Councils.

It is matter of faith that the whole Church shall never be led into any formal acceptance of error by virtue of our Lord's promise; and on this ground the Church of England receives the Six General Councils. But it is not matter of faith that the Church will always be able to hold General Councils, as in fact, important as the issues were, God allowed a time to elapse before the Second and Fourth General Councils could be called.

Meanwhile God the Holy Ghost exercises the office of Teacher, which He vouchsafed to take, both by teaching the children of God (as it is said, "they shall all be taught of God"), and by giving them the supernatural gift of faith, as of grace; and He maintains in the Church every where the tradition of the great body of the faith, infallibly fixed. And this is not impaired, although there are other points not yet cleared up, both with the Greek Church and our own, e. g. as to the Papal claims, so different from the relation of the Patriarchates to one another in early times, or indulgences which the Greek Church never knew, or the denial of the cup, which the Greek Church ever gave, or the marriage-law of the Council of Trent, which allows what the whole Church from the first, until the miserable Alexander VI. (Borgia), held to be incest. Largely, moreover, as invocation of the Blessed Virgin is used in the Greek Church, it has nowhere adopted that vast formulized theory as to her place as the channel of all grace to the Church, and to each single soul, which is to us the especial "crux" in the Roman system. It has protested against the doctrine of the Immaculate Conception[8] of the Blessed Virgin, which Pius IX. defined, as "attested" by "the monuments of the Eastern Church," as well as "the Western."

Dr. Manning has invented a new heresy, which he charges upon us. The Church of England nowhere denies that General Councils can be held, nor that any doctrine could be vindicated simultaneously throughout the whole Church. The time may come, when this will have to be done. True, that the first office of a General Council *now* would be to reunite Christendom. But until this be

[8] See Note B at the end.

(which may God, in His mercy, bring to pass), truth, when occasion shall require, may be vindicated by the whole Church simultaneously, without any meeting, as was done in the early Church, after the Council of Nice as well as before. There are indications of clouds lowering on the horizon of the Roman Church, in regard to Holy Scripture, which have discharged their first burst upon ourselves. There have appeared already among Roman Catholics symptoms of a tendency to hold cheaply by Holy Scripture, as being comparatively unimportant to them, who have the authority of an infallible Church, forgetting that the authority of the Church depends upon Holy Scripture. There are those among them who seem inclined to indemnify themselves for their submission to the Church in things formally laid down by it, by a licence as to things, not so distinctly defined. Whereto this may grow, or whether He will nip it, God alone knows! But the need may arise among them, as well as among ourselves, to lay down formally the truth of all Holy Scripture, as given by inspiration of God, which has been presupposed by all, everywhere, at all times, from the first. Such a simultaneous decree would, by general consent, have the authority of a General Council, as without any General Council Pelagianism was condemned by the whole Church.

Why then, since we believe the teaching of God the Holy Ghost in the Church to be infallible, is it to be made a heresy to say that man does not use the gift as much as he might, as e. g. if God's constraining grace were to move the whole Church everywhere to seek visible reconciliation? The question does not relate to that which has once been settled by the whole Church. Nothing, of course, can add to the authority of what has ever been ruled by an infallible authority. We ourselves have, equally with those in the Roman Church, infallible truth, as resting on infallible authority. We do not need the present agency of an infallible Church to assure us of the truth of what has been ruled infallibly. Nor, in fact, have Roman Catholics any more infallible authority for what they hold than we, seeing that it was ruled by the Church in past ages, to whom, so far, the present Church submits. The later General Councils began by accepting what had been ruled before them. The second received, while it enlarged, the creed of the first; the third premised to its own acts the confession of the creeds of the two first; the fourth received the decree of Ephesus too, and accepted the wonderful clearness of the exposition of faith by St. Leo, *as agreeing with those previous authorities.* They accepted those creeds before them, not thereby adding to their authority, but as authenticating their own orthodoxy. The question, then, is not whether the doctrine laid down in General Councils, and received by the whole Church, is certain truth (on this both agree); nor whether the whole doctrine of the Holy Trinity, of the Incarnation, of Grace, and whatsoever else has been received formally by the whole Church, is infallibly settled (on this too both are at one); nor whether an Œcumenical Council, if such were now held and received by the whole Church, would, by that reception, have the seal of infallibility (on this, too, according to the principles of the Gallican Church and our own, there is no question); nor whether, in fact, if the same doctrines were enunciated at once by the whole Church, the East, West, our own, separately, but concordantly (e. g. as to the character of the inspiration of Holy Scripture), the doctrine, so simultaneously enunciated, would be infallibly certain (which it would be);—but whether what should be enacted, either by the Greek or Roman Church, would be infallible, unless received by the other. This (granted that the Eastern Church is a part of the Church), it would not be according to the principles of the Gallican divines too, because there would not be universal reception.

This, then, which is to destroy the whole faith among us, resolves itself into the fact, that we acknowledge the Greek Church, as well as the Roman, to be part of the Church of Christ. If it is, the Western Councils alone, not having yet had universal reception, have not received the seal of infallibility; and the Roman Church itself owned that those intermediate Councils might be counted to be wanting in something, since it was willing, in prospect of union with the East, to ignore them as General Councils.

vii. But is there then no issue to the present division of Christendom? Is disunion to be the normal state of the Church, for which we all pray that God would give her unity, peace, and concord? God forbid! I have never expected to see that external unity of intercommunion restored in my own day; but I have felt it to be an end to be wished for, and prayed for. I doubt not that the Roman Church and ourselves are kept apart much more by that vast practical system which lies beyond the letter of the Council of Trent, things which are taught with a quasi-authority in the Roman Church, than by what is actually defined. Nothing could be more unpractical than for an individual to throw himself into the Roman Church, because he could accept the *letter* of the Council of Trent. Those who were born Roman Catholics have a liberty, which, in the nature of things, a person could not have, who left another system, to embrace that of Rome. I cannot imagine how any faith could stand the shock of leaving one system, criticizing *it*, and casting himself into another system, criticizing *it*. For myself I have always felt that had (which God of His mercy avert hereafter also) the English Church, by accepting heresy, driven me out of it, I could have gone in no other way than that of closing my eyes, and accepting whatever was put before me. But a liberty which individuals could not use, and explanations which, so long as they remain individual, must be unauthoritative, might be formally made by the Church of Rome to the Church of England as the basis of reunion. I have already hinted at several such explanations which might, I should have thought, be made. The Council of Trent laid down, in many cases, what is very far below the practical system, encouraged, at present, every where in the Church of Rome, taught in her name and with her authority, but which, on being questioned, no Roman Catholic, I believe, would declare to be *de fide*. And yet, take not ourselves only, but the general body of Englishmen, whether instructed or not instructed, it will be of this as yet undefined body of practical belief that they will be thinking when they speak of our "reformed" Church, or against becoming Roman Catholics. If they speak against Papal authority, it is not in itself (which would be a matter of indifference), but as an authority, which, if they submitted to it, would enforce upon them that practical system. Probably, too, there is an hereditary dread of the renewal of the fires of Smithfield, the sinfulness of which has never been disowned.

I would explain what I mean with reference to Art XXII.

vii. *a.* In regard to the Invocation of Saints, the Council of Trent lays down this only, "It[1] is good

[1] Sess. xxv. Bishop Latimer is quoted as agreeing altogether

and useful suppliantly to invoke the saints, and to have recourse to their *prayers*, help, and assistance, to obtain favours from God, through His Son Jesus Christ our Lord, Who is alone our Redeemer and Saviour;" and direct prayer to the saints to "give us good things, and deliver us from evil things," seems to be directly prohibited by the Catechism of the Council[2]. And there is the popular explanation, that we are to ask for their prayers in no other sense than we ask for each other's prayers, and that "they[3] do nothing for us mortals in heaven, but what they did while they were here on earth, and what all good Christians are bound to do for each other, namely, they help us by their prayers. The only difference is, that as the saints in heaven are free from every stain of sin and imperfection, and are confirmed in grace and glory, so their prayers are far more efficacious for obtaining what they ask for than are the prayers of us imperfect and sinful mortals."

with the *words* of the Council of Trent. "Take saints for inhabitants of heaven, and worshipping them for praying to them, I never denied but that they might be worshipped, and be our mediators, though not by way of redemption (for so Christ alone is a whole mediator, both for them and us), yet by way of intercession."—Foxe, Acts and Monuments.

[2] "God and the saints are not to be prayed to in the same manner, for we pray to God that He Himself would give us good things, and deliver us from evil things: but we beg of the saints that they would be our advocates, and obtain from God what we stand in need of." Cat. of C. of Trent, quoted by Milner, End of Contr. Lett. xxxiii.

[3] Milner, ib.

Now, were this all, the difficulty never could have arisen. The mere "ora pro nobis," *so explained*, could not have led any to stop short in the Saints, nor have called forth any protest, out of zeal for God's honour. But, along with this, was that vast system as to the Blessed Virgin, which to all of us has been the special "crux" of the Roman system. This we have often insisted upon[4], as did those before us. It is impossible to condense the statements of a doctrine which presents itself in so many startling forms, co-extensive with the present Office of our Dear Lord for us. His Precious Blood, they of course say with us, is alone the meritorious cause of our salvation. But her intercession is held to be co-extensive with His, "Who ever liveth to make intercession for us," our Divine Lord, and to be the access to His Intercession. And this is taught, not as the glowing expression of Southern feeling, but as the deliberate mind of the present Roman Church. It was one who has since been beatified[5], who formally rejected the "opinion of a certain modern author, who has written with great piety and learning on true and false devotion," that "the proposition, 'God gives no grace except through Mary,' is an hyperbole and exaggeration, which fell from some of the saints in a moment of fervour, and is to be understood

[4] Dr. Pusey's Letter to Dr. Jelf, pp. 187—216, and Sermon, Rule of Faith, pp. 55—61.

[5] Liguori, Glories of Mary, v. 1, quoted Rule of Faith, p. 57.

to mean that from Mary we have received Jesus Christ, through Whose merits we receive all graces." God, it is granted, "*could* grant His graces without the intercession of Mary[6];" but it is asserted that "He *will* not." It is one of their most learned writers[7] who says, "it is the universal sentiment of the [Roman] Church that the intercession of Mary is not only useful, but also in a certain manner necessary;" "necessary, with a *moral* necessity, because the Church seems to think, with St. Bernard, that God has determined to give us no grace except through the hands of Mary[1]." So, then, it is taught in authorized books, that "it is morally impossible for those to be saved who neglect the devotion to the Blessed Virgin[2];" that "it is the will of God that all graces should pass through her hands;" that "no creature obtained any grace from God, save according to the dispensation of His holy mother[3];" that Jesus has, in fact, said, "no one shall be partaker of My Blood, unless through the intercession of My mother[4];" that "we can only hope to obtain perseverance through her[5];" that "God granted all the pardons in the Old Testament absolutely for the reverence and love

[6] Ib.

[7] Suarez, T. ii. in 3 P. Disp. 23, § 3.

[1] Liguori, ib. [2] See the Proofs in Rule of Faith, p. 55.

[3] Bernardine Sen. Serm. 61, Tr. i., Art. 8, quoted by Lig.

[4] Contensonius, Theol. Mentis et Cordis, T. ii. L. x. D. iv. c. 1, in Lig.

[5] See in Rule of Faith, p. 58.

of this Blessed Virgin[6];" that "our salvation is in her hand[7];" that "it is impossible for any to be saved, who turns away from her, or is disregarded by her; or to be lost, who turns to her, or is regarded by her[8];" that "whom the justice of God saves not, the *infinite* mercy of Mary saves by her intercession[1];" that God is "subject to the command of Mary[2];" that "God has resigned into her hands (if one might say so) His omnipotence in the sphere of grace[3];" "that it is safer to seek salvation through her than directly from Jesus[4]."

[6] Bernardine Sen., Serm. 61, c. 8.

[7] Ric. a S. Laurent. de Laud. Virg. L. 3, p. 1, and others in Lig.

[8] Eadmer de Excell. Virg. cxi., quoted as St. Anselm, in Lig. St. Antonin. ib.

[1] Ascribed to St. Chrys. if not to St. Ignat., but spurious, in Lig.

[2] "All things are subject to the command of the Virgin, even God Himself." Bern. Sen. Serm. 61, Art. i. c. 6. Ussher, p. 417. "The Blessed Virgin is superior to God, and God Himself *is* subject unto her, in respect of the Manhood which He assumed from her." Bern. de Bust. Marial. p. 9, Serm. 2, ib. "However she be subject unto God, inasmuch as she is a creature, yet she is said to be superior and preferred before Him, inasmuch as she is His mother." Ib. p. 2, s. 2, ib. "You have over God the authority of a mother, and hence you obtain pardon for the most obdurate sinners." Gl. of M. in Letter, p. 209.

[3] Glories of M. p. 85, quoted Letter, p. 208. See also Treatise on the Scapular, c. 7, p. 43. Gl. of M. p. 130. On "participated omnipotency," ib. 207.

[4] As "in the vision which Burn. de Bust. reciteth as shown to St. Francis touching the two ladders, that reached from

It seemed to me to bear very closely upon the mediatorial Office of our Lord, when M. Olier, founder of the seminary of St. Sulpice, said, "*The intention of the Church is*, that we seek Jesus Christ in His saints; and we are much more sure of finding Him in His saints, for instance, in the Blessed Virgin, St. Joseph, St. John, St. Peter, than when we seek Him immediately and of ourselves.—We are very unworthy to draw near unto Jesus; and He has a right to repulse [rebuter] us, because of His justice, since, *having entered into all the feelings of His Father from the time of His blessed Resurrection, He finds Himself in the same disposition with the Father towards sinners, i. e., to reject them; so that the difficulty is to induce Him* to exchange the office of Judge for that of Advocate; and, of a Judge, to make Him a suppliant. Now this is what the saints effect, and especially the most Blessed Virgin." To me this seemed unintentional heresy, sanctioned by the two Gallican Bishops who recommended the book. I understand that an apology has been made for it, that M. Olier was a devotional, not a dogmatic writer,

earth to heaven, the one red, upon which Christ leaned, from which many fell backward and could not ascend; the other white, upon which the holy Virgin leaned; the help whereof such as used, were by her received with a cheerful countenance, and so with facility ascended into heaven." Marial. p. 9, Serm. 2, Assim. 2; also (as shown to Fr. Lion) Spec. vit. Franc. et soc. p. 2, c. 45, Spec. exempl. dist. 7, exempl. 41, in Ussher, p. 429, repeated in Glor. of M. p. 180.

and so did not express himself with formal accuracy. Of course, I never thought of imputing to a pious writer, like M. Olier, conscious heresy. The assertion itself, however, that "our Lord had changed since His Resurrection, and was now of one mind with the Father," in a way in which He had not been before, must, in any plain meaning of the words, be heretical. The statement, moreover, that the saints are more ready to intercede with Jesus, than Jesus is to intercede with the Father, is, in fact, a denial of His mediatorial office, and is by no means peculiar to M. Olier. It was said of old, too, "no sinner doth deserve that Christ should any more make intercession for him with the Father, without Whose intercession none can be delivered either from the eternal punishment or the temporal, nor from the fault which he has voluntarily committed, and therefore it was necessary that Christ should constitute His well-beloved mother a mediatrix betwixt us and Him,—that she would appease the wrath of her Son[5];" "that God retained justice unto Himself, and granted mercy to her[6];" that "she is the throne of grace, whereof the Apostle speaketh;[7]" that "she appeaseth the just anger of her Son[8];"

[5] Jac. de Valent. in Expos. *Magnificat.* Ussher.

[6] Gabr. Biel in Can. Miss. Lect. 80. Bernardin. de Bust. Marial. p. 3, s. 3, de excell. 4, in Ussher.

[7] Bern. de B. ib. Exc. 5, and p. 5, Serm. 7, fin. Ussher.

[8] "I shall no longer fear your Son justly irritated, since one word from you [Mary] will appease Him." Gl. of M. p. 74.

that "to sinners, who have lost Divine grace, there is no more sun" (the symbol of Jesus) "for him, but the moon is still on the horizon; let him address himself to Mary[9];" that "she is the only refuge of those who have incurred the Divine indignation[1];" that "Jesus, being no less our Judge than our Saviour, He *must* avenge the wrongs we do Him by our sins; while the holy Virgin, being solely our Advocate, is obliged to entertain only sentiments of pity for us[2]."

It is commonly said, that if any Roman Catholic acknowledges that "it is good and useful to pray to the saints," he is not bound, himself, to do so. Were the above teaching true, it would be cruelty to say so; because, according to it, he would be forfeiting what is morally necessary to his salvation. So then it seems as if the Roman Church must either advance in her theoretical teaching, or recede in her practical teaching. At present this sort of teaching is in the advance. One should have thought that, at least, when our Lord gives Himself to us in the Holy Eucharist, *this* must be direct communion with Himself. But

Letter on Tract 90, p. 211. "If my Saviour drive me off because of my sins, I will go and cast myself at the feet of His mother; thence I will not rise till she has obtained my pardon. For she does not know what it is to be insensible to the voice of misery, and her pity will mitigate the anger of her Son." Gl. of M. p. 89. Ib.

[9] Innocent III. in Glories of Mary, p. 69; Letter, ib.

[1] Blosius in Glories of Mary, p. 93, quoted ib.

[2] Eadmer, de Exc. B. V., ib. p. 212.

a new ritual has arisen, which seems to be intended to symbolize that we do not gain access even to Holy Communion, except through the Blessed Virgin. This is but the carrying out of the old principle, that "it is the will of God that all graces should come through her hands." Before, it had been taught, "Jesus[3] Christ is, in the Holy Sacrament, risen again and full of glory; and though He be in a sacrament of goodness and mercy, He nevertheless therein exercises His judgments very commonly by condemnations. We must then go to a sacrament solely of mercy, wherein Jesus Christ exercises no judgments. This sacrament is the most Blessed Virgin. It is through her that we have access to Jesus Christ in full confidence." But now, those colossal figures of the Blessed Virgin, which are carried in procession, and placed before or by the side of the Altar, seem intended to represent, that, through her mediation only, those who are in the grace of Christ become fitted to become partakers of His blessed Body and Blood. In Southern India and Ceylon, our Churches are called by the natives "Jesus-Churches;" the Roman Catholic Churches "Mary-Churches."

It is, of course, an abuse of this teaching, when any *confine* their prayers to the Blessed Virgin. A certain proportion, it has been ascertained by those who have inquired, do stop short in her. I have myself been asked by Roman Catholics to

[3] M. Olier, Catéchisme Chrétien, quoted Rule of Faith, p. 60.

pray for my conversion: once only I was asked to pray our Lord. On the other occasions, I was exclusively asked to pray the Blessed Virgin for it[4]. In an edition of "the Glories of Mary," I have seen one objection so far attended to, that notes were added upon the direct prayers to the Blessed Virgin for spiritual graces, stating that it was meant only that she should obtain these graces by her intercession. Still, the teaching remains, that we are even surer to obtain them from her, than if we go directly to the One Mediator between God and man, our Divine Lord, "Who ever liveth to make intercession for us."

The Homilies illustrate what it is, which our Articles condemn, viz., Invocations, which seem to interfere with the all-sufficiency of the Intercession of our Divine Redeemer, or any act of devotion which is "proper unto God[5]." Bishop Andrewes also, in his summary, explains what those of his day believed to be condemned by the article, not requests for the prayers of saints departed, but

[4] A friend of mine, in like way, was asked to pray to the Blessed Virgin in a form framed on the beginning of the Litany: "Mary, daughter of the Father, give me light; Mary, Mother of the Son,—Mary, Spouse of the Holy Ghost,"—the especial prayers I forget; but they were exactly the same prayers which we should have addressed to the Holy Trinity.

"These English are but half converts!" was the exclamation of an Italian priest by a devout deathbed, when the dying person commended herself to "Jesus," instead of to "Jesus and Mary."

[5] On Prayer, p. 277.

direct addresses to them, as if they could themselves give what we ask. "They[6] say to the Blessed Virgin, 'Sancta Maria!' not only 'Ora pro nobis,' but 'Succurre miseris, juva pusillanimes, refove flebiles, accipe quod offerimus, dona quod rogamus, excusa quod timemus.'—All which and many more show plainly that the *practice* of the Church of Rome, in this point of invocation of saints, is far otherwise than Cardinal Perron would bear the world in hand; and that *prier pour prier* is not all, but that, 'Tu dona cœlum, Tu laxa, Tu sana, Tu solve crimina, Tu duc, conduc, induc, perduc, ad gloriam, Tu serva, Tu fer opem, Tu aufer, Tu confer vitam,' are said to them, *totidem verbis;* more than which cannot be said to God Himself. And again, 'Hic nos solvat a peccatis, hic nostros tergat reatus, hic arma conferat, hic hostem fuget, hic gubernet, hic aptet tuo conspectui,' which, if they be not *direct* and absolute, it would be asked of them, What is absolute or direct?" And this impression, that more is intended than the asking of their prayers, as we do those of members of Christ still in the flesh, is strengthened by the statement, not contained in the Council of Trent, that invocation is "an eminent kind of adoration[7];" that "we [Roman

[6] Answer to Card. Perron's Reply, end, pp. 58. 62 [pp. 76. 80, ed. Ang. Cath. Lib.].

[7] "Eximium adorationis genus." Bellarm. Præf. in Controv. Eccl. Triumph. quoted by Ussher, p. 402.

Catholics] do not honour the saints with that worship only, wherewith we do men which excel in virtue, &c., but also with *Divine* worship and honour, which is an act of religion," only that they "do not give Divine worship and honour unto the saints for themselves, but for God Who hath made them saints[8]."

The large system as to the B. V., of which I have given specimens, unknown as it was to the Ancient Church[9], has a quasi-authority in the Roman Church, (at least, it is set forth in her name), moulds, and necessarily must mould, a great part of the

[8] Azor. Inst. Mor. T. i. L. ix. c. 10, quoted ib.

[9] The one exception is a relation given by S. Gregory as to S. Justina, out of some spurious Acts belonging to the latter half of the fourth (his own) century. The Acts, from which he takes his account, agree in substance with those which S. Prudentius also had (Peristeph. 13), and which the Empress Eudoxia versified (Phot. Cod. 184, p. 215, Hoesch.). All alike, on the ground of those Acts, confound S. Cyprian with an Eastern martyr, whom the Acts make a magician before he was converted. Besides historical inaccuracies, the Acts have plainly fabulous stories about magic. (See Baluz. Præf. ad S. Cypr. xxxiii.) As extant, however, they have not the history related by S. Gregory, that, at the close of long prayers to God, Justina "besought the Virgin Mary to succour a virgin in peril from the assaults of Satan" (Orat. 24, § 11). S. Gregory relates the fact as he found it in his Acts, without comment, not remarking on the Acts of a martyr. The Acts are most full, in Latin, in Martene, Anecd. iii. pp. 1621, sqq.; the Conf. S. Cypriani exists in Greek, App. to S. Cypr. p. ccxcv, Ben. In no instance, among the genuine Acts of Martyrs, edited by Ruinart, is any martyr related to have asked for help amidst those super-human sufferings, or otherwise, except from God generally, or from our Lord.

private devotions in the Roman Church. Yet Dr. Manning too, I suppose, would not allege it as the teaching of God the Holy Ghost, which a man could not reject without sin: for then it would be *de fide* and infallible, which yet it is alleged not to be. Yet devotions to the Blessed Virgin have been and are assigned as penance in the Roman Church, and consequently as a condition of forgiveness of sin. It is notorious that this system is the great barrier and ground of alienation of pious minds in England. "It comes," said one who appreciated highly what is good and holy in the Roman Church, "as near to idolatry, as can be supposed in a Church, of which it is said, 'the idols He shall utterly abolish.'" I have often myself had to try to remove the rooted conviction that Roman Catholics are actual "idolaters." Since then the lawfulness or usefulness of asking the saints to pray for us is alone laid down as "of faith," there is a large scope for providing that, in case of a reunion, our people should not be flooded with these devotions, which to us are most alien. Nothing which seems to interfere with exclusive trust and reliance on Jesus will, without some great revolution, gain hold of the hearts of the English people.

And here, for the sake of others, it may perhaps be well to repeat a statement which I made above seventeen years ago, why, in a book of devotions [1],

[1] Paradise for the Christian Soul, Advertisement.

which I transplanted into the English Church, I "omitted all mention of the Invocation of Saints." I said:—

"However it may be explained by Roman Catholic controversialists, to be no more than asking the prayers of members of Christ yet in the flesh, still, in use, it is plainly more; for no one would ask those in the flesh to 'protect us from the enemy,' 'receive us in the hour of death,' 'lead us to the joy of heaven,' 'may thy [the Blessed Virgin] abundant love cover the multitude of sins,' 'heal my wounds, and to the mind which asketh thee, give the gifts of grace[2],' or use any of the *direct* prayers for graces, which God Alone can bestow, which are common in Roman Catholic devotions to the Blessed Virgin. No one can look uncontroversially at such occasional addresses, as there are to martyrs in the fourth century (and those chiefly prayers at their tombs through their intercession for miraculous aid of God), and such books as 'the Glories of Mary,' 'the Month of Mary,' and say that the character of the modern reliance on and invocation of Saints was that of the ancient Church. No one could (it should be thought) observe how through volumes of S. Augustine or S. Chrysostom, there is no mention of any reliance except on Christ Alone; and how in modern books, S. Mary is held out as '*the* refuge of sinners,' as having 'the goats committed to her, as Christ the sheep,' as 'the throne of grace,' to whom a sinner may have easier access than to Christ[3], and seriously say, that the ancient and

---

[2] Or say, "If I walk through the midst of the shadow of death, I will fear no evil, for she is with me. If war arise against me, in this will I be confident. If my father and mother forsake me, the Mother of my Lord shall take me up."

[3] "Christ is not our Advocate only, but a Judge; and since the Just is scarcely secure, how shall a sinner go to Him, as an Advocate? Therefore God has provided us of an advocatress, who is gentle and sweet, in whom nothing that is sharp is to be found."—Antonin. quoted by Taylor, Dissuasive, I. ii. 8.

modern teaching and practice are the same. *We* could preach whole volumes of the sermons of S. Augustine or S. Chrysostom to our people to their edification and without offence: were a Roman Catholic preacher to confine himself to their preaching, he would (it has been said among themselves) be regarded as 'indevout towards S. Mary,' as 'one whose religion was more of the head than of the heart.' The Editor, then, has not ventured even upon the outskirts of so vast a system, which, even according to Roman Catholic testimony which he has had, does practically occasion many uninstructed minds to stop short in the mediation of S. Mary. When Holy Scripture is not even alleged (as no text for the invocation of saints either is or can be quoted by Roman Catholic controversialists), and primitive antiquity is equally silent (now that passages as to S. Mary once attributed to S. Athanasius, S. Augustine, S. Ephrem, S. Chrysostom, under the shadow of whose great names this system grew up, are acknowledged to be spurious), and the language of great fathers (as S. Cyril of Alexandria) has to be explained away; there was no authority to which the Editor dared to yield his faith. Taught by the Church to receive that and that alone, as matter of faith, which was part of the 'good deposit,' 'once for all committed to the saints,' and which had been held 'always, every where, and by all,' he did not venture to receive what was confessedly of a more recent origin, and whose tendency seemed at variance with Holy Scripture itself. While acknowledging the 'authority of the Church in controversies of faith' (Art. XX.), he could not understand on what ground that vast system, as to S. Mary, could be rested, except that of a new revelation. 'Developement' must surely apply to the expression, not to the substance of belief. It must be the bringing out in words of what was always inwardly held; the securing of the old, not the addition of any thing new. However the language of the Church on the doctrine of the Holy Trinity may have, in time, become more fixed and definite, any one would think it an impiety to imagine that S. John and S. Peter had not received, and did not deliver, all which has ever since been believed. He 'who lay on Jesus' Breast,' and he on whose confession of faith the Church was built, could not be ignorant of any thing belonging to that faith[4]. Neither can it be believed that they withheld any thing belonging to that faith[5]. To imagine either, was of old accounted to be 'subjecting[6] Christ to reproach.' Yet it seems inconceivable that S. Peter, S. John, and S. Paul should have believed what is now earnestly taught and believed upon authority *within* the Roman Church, as to the *present* office of the Blessed Virgin, or that believing it, they could have written as (e. g.) S. Paul wrote through the Holy Ghost, in the Epistle to the Hebrews; or that, if Almighty God had willed it to be believed in the Church, it should have been so excluded from Holy Scripture, and the doctrine itself not have appeared for centuries. The Editor, then, in a former work, while excluding invocations, admitted what is involved in the word θεοτόκος, as sanctioned by an Œcumenical Council, to whose authority the English Church yields unquestioning submission. In the present, he has omitted the whole second section 'Of the Worship and Veneration of Saints,' and half of the seventh, 'On the Worship and Veneration of the Blessed Virgin Mary.' And, generally, for members of the English Church, who desire the prayers of the departed, it has to him ever seemed safest to pray for them to Him, 'of Whom and through Whom and to Whom are all things,' our God and our All, Who, according to the current Roman explanation also, reveals to them the desire of those below to have their prayers."

In the years which have passed since I wrote that Preface, the actual state of the Cultus of the

[4] "'For after that our Lord arose from the dead, and they were endued with the power of the Holy Spirit coming upon them from on high, they were fully filled as to all things, and had perfect knowledge.' 'It is unlawful to say that they preached before they had perfect knowledge.' S. Iren. iii. 1. 1. 'According to these' [the heretics], 'Peter was imperfect; imperfect also the other Apostles. And were they to live again, they must needs become the disciples of these, that they too may become perfect. But this were absurd.'" Ib. 12. 7. See also in the same book, 11 ult.

[5] Id. iii. 3. 5.

[6] Tert. de Præscr. Hær. c. 22.

Blessed Virgin within the Roman Communion has been set forth in an authentic and official way in the answers sent by the Archbishops and Bishops to the inquiry of Pius IX. in regard to the doctrine of the Immaculate Conception. It appears from those answers, that the poorer classes are not, for the most part, even acquainted with the distinction between what is to be believed to be *de fide*, and what is popularly taught them as truth. They receive all which they are taught, alike as matter of faith, whether in the minds of their teachers it is a pious opinion or *de fide*. There was even a difficulty or a risk in acting upon the Pope's desire, that the Bishops would have public prayers in their Dioceses, that God would "pour on him the heavenly light of His Divine Spirit, that in a matter of so much moment he might take that counsel which should be to the greater glory of His Holy Name, to the praise of the most Blessed Virgin, and to the advantage of the Church militant[7]." The difficulty (at least in some places or countries) was, lest it should shake the people's faith, if they were told plainly, that the doctrine which they had always been taught to believe, had never been declared to be matter of faith, and that its being so made was yet uncertain. So, some of the Bishops reported to the Pope that they had veiled the object of the public prayers; some, I think, had not ventured to direct any

[7] Ep. Encycl. Pii IX. A.D. 1849.

public prayers at all. I fear that an opening has been made for the extension of that cultus, both in regard to the doctrines which shall, in fact, be part of the faith in the Roman Communion, and their relation to other fundamental doctrines of the faith, which is altogether incalculable. A very popular devotional writer, once among ourselves, spoke lately of "[8] the speedy coming of that great age of the Church which is to be the Age of Mary," with which he prayed that "the Holy Ghost, the Divine Zealot of Jesus and Mary, may be pleased quickly to console us;" and of one, "an Elias-like Missionary of the Holy Ghost and of Mary," who "proclaims that he brings an authentic message from God about the greater honour and wider knowledge and more prominent love of His Blessed Mother and her connexion with the second advent of her Son." Here, in England, we are told, that Roman Catholics too know little or nothing of the true devotion to the Blessed Virgin, because it is kept in check by what F. Faber calls "the sneers of heresy," and what we believe to be sensitiveness to the honour and glory of Jesus.

I remember that the late Cardinal Wiseman, many years past, blamed English Roman Catholics as having been ashamed of their distinctive doctrines[9]. The doctrine of the Immaculate Con-

[8] Faber, Preface to transl. of De Montfort on the true devotion to the Blessed Virgin, pp. xi. xii., vi. vii.

[9] In his controversial Lectures.

ception, if I understand the statement aright, has only been introduced of late years into their public services, and that, through an impulse given by an individual[1]. F. Faber, in his popular books, is always bringing in the devotion to the Blessed Virgin. He believes that the shortcomings of English Roman Catholics is owing to the inadequacy of their devotion to her. After instancing people's failures in overcoming their faults, want of devotion, unsubmission to God's special Providence for *them*, feeling domestic troubles almost incompatible with salvation, and that "for all these

[1] Bishop Nicholson, Coadjutor of Corfu, says, "I persuaded many Bishops of Italy, Germany, England, Ireland, to ask for the word 'Immaculate' to be added to the Mass of the Conception, and 'Queen conceived without original stain,' in the Litany of Loretto, and to supplicate the Vicar of Jesus Christ to declare the Immaculate Conception ex cathedra." Pareri dell' Episcopato Cattolico sulla definizione dogmatico dell' immacolato concepimento della B. V. Maria, i. 403. The Roman Catholic Bishops of Cashel, Killaloe, Cork, Elphin imply that the people had not been taught the doctrine. The R. C. Archbishop of Cashel said, that "they had not *explicit* faith, but that they had *implicit*," since they so venerated the Blessed Virgin, that they would believe any thing to her honour (Ib. i. 487); the R. C. Bishop of Killaloe, that the clergy had been silent about it, on account of various Bulls (Ib. i. 500); of Cork, that the laity were not versed in theological questions (Ib. ii. 85); of Elphin, that he did not ask people, as they did not understand the question (Ib. ii. 204). The R. C. Bishop of Meath said, that both "priests and people believed it" (Ib. iii. 211), and the Bishop of Clonfert, that they would reject the contrary, which, however, he as well as others put in the form, that she had been "a child of wrath" (Ib. iii. 214).

things prayer appears to bring so little remedy," he asks,

"[2] What is the remedy that is wanted? what is the remedy indicated by God Himself? If we may rely on the disclosures of the saints, it is an immense increase of devotion to our Blessed Lady, but remember, nothing short of an *immense*[3] one. Here, in England, Mary is not half enough preached. Devotion to her is low and thin and poor. It is frightened out of its wits by the sneers of heresy. It is always invoking human respect and carnal prudence, wishing to make Mary so little of a Mary, that Protestants may feel at ease about her. Its ignorance of theology makes it unsubstantial and unworthy. It is not the prominent characteristic of our religion which it ought to be. It has no faith in itself. *Hence* it is, that *Jesus is not loved*, that heretics are not converted, that the Church is not exalted; that souls, which might be saints, wither and dwindle; that the sacraments are not rightly frequented, or souls enthusiastically evangelized. Jesus is obscured, because Mary is kept in the background. *Thousands of souls perish, because Mary is withheld from them.* It is the miserable unworthy shadow which we call our devotion to the Blessed Virgin, that is *the cause of* all these wants and blights, these evils and omissions and declines. Yet, if we are to believe the revelations of the saints, God is *pressing*[3] for a

[2] Pref. to De Montf. p. ix. x.

[3] Faber's Italics.

greater, a wider, a stronger, *quite another devotion* to His Blessed Mother."

It must often come to us to ask on reading such statements,—"If devotion to the Blessed Virgin *were* so essential to salvation, how could it be, that God, in His last and final revelation of Himself, is so wholly silent about it?" Christians had "fiery trials[4]" then, and were to count them no "strange thing." The sufferings of the martyrs are almost past our powers of conception; yet there were slight and easy and self-deceiving ways, by which to deny Christ. Converts had temptations, from which, if we will, we are exempt, the memory of heathen sins and evil habits, antecedent to grace. How can it be thought by any, that Jesus,—Who "ever liveth to make intercession for us[5]," Who crowned His own and was crowned in them; Whose words in His everlasting Gospel are, "[6] Come unto *Me*, all that are weary and heavy laden, and I will give you rest;" "Whatsoever ye shall ask the Father in My Name, He will give it you;" "Whatsoever ye shall ask in My Name, that will I do, that the Father may be glorified in the Son; if ye shall ask any thing in My Name, I will do it[7],"—is not willing to hear us, unless we seek a Mediatrix with Him, who is to dispose Him to hear us?

However, to judge from the official answers of the Bishops to Pius IX. in answer to his inquiry,

[4] 1 Pet. iv. 12; i. 7.
[5] Heb. vii. 25.
[6] S. Matt. xi. 28.
[7] S. John xvi. 23; xiv. 13, 14.

"with what devotion your Clergy and faithful people are animated towards the Conception of the Immaculate Virgin," Faber was right as to the immensely greater devotion and trust in the Blessed Virgin, at least in countries where there is no check from the contact with Protestants. Certainly the prominent impression in my mind from reading those answers (they occupy more than three close volumes) was, "if the devotion to God were like that to the Blessed Virgin, it would be a world of saints." "In this Diocese," says the Bishop of Cochabamba [8], "as in the whole of civilized America, it has attained to the highest degree, so that nothing more can be desired." "Our only hope in these countries, tried by divers tribulations," says the Vicar Apostolic in Cochin China [9], "is placed in our most holy Mother, from whom we expect salvation [salus]." "The devotion to the Blessed Virgin is such as is to be defined by no bounds," says the Bishop of Scutari [1]. In Spain and Portugal devotion to the Blessed Virgin is in its natural home. They are familiarly called Marian kingdoms [2]. I fear that F. Faber is right in another point too, that this cultus of the Blessed Virgin is about to receive "an immense increase."

[8] Pareri, iii. 149. [9] Ib. iii. 344.

[1] Ib. i. 159. "Ut nullis terminis sit definita."

[2] e.g. The Bishop of Lerida, "in hoc Mariano regno," Par. i. 168. In like way the Bishop of Guadalaxara speaks of Mexico as "Marian" (iii. 76), and so others.

You will well remember, with what a deep pang we heard of the Encyclical Letter of Pius IX. from Gaeta, in which he expressed to the Bishops in the Roman Communion, his "vehement wish, that with the greatest possible speed you would signify to us, with what devotion your clergy and faithful people are animated towards the conception of the Immaculate Virgin, and with what longing they burn, that the matter should be decreed by the Apostolic See; and most especially we desire to know, what you yourselves, in your excellent wisdom, think on that matter and what you desire." We felt that the decree, if passed, would be one more difficulty in the way of the reunion of Christendom, one more ground of severance between the Roman and the Greek Church; an insoluble difference between the modern Roman and the ancient Church. Even amid our own recent troubles, we heard of the decision in 1854 in silent sorrow.

The object of the decree was (as some of the Roman Catholic Bishops pointed out in their answers) new in the history of the Church. It was not to allay any controversy. In the Roman Communion, controversy had long since been hushed by authority; outside of it, there was the less ground for controversy, because the doctrine occupied no apparent prominence. Several Bishops expressed their fears, lest the definition should awaken the controversy. *The* ground, put forward by Pius IX., was of this sort, that as we believe that what is done purely for the Glory of God draws down fresh favours from God, so, "the Blessed Virgin being placed," as they hold, "between Christ and the Church," what should be done for the glory of the Blessed Virgin would draw down from her fresh favours for the Church. He wrote,

"[8] On this hope we chiefly rely, that the most Blessed Virgin,—who raised the height of merits above all the choirs of Angels to the throne of the Deity, and by the foot of Virtue 'bruised the serpent's head,' and who, being constituted *between Christ and His Church*, and, being wholly sweet and full of graces, hath ever delivered the Christian people from calamities of all sorts and from the snares and assaults of all enemies and hath rescued them from destruction, and, commiserating our most sad and most sorrowful vicissitudes and our most severe straits, toils, necessities with that most large feeling of her motherly mind—will, by her most present and most powerful patronage with God, both turn away the scourges of Divine wrath wherewith we are afflicted for our sins, and will allay, dissipate the most turbulent storms of ills, wherewith, to the incredible sorrow of our mind, the Church every where is tossed, and will turn our sorrow into joy. For *ye know very well*, Ven. Brethren, *that the whole of our confidence is placed*

[8] Ep. Encycl. A.D. 1849.

in the most Holy Virgin, since God has placed in Mary the fulness of all good, that accordingly we may know that *if there is any hope in us*, *if any grace*, *if any salvation*, *it redounds to us from her*, because such is His will Who hath willed that we should have every thing through Mary."

Much the same language had been addressed to Gregory XVI. and to Pius IX. himself by Bishops [4], (almost exclusively Italian and French,) who had asked them successively to proclaim the doctrine of the Immaculate Conception to be *de fide*. They hoped (as some expressed it), that "she who requited every the least office towards her [5]," and who,

[4] 88 Italian Bishops wrote, 54 French, 11 only from Spain and Portugal, including Spanish and Portuguese America; 5 English, including Australia; 1 Irish; 9 European Missionary Bishops in China, the East Indies, &c., 1 from Senegal, 1 of Corfu. 20 French Bishops, who wrote subsequently, did not write then; 13 French, and 25 Italian (chiefly Neapolitan), who wrote then, sent no answer to the Encyclical. Gregory XVI. assigned the silence of Bishops from other nations as a ground for not proceeding then. The Bishop de la Rochelle gives an extract from his letter to himself.

"He (Gregory XVI.) added, that except the Bishops of France, and some of Venetia, Lombardy, and Spain, the Bishops of other nations had hitherto kept silence; Germany, England, and Ireland had been silent; that there seemed to him ground to fear, lest the judgment asked for, if then solemnly promulged, would render the Apostolic See odious to certain nations; that complaining and almost threatening sounds, emanating from different countries, had been heard at the Canonization of some whom Pius VII. had placed among the saints." Par. i. 13.

[5] This seems to be almost a proverbial saying. It occurs in the Bishop of Bayeux, i. 289. Lipari, i. 347. Iaca, i. 480, &c.

they say, was and is to "bruise the serpent's head [6]," and is "the destroyer of all heresies [7]," would establish the truth, restore peace, destroy heresy. The Encyclical of Pius IX. was, so far, a response to those Bishops who had applied to Gregory XVI. and to himself, to define, "by his infallible authority," the doctrine of the Immaculate Conception, as a matter of faith. But it is not the less a great change, both in the constitution of the Church and the principles upon which it declares any matter to be *de fide*. "In the constitution of the Church," because the personal infallibility of the Pope, by himself, comes out in the strongest way, despite of the terrible denial of the faith by Liberius, and the formal error of Honorius, with the anathema of the Sixth General Council. The Bishops who applied to the two Popes asked each severally to set the seal of infallibility upon the opinion, by virtue of his own act. Those who answered the Encyclical

[6] "She shall bruise His head," for, "He shall bruise." *Ipsa*, for *ipse*, an error which came into the Latin about the time of S. Augustine. See De Rossi Varr. Lect. T. ii. App. pp. 210, 211. The frequent allusions to this "protevangelium," in the letters of the Bishops and in controversy, as though it ascribed to the Blessed Virgin directly and personally, what God promised as to the Person of our Lord, shows how deeply this mistake of the Vulgate has worked into the Marian system.

[7] "The destroyer of heresies throughout the whole world" is a received title of the B. V. in the Roman Church, applying to her present personal power, what was originally said of the Incarnation, that It, rightly believed, is the destruction of all heresies.

letter, spoke of the act, as his, not theirs; those who dissented from its expediency, declared themselves ready to submit to his judgment; some Spanish and Portuguese Bishops, while they declared that "no injury could arise to" their own countrymen who could not imagine the doctrine not to be of faith, professed not to be able to judge as to its effects on the whole Church, and left the decision to the Pope. The Bishops did not meet in Council, either to address the Pope, or to consider his Encyclical letter, except in Ireland, where the Roman Catholic Bishops, to inaugurate their restored synods, chose an act which should do honour to the Blessed Virgin. The Pope asked the opinion of each Bishop individually; the Bishops answered, as sons who had but a delegated authority, to an infallible head. What advice could any individual give to one, who, as all believed, was to give an inspired decision, to reject which, was, they held, to reject God?

The full weight of Papal authority was given beforehand to the conclusion, to which Pius IX. wished to bring the Bishops in the Roman Communion. Not his wishes only, but the great fervency of those wishes were expressed in the Encyclical letter, addressed severally to each Bishop. Any Bishop, who should hesitate to accede to those wishes, must have felt that he was going counter to the whole mind of him whom he owned as the Vicegerent of God upon earth. Nothing but the strong imperative voice of conscience could induce any one, in any degree, to oppose him. It was not imperative to answer, and many took refuge in silence. But each was bound to submit himself to the decision, whatever it might be. In a Council, any considerable number of orthodox Bishops who dissented from a point not yet ruled, could not but have weight. The wording of at least one decree of the Council of Trent was modified in order not to condemn the opinion of a single Bishop [8]. We all know how a minority makes itself felt; much more, when any thing affecting men's souls is at issue, and Bishops can plead, in fervid living words, that they fear the effect of a decision on the souls of their fellow-men committed to their care. In the individual collecting of opinions by letter, minorities had no voice. They had no collective existence. Each Archbishop or Bishop was but an unit, which could scarcely put forth itself, and which certainly could not assert itself in presence of infallibility [9]. Pius IX., in his "Constitution," ignored the minority, as if it had never existed. "We were touched with no slight consolation when

[8] Catharinus.

[9] The Bishop of Massa di Carrara doubtless expressed the mind of many, when he said, "In a matter of such moment, to be defined by the supreme and infallible judgment of the Holy See, I dare not open the sentiment of my mind" (i. 319). The same feeling is apparent in many other responses.

the responses of those venerable brethren [the Bishops] came to us. For, writing back to us with an incredible happiness, joy, and eagerness, they not only asserted anew their own singular piety and mind, and that of the clergy and people of each, towards the Immaculate Conception of the Blessed Virgin, but also asked of us, as it were, with a common vote, that the Immaculate Conception of the Virgin herself should be defined by our supreme judgment and authority."

The wishes expressed by the Italian, Spanish, Portuguese Bishops were nearly unanimous; and these formed near three-fifths of those who sent answers [1]. Yet even from Italy came a distinct, well-worded objection from the Bishop of Mondovi [2], who "could not dare," even after the prayers of his Diocese, to decide that there was evidence enough to erect the "pious opinion" into a matter of faith, or that *then* was the best time to define it. Doubts were also expressed by the Cardinal Bishop of Viterbo and Toscanella [3], the Cardinal Archbishop of Urbino [4], "with some of the most pious and learned of his clergy," "fearing loss of souls." The Cardinal Bishop of Ancona and

[1] There were answers from 178 Bishops of Italy, and the adjacent islands; 101 from Spain and Portugal, with Spanish and Portuguese America. The whole number was about 490.

[2] iii. 144. See B. n. 36. The Pareri, &c., being now a very scarce book, extracts from this and most of the following letters are given in Note B., at the end.

[3] iii. 34. B. n. 37.

[4] iii. 44—46. B. n. 38.

Umana[1], the Bishops of Cervia[2] and Otranto[3], and the Archbishop of Perugia[4], wished the decree to be tempered, and made indirect; the Bishop of Majorca felt the difficulties and dissuaded[5]; the Archbishop of Milan, and five Bishops in the North of Italy[6], left the decision "in these most difficult times" to "the Holy See, to which is promised the special assistance of the Holy Spirit." In Spain, the Bishop of Lugo[7] wished the decree to be made indirect, if it should be given at all, his own mind being against it. The Bishop of Zamora wished that no note should be set on those who had maintained the contrary, before or after the Council of Trent[8]. Two very remarkable answers came from the Bishops of Iaca, in Portugal, and of Chiapo in Mexico. The Bishop of Iaca[9] much desired that the definition should be delayed until two learned works of divines of Salamanca, written in disproof of the testimonies of the Fathers alleged by Maracci, could be examined; the Bishop of Chiapo[10] was constrained, though with much regret, to oppose the decision, as being unsupported by any clear testimony from Scripture, or

[1] ii. 153. B. n. 39. [2] ii. 218. B. n. 40.
[3] ii. 366. B. n. 41. [4] ii. 290. B. n. 42.
[5] ii. 158. B. n. 43.
[6] The Bishops of Bergamo, Como, Crema, Lodi, Mantua, with the Vicars General of the chapters of Cremona, Pavia, and Brescia, i. 222, 223.
[7] ii. 99. B. n. 44. [8] i. 415. B. n. 45.
[9] i. 481. B. n. 46. [10] ix. App. 17. B. n. 47.

from Tradition. Yet more striking, perhaps, is the answer of the Bishop of Ventimiglia from Italy itself, resting his doubt on the probable intention of God the Holy Ghost, as evinced by His silence in Scripture. "[1] For that not without a purpose the origin of the most holy Mother is passed over by the Evangelist, her Nativity is not described, nor is it recorded how she was conceived (as the holy Bishop of Valence observes[2]), and the whole praise of her is touched upon in the very few words, in which her Divine Maternity is declared, forces on me grave fear, lest the Holy Ghost, in the inscrutable counsel of His Wisdom, willed that her holy origin should remain hidden; so that the only cause of her singular honour revealed should be the glory of the Immaculate Conception of Him, the Holy and Immaculate High Priest, Who was to bring cleansing to all besides."

The Irish Roman Catholic Bishops agreed[3] (although the Roman Catholic Archbishop of Dublin reports the remarkable dissent of "the Jesuit Fathers at Dublin, and almost all the Professors of Maynooth[4]"), so did the five Vicars Apostolic in Scotland (who reported that the cultus of the Blessed Virgin was the dearer to their people, because they alone in Scotland had it[5]), and the

[1] iii. 374.
[2] Thom. Valentin. conc. 2 de Nativ. B. M. V.
[3] iii. 376—379. [4] ii. 143. B. n. 50. [5] ii. 148.

one Vicar Apostolic of Norway and Sweden with his five priests [1].

Of the Archbishops and Bishops of France, no answer came from one-fourth [2]; the Archbishops of Paris [3] and Rouen [4] wrote earnestly to deprecate any decision, as did the Bishops of Coutances [5], and Evreux [6]; Chartres [7] was anxious; Anneçy [8], Meaux [9], Carcassonne [10] doubted. The Archbishop of Rheims [11], with the Bishops of Soissons [12], Amiens [13], Beauvais [14], Blois [15], wished the decree to be softened so as to leave those who disbelieved it free from the note of heresy (which would, I suppose, have left things much as they were before). Of those who had asked Gregory XVI. to define the doctrine, after nine years the Archbishop of Bourges feared that "[16] more evil than good would come from it;" the Bishop of Versailles hesitated, lest it should be an additional hindrance to the return of the Protestants, whom it was difficult to make believe what was already of faith in regard to her [17]; the Bishop of Périgueux,

[1] iii. 309.

[2] Viz. 22. France has 14 Archbishops, 66 Bishops; in all, 80 (Moroni, T. 27, p. 141).

[3] ii. 26—46; iii. 310, 311. 338. B. n. 1.

[4] i. 357—359. B. n. 2.

[5] i. 362, 363. B. n. 3.

[6] i. 100, 101. B. n. 4.

[7] i. 175, 176. B. n. 5.

[8] i. 445, 446. B. n. 6.

[9] ii. 362, 363. B. n. 7.

[10] iii. 333. B. n. 8.

[11] i. 121. B. n. 9.

[12] iii. 290. B. n. 10.

[13] i. 135. B. n. 11.

[14] i. 321. B. n. 12.

[15] i. 211, 212. B. n. 13.

[16] i. 498. B. n. 14.

[17] ii. 103. B. n. 15.

much as he wished it, yet "[1] in these most difficult times, in which we live," left the matter to the Pope, as did the Bishop of Angoulême[2]. The Bishop of Angers[3] expressed his doubts, stating that "the same thoughts and fears were shared by some at least of his colleagues in the Episcopate, and by priests, not less distinguished by learning than by piety towards the Blessed Virgin." The statement is the more remarkable, on account of his strong opposite bias. "We fully trust that she [the Blessed Virgin] will bestow on the holy Church of God and the whole world new and unheard-of benefits, when, a decree supervening from the Holy See, so many men and women, so loved by God and His Son Jesus Christ, shall with one mouth, firm faith, exulting minds, confess that Mary was immaculate in her Conception," &c. The Bishops, then, who requested the definition, were but a bare majority of the Bishops of France (41 out of 80). In a Gallican Council, it can hardly be doubted, that the earnest pleadings of the Archbishops of Paris and Rouen, and of the Bishop of Evreux, would have prevailed, and the question would have remained undecided.

In Germany the Apostolic Nuncio at Vienna wrote to Cardinal Antonelli that he had tried to elicit a favourable opinion from the Archbishops, and had failed. He said[4]:—

[1] i. 361.
[2] i. 258, 259. B. n. 16.
[3] ii. 11.
[4] ii. 464, 465.

"I have written anew confidentially to the Archbishops of this monarchy to excite them to express their own opinion, and that of their Suffragans, on the important subject of the Immaculate Conception of the Madonna. Their silence hitherto, as I have had the honour to point out to your Eminence, can only be an argument, that they are not inclined to a determination, directed to declare the pious belief of the Immaculate Conception as a dogma." The Archbishops and Bishops of the Austrian Empire are counted at 121 [5], exclusive of those in the Austrian possessions in Italy, and of those in Carinthia, Carniola, Transylvania, whose numbers I do not know. Three [6], out of nine [7] Dalmatian Bishops, wrote, expressing their assent; but these also are Italian. Of the 121 Archbishops and Bishops (any how, of the Bishops of the rest of the Austrian Empire out of Italy), only four (out of 21) Hungarian Bishops [8] expressed agreement. From Moravia, the Archbishop of Olmütz and the Bishop of Brünn wrote earnestly, "[9] after mature deliberation, and fervidly imploring light from above," expressing their wish that the decree

[5] This and the following numbers are taken from McCulloch's Geography, upon whose numbers (he being "a member of the Institute") I concluded that I might rely.

[6] Sebenico, Zara, Spalatro.

[7] Moroni, T. xix. pp. 75, 76.

[8] Colocsa and Bayia, Fünfkirchen, Sabaria, Scepusio.

[9] iii. 232, 233. B. n. 24, 25.

should be delayed on account of the peril of souls among their people. The four Bohemian Bishops expressed the same desire on the same ground [1]. The Archbishop of Gorizia and Gradisca [2], the Cardinal Archbishop of Salzburg [3], and the Bishop of Trieste [4] (which three alone wrote from Austria proper), wrote, with different degrees of strength, requesting that things should remain as the Council of Trent had left them.

From the Prussian territory the Archbishop of Breslau wrote against it with a respectful, but touching solemnity, "Dixi et salvavi animam meam [5]." Doubts were expressed by the Bishop of Munster [6]; the Bishop of Paderborn expressed his wish that any decision should be delayed [7]; the Bishop of Warmia mentioned the opinion of many (among others his chapter) in favour of delay, gave no opinion, but declared that whatever the Pope "might decree, would be received as a Divine oracle [8]." The Bishop of Trèves doubted for a time on account of the un-Catholics [9], but decided that the decree would be advantageous, "since it was the Blessed Virgin alone who destroyed all heresies in the whole world."

In Hanovèr, the Bishop of Hildesheim reported

[1] ii. 404. B. n. 25 b.
[2] i. 177—179. B. n. 21.
[3] i. 327. B. n. 22.
[4] i. 436. B. n. 23.
[5] ii. 467. B. n. 26.
[6] vii. cxxxviii. cxxxix. B. n. 28.
[7] iii. 184. B. n. 29.
[8] i. 278—280. B. n. 27.
[9] vii. clvii. B. n. 30.

that the greater part of his Clergy thought that, at least in those parts, a dogmatic decree was neither necessary nor desirable. He himself left it to the Pope's "wiser judgment[1]."

In Hesse, "Clergy, distinguished for knowledge, full of piety towards Mother Church," dissuaded it. The Bishop of Fulda, like the Bishop of Trèves, held that, "the greater the number of adversaries, the more the Church, who had to strive against the powers of darkness, ought to pray for *her* help and aid, who bruised the serpent's head, the more extol and venerate by prayer her who, praying her Son, alone destroyed all heresies in the whole world[2]."

In Nassau, the Apostolic Administrator of Limburg gave strong reasons against the decision, but acquiesced, because, the question having been raised, things could not remain as they were[3].

The Card. Archbishop of Malines stated, that "'in these parts, and especially in the neighbouring kingdoms of France and Holland, ecclesiastics, conspicuous for piety, knowledge, and prudence, feared, lest heretics and unbelievers should take fresh occasion to calumniate the Catholic Church, as though she invented new dogmas, and paid undue worship to the most holy Mother of God, whence many, who were inclined to embrace the faith, might turn back."

[1] iii. 346, 347. B. n. 31.
[2] ii. 439. B. n. 32.
[3] iii. 307, 308. B. n. 33.
[4] ii. 447. B. n. 34.

In Bavaria, the Archbishop of Munich "[5] could not decide about the expediency of defining, in the present circumstances of the Church, for fear of occasioning fresh dissensions where Catholics were mixed with heretics;" the Bishop of Bamberg held that the evidence was not strong enough. "[6] To the body of the more erudite and learned in our Germany the matter does not seem so clear, that (whatever the very learned and illustrious Tramontanes have recently written) they can think that this opinion, which has hitherto been cherished as pious, should be inserted among dogmas which no one may doubt." He begged that the decision might be left to a General Council at some future time.

In Switzerland and Savoy, the Bishop of St. Gall[7], with his counsellors, thought that the dogmatic definition would not increase the devotion towards the Immaculate Conception, and was superfluous at that time, and ill-advised. The Archbishop of Chambéry held that the "[8] tradition was not sufficiently clear to make it an article of faith and a true dogma, to be believed by all under pain of mortal sin;" and so thought it best to "follow the prudent line of the Council of Trent by either abstaining from defining, or at least defining the question only indirectly and broadly, by asserting that the cultus of the Catholic Church

[5] ii. 417. B. n. 19.
[6] ii. 59. B. n. 20.
[7] iii. 803. B. n. 18.
[8] i. 411, 412. B. n. 17.

towards the Conception of the Blessed Virgin Mary was pious and holy."

Even the [9] Patriarch of the Melchites in the Patriarchates of Antioch, Alexandria, and Jerusalem reported, "Some of my Bishops think best, on account of the very many heretics, abounding here in the Levant, not, without great necessity, to multiply the articles of faith, in order to give them no motive to speak, however unjustly, against the Apostolic See." The Vicar Apostolic of Constantinople dissuaded the definition on theological grounds: "[10] Notwithstanding the weight of the recent theological dissertations on this point, the reserve of the Scriptures in regard to this privilege, the hesitation of the Holy Fathers to treat the said question, the delays of the Church itself to decide it, united to the dispositions of spirits in various countries, amid Catholics too, in this century, in which reason, priding itself, burns to wage war with faith, make me judge before God, that the question ought to remain undecided; and even should the Church support the instruction that Mary was conceived immaculate, that it should not impose the obligation to believe this as a doctrine of faith."

A remarkable response, objecting to the decree with much solidity and clearness, came from the Vicar Apostolic of Mysore [11], and another from

[9] ii. 370. [10] i. 266. [11] iii. 351. B. n. 48.

Coimbatoor[1]. The Vicar Apostolic of Patna (a German) sent his adhesion, with the remarkable addition, "[2]*If* the tradition be established by recent authors." The Coadjutor Bishop at Calcutta falls in with "the greater number of Bishops[3]." The Vicar Apostolic of Central Tonkin said that he could neither affirm nor deny that the pious opinion should be placed among the articles of faith, having no means to examine the subject duly, and that, for himself, he trusted the infallibility of the Apostolic See[4].

A remarkable hiatus occurs in the United States. In 1849 there were twenty-eight Roman Catholic Bishops in those States[5]. One only answer came, from Oregon[6], containing the assent of the Roman Catholic Archbishop of Oregon-city, the Bishops of Vancouver, and Wallavalla.

The European Missionary Bishops for the most part followed their nation, or, as the Vicar Apostolic of Ispahan[7], refer the decision to the head of the Church.

I have entered into all this detail, because it gives two remarkable aspects of things in the Roman Communion. On the one side were those, chiefly Italians, Spaniards, Portuguese (whether in Europe or America), and the Irish who set their hope in the

[1] iii. 354. B. n. 49.
[2] ii. 385.
[3] ii. 398.
[4] iii. 172.
[5] Moroni, T. 95, p. 76.
[6] iii. 23.
[7] iii. 321.

Blessed Virgin, as being "placed between Christ and the Church," and whose one thought is, that whatever shall exalt the Blessed Virgin will obtain fresh favours from her. Of those, who asked that the Immaculate Conception might be made an article of faith, I counted 130 who expressed this as the ground of their desire, more or less strongly, besides such as only echoed the language of Pius IX., "to the glory of God, *the praise of the most Blessed Virgin*, the benefit of the Church militant." Of these, 70 were Italians, 23 Spanish and Portuguese, 25 the Irish Roman Catholic Bishops. The sentiment itself was often clothed in very strong words; and benefits, which Holy Scripture ascribes directly to God, seem to be purposely ascribed to the Blessed Virgin (of course, as *the* instrument of God in dispensing them, but still as their dispenser): "Glorify the Mother of God," wrote the Bishop of Bova to the Pope [8], "that the Mother of God may glorify thee;—she will render thee glorious who hast glorified so great a lady. For, I doubt not, in order that you may be confirmed in this hope, the Virgin herself makes thee certain of this promise, by a voice brought down from heaven, by those words, 'I have glorified thee, and will glorify thee again.'" "She," writes the Vicar Apostolic of Uraguai [9], "will direct the goings of your Holiness into the way of peace. She will

[8] ii. 18. [9] ii. 25.

command her angels, that they keep your Holiness in all your ways, that you may walk on asp and basilisk, and tread on lion and dragon; and because your Holiness will hope in her, therefore she will deliver and protect you, because you have known her name, i.e. the fitting time foreordained by the Father of lights for defining her Immaculate Conception. Your Holiness, crying aloud to her, will doubtless hear, 'she will be in the trouble,' which you now experience, out of which she will infallibly deliver you; she will glorify your Holiness, filling you with length of days, and at last showing you her salvation, i.e. her Son Jesus." "We," said the Bishop of Perpignan[1], "rely upon the hope, that the most Blessed Mother, the Queen of heaven and Mistress of the world, in return for the solemn declaration of her Immaculate Conception, will be pleased to dissipate all our sad and sorrowful vicissitudes, and sharpest anguish, labours, necessities, compassionating us with that most large affection of her motherly mind, as is her wont, by her most present and most powerful patronage with God, and will quell, dissipate those most turbulent storms of ills wherewith the Church is tossed every where, and turn our sorrow into joy." "In these most difficult times," said the Bishop of the Canaries[2], "in

[1] i. 55, 56.

[2] i. 293. In like way the Archbishop of Orviedo: "In this most turbulent tempest, wherewith the Church of Christ is

which the ship of the Church is tossed in all directions by furious waves, upraised not by those only who are without, but very chiefly by those who have been reborn of water and the Holy Spirit in the bosom of the Catholic Church, and who as yet do not disdain openly to call themselves Catholics, yet with wolf's heart under the sheep's skin, let a most firm anchor be sought for her, that the ship of Peter may abide secure, &c. But what is this anchor? Mary."

"The great one[3] herself," said the delegate Apostolic of Greece[4], "will requite you, and by her most powerful patronage will disperse these horrible tempests, wherewith, in these most sad times, your Blessedness, with the whole Church, is tossed. Winds and storm will cease; and there will be a great calm." "I daily," said the Bishop of Cesena[5], "most earnestly and unintermittingly implore the most merciful and holy Virgin, the consoler of the sorrowful, that she, assenting to our prayers, would restore thee very speedily to thy kingdom and august see." "She

tossed every where, the eyes of all are turned to Mary, who slew all heresies in all the world, as to a polar star; and this is perhaps the counsel of Divine Providence, that she should then at length calm and disperse the storm, when she shall be adorned with this new honour by the oracle of the Church itself."—ii. 461.

[3] Perhaps a misprint, "magna" for "magnas." "She herself will yield thee great thanks," &c.

[4] i. 301. [5] Ib. 323.

loves those who love her," said the Archbishop of Granada[6], "and most abundantly builds up with graces, and disposes her servants to become the habitation and temple of her Blessed Son and the Holy Spirit. She was full of grace, that 'of her fulness' all creatures may 'receive,' and have a large shower of heavenly gifts infused into them. She is the Mother of fair love, and fear, and knowledge, and holy hope, and in her is all grace of the way and of truth, all hope of life and virtue. Since then the most Blessed Virgin has been enriched with such endowments by God, it is to be hoped most exceedingly, that, propitiated and conquered by such praises and deferences most grateful to her, she, turning her eyes of mercy to us, will powerfully rescue us from the ills with which in the present most horrible tempest we are oppressed." "For all heresies," said the Bishop of Firenza[7], "in the whole world were slain by Her; She is terrible as an ordered host to protect the universal Church of Her Only Begotten Son, and to put its enemies to flight; in Her is all hope of life and virtue." "The preparation of the heart," said the Bishop de la Rochelle[8], "the Immacu-

[6] iii. 202.

[7] i. 281, 282. "I hold for certain, that the Most Holy Mother of God, adorned at length with this honour on earth, will rescue the Church of her Son safe out of such calamities and perils."—Tivoli, i. 237.

[8] i. 13.

late Mother of the Redeemer will hear." "If an opportune and fitting time were to be desired for decreeing this honour of the most Holy Virgin," said the Bishop of Leon[9], "none could be found more opportune and fitting than this wherein we live. For in this most immense mass of errors, calamities, and troubles, wherewith we are oppressed and shaken on all sides, our whole hope is to be placed in that most powerful Virgin, which bruised the dragon, to whom it was given to destroy all heresies, and at whose free will all the treasures of heaven are dispensed." "We have little hope," said the Bishop of Lerida[1], "that human remedies will profit us, unless the Most Blessed Virgin Mary, who is our true health, apply her healing hands, and she, most tender one, will, if," &c.

These and the like expressions are the necessary consequences of the doctrine, that "God does not will to give any thing except through the Blessed Virgin;" "He has placed her between Christ and the Church." Our Lord has bidden us ask the Father in His Name; and *we* should not expect to be heard except through our Divine Redeemer. In like way, if God had "placed the Blessed Virgin between Christ and His Church," then, so far from there being any thing amiss in the exclusiveness of

[9] i. 115, 116. So the Bishop of Squillace, i. 113.
[1] i. 169.

these prayers, it would rather seem, that to pray "to Mary," or "through Mary," would be the only legitimate form of prayer, as our prayers are to God "through Jesus," or "to Jesus," God and Man. It is the natural result of this belief, that, in almost every case, the hopes are expressed, that "Mary will do this or that." I remember few cases only, in which any Bishop said[2], "God would do it" (there may of course have been more), and one or two, that "the prayers of Mary, solemnly declared by the Holy See Immaculate in her Conception, will draw her Son out of that deep sleep which He seems to take in that boat[3]." "The Virgin Mother of God, helping our infirmities, will entreat her Son for us with groanings which cannot be uttered[4]." Where *our* natural language would be, "God will do this or that," there it seems equally natural to Roman Catholics to say, "Mary will do it." At least, where we expect beforehand, in the unfinished sentence, to find "God," or "Jesus," we find "Mary."

The ways in which the declaration of the Immaculate Conception as matter of faith was to obtain these benefits to the Church were twofold, either as the direct fruit of the honour so shown to

[2] As the Bishop of Casale, iii. 62; Rottenburg, i. 276; Warmia, i. 280; Durango, iii. 156; *Jesus*, Massa et Popul. i. 273.

[3] Coadj. Bishop of Montreal, ii. 268. Nevers, iii. 245.

[4] Archb. of Cuba, i. 142.

the Blessed Virgin in propitiating her, or (more rarely) by increasing the devotion of the people to her. Thus the Bishop of Sion urged it as an argument for the direct definition of the doctrine, that the "[5] indirect definition of it would not increase devotion to the Blessed Virgin."

The results hoped from the definition were most large. The most common, perhaps, was the destruction of heresies throughout the world; a Missionary Bishop in China expected "[6] the conversion of idolaters speedily;" the Patriarch of Venice looked for "[7] universal peace and love and duty;"

[5] ii. 486, 488.

[6] Adm. of Nankin, iii. 23.

[7] iii. 37, 38, 39. The Archbishop of Cuba expected as the result that "all would be one fold and One Shepherd," i. 142. The Bishop of Isernia, "that there would be peace to the whole Church," i. 162. The Bishop of Valladolid, "extirpation of heresies, peace of the Church, increase of true faith and piety," i. 195. The Bishop of Gubbio, "conversion of sinners and unbelievers," i. 147, 148. "Those many lost benefits will return to the human race, and to the Church tranquillity, peace, security, splendour," Coadj. of Corfu, i. 409. "Faith, charity, religion," S. Fé di Bogota, ii. 432. "She, with her virgin and immaculate foot, will bruise the head of the Infernal Serpent, will bring to nought the snares of the Prince of darkness, scattered wide, in these our times, by the most impious sects, and by her potent virtue will restore peace to the Church, and its own rights, power, liberty, glory to the Holy Apostolic See, and thee, the head of the whole Church and the foundation, she will preserve;" Abb. Commendat. of S. Vincent and Anastasius, i. 173. "Innumerable riches of grace will be diffused to the whole Christian people, and our sorrow will be turned into joy," Ugento, i. 228. The Bishop of Aire advocated it because "never was the bruising of the serpent's head more needed," i. 272.

the Bishop of Pampeluna, "[8] that the wicked one would be slain by the breath of the mouth[9] of Mary;" the Archbishop of Ferrara, "[10] that she would complete the conquest of the infernal Serpent[1]."

The Irish Bishops expected, "The Mother of Mercy will arise, when she shall understand that her glory is at our hearts, and stretching forth the right hand of her might, amid the most dire storms and tempests wherewith we are tossed, she will lead us to the port of safety; she will arise and utterly destroy all heresies, which, to the detriment of our faith, carry their inroads boldly and with impunity[2]."

On this side, there seem to be no limits to the extent, either of the increase of the devotion to the Blessed Virgin or the subjects which may be made doctrines of faith. Devotion to the Blessed Virgin is to be the great means of obtaining favours from God, Who "wills that all favour should come through her;" one chief means of showing that devotion is held to be, to declare what had been held as "pious opinions," or were taught with a quasi-authority in the Church, to be matters of saving faith. The existence of such teaching, spreading in the Church, is itself to be a proof that it is true. The natural issue of the precedent now set is, step by step to declare as matter of faith any and every thing which is taught about the Blessed Virgin,

[8] i. 491. [9] Said of Jesus, Isa. xi. 4, 1 Thess. ii. 8.
[10] i. 298. [1] See above, p. 124. [2] iii. 370.

so soon as it has, through the constant and diligent teaching of the priesthood, taken root enough.

And this decision, by a further precedent, now made, would depend not on a General Council, not on the consent of the whole Roman Communion, but on the will of the Pope of that time.

And not only this, but the way also in which any decree on any given subject is to be framed, would, according to this precedent, rest with the Pope or his Consistory. That wonderful exposition of the doctrine of the Incarnation, the "tome" of Leo I., was accepted by the Council of Chalcedon, on the ground that it agreed with the faith, expressed or accepted by the Councils before it[3]. The terms in which the decree as to the Immaculate Conception of the Blessed Virgin was framed, were settled, not by any Council, nor by any consent of the Church, but by Pius IX. and his Theologians at Rome.

Yet it was a very delicate point. According to the physical theories of those times, a distinction had been made between what was called the active and the passive conception of the Blessed Virgin; the active conception relating to the derivation of the body from her parents, the passive being the infusion of the soul from God. It used to be thought that there was an interval between the first

[3] See Bossuet, Def. Cler. Gall. vii. 15—17, translated too by Allies, "Church of England cleared from Schism," pp. 282—287.

formation of the body and the infusion of the soul; so that the body might have been conceived in original sin, according to the law of the transmission of this inherent sin, but have been cleansed from its stain before the soul was infused into it by God, so that it should not communicate itself to the soul. Probably the distinction was altogether wrong. Yet some of the Bishops expressed that they wished it to be declared that "the passive Conception" was immaculate, in other words, that the soul of the Blessed Virgin, being infused pure by God, was preserved pure from the stain of sin. The decree itself ignores all such distinctions, and defines that it is revealed by God, that "the most Blessed Virgin Mary was, *in the first instant of her conception*, by the singular grace and privilege of Almighty God, in view of the merits of Christ Jesus, the Saviour of the human race, preserved free from all taint of original guilt." The words "in the first instant of her conception," are a known phrase among the Schoolmen. S. Thomas, e. g. inquires whether, contrary to the Aristotelian physics, "the body of Christ was animated *in the first instant of His conception*;" and answered[4], of course, that the Word of God took, at one and the same instant, body and soul. In like way he shows, that "*in the first instant of conception* Christ had the fulness of grace sanctifying His Soul and Body;" "[5] *in the first instant of His conception* Christ had

[4] p. 3, q. 34, art. 1.

[5] Ib. art. 2.

the use of free-will;" "*in the first instant of His conception* He merited;" "*in the first instant of His conception* He beheld God in His essence clearer than all creatures." What then Pius IX. has, in fact, decreed, is that the Blessed Virgin Mary, although conceived after the way of nature, had "in view of the merits of Christ" precisely that same privilege which our Lord had, being "conceived of the Holy Ghost," in that, "in the first moment of her conception," she was not only sanctified, but kept absolutely free from all taint of original sin. This certainly was not what some of the Bishops meant, who concurred in asking for the definition, in that they spoke of the "passive conception" only, as immaculate.

In fixing this doctrine, as matter of faith, the principle of the Council of Trent was maintained in words, that the faith must be contained in Scripture or continuous tradition from the Apostles, having been taught by our Lord or by God the Holy Ghost. But another principle came in, which made all evidence as to fact superfluous. It was this, that the Church being incapable of erring, any thing taught throughout the Church, although not defined by any authority, or representing any thing beyond the opinion of the actual clergy, was necessarily true. In the old words, the "*quod ubique*" was to be, *ipso facto*, a test of the "*quod semper.*" Any doctrine being taught "every where" at this present moment was to be a proof of a Divine tradition that it had been "always" taught. The present reception of any "pious opinion," especially at Rome, — "the mother and mistress of all Churches, in which *alone* religion hath been guarded inviolably, and from which all other nations must needs borrow the transmission of faith,"—is apparently, according to the principles of that decree, a guarantee, that that opinion has always (however or by whomsoever contradicted) been part of the Divine revelation.

In like way, to those who believed the personal infallibility of the Pope, the fact that he pronounced any thing to be true was to be a proof that it had been always taught. Only, *in that case the heresy contained in the formal letter of Honorius would be true*[6]. This argument was used again and again by the Bishops,—the doctrine of the Immaculate Conception must be true, because the Church teaches it every where, and the Church cannot err. They urge continually, if the people were to think that *this*, which has been taught confidently as Divine truth, was doubtful, they might doubt every thing.

We have been often told that it was enough for any one in the Roman Communion to believe the Canons of the Council of Trent. The Bishops of Spain and Portugal, especially, tell us of a vast practical system, which the Bishops and Priests teach, and the people believe, as matter of faith.

[6] See Bossuet, Def. Cler. Gall. vii. 22, sqq.

And this system being taught every where, then, on the principle upon which the Immaculate Conception was affirmed, it too might be, and must be assumed to be, of Divine tradition, and might be declared to be matter of saving faith. Some of the Bishops observed that the doctrine of the Assumption of the Blessed Virgin Mary, i. e., as it is now understood, of the taking of the body up into heaven without seeing corruption, rested on the self-same authority. The feast of the Assumption, as well as that of the Conception, has been changed from its original meaning, and, having originally denoted the removal of the soul of the Blessed Virgin Mary to heaven, is now held in honour of the Ascension, soul and body. There is the same practical teaching of the Assumption as there was of the Immaculate Conception. Indeed, the doctrine that her "flesh saw no corruption" is the legitimate consequence of the freedom from sin, original as well as actual. For death is the penalty of sin. The bold conception of some, that her death was but the dissolution of soul and body through ecstasy of love, and that her body, though buried, rose from the closed tomb before it could "see corruption," and was taken up to the Right Hand of her Son, as He to the Right Hand of God, is but the complement of the other doctrines about her. It is said that it is to the honour of the Son that His Virgin Mother, of whom He vouchsafed to be born, should not undergo corruption, the penalty of sin, as that she should not, in the first moment of her conception, have had original sin.

To us, the most startling part of this system is its completeness. It shocked us to find that she was accounted to be "placed by God between Christ and the Church" (and so, of course, between Him and each individual); but the one half of the ground alleged for this, that we, as sinners, were of ourselves too unworthy to approach to Christ, found too much response in the hearts of us, miserable sinners. We know that we are unworthy to approach Him, but that He said—not, Go to My Mother, but—"come unto Me," and "whoso cometh unto Me, I will in no wise cast out." But now we find, over and above this, a studied identification of her, in all but what follows from the Hypostatic Union, with her Divine Son. And this, partly because, in the offices in honour of her, passages of Scripture which relate to Divine Uncreated Wisdom are recited; in some degree also, because what has been said of her by the Fathers, as the chosen vessel of the Incarnation, was applied personally to her; yet more on account of spurious passages attributed to Fathers of great name.

We had heard before, repeatedly, that she was the Mediatrix with the Redeemer; some of us, who do not read Marian books, have heard now for the first time, that she was ever our "Co-Redemptress." The evidence lies, not in any insulated passage of a devotional writer (which was alleged in plea for the language of M. Olier), but in formal answers from Archbishops and Bishops to the Pope as to what they desired in regard to the declaration of the Immaculate Conception as an Article of Faith. Thus the Archbishop of Syracuse wrote, "Since[7] we know certainly that she, in the fulness of time, was Co-redemptress of the human race, together with her Son Jesus Christ our Lord." From North Italy the Bishop of Asti wrote of "the[8] dogma of the singular privilege granted by the Divine Redeemer to His pure mother, the Co-redemptress of the world." In South Italy the Bishop of Gallipoli wrote, "the[9] human race, whom the Son of God, from her, redeemed; whom, together with Him, she herself co-redeemed." The Bishop of Cariati prayed the Pope to "command[10] all the sons of Holy Mother Church and thy own, that no one of them should dare at any time hereafter to suspect as to the Immaculate Conception of their co-redeemer." From Sardinia, the Bishop of Alghero wrote, "It[1] is the common consent of all the faithful, and the common wish and desire of all, that our so beneficent Parent and Co-redeemer should be presented by the Apostolic See with the honour of this most illustrious mystery." In Spain, the Bishop of Almeria justified the attribute by appeal to the service of the

[7] ix. 201.

[8] Ib. i. 325. "She deserved the name and glory of Co-redeemer," Archbishop of Trani, ib. i. 10.

[9] "Quem simul cum Eo Ipsa corredemit," ib. i. 218.

[10] ix. 160.

[1] ix. 7.

Conception. "The[2] Church, adapting to the Mother of God in the Office of the Conception that text, 'Let Us make a help like unto Him,' assures us of it, and confirms those most ancient traditions, 'Companion of the Redeemer,' 'Co-Redemptress,' 'Authoress of everlasting salvation.'" The Bishops refer to these as ancient, well-known, traditionary titles, at least in their Churches in North and South Italy, Sicily, Sardinia, Spain.

This doctrine, which is here alluded to, is drawn out by Roman Catholic Divines of every school. It occurs in à Lapide, a repertorium for sermons, as well as in the most Marian writers. Proceeding on that same ground of the Scriptures adapted to the Blessed Virgin, Salazar writes,—

"It[3] was not fitting that Christ Alone should give Himself to the regeneration of man; and so it was necessary that a woman, Mary, like unto Him, should be given Him, that, with her and by her, all the regeneration and adoption of the sons of God should take place."

"She[4] merited by congruity the salvation of the whole world; not only because she bare Christ, but because she gave to us Him Whom she had borne and Who was truly hers, and for us she offered Him to death. For each will of the Mother and the Son, throughout concordant and conspiring, sacrificed

[2] Ib. i. 186.
[3] Pro Immac. B. V. Concept., c. 19, n. 7.
[4] Id. ib. c. 21, n. 2.

to God one and the same holocaust for the salvation of the world."

"The[5] ways in which the Blessed Virgin co-operated with Christ to the salvation of the world may be classed as three:—

"1. As far as she so sacrificed herself to God for the salvation of the world by the wish and longing for death and the cross, that, if it could be, she too, for the salvation of the universe, was willing to co-die (commori) with her Son, and to meet a like death with Him.

"2nd, and chiefly, whereby the Virgin gave her help to Christ for the common salvation, in that she, exhibiting a will altogether conformable and concordant with the will of Christ, gave her Son to death for the common salvation. And her zeal for the human race is not seen only therein, that it made her will conspire with the will of her Son, but also in that she excited and impelled Him to undergo death.

"3rdly, That she acted as mediatrix with the Mediator. The work of our salvation was so wrought. The Virgin expressed to her Son the wishes and desires which she had conceived for the salvation of the human race; but the Son, deferring to the Mother, received these, and again presented to the Father the desires both of His Mother and His own; but the Father granted what was wished, first to the Son, then to the Mother.

[5] Ib. n. 3—7.

"It is clear from this, that the salvation of the world was granted by the Eternal Father, not only to Christ, but also to the Virgin; yet so that the Son, as the first and principal cause, gave the price of condignity for our redemption; but the Virgin obtained the same redemption by a sort of congruity. So Mary was an aider and helper to Christ the Lord for our redemption; not that Christ needed that help or aid, since the value of His Blood surpassed by a boundless interval the compensation of our debts, but because the authority and dignity of the mother demanded this, that her merits, prayers, and desires should be united with the desires and merits of Christ, so that the salvation of men should be bestowed on both.

"But if you ask how much of help and aid the Virgin gave to the common salvation, I have said boldly, that Christ the Lord obtained nothing by His merits, either for us or for the Virgin herself, which the Virgin Mother of God did not also gain out of congruity (excepting always the original and first grace wherewith the Virgin was gifted; for *this* the Virgin could not obtain by any way of congruence). Thence it follows that the Virgin Mother of God, from the aforesaid congruence, so obtained of God the common salvation of the human race, that even the extinction of original sin is also to be referred to her."

Whereas the Fathers speak of the Blessed Virgin as the instrument of our salvation, in that she gave birth to the Redeemer, the modern Marian writers expressly reject this. "This," they say[6], "was an act of nature only; to have merited the Incarnation '*ex congruo*,' and so to have accelerated it, was," they say, "common only with Patriarchs and the old Fathers; to have prayed for the salvation of mankind was also common with others. In order, then, to establish that she had something special to herself, it must be laid down that 'Christ, God and Man,' was the true Son of Mary, and so was something of her own, placed under her parental authority, and, as it were, dominion. She, then, is to be said to have given of her own; and of Mary it may be said, 'So' Mary 'loved the world, that she gave her only begotten Son.' The Virgin not only, concordant with the Father, gave her Son to the world, but also, in conformity with her Son, with priestly piety offered Him up as a Sacrifice for the world. We owe then to the Virgin Mother of God, not only that she bare Christ to the world, but also that she truly gave to the world, and voluntarily offered Him for the salvation of the world, as something which was her own." "After the manner of a Priest, acting in a manner together with her Son the Priest, she offered to the Eternal Father the Sacrifice of redemption. Christ the Lord was offered once upon the cross; but in her heart a thousand times, i. e., so often as

[6] De Salazar on Prov. viii. 19, pp. 621—629.

she voluntarily assigned Him to death. The life, the Passion of Jesus Christ, and His Death itself, were the price of our redemption, so far as they were voluntarily undertaken by Christ; but the will of the Virgin, whereby she offered her Son, related to that same life and Passion. Wherefore it was meet, that, as that life and Passion, as being voluntary in the Son, merited the salvation of all, 'of condignity;' so the same life and Passion, as being voluntary in the Mother, should merit that same salvation, 'of congruity.' To speak more plainly, it is equitable, that, as the Son voluntarily enduring death satisfied for all, so the Virgin, voluntarily offering her Son to that same death, obtained the salvation of all. That act, whereby the Virgin both gave her Son to us and offered Him for us to the Father, was most surpassing and especially meritorious, and so, worthy to be computed together with the Passion of Christ. So that, as the Passion of Christ is said to have satisfied for the common salvation of all, so this so great action of Mary may be said in a special manner to have obtained it. On the ground of this action of such value and merit, the Virgin Mother of God was worthy that the common salvation and redemption of the whole human race should be ascribed in a manner to her. And since she had this in common with Christ, that she is said really and properly to have given and offered the price of our redemption, *therefore* she bears, together with Him, *all the titles and names which are wont to be ascribed to Christ*, and is rightly called Redemptress, Restoress, Mediatress, Authoress, and Cause of our salvation.

"In another way, she may be called co-operatress and helper of Christ, viz., that as *many other things* made death not a little difficult and arduous to Christ, moved whereby He burst out into those words, 'Father, if it be possible, let this cup pass from Me,' nothing could more load His mind and make death more difficult to Him, than that it should be displeasing to His most loving Mother. Who sees not this? Wherefore, contrariwise, nothing so took a load off His mind, and so incited Him to suffer death, as that ready will of His Mother, altogether concordant with the will of His Father; so that I should venture to affirm that, besides the will of His Father, than which nothing was dearer to the Son, and which He wished in the first instance to execute, nothing stood nearer than this will of His Mother, to whom He deferred next to the Father. So, then, He Who addressed His Father, 'Not My will, but Thine be done,' and, owning the will of His Father, willingly offered Himself to death, did also gain great courage to endure death, in that He knew that His Mother willed the same; yea, we may say that *by dying He obeyed not only His Father, but also His Mother*. I add, that it may be questioned whether, if, 'per impossibile,' there had been no will of the

Father, and His Mother alone wished and *decreed* that her Son should die for men, this would suffice that Christ, obeying His Mother, should willingly undergo death. I believe that Christ so deferred to His Mother, that it would have sufficed. Let others think as they will. I add that the Mother of God herself embraces the human race with so much love and affection that if, according to the aforesaid supposition, that will of the Eternal Father were wanting, she would yet, of her own will, choose that her Son should die for men. Therefore, since the Virgin Mary much strengthened her Son to endure death, and lightened to Him death itself, exhibiting her will in that respect conformable to the Divine will, therefore she ought rightly to be called His helper. So that it might be said much more truly of the Second Adam, that 'a help like unto Him was given to Him'—like, I say, not in dignity or merits, but in will and mind towards men, because she so ardently desired the salvation of the human race, that by her own will, perhaps by exhortation also, she confirmed in some measure her Son Who willed to die. 'A help meet,' I say, because that salvation of the whole human race which her Son merited '*de condigno*,' she, '*de congruo*,' in a certain excellent way obtained and promoted."

This is altogether deliberate dogmatic language, touching upon the character and attributes of our Lord and God, His office as our Redeemer and the very centre of the faith. It gives the same aspect of our redemption, as other language does of our Lord's perpetual Intercession for us sinners,—that the Blessed Virgin had authority over our Blessed Lord in regard to this His Divine work, and that it was accomplished, in part, in obedience to her maternal authority. It is the "Monstra te esse Matrem" applied to His office for us on earth; and that, not as any hyperbole, but with dogmatic preciseness. "Since[7] the Blessed Virgin is the Mother of God, and God is her Son, and every son is naturally inferior to his mother and her subject, and the mother is set over and superior to her son, it follows that the Blessed Virgin herself is superior to God, and God Himself is her subject, in regard to the Humanity which He took from her." This doctrine, again, bears very closely upon the doctrine of our Redemption, in that our Blessed Lord's perfect Obedience paid the Price of our disobedience, and "by[8] the Obedience of One many were made righteous." "He[9] became obedient unto death, the Death of the Cross." But now we are told of another obedience, not as the ensample which He gave us in His Holy Childhood by being subject to His parents, the real and the reputed alike[1], but, in His office as our Redeemer, to her whom He redeemed. The Blessed Virgin stands

[7] S. Bernardin. de Bust. Marial. P. IX. Serm. ii. in Ussher, l. c., c. ix.

[8] Rom. v. 19. [9] Phil. ii. 8. [1] S. Luke ii. 51.

out in this system, not only in her own special gifts, but as already, before the Price was paid for her redemption, subject to no law of humanity, except of suffering together with her Son, and interceding for our fallen race, as one who did not belong to it.

It seems to be a part of this system, to parallel the Blessed Virgin throughout with her Divine Son, so that every prerogative which belonged to Him by nature or office should be in some measure imputed to her. As His Conception, not in the way of nature, but by the Holy Ghost, was Immaculate, so, it is said, was hers by the Divine interference, her birth of barren and aged parents being (it is said) scarcely by way of nature; as He was the Son of God by Nature, so, they say, was she "[2]by a more noble right than that of adoption only, a right which emulates in a manner natural filiation;" as He was perfect[3], so was she, in such sense, perfect, and "[4]such must needs be the virtues of the Virgin, that Christ, *imitating* them, fulfilled the office of Saviour; that as Christ, both as God and Man, bore the image of the Eternal Father, so it was meet that, God and Man, He should bear the character of His Mother. As God in Christ, by 'interchange of properties,' is called

[2] Salazar in Prov. viii. 30, p. 696, and Ind. v. Maria.

[3] Ib. p. 649.

[4] Ib. p. 544. The terms are known terms, "patrizo" and "matrizo."

Son of Mary, so He is said to have the character of His Mother on that same principle. In order, then, that we might say, that not Man only but God also should have the character of His Mother, need was that the Virgin should by the bounty of God have many properties and conditions of God, whereby she might be as like as possible to Him." As Jesus, our High Priest, had no need to offer sacrifice for Himself; so she is spoken of, as desiring nothing but the salvation of mankind; as Jesus merited our salvation, of condignity, so she, of congruity; as He died for us in act, so she in will; as He offered "a full, perfect, and sufficient, sacrifice, oblation, and satisfaction for the sins of the whole world," viz. Himself, so she, they say, sacrificed her Son for us all. As our Redemption gained its sufficiency and might from Jesus, so, they say, did it gain its beauty and loveliness from the aid of Mary[5]. As

[5] "As I have often inculcated, Christ so wrought our redemption, as to call in Mary, as an aid in this work. Wherefore as the birth, nature itself guiding, derives strength from the man, but, from the woman, form and beauty; so also our redemption, (which was borne, as it were, by Mary and Christ,) derives from Christ sufficiency, strength, and consistency, but from Mary, beauty and loveliness. For as therefrom, that Christ the Lord worked our redemption, we infer rightly, that nothing of sufficiency or might should be wanting to it; so therefrom, that the Virgin co-operated to the same, we rightly deduce, that nothing of form or beauty could be missed in it. For in some way the grace and beauty of the redemption would fade, if the aforesaid co-operation of the Virgin were lacking." Salaz. pro Immac. Virg. Conc., § 14, n. 171.

we are clothed with the merits of Christ, so also, they say, with the merits of Mary[6]. As Jesus rose again the third day without seeing corruption, so they speak of her Resurrection "[7]so as to anticipate corruption, in some three days;" as He was the first-fruits of them that slept, so is she[8]; as He was taken up into heaven in the body, so, they say, was she; as He sits at the Right Hand of God, so she at His Right Hand; as He is there our perpetual Intercessor with the Father, so she with Him; as "no man cometh to the Father," Jesus saith, "but by Me;" so "no one cometh to Jesus," they say, "but by her;" as He is our High Priest, so she, they say, a Priestess[9]; He, our High Priest, gave us the sacrament of His Body and Blood; so, they say, did she, "her will conspiring with the will of her Son to the making of the Eucharist, and assenting to her Son so giving and offering Himself for food and drink, since we confess that the sacrifice and gifts, given to us under the form of bread and wine, are truly hers and appertain unto her[10]." As in the Eucharist He is present and we receive Him, so she, they say, is present and received in that same sacrament[1]. The priest is "minister of Christ," and

[6] De Montf. p. 143.

[7] Oswald, Mariologie, 171. De Montfort speaks of her resurrection. True devotion, &c., p. 1.

[8] Oswald, p. 174. [9] Ib. p. 198.

[10] Salazar in Prov. ix. 4, 5, p. 769.

[1] Oswald, 174—186. Oswald speaks of her office to us in

"minister of Mary[2]." They seem to assign to her an office, like that of God the Holy Ghost, in dwelling in the soul. They speak of "souls[3] born not of blood, nor of flesh, nor of the will of man, but of God *and Mary*;" that "the[4] Holy Ghost chose to make use of our Blessed Lady to bring His fruitfulness into action by producing in her and by her Jesus Christ in His members;" that "according[5] to that word, 'the kingdom of God is within you,' in like manner the kingdom of our Blessed Lady is principally in the interior of a man, his soul;" that "when[6] Mary has struck her roots in the soul, she produces there marvels of grace, which she alone can produce, because she alone is the fruitful Virgin, who never has had, and never will have, her equal in purity and fruitfulness." "She alone[7]," we are told, "can produce, in union with the Holy Ghost, singular and extraordinary things. When the Holy Ghost, her Spouse, has *found Mary in a soul*, He flies there. He enters there in His fulness; He communicates Himself to that soul abundantly, and to the full extent to which she makes room for her Spouse. Nay, one great reason why the Holy Ghost does

Baptism, ib. 187,—"Through it, the woman has a right to that special blessing, deposited for her in the Church through the merits of Mary."

[2] Ib. 200.

[3] De Montfort, pp. 74 and 126.

[4] Ib. p. 11.

[5] Ib. p. 21.

[6] Ib. p. 19.

[7] Ib. p. 20.

not now do startling wonders in our souls is, because He does not find there a sufficiently great union with His faithful and indissoluble Spouse." At Holy Communion, the soul is taught to desire that she will come and dwell with it in order to receive her Son, which "she[8] can do by the dominion she has over all hearts, and her Son will be well received by her without stains and without danger of being outraged or destroyed." To the Son, the soul is to "pray[9] to have pity upon you, that you may introduce Him into the house of His own Mother and yours, and that you will not let Him go without His coming to lodge there." The Holy Ghost "you[1] can pray to come Himself in Mary, His indissoluble Spouse, telling Him that her bosom is as pure, and her heart as burning as ever, and that, without His descent into your soul, neither Jesus nor Mary will be formed, nor yet worthily lodged."

These details show, that it is in no figurative or general way that one lays down, "What[2] I say absolutely of Jesus Christ, I say relatively of our Blessed Lady. Jesus Christ, having chosen her for the inseparable companion of His life, of His death, of His glory, and of His power in heaven and upon earth, has given her by grace, relatively to His Majesty, all the same rights and privileges which He possesses by nature. 'All that is fitting

[8] Ib. p. 186.
[9] Ib. p. 187.
[1] Ib. p. 188.
[2] Ib. 49, 50.

to God by nature is fitting to Mary by grace,' say the Saints; so that, according to them, Mary and Jesus, having but the same will and the same power, the two have the same subjects, servants, and slaves."

And so they declare her the centre of creation. "Mary[3]," they say, "is that ring in the chain of creatures, wherein, seizing, the Son of God drew up the universe again to the Godhead. Therefore, Mary is not only the middle point of mankind, but the centre of the whole universe." Again, an expression, whose whole force is derived from applying to the B. V. what belongs to our Lord Alone, "in[4] Whom God gathered together in one all things, both which are in heaven and which are on earth." Blessed be His goodness that He, being God, for our sake became Man, and, by the ineffable condescension of the Incarnation, knit in one the Creator and the creature! But plainly He, in Whose Divine Person the Godhead and Manhood, the Uncreated and the created nature, were united, not His creature, is the Centre of creation.

Nay, one ventures to state, that she, to be born of a fallen race, obtained grace for those who never fell. "The[5] Virgin, the associate and co-operatress of the merits of Christ, obtained for the angels themselves and our first parents that grace wherein

[3] Salazar, l. c. p. 213. [4] Eph. i. 10.
[5] Salazar pro Imm. Deip. V. Concept. c. 3, p. 28.

they were first created." "The [6] Virgin is mediatress not of men only, but of the Angels."

The title, "the Complement of the Trinity" (founded originally on a strange mistake of the meaning of an unknown author), is still said to be one which she has merited [7]. It was (and I sup-

[6] Ib. in Prov. xxx. n. 200.

[7] Archbishop of Trani, Par. i. 10. The title is a mere mistake, drawn from a Latin translation of a homily attributed to some Hesychius, Presbyter of Jerusalem, in which he contrasted Mary with Noah's ark. "*It* was an ark of living things, she of life; it, of perishable animals, she, of imperishable Life; it bare Noah, she bare the Maker of Noah; it had two or three stories, she the whole fulness of the Trinity; inasmuch as the Spirit too came upon her, and the Father overshadowed her, and the Son dwelt in her, borne in the womb." Bibl. Patr., Paris 1624, T. ii. p. 421.

Whereas the writer (whoever he was) spoke of the whole Holy Trinity as concerned in the Incarnation, a celebrated Jesuit preacher, first-court-preacher of Philip III., attributed the saying, as altered into "Mary is the Complement of the whole Trinity," to the celebrated Hesychius of Jerusalem. He explained it to mean that she "added the last complement to the Holy Trinity, in that, through the Incarnation of our Lord in her, the Virgin Mother of God filled up the capacity which the Trinity had of a natural paternity and a natural filiation, and a bond of both in time, in addition to the eternal relations of natural Paternity and natural Filiation, and the Indissoluble Bond of both." Other solutions were: 1) That the attributes and perfections of the Trinity shone forth most in her, and showed forth their virtue and efficacy most in her. (Salazar rejects this, because Hesychius is said to have affirmed, that the Virgin was "the complement, not of the attributes of God, but of the very Trinity itself.") 2) "That the Father imparts His infinite Essence to the Son, and the Son, with the Father, communicates the same to the Holy Ghost; but that there is no fourth person to whom the Holy

pose is) the basis of speculations as to the way in which a creature, however exalted, could be said to fill up the eternal and infinite God. Again, the belief (founded on what is now owned to be an error, which crept into the Latin translation about the close of the fourth century [8]), that the Blessed Virgin was prophesied of as "*she*" who should "bruise the serpent's head," became the support of the doctrine of the Immaculate Conception [9], and gives rise to the statements, "God [1] has never made or formed but one enmity; but it is an irreconcileable one, which shall endure and develope even unto the end. It is between *Mary*, His worthy Mother, and the devil; between *the children* and the servants *of Mary* and the children and instruments of Lucifer."

This system is, I understand, developing. Certainly the Bishops, in their answer to the Encyclical, speak of the diligence of the priests in preaching it. Some who did not wish the doctrine to be defined, wished the more that it should be diligently preached. As one instance of this

Ghost can pour Himself forth without measure. Mary then gave a complement to the Trinity, in that the Holy Ghost could lighten that infinite desire of communicating Himself by the wonderful affluence of His gifts to Mary." Salazar in Prov. viii. 23, n. 300—306.

[8] See above, p. 124.

[9] It was put forward by many of the Bishops in their answer to the Encyclical.

[1] De Montfort, pp. 30, 31.

development, in 1841 I mentioned a belief, said to exist among the poorer people in Rome, that in the Holy Eucharist not only our Lord, but His mother is present [2]. True, that Jesus took the Flesh of His Mother; but in those gracious thirty-three years it was all changed by the laws of our mortality. Yet the belief is defended by one who writes with confidence, as a necessary consequence of their theory as to the Blessed Virgin. "We [3] *maintain* a (co-) presence of Mary in the Eucharist. This is a necessary inference from our Marian theory, and we shrink back from no consequence." "We are much inclined," he says afterwards [4], "to believe an essential co-presence of Mary in her whole person, with body and soul, under the sacred species. Certainly to such a presence in the Eucharist 1) there is required a glorious mode of being of the Virgin body of the Holy Mother. We are not only justified in holding this as to Mary, but we have well-nigh proved it. 2) The assumption of a bodily presence of Mary in the Eucharist compels self-evidently the assumption of a multilocation (i.e. a contemporaneous presence in different portions of space) of Mary, according to her flesh too. 3) One who would receive this must be ready to admit a compenetration of the Body of Christ and of that of the Virgin in

[2] Letter to Dr. Jelf, p. 209. It was said on the authority of one who had been staying at Rome.

[3] Oswald, Dogmat. Mariologie, p. 177.

[4] Ib. p. 179.

the same portion of space, i.e. under the sacred species." The writer subsequently explains that "the 'lac virginale' must be looked upon as that of Mary, which is primarily present in the Eucharist, whereto, in further consequence, the whole corporality of the Blessed Virgin, as also her soul, would be joined." "The[5] Blood of the Lord, and the lac of His Virgin Mother, are both present in the Sacrament."

This same doctrine was indeed stated of old by one of their most popular and careful Commentators on Holy Scripture[6]. "As this saying, 'Those who eat me, shall still hunger,' is literally true of Christ, Whom we eat in the Eucharist, and again hunger for Him and long again to eat Him; so can it in like way be said truly and literally of the Blessed Virgin. Wondrous is this, but true. For as often as we eat the Flesh of Christ in the Eucharist, so often do we in it really eat the Flesh of the Blessed Virgin. For the Flesh of Christ *is* the flesh of the Blessed Virgin. Yea, that very Flesh of Christ, before it was detached from the flesh of the Blessed Virgin in the Incarnation, was the own flesh of the Blessed Virgin, and was informed and animated by her soul. As then we daily hunger after the flesh of Christ in the Eucharist, so too we hunger for that same flesh of the Blessed Virgin that we may drink her virgin endowments and

[5] Ib. pp. 182, 183.
[6] Corn. à Lap. on Ecclus. xxiv. 29.

ways, and incorporate them in ourselves. And this do not only priests and religious, but all Christians; for the Blessed Virgin feeds all with her own flesh equally with the Flesh of Christ in the Eucharist. And *hence* that love of virginity and angelic purity in those who worthily and frequently communicate. For this cause all the faithful ought to bear about the Blessed Virgin, as well as Christ, assiduously in heart, in word, and in work; yea, as it were, to pass into and be transmuted into the Blessed Virgin, as iron glowing with fire passes into fire, or as bread seasoned with leaven, passes, as it were, into leaven."

This same conclusion, the presence and consequent reception of something at least of the Blessed Virgin in the Holy Eucharist, appears to be involved in the statement of one whose writings have a large circulation in England, at least, and America:—

"There[7] is some portion of the Precious Blood which once

---

[7] Faber, "The Precious Blood," pp. 29, 30. Salazar mentions a meditation of S. Ignatius, which he thought to have been given him by God, but which rested on human reasoning on physics; viz., that, on Aristotle's maxim, that "the son is a great part of his father and mother," "in the Eucharist he received the flesh and blood, not only of Christ, but also a great, yea, chief, part of Mary. For if the flesh and blood of the son and the mother be one, he who receiveth the flesh and blood of the son, must needs also receive the flesh of the mother. And if the son is a part of his parents, whoso eateth the son, eateth also a part of his mother. Hence, he said, that all they who

was Mary's own blood, and which remains still in our Blessed Lord, incredibly exalted by its union with His Divine Person, yet still the same. This portion of Himself, it is piously believed, has not been allowed to undergo the usual changes of human substance. At this moment, in heaven, He retains something which was once His Mother's, and which is, possibly, visible, as such, to the saints and angels. He vouchsafed at mass to show to S. Ignatius *the very part of the Host which had once belonged to the substance of Mary.* It may have a distinct and singular beauty in heaven, where, by His compassion, it may one day be our blessed lot to see it and adore it. But with the exception of this portion of it, the Precious Blood was a growing thing, &c."

The way in which the practical Roman system has been enlarged by later visions or revelations, is a perplexing subject. 1) Because the Roman Divines themselves do not allege them as grounds of faith. For, as such, the Council of Trent alleges only Scripture and continuous tradition. 2) These revelations contradict one another; as when the Immaculate Conception is supported by a revelation of S. Brigit, contradicted by one of S. Catherine of Sienna. 3) Roman Divines accept one revelation, as establishing what is contained in it, and set aside another. Thus, Bellarmine quotes one revelation of S. Brigit in support of a matter of belief, and sets aside another as contrary to the received belief. But the same revelations cannot be, and not be, an authority for our belief.

are worthily refreshed with the Body and Blood of Christ, become one flesh not only with the Lord Christ, but pass into one flesh with the Virgin." Salazar in Prov. ix. 4, 5, n. 144, 145.

Benedict XIV. lays down, "The approbation of such revelations is no more than a permission, that, after a mature examination, they may be published for the benefit of the faithful. Though an assent of Catholic faith be not due nor can be given to these revelations so approved, a human assent is due to them according to the rules of prudence, by which such revelations are probable and piously credible, as in regard to the revelations of B. Hildegardis, which are said to have been approved by Eugenius III., Boniface IX., S. Brigit, S. Catherine of Sienna, and Gregory XI.[8]" Yet the revelations of S. Brigit have been a support of the doctrine of the Immaculate Conception, as other visions were of details as to Purgatory, which visions were, however, set aside in other points, as those ascribed to S. Fursey.

[8] De Canoniz. Sanct. ii. 32. 11, quoted by A. Butler, Oct. 8, S. Brigit, from Araus., Decis. Mor., Tract. 3, qu. 23, § 2. Gerson, Opp., T. i., col. 24, says, that two contradictories may, in different respects, be piously believed: quoted by Bened. XIV. ib. "For although no one ought to believe or to propose to be believed, what he knew to be certainly false, yet so long as it was not certainly known to be false, the pious belief was independent of its truth or falsehood." Fleury, H. E. 70, n. 161, quotes Papebrock (app. ad Vit. S. Mariæ de Pazzi), as showing by instances that visions are no dogmatic authority. Yet they themselves claim this most energetically as an authority beyond all other. In the Revelations of S. Brigit, the Blessed Virgin is supposed to have said, "If ye believe not Scripture, the Church, the Fathers, at least believe ye me, who have often revealed, that all sin of Adam was severed from me, &c." Revel. S. Brig. c. 12. 45. 49. T. ii. quoted by Bishop of Marsi, Par. ii. 311.

I see not why this doctrine, then, of the reception of the blood of the Blessed Virgin in the Holy Eucharist should not prevail, on the ground of the revelation alleged to have been made to S. Ignatius Loyola; as that of her Immaculate Conception was upheld by the revelation to S. Brigit. Nay, further, it is involved in the "pious belief" mentioned by Faber, that Jesus shed, for us sinners, the unchanged blood of Mary; which, whereunto it may lead, one had rather not think.

No one, of course, is responsible for the bold imagination of one who had as yet joined neither Greek nor Roman communion, although he despised our own. Still the conception is illustrative, the more, since prayers originally addressed to God have been altered into prayers to the Blessed Virgin.

"Whatever[9] point," Mr. Palmer wrote, "may have been reached, there must always be room in what is of its own nature limited for further addition and increase; and it is not difficult to imagine to ourselves very considerable additions and developments which might yet be made to the worship of the Blessed Virgin." And then Mr. Palmer gave as instances;

"Assuming that, in and under Christ the Head, the Blessed Virgin is, after her Assumption, as it were, the neck of the Church, so that all grace

[9] Palmer, Diss. on the Orthodox Comm., pp. 248, 249.

whatever flows to the Body through her, that is, through her prayers, it might be argued, that, for such as have this belief to ask any thing of or through her, is identical in sense, but in point of form better, than to ask it directly of Christ, in like manner as to ask any thing of or through Christ, is identical in sense, but clearer and fuller in point of form, than to ask it directly of the Father. And hence, it might seem that it would be an improvement, if, reserving only the use of the appointed Forms for the making of the Sacraments, and an occasional use of the Lord's Prayer (and this rather from respect to the letter of their outward Institution than from any inward necessity or propriety), every prayer, both of individuals and of the Church, were addressed to or through Blessed Mary, a form beginning, 'Our Lady, which art in heaven,' &c., being preferred for general use to the original letter of the Lord's Prayer; and the Psalter, the Te Deum, and all the daily Offices, being used in preference with similar accommodation."

We see the growth. The doctrine of the Immaculate Conception has prevailed, although opposed at its first appearance by S. Bernard [1], with no foundation in antiquity [2], grounded on the fact of the

[1] Ep. 172, ad Canon. Lugd. Opp. i. 169.

[2] "All the saints, who speak of it, say with one voice, that the Blessed Virgin was conceived in original sin." Melchior Canus (a Tridentine Doctor), Loci Theol. vii. 1. "Arguments (from reason) do not place the opinion as to the Immaculate

celebration of the Feast of the Conception[3] (which yet

Conception of the Blessed Virgin in any degree of certainty, since neither any convincing place of Scripture, nor the traditions of the ancient Church, nor consent of fathers or schoolmen favour it." Card. Pallavacini, in MS. Diss. lent to Perrone. See Episcopato Cattolico, vi. 520. S. Augustine, in his often-quoted passage (in answer to Pelagius, who had alleged the Blessed Virgin with many others to have lived free from sin), manifestly refers to "actual sins," as the use of the plural "sins" in itself shows. "Excepting then the holy Virgin Mary, of whom, out of honour to the Lord, I wish no question to be made when sins are treated of,—for how do we know what more of grace, wholly *to conquer* sin, may have been bestowed upon her, who was found meet to conceive and bear Him, of Whom it is certain that He had no sin?" (De Nat. et Grat. c. 36.) S. Augustine does not even rule that she never sinned actually, by any sin of infirmity; he marks it to be uncertain, by the contrast which he draws with our Lord, of Whom he says, "it is certain (constat) that He had no sin." On the other hand, S. Augustine most distinctly says, that the Blessed Virgin was born in original sin (de Gen. ad lit. x. 18 and 20; de Pecc. Mer. et Rem. ii. 24; cont. Julian. Pelag. iv. 122; v. 15; vi. 22; in Ps. 34, § 2, n. 3). In the Greek Church, S. Johann. Damasceno speaks of her (as we should), as purified by the overshadowing of God the Holy Ghost. "After the consent of the Holy Virgin, the Holy Ghost came upon her, according to the Word of the Lord which the Angel spake, purifying her." De Orthod. Fide, iii. 2.

[3] Some make a fifth festival, viz. of the Conception of the Blessed Mary, saying, 'that as the death of saints is celebrated, not on account of their death, but because they were then received to the everlasting nuptials, so may the Conception be celebrated as a festival, not because she was conceived (since she was conceived in sin), but because the Mother of the Lord was conceived.' Durandus à S. Porc. (A.D. 1320.) Rational. D. Offic. vii. 7. Bellarmine agrees that this is admissible. De Cult. Sanct. iii. 16. The explanation that the festival was kept only as "the Conception of the Immaculate Mary,"

related at first to "the *sanctification* of the Blessed Virgin[4]," the contradictory of her Immaculate Conception), opposed by a chain of later writers whom Rome too has canonized[5], and even at the last by

not as "the Immaculate Conception of the Blessed Mary," was forbidden by Alexander VII. (A.D. 1661.) Bullar. Rom., T. vi. par. v. p. 182, § 4. He declared that the feast "did not relate to her sanctification, but most strictly to her preservation from original sin at the first moment of her Conception." Archbishop of Sassari, i. 388.

[4] Alv. Pelagius, (Bishop) in the fourteenth century, says, "The Roman Church does not celebrate, though it tolerates, the Feast of the Conception. The feast ought to be referred to the sanctification of the Virgin, not to her Conception; and so says the prayer which is said in this feast at Rome in the Church of S. Maria Major, 'Deus, qui sanctificationem Virginis,' &c., as I saw and heard when I preached on that sanctification, on that feast of the 'sanctification which is kept in December fifteen days before the Feast of the Nativity.'" De Planctu Eccl. i. 51. Turrecremata attests that in the office then used in Germany on the Feast of S. Elizabeth there were these words, "The Blessed Virgin Mary, although full of grace, was yet born with the fomes [peccati], which, however, the virtue of the Highest extinguished at the very time of the Conception of Christ." Preuss, p. 1017. Gregory XV., A.D. 1622, forbade the use of any other word than "Conception" in any office, public or private (i.e. forbade the word sanctification). Bullar. T. v. 65, § 4, pp. 45, 46. He expunged the word "sanctification" from the liturgies. Archbishop of Albano, Pareri, &c., ii. 237. Yet some Bishops argued that the Immaculate Conception was matter of faith, on the ground that the festival had always been celebrated at Rome.

[5] S. Anselm, Cur Deus homo, ii. 16 A,—"The Virgin herself, whence He was assumed, was conceived in iniquity, and in sin did her mother conceive her, and with original sin was she born, because she too sinned in Adam, in whom all sinned." S. Peter Damian., Opusc. vi. 19,—"From that very flesh of the Virgin, *which was conceived of sin*, the Flesh came forth without

grave bishops[6] on the ground of the inadequacy of the proof or the injury which they apprehended to their flocks, or the increased difficulties to those external to the Roman Communion. The decree which defines that the doctrine, that "the most Blessed Virgin Mary was, in the first instant of her conception, preserved free from all stain of original sin by the singular grace and privilege of Almighty God, in view of the merits of Christ Jesus, the Saviour of Mankind, was revealed by God, and is therefore to be firmly and stedfastly believed by all the faithful;"—that same decree exhorts all in the

sin, which also abolished the sins of the flesh." So in the ninth century Paschasius Radbertus, de Perp. Virg. S. Mariæ,—"But the Blessed Mary, although she was born and procreated of the flesh of sin, and *herself was flesh of sin*, was she not then, from the forecoming grace of the Holy Ghost, called by the angel blessed above all women? 'The Holy Ghost shall come upon thee, and the power of the Highest shall overshadow thee.' Else if she was not sanctified and cleansed by the same Spirit, how was not her flesh, flesh of sin?" In like way P. Lombard, Hugh and Richard à S. Victore, Alexander of Ales, S. Thomas Aquinas, S. Bonaventura, Albertus Magnus, &c., and, earlier, the two S. Fulgentius. Rusp. de Inc. et Grat. c. 6: "The flesh of Mary, because she was conceived in iniquity after the manner of men, was flesh of sin. If it is not called untruthfully flesh of sin, the flesh hath in itself sin." S. Fulg. Ferr., "The flesh of Christ was like and unlike to the flesh of Mary; like, because He was born of it; unlike, because He did not contract thence the contagion of a vitiated origin." From Pet. de Inc. xiv. 2. Add Bede Hom. sup. Missus, Rup. in Cant. c. 1, i. p. 986. Melchior Canus quotes also S. Erhard, or Eberhard, S. Antonius of Padua, S. Bernardine, S. Vincent Ferr., S. Antoninus, &c.

[6] See above, pp. 127—137, and Note B at the end.

Roman Communion, to what, it seemed to us, most Roman Catholics are of themselves inclined, an exceeding devotion to the Blessed Virgin. "Our mouth is filled with joy and our tongue with exultation, and we do render and ever will render most great and most humble thanks to our Lord Jesus Christ, that, of His singular goodness, He has granted to us, although unworthy, to offer and decree this honour and this glory and praise to His most holy Mother. But we rest our most certain hope and certain confidence, that it will be, that that Most Blessed Virgin—(who, all beautiful and immaculate, bruised the poisonous head of the most cruel serpent[7], and brought salvation to the world; who is also the glory of the Apostles and Prophets, and the honour of Martyrs, and of all the saints the joy and crown; who also, being the safest refuge of all in peril, and most faithful helper, and the most powerful mediatress and reconciless (conciliatrix) of the whole world with her only-begotten Son, and the most illustrious glory and ornament and most firm protection of the Holy Church, ever slew all heresies[8] and delivered the faithful people and nations from the greatest calamities of all sorts, and has freed us too from so many gathering perils)—will, by her most mighty patronage, effect, that the holy mother, the Catholic Church, all difficulties removed and all errors dispersed, may, throughout all nations and all places,

[7] See above, p. 140. [8] See above, p. 140.

daily more thrive, flourish, and reign from sea to sea, and from the river to the ends of the earth, so that the guilty may obtain pardon; the sick, healing; the faint-hearted, strength; the afflicted, consolation; the imperilled, help; and all in error, the darkness of mind being dispersed, may return to the way of truth, and there be one fold and one Shepherd." "Let all the sons of the Catholic Church, most dear to us, hear these our words, and *with a yet more ardent* zeal of piety, religion, and love, continue to worship, invoke, pray, the most blessed Mother of God, the Virgin Mary, conceived without original stain, and to flee unto this most sweet Mother of mercy and grace, in all perils, distresses, necessities, and doubtful and anxious circumstances. For nothing is to be feared, nothing despaired of, when she is the Captain, she the Author, she propitious, she protecting, who, bearing a motherly mind towards us, and having in hand the affairs of our salvation, is anxious about the whole human race, and having been made by the Lord Queen of heaven and earth, and exalted above all the orders of angels and saints, standing at the Right Hand of her only-begotten Son our Lord Jesus Christ, does by her mother's prayers, most potently impetrate and find what she seeks, and cannot be frustrated."

It may be, in God's Providence, that disappointment may check this course. The hopes have not yet been realized. For the years which have elapsed since that decree, have been years of singular trouble. Else this decree, in the legitimate application of its principles, would be but the beginning of a vast transmutation of doctrine, now practically taught with all authority in the Roman Church, into matter of faith, as to the Blessed Virgin, until she be proclaimed as "bearing all the titles and names which are wont to be ascribed to Christ," as the Co-Redeemer of the human race, the only access to Jesus, the Indweller of the soul, to prepare it for the Indwelling of God the Holy Ghost[9]. In the doctrine of the Immaculate Conception there was the more difficulty, because it bore closely upon the doctrines of the transmission of original sin and the universality of redemption, and so, careful and deliberate judgments, stating the exact contrary of the doctrine, had been elicited by the Pelagian controversy. This having been surmounted, there is no fresh difficulty as to any other. The tendency of every decisive act, moreover, both in a body and in an individual, is to produce other similar acts. And that portion of the Roman Church, which is most devoted to the cultus of the Blessed Virgin, is most persuaded of the personal infallibility of the Pope, and of a continual flow of inspiration, which may at any time change popular opinion into infallible truth.

This question of reliance upon the Blessed Virgin as *the* being in whose hands our salvation is virtually

[9] See above, pp. 151—165.

to be placed, is quite distinct from that other question of the nature of the worship paid to her. The one is a practical question, affecting our whole eternity, "What shall I do to be saved?" The practical answer to the Roman Catholic seems to me to be, "Go to Mary, and you will be saved;" in our dear Lord's own words, it is, "Come unto Me;" in our own belief it is, "Go to Jesus, and you will be saved."

The answer which is commonly made, that devotion to the Blessed Virgin is but relative, does not touch this. No one would impute to the Marian writers that they mean that she is Dea, although, notoriously, some of them have called her so. But they speak of what comes to the same, of her "delegated omnipotency;" and a recent writer says, "when[10] Mary, in her office of Advocate, is named 'Omnipotency kneeling,' or 'interceding Omnipotency,' this will now, I hope, appear to be saying not too much but too little." The human mind is narrow, and easily filled with one thought, especially when that thought relates to one's all. When, then, the soul is taught that the devotion to Mary is essential, that she is "the[1] nearest to us, and the most suited to our capacity," that "to go to Jesus, we *must* go to Mary; she is our Mediatrix of intercession;" that *she* repels none; "*she* is good and tender; *she* has nothing in her austere and repul-

[10] Oswald, Mariologie, p. 216.
[1] De Montf. p. 171.

sive;" it seems inconceivable that many should not stop short in her, with, at best, a more or less indistinct reference to Jesus. It is difficult to see how direct heresy should not be suggested by sentences such as these (and they are so common): "If[2] we fear to go directly to Jesus Christ our God, whether because of His infinite greatness or because of our vileness, or because of our sins, let us boldly implore the aid of Mary our Mother. *She* is so charitable that she repels none of those who ask for her intercession, no matter how great sinners they have been; for, as the saints say, never has it been heard, since the world was the world, that any one has confidently and perseveringly had recourse to our Blessed Lady and yet has been repelled." For, for this argument to have any force, it must be implied to be possible that any could "confidently and perseveringly have recourse to

[2] Ib. p. 58. Oswald says, "Ascending, the ladder to heaven leads first to the Mother; from the Mother to the Son, from the Son to the Father. We might, indeed, passing over the lowest Court, turn direct to the Son; but we can also spring over the middle step and go direct to the Godhead." Yet, so we should directly contradict our Lord, "No one cometh to the Father but by Me." It is not God, but man, who says, "no man cometh unto Jesus but by Mary." Oswald proceeds, "The natural order is that which I have named. I believe that this way of looking at it, will occasion milder judgment as to a certain equalizing, nay, *apparent* preference of the devotion to Mary to that to Christ. As long as it is genuine, it can only have the meaning, that Mary, in this valley of tears, is nearer to us, and so is approached most gladly."—p. 216. He himself asserts that "Mary is always—more dimly or more clearly, this does not matter—thought of in connexion with her Son."

our Divine Lord and yet be repelled," which is, of course, directly against the Gospel.

But also, in regard to the mode of worship itself, the "more than servitude," the "hyperdouleia" which is intended to separate the cultus of the Blessed Virgin from all advocacy of the Saints or asking for their prayers, "douleia," melts very much into the "latreia" or the worship due to God. "Jesus[3] is altogether in Mary, and Mary is altogether in Jesus," so that to pray to Mary is to pray to Jesus in her. "Some[4] say that that special worship to her is a sort of latreia[5], so that the cultus of the Blessed Virgin proceeds from the same habit of religion, from which arises the adoration of God and Christ. They prove it, first, because although the excellence of the mother is created, yet it has respect to the uncreated excellence, from which it takes its value; secondly, because this dignity appertains to the order of the Hypostatic Union, on the ground whereof the adoration of latreia is due to the Humanity of Christ. So then, by reason thereof, there is due to the Blessed Virgin, as the Mother of God, the same adoration, but inferior; whence Caietan[6] teaches that the Blessed Virgin

[3] De Montf. p. 171.

[4] Corn. à Lap. on Cant. v. 11, p. 247.

[5] "Franc. Suarez thinks this very probable (3 p. q. 37, disp. 22, S. 3, sub fin.), and from him Mendoza (in Viridario, L. 2, Probl. 4), though G. Vazquez thinks the contrary, de Adorat., disp. 8, c. 2." Ibid.

[6] "2. 2. q. 103, art. 4, ad 2."

has a consanguinity with Christ, as God, and so that a special adoration is due to her, because 'by an operation of her own she touched the bounds of Divinity,' i. e. because she conceived, bore, nourished God. And the fathers often assert that 'the whole honour of the Mother is referred to the Son.' Thirdly, because in human things the same habit, which inclines to honour a king, inclines also to honour the king's mother, as such. But this adoration is not absolute, which is due to God only; but diminished, participated, and respective: for it has respect to the dignity and Divinity of the Son, for which the mother of God is honoured, as such: wherefore this honour does not stop in the Mother, but through her tends to the Son; and the Mother is not so much adored in herself, as the Son is adored in the Mother." Yet we are told, that "[7] after devotion to our Lord in the Blessed Sacrament, devotion to our Lady is the holiest and solidest of all devotions;" that the devotion to the Blessed Virgin comes first in order[8]; that "[9] the difference between the 'pray for us' and the 'have mercy upon us,' is not so complete, as is commonly thought. As it is dogmatically admissible, to approach the God-Man, Who in the days of His Flesh prayed the Father for us, and Who now too, as the

[7] De Montf. p. 68. [8] Ib. p. 65.

[9] Oswald, Mariologie, p. 216. The "Ora pro nobis," as said in the litanies to the saints; "Miserere nobis," as said in the litanies to the Holy Trinity.

Apostle says, 'intercedeth for us,' with a 'Pray for us,' so perhaps there would not be much to be objected to, if only rightly understood, were one to cry out to the Queen of heaven, 'Have mercy upon us.'" But as, practically, no one would say to our Lord, "Pray for me," because it would be a passing by of His Divine Nature and irreverence to Him[1]; so, to say to the Blessed Virgin, "Have mercy upon us," is indistinguishable, except in intention, from prayer to the Holy Trinity.

We have been told that the devotion of the people to the Blessed Virgin outruns the judgment of the priests; but if the whole weight of Papal authority is added to the popular devotions, and the people are bidden, on what is to them the highest authority, to be still more devoted to the Blessed Virgin as *the* mediatrix with "*the* One Mediator between God and man, the Man Christ Jesus," our Adorable Lord, one sees not where there shall be any pause or bound, short of that bold conception that "every prayer, both of individuals and of the Church, should be addressed to S. Mary." Popular devotion now is already very different from what it was in the time of S. Bernard. S. Bernard has strong passages, grounded on what the Breviary stated to be the language of S. Athanasius, S. Augustine, &c., which Roman Catholic critics have discovered not to be theirs. But the devotion of S. Bernard is concentrated on Christ crucified. In S. Bernard on

[1] Pétau de Inc. xii. 8, fin. speaks against it.

the Canticles, one is in a different atmosphere from that of e. g. Faber. Pius IX. gave permission throughout the Roman Communion to substitute special Hours recently composed on the Immaculate Conception of the Blessed Virgin for those in the common Breviary, apparently in order to give an impulse to this devotion [2]. At the beginning of the last century, De Montfort complained of two classes of "false devotees to our Lady," the "critical devotees" and "the scrupulous devotees," both of whom checked in some degree the devotion to the Blessed Virgin. The "critical devotees," he says [3], "do an infinite wrong to the devotion to our Lady; and they are but too successful in alienating people from it, under the pretext of destroying its abuses." "The scrupulous devotees are those who fear to dishonour the Son by honouring the Mother, to abase the one by elevating the other; they say, 'We must have recourse to Jesus Christ; He is our only Mediator. We must preach Jesus Christ, this is the solid devotion.'" "[4] Instead of the

[2] "Since we have already allowed the Roman Clergy to recite the special Canonical Hours, quite recently composed and printed, on the Conception of the most Blessed Virgin, in place of those contained in the common Breviary, therefore by these letters we give you, venerable brothers, the faculty, that, if it seem good, all the Clergy of your diocese should be free to render the same canonical hours on the Conception of the most holy Virgin, which the Roman Clergy now use, without needing to implore leave from us or from our Congregation of sacred rites."—Ep. Encycl. Pii IX. A.D. 1849.

[3] Pp. 62—64.

[4] P. 41.

Rosary, they counsel to any poor client of our Lady the seven Penitential Psalms. Instead of devotion to the holy Virgin, they counsel him devotion to Jesus Christ." Both these classes seem to have passed away; there seem to be now those only who are silent, or who intensify the devotion to the Blessed Virgin. The Clergy, according to the answers of the Bishops to the Pope, seem to be every where earnest in promoting it. If the system should grow, as seems likely, and it should be discovered in Roman Catholic countries, that this vast range of doctrine which the people have been taught or encouraged in, in the name of the Church, has no foundation in either of the two authorities alleged by the Council of Trent—Holy Scripture or continuous tradition from our Lord or His Apostles—it is an anxious thought what the result might be. Such an authoritative explanation, as might be satisfactory to the English Church, might hereafter be of benefit to the Roman also. The Saxon mind is a large element in the Christian body.

The solemn words addressed to Pius IX. in answer to his Encyclical Letter by the Metropolitan of Gorizia and Gradisca in Austria, (and that, as it seems, from a synod of several bishops[5],) shows that the anxiety for the faith of those now outwardly Catholics is shared by some in the Communion of Rome too.

"If," he says[6], "the present state of all Ger-

[5] "In actuali plurimorum Episcoporum congregatione præsentem."

[6] Pareri dell' Episc. Cattolico, i. 178, 179.

many, and the condition of the Austrian provinces in particular, be considered attentively, as it ought, the proposition about deciding the scholastic question as to the Immaculate Conception of the Blessed Virgin Mary, in such wise, that a pious belief should be transformed into an article of Faith and a Catholic dogma, in face of, or rather over against, the Protestants, but especially over against that sect which presumes to be called German Catholic, and which strains day by day with incredible effort to extend itself more and more, and in sight of such numbers of languid Catholics, who, both in Germany and Italy, call themselves Catholic Christians, but who have, in fact, either cast off all faith in God, or have abandoned themselves to absolute religious indifferentism, in the actual state of political liberty, seems to me a matter full of peril.—

"Under these circumstances, (as far as I can see,) you must direct your mind, and strive, with all the effort you can by the help of God, together with the fathers of the Society of Jesus, that the Catholic faith should by the gift of God be more and more established in that sense in which it was excellently declared and established in the Council of Trent, and that it should take deeper root in men's hearts, that, according to the Apostle, we may have 'faith working by love' to life eternal; but you must abstain, at least for the present, from forming new articles of faith, and so leave the question of the Immaculate Conception of the Blessed Virgin in that state, in which the Catholic Church has hitherto kept it. There is still found in Europe a sufficient number of Catholics; but, alas! perhaps the greater part of them does not from the heart believe even the articles of faith necessary, *necessitate medii*, to salvation [7]. What avails it to establish that the most Blessed Virgin Mary was conceived without spot, when it is not believed that Jesus is the Son of God?"

vii. *b*. The same distinction between the popular system, and that which is laid down as *de fide*, recurs as to the doctrine of Purgatory. The Council of Trent states a minimum as to the doctrine of the Western Church: "There is a Purgatory, and the souls detained there are helped by the prayers of the faithful and the acceptable sacrifice of the Altar [8]." It is stated, moreover, that the Roman Church does not require "any belief of the *opinion* that the souls there are punished by material fire [9]."

On the other hand, what the popular mind in England objects to, is clearly expressed by Hooker, whom our friend quoted. "The [1] other punishment, which hath in it not only loss of joy, but

[7] The Archbishop of Breslau, who, in the most solemn and earnest manner, opposed the decree, spoke of "a part of the clergy, imbued with neologism, in the Rhine provinces, in Baden, and in Bohemia."—Pareri, &c., ii. 467. The Bishop of Clermont said, "Although the days are evil, and the number of those who, tainted with unbelief or ignorance, care little as to things pertaining to salvation but too increased, &c."—Ib., ii. 471.

[8] Sess. xxv. [9] Milner, End of Contr., Letter 43, n. 2.

[1] Sermon on Pride, Works, iii. 798, quoted in Tract 90, p. 27.

also sense of grief, vexation, and woe, is that whereunto they give the names of purgatory pains, *in nothing different from those very infernal torments, which the souls of castaways, together with damned spirits, do endure*[2]; save only in this, that there is an appointed term to the one, to the other, none; but for the time they last they are equal." Hooker must mean, as his context implies, that the *physical* sufferings are equal; for the sufferings, as a whole, could not but be different, according as there should be hope or knowledge, that those sufferings should, at some time, end in the beatific vision of God, (for it was held by some, that some souls shall not be certain of their salvation until the Day of Judgment,) or knowledge that the suffering is eternal.

On our side, to thoughtful minds, whom the grace of God has taught something of what sin is, and of the holiness and love of God and of Jesus, it is absolutely inconceivable that,—when the soul shall first behold Jesus, and, in His sight, with its powers quickened by Him, shall behold its past life as a whole; when, in His countenance, it shall behold all which it never before saw of His goodness, and, in contrast with this, all its own ingratitude, baseness, rebellion, negligence, discontent, murmurings, not to speak of deadly, forgiven sin,—it should not have intense pain, pain so intense,

[2] Aquinas held this; and that the difference was, that "the damned, as being worse in merits, are to be reckoned worse in place." See in my Letter to Dr. Jelf, p. 85.

that one should think that, in this life, soul and body would be severed by its intensity. There seems also to be an instinctive feeling, that a soul, which here has had no longings for God, even if the man himself should die in a state of grace, would not be at once, and might not for some long period be, admitted to the sight of God. It is a common saying, that a number of souls "seem to be fit neither for heaven nor hell," and that purgatory seems to meet the case of this class of souls. This cannot mean, necessarily so. For this would be to limit the Omnipotence of God. The ordinary belief in England must be, that God, in one act at the particular judgment, at once frees the soul, which dies in His grace, from all sinfulness which clung to it while yet in the body, and fits it for its abode in Paradise. The Roman doctrine of purgatory presupposes, that exactly the same number of souls will be saved, viz. those, and those only who die in a state of grace, and that the capacity of loving God will receive no accession there. The time of gaining grace, in the belief of the Roman Church equally with our own, is over with this life, and the place of the soul in bliss is then fixed for ever. Suffering and preparation for the sight of God, which, here, would have been the channel of large grace, would, *there*, be without any increase of grace. Yet many of us, for our misdeserts, may be unfit for the immediate presence of God; or, in the great words of S. Irenæus, "capere Deum[3]," "to contain God," who yet, for the Merits of Jesus, may, we trust, in His mercy be saved. God can, "[4]in a short time, fulfil a long time." Publicans and harlots shall enter into the kingdom of God before the self-righteous. We know not what God may do, in one agony of loving penitence, for one who accepts His last grace in that almost sacrament of death. The question, however, is not about individuals. As a class, we could not affirm that those, who bring forth no worthy fruits of repentance, with whom, after a long period of deadly sin, repentance has been but a superficial work, may not, after death, be in a state of privation of the sight of God (the "pœna damni"), not being admitted at once to the sight of *Him*, Whom on earth they little cared to think of or speak to, and Whom they served with a cold and grudging service. And the absence of the sight of God, Whom the soul in grace knows to be its only Good, would, when the distractions of this world no longer dazzled it, be an intense suffering, above all the sufferings of this life, while the *knowledge* that it was saved, and that it belonged to Jesus, and that it would, in all eternity, behold God and be the object of His infinite love, would be "[5]joy and felicity" above all the spiritual joys in this life, even apart from all those consolations which God might bestow on the soul which He had made His own for ever.

[3] Adv. Hær. v. 32. 1. [4] Wisdom iv. 13.
[5] Burial Service.

The Greek Church, too[6], while it states that such souls as have departed with faith, but without having had time to "bring forth fruits worthy of repentance," "may be aided towards the attainment of a blessed resurrection by prayers offered in their behalf," still holds that "the souls of (all) the righteous are in light and rest, with a foretaste of eternal happiness."

A modern approved German Catholic writer on Dogma excludes from Purgatory the idea of physical fire, or of any other than mental sufferings. "About[7] *any*, or *the*, place of purifying, nothing has been decided as matter of doctrine. So neither as to the mode of purifying. About the last, the fathers have expressed themselves only problematically and hypothetically, and Doctors and believers have only assumed a fire as matter of opinion; in which mention ignorance only or malice (in order to make room for irony) can find occasion to think of our common fire. Purifying, as the sloughing-off of the imperfection ingrown as it were with the soul; the straining of the soul to become free from all earthliness on her; the longing for the vision of God, from which the unbefittingness, yet cleaving to her, still excludes her; her struggle towards the full death of the evil in her, and towards the full life of the good in her; this up-stirring of her deepest and inmost self implies fire, fiery pain enough."

[6] Longer Catechism, P. i. p. 98, 99, Blackmore's Transl.

[7] Klee, Dogmatik, ii. 429, 430.

Tetzel, on the contrary, preached, "Ye[8] hear not your parents and other deceased crying, Have mercy, have mercy on me, &c., for the hand of God hath touched me. For we are in the severest pains and torment, from which ye could free us by a slight alms. And ye will not. Ye permit us to lie in the flames, deferring the glory promised to us." And[9], "let them observe that, seeing that mortal sins in the whole period of life are almost infinite, they have to endure an infinite punishment in the burning pains of purgatory." In England, when private masses were being discontinued, Sir Thomas More appealed in behalf of the souls in purgatory, speaking of "pains, which else [unless the masses should be purchased] will hold them here with us in fire and torments intolerable, only God knoweth how long." He wrote of them as "never resting[1]."

The Catechism of the Council of Trent (which, I suppose, comes as near to a binding authority as any writing which has not absolute authority) supports the received practical teaching of a material fire—"There is a Purgatorial *fire*, in which the souls of the *pious* are *tormented* for a certain time, and expiated, in order that an entrance may be open to them into their eternal home, where nothing defiled can enter." Besides

[8] Instructio pro Sacerd., Serm. 2, in v. d. Hardt, Hist. Ref.

[9] Id. Serm. 3, ib.

[1] Supplication of Souls. Works, p. 316. See Letter to Dr. Jelf, p. 87.

this, the system as to the Blessed Virgin reappears here, rested upon I know not what, yet taught as absolutely certain, that Purgatory is especially her kingdom. Liguori mentions no writer, except S. P. Damian (A.D. 1057), earlier than the latter half of the fourteenth century, who speaks of the Blessed Virgin in relation to Purgatory. The opinion gained its chief impulse from two writers, who seem to have been the chief authors of the modern theories as to her authority, the two S. Bernardines. Yet recent devotional books speak with as much certainty of "[2] S. Michael as Prince of Purgatory and our Lady's regent," "The moonlight of Mary's throne lighting up their land of pain," as if this had been revealed in God's Word.

There is then here again, if the Church of Rome were so minded, scope for proposing to us a doctrine which our Church in no way intends to contradict, and which (strangely enough) commends itself even to minds the most alien from Catholic truth[3]. There is no ground for thinking that, in rejecting the popular "*Romish* doctrine of purgatory," the

[2] The language is that of the late F. Faber.

[3] The case of this class of souls is the stock argument among those who are denying Hell, "those who *die in ignorance*, like the thousands of the London poor." Who ever said or suggested that they would necessarily be lost? Mr. Wilson, in his Defence (p. 147), maintained that the Roman doctrine of Purgatory made the belief in Hell more reasonable in the Roman, than in the English Church; as though the English Church held that any whom the Roman Church assigns to Purgatory would be cast into Hell!

Church of England meant to reject all suffering after this life, since the Day of Judgment is, in Holy Scripture, so plainly spoken of as "a great and terrible day." But Cardinal Wiseman, when consulted by one who related the fact to me, after taking a day to reflect, stated that the belief that there would be suffering in the Day of Judgment, would satisfy the doctrine of Purgatory. The Greeks formally rejected the doctrine of material fire, and hold only that there is spiritual pain for some souls. The fact, that, after that rejection, the Roman Church did not, at the Council of Trent, introduce any mention of the fire of Purgatory, has been noticed as an acquiescence in its exclusion from matters of faith. Still it is as much the popular belief as if it had been so decreed; devotional writers keep up that belief as about a thing certainly true; and it might, like the doctrine of the Immaculate Conception, be affirmed as a matter of faith at any future time.

Now too, in the face of those express words of God, "I exhort therefore, that first of all, supplications, prayers, intercessions, and giving of thanks be made for all men, for this is good and acceptable in the sight of God our Saviour, Who will have all men to be saved and to come unto the knowledge of the truth[4]," it is taught, that it is more acceptable to God to pray for souls in Purgatory[5], than

[4] 1 Tim. ii. 1—4.

[5] Rosignoli, Opere, i. 710, as quoted in Faber, "All for Jesus;" "Purgatory," pp. 354—356.

for the conversion of sinners, that they fall not into Hell; and to pray exclusively for them, as far as relates to prayers at a priest's own disposal.

vii. *c.* "Pardons," or "indulgences" are in principle, it is agreed, only "relaxations of Canonical Penance," i. e., of a portion of that severity, which the Ancient Church thought good to impose on those who had greatly sinned; that "[6] being punished in this world, their souls might be saved in the day of the Lord." The Church, at times, shortened the period of public penance, restoring the offender sooner to Communion, in view of his penitence or the necessity of the case; as when the lapsed were restored under the prospect of renewed persecution, or to other penitents death seemed near, that they might be fortified by the Body and Blood of Christ[7]: or the Canonical punishment was exchanged for some other, in consideration of infirmity either of body or will. This was done either by Synods or by the single Bishop, by virtue of our Lord's words, "Whatsoever ye shall loose on earth shall be loosed in heaven[8]." And so (the sincerity of the penitent being presupposed) the Church hoped that her acts would be ratified by Him Who gave her this power. Writers cite, as instances, St. Paul's[9] forgiveness and restoration of the incestuous Corinthian at the prayers of the

[6] Commination Service.

[7] S. Cyprian, Ep. 57, ad Corn. p. 136, Oxf. Tr.

[8] S. Matt. xvi. 19; xviii. 18.

[9] 2 Cor. ii. 10.

faithful, or that of the lapsed in S. Cyprian's time, at the intercession of the Confessors, who were expecting martyrdom for the testimony of Jesus. The *term* "indulgence" occurs only in these passages of S. Cyprian, until the eleventh century. The *thing* continued, as being, in fact, inseparable from any system of canonical penance. The general rule of the Church had to be adapted to the case of individuals. Thus, the Council of Neo-Cæsarea, A.D. 314, "enacted that the period of penitence for those who had fallen into the sin of polygamy, should be abridged on account of "the faith and penitence of individuals[1]." Or when fervour and discipline were weakened, the Church permitted lighter penances[2], sooner than that the offender should refuse all acts of penitence, and so risk the loss of his soul. "Such," Amort also agrees[3], "were the chief instances of Indulgences for the first thousand years after our Lord." In the latter part of the thirteenth century "the Bishop could still give Indulgences in his own diocese as much as he willed, unless he were limited by the Pope. But the limitation, as seems to me (he

[1] Can. 3. So Conc. Ancyr. c. 2. 7. 16. Nic. i. c. 12. Arelat. ii. c. 10. Canons of S. Basil, Ep. ad Amphiloch. c. 2. 7. 53. 74. 84. S. Greg. Nyss., Ep. Canon. ad Letoium, can. 8. 11. Conc. Carth. can. 75, 76. Aur. iv. c. 8. 27. Wormat. (A. 868), c. 25. Tribur. (A. 890), c. 52. These are the chief instances given by Amort, Hist. Indulg. P. ii. c. iv. § 31—52.

[2] As in the Pœnitentials of Bede, Theodore, Burchard, the Roman.

[3] Ib. § 57.

adds), is reasonable, according to the excessive abuse of indulgences which now are given; whence it seems well that several Bishops together should not give (indulgences) beyond forty days[4]."

The "modern indulgences" (as Amort too and others call them) were of two sorts; (1) a plenary forgiveness of all guilt as well as punishment, chiefly in connexion with Crusades. These being holy wars, death, incurred in them, was a sort of martyrdom, which was accounted to be "a baptism of blood," and so to carry with it remission of sins. The abuse of these Indulgences, and the exceeding wickedness incident thereon, was probably one cause of the failure of the Crusades. The other sorts were founded upon precedents which were, unhappily, by mistake[5] or fraud[6], attributed to earlier Bishops of Rome. Yet Amort says, that "until A.D. 1391 no plenary indulgence was granted to all the faithful, which should exempt them from all obligation of making fitting amends."

The indulgences, in their modern form, were condemned at the time in terms much stronger than those used by the Church of England. Bert-

[4] Alb. M. in iv. dist. 20, art. 21. Aq. iv. dist. 24, q. 3. art. 2.

[5] Because S. Gregory I. instituted certain stations, it was inferred, by mistake, that he annexed indulgences to the visiting of the stations, which no old writer mentions. See Pagi in Leo IV. 1, n. 4.

[6] The indulgences ascribed to Leo III. A.D. 803, Sergius, A.D. 847. See Mabillon, Præf. ad Sæc. 5 Bened. n. 107, Papebroch. Conat. Chron.-Hist., Diss. 17, quoted and extracted, in part, in Amort, Hist. Indulg. P. i. n. xlv. xlvi., pp. 43—53.

hold, a fervent Franciscan preacher at the close of the thirteenth century, a man "of[7] holy life and great learning, who, by word and example, converted countless sinners to the Lord, whose memory was blessed, and was still most fresh among men" half a century after his departure, said of the sellers of them, "They[8] arose but of late. When I was yet a little child, there was not one of them any where. They are called 'Penny Preachers,' and are among the favourite servants of the Devil. He goes forth among the simple people, preaches and calls out, so that all present weep. And he says he has power from the Pope to take away all thy sins for a halfpenny. And he lies, that men are for this free before God; and he crowns the devil daily with many thousand souls. Ye must give them nothing; then must they cease from this cheating. While ye give to them, ye sell yourselves to eternal death. And they murder you, and turn you from the right repentance which God has hallowed, that ye should repent no longer." And another celebrated, though peculiar, preacher of the 15th century says, "Theologians[9] have made little or no mention of indulgences. But hypocrites only have preached them with infinite lies to deceive the people. Thou must go to the great indulgence,

[7] Jo. Vitoduranus, Chron. ad A. 1265, in Gieseler, ii. 2, § 80, n. c.

[8] Berthold, Deutsche Pred., p. 384, ed. Kl.

[9] Menot, Serm. Quadr. f. 147 b, in Gies. K. G. Par. 3, § 147, n. ee.

which is contrition. Do this, and I promise to thee what was promised to Magdalene. Go to the tears of the heart; shed them abundantly. God said not to her, that she should put five shillings in the chest, but He said to her, 'Thy faith hath saved thee.'"

The difficulty as to indulgences, apart from the special abuses before the Reformation, relates to this: "In what way they can be thought, consistently with the previous acts of the Church, to avail for the departed?" It is now conceded, that "until the end of the fifteenth Century, there was scarcely any, or any how very rare use of indulgences for the departed." Those who defend indulgences, see that the modern discipline of the Church cannot in any way be reconciled to the ancient, except on the supposition, that indulgences avail only by way of prayer to God, which prayer God would hear, or not hear, according to His Infinite Wisdom, and His knowledge of the condition of souls.

Amort says[10], "there are four opinions, as to the value of indulgences to the departed." The first, "rejected by almost all Theologians, that the Pope has jurisdiction in Purgatory." This (most remark) is contrary to our Lord's limitation, "Whatsoever ye shall loose *on earth.*" "The second, of some older writers, that they only avail in the way of deprecation, in that the Church undertakes to pray

[10] Hist. Indulg. P. ii. S. v. § 2, p. 289.

God for the soul of a certain departed. The gain then is, that the Pope specially prays God in the name of the whole Church, together with him who gains the indulgence. The third, and most common among Theologians, is that they avail by way of payment, in that the Church takes the satisfactory merits of Christ and the Saints, and pays them to God for the soul which is being purified, and that God is bound to release that soul." The fourth, "that they avail by way of payment, but that God is not so bound."

Amort's own opinion is, that "the indulgence for the dead is a solemn deprecation, with a pleading before the Throne of the merits of Christ and of His saints, but that it does not involve the success of the deprecation [1]." Scavini adds to this, "Most think that indulgences benefit the departed more or less, according as they, in their lifetime, deserved by their own acts that the indulgences should be applied to them."

Thus reduced, indulgences differ from other prayers for the departed, only in that they are more solemn deprecations in the name of the whole Church. The Council of Trent, being about to

[1] Theol. Eclect. T. iii. p. 189. The divine who supplied me with this last quotation, adds, "I believe this to be the common doctrine now. Thus Scavini says, 'that they are given by way of suffrage or of simple payment, in so far as God is prayed to vouchsafe to accept them. But in what measure God accepts them, we know not.'"

disperse, did not explain what indulgences are; only affirming that they "ought to be retained in the Church." It condemns those only "who assert that they are useless, or deny that the Church has any power to grant them[2]." There is then ample scope for explanation on this subject also; the more so, since the Council of Trent condemned that sale of them which had so large a share in bringing about the Reformation.

"In granting indulgences the Synod wishes moderation to be used according to the old and approved custom in the Church, lest ecclesiastical discipline should be enervated by excessive easiness." If the Roman Church wishes to go back to the ancient custom, then the British, which expresses the same wish, is so far at one with her. It proceeded,—

"But abuses, which have crept in here, on occasion of which this eminent name 'Indulgences' is blasphemed by heretics, the Synod, wishing to see corrected, enacts generally by this present decree, that all perverse gains for obtaining the same, from which a very large occasion of abuses flowed among the Christian people, should be altogether abolished. But as to other abuses, which have arisen from superstition, ignorance, irreverence, or any other cause whatsoever, since, on account of the multiplicity of places and provinces where they are committed, they cannot be specially prohibited, the Synod commands all Bishops, each diligently to bring together such abuses in his own Church, and to relate them in a Provincial Synod, in order that, the judgment of other bishops too being ascertained, it may be forthwith brought before the Supreme Roman Pontiff,

[2] Sess. xxv. continuat.

by whose authority and prudence *that* may be enacted which shall be expedient to the Universal Church, that so the gift of holy indulgences may be dispensed piously, holily, and uncorruptly to all the faithful."

In regard to "indulgences" we are at one with the Greek Church, which never heard of them in the sense in which they, and very chiefly, caused the Reformation. I mean, the Greek Church abridged Canonical Penance in this life, according to the earnestness or necessities of penitents, but never thought of such abridgments or Indulgences to penitents, with reference to the intermediate state.

vii. *d.* The veneration of images and relics as condemned by our Article, need not detain us long. Our friend has illustrated, from the homilies, what was probably the meaning of the Article. The writers of that homily had had before their eyes what the writers of the Articles desired to reject. The Council of Trent, as he observed, condemned in part the self-same things,—

"[3] All superstition also in invocation of saints, veneration of relics, and sacred use of images, be put away; all *filthy lucre* be cast out of doors; and *all wantonness* be avoided; *so that images be not painted or adorned with an immodest beauty;* or the celebration of saints and attendance on relics *be abused to revelries and drunkennesses;* as though festival-days were kept in honour of saints *by luxury and lasciviousness.*"

Dr. Milner[4] also referred to their first Catechism

---

[3] Sess. 25. Tract 91, p. 36.

[4] End of Controv., Let. xxxiv.

for the instruction of children. "*Qu.* May we pray to relics or images? *Ans.* No, by no means; for they have no life or sense to hear or to help us;" and to the Anathema of Gother and Challoner, "Cursed is he that commits idolatry; that prays to images or relics, or worships them for God. Amen." The Council of Trent requires only that "*due* honour and veneration should be paid them; not that we believe there is any divinity or *power in them*, for which we respect them, or that any thing is to be asked of them, or that trust is to be placed in them, as the heathen of old trusted in their idols." On the other hand, we know that, in kissing the outside of the material Bible, we mean only to express reverence for the Word of God; in the traditional custom of bowing to the Altar (when the Holy Sacrament is not there), we mean only reverence to it, as having been "the Throne of God[5]," (as Peers bow before the Throne in respect for the absent Sovereign.) So also, if any should kiss the feet of the Crucifix, it would be in reverence to the Crucified. Even Dr. Arnold "rather envied" the simple faith of a child who did so.

"In the crypt is a Calvary and figures as large as life, representing the burying of our Lord. The woman who showed in the crypt had her little girl with her, and she lifted up the child, about three years old, to kiss the feet of our Lord. Is this idolatry? Nay, verily, it may be so; but it need not be,

---

[5] Laud, Speech at the Star-Chamber, 1637, p. 47.

and assuredly is *in itself right and natural.* I confess I rather envied the child[6]."

There is then nothing in this respect which might not easily be reconciled; the more, since Petavius says, "we must lay down in the first instance, that images are to be reckoned among the 'adiaphora,' which do not belong to the substance of religion, and which the Church may retain or take away, as she judges best[7]."

viii. The earlier explanations of the Articles I set down, in order to show that the Articles in no way contradict any Catholic truth, as was alleged by Dr. Manning. In these last I have had the further object of showing that the breach between us and Rome is not so wide as is commonly thought, or as, in the period of my youth, the Articles were unconsciously strained to make out. Plainly, on the surface, by the force of the terms, "the Romish doctrine," as to these subjects, cannot include any doctrine upon them which is not "*the Roman* doctrine." Without entering into any details, or any discussion of its claims, it cannot include any doctrine of "the Greek Church," e. g. as to Purgatory, which is *not* Roman, nor any "opinions" floating in the Early Church. Else it would have run, "*all* belief in Purgatory, &c." But while any opinion, held in the Ancient Undivided Church or by the Greek Church upon any of these subjects,

[6] Dr. Arnold's Life, ii. 402. [7] De Incarn. xv. 13. 1.

cannot, on the ground of the language itself, be intended by the Article, which speaks of "the *Romish* doctrine;" neither is there any ground to assume that the Article was directed against the canons of the Council of Trent. For, on the one hand, upon some of the subjects there is very little to be found in those canons; on the other hand, the entire practical system floating in the Roman communion was all around the writers of the Articles. They had themselves been familiar with it before the Council of Trent. Yet any one would, *à priori*, suppose that a protest published in the language of the people would relate to what was known and familiar, what *was* the subject of controversy, not to what was unknown and recondite, and would have to be put together out of a foreign document. Men protest against what they have before them, what presses upon them. The Twenty-second Article was not drawn up with reference to the Council of Trent, having been framed before it. The only change, after the Council of Trent, was the substitution of the terms "the Romish doctrine" for "the doctrine of the Schoolmen." The body of the Article did not refer to formal decrees before; there is nothing to make it refer to formal decrees afterwards. It does not contain a single hint as to the special character of the doctrines which it rejects. It assumes that doctrine to be popularly known. English controversialists afterwards, as well as before, wrote about the popular doctrine. Indeed, so far from the doctrine of the Council of Trent being the subject of controversy, it has happened that Roman controversialists have pared down the popular statements of English writers, because they alleged what was beside or against Tridentine doctrine. I am not aware that Jewell, although he makes his statements against the authority of the Council of Trent, any where animadverts upon formal expositions of doctrine. He continued his charges, as before, against the popular system.

This system, going beyond the letter of the Council of Trent, remained as it did before. The Council of Trent gave an indirect sanction to it, in that, while a large portion of Europe was complaining of it, the Council removed certain practical abuses (such as the trade in Indulgences), but, else, left the whole practical doctrine unexplained and unlimited, while it laid down, as *de fide*, certain statements which lay at the root of that practical system. On the other hand, it tacitly allowed that this system was not *de fide*, in that, after the objections had been raised against it, it did not erect any portion of it into Articles of Faith. In like way, it has been observed that the opinion as to a material fire of Purgatory was the more left an open question, in that, after the Greeks at the Council of Florence had denied it, the Latins did not define it. So long, however, as the Church of Rome places no restriction upon this practical system, she remains responsible for it. For it is taught by her priests, put forth as certain truth and as her teaching, in books which have the sanction of her Bishops, and by writers who have been canonized. Yet Rome need not make such doctrines terms of communion, nor need she insist that the Church of England, if united with her, should receive them, but provision might be formally made on both sides that she need not.

This has been often said to individuals, although it seems to me to be a psychological impossibility for one who has already exchanged one system for another to make those distinctions. One who, by his own act, places himself under authority, cannot make conditions about his submission. But definite explanations of our Articles have, before now, been at least tentatively offered to us, on the Roman and the Greek side, as sufficient to restore communion; and the Roman explanations too were, in most cases, mere supplements to our Articles, on points upon which our Church had not spoken.

The proposal for union with the Gallican Church in Archbishop Wake's time, came, in the first instance, from Du Pin and three other doctors of the Sorbonne. "[8] They wished for an union with the Church of England, as the most effectual means to unite all the Western Churches."

The correspondence between Du Pin and Arch-

[8] M. Beauvoir's Letter to Wake, Dec. 11, 1717. No. 2 in Maclaine, Trans. of Mosh. vi. 98.

bishop Wake was shown to the Cardinal de Noailles, the Procureur Général, D. D. Joly de Fleury[9]. A detailed account was given to the Regent and the Court[1], which also did not, for the time, appear to disapprove of it. An oration, made by De Girardin to the Doctors of the Sorbonne, to recommend the union, and to prepare them for the treatise itself, was favourably heard and applauded[2]. Du Pin wrote, Jan. 13, 1719, "The[3] Theological Faculty at Paris, whose authority is great in this realm, will not be out of harmony with our object. This seems to me a thing to be earnestly set about in these times, but maturely weighing and discussing every thing accurately. To accomplish the work belongs to God, in Whose hand are the hearts, not of kings only, but of all men." De Girardin gives an account of the reception of a letter of Wake's by the Doctors of the Sorbonne, with which they were much delighted, and said, that "the foundations of concord had been laid by him, and that

[9] Du Pin's "Rélation de ce qui s'est passé entre M. Du Pin et M. l'Archevêque de Cantorbery, au sujet des lettres qu'ils se sont mutuellement écrites," in Wake's MS. letters, Christ Church Lib., T. 25, n. 139.

[1] Letter of M. Beauvoir, Feb. 8, 1719, Ib. n. 190 (it stands as 110). For these notices I am indebted to the Rev. E. Ffoulkes.

[2] Letter of M. Beauvoir (no date), and in another letter of April 5, 1718, O. S., Wake, Ep. T. 28. The Oration itself is in T. 25, n. 67, and M. Girardin's letter, with which he sent it to Wake, Ib. n. 66, April 30, 1718.

[3] Ib. n. 99.

they must make their contribution towards so beautiful a work[4]." It is said that "[5] the treatise itself was read to the Doctors of the Sorbonne." It had the hearty concurrence of De Girardin. Du Pin stated to M. Beauvoir, that "he[6] had communicated his design to the Cardinal de Noailles, who had approved of it." In his official account Du Pin says, that Wake "sent" him "[7] the Confession of Faith and the Liturgy of the English Church, and that M. Du Pin formed thereon a memorial, containing the Articles upon which they were agreed, those which were indifferent, and those upon which it was necessary to confer, in order to explain them;—articles, which came to few." This was in accordance to Du Pin's previous conviction, "[8] that we [the two Churches] were not so far apart as to preclude reunion; that there were many articles upon which we were agreed; others which related to discipline only, in regard to which there could be no dispute on either side; and that in regard to the other articles, few in number, upon mutual explanation the two parties might agree." The "Commonitorium" then of Du Pin was no common document; it may be supposed to represent the mind of the moderate Gallicans of 1719.

[4] Ib. n. 92, dated VI. Kal. Sept.

[5] Maclaine, App. to Mosheim, vi. p. 75.

[6] Letter of M. Beauvoir to Archbishop Wake, Sept. 17, 1718, T. 29, n. 5.

[7] Du Pin's Rélation, l. c.

[8] Beauvoir to Wake, T. 28, July 16, 1718, O. S.

Cardinal de Noailles had desired to peruse it before it should be sent. It is exceedingly to be regretted that, at present, the "Commonitorium" cannot be found, and that so little of it is preserved *verbatim*. But, as appears from Maclaine's epitome of it[9], Du Pin approved unconditionally of twenty-three of our Articles[1]; passed over that on the Homilies, as not knowing them; proposed slight explanations of ten; so that there remained a difficulty in regard to five only, and on these also he mostly offered explanations of the Roman Doctrine.

On the VIth he agrees as to the principle, that "Scripture contains all things necessary to salvation," and affirms no more as to tradition than many of our Divines have done. "This (viz., that Scripture contains all things necessary to salvation) we will gladly admit, provided that tradition be not excluded, *which does not exhibit new articles of faith, but confirms and explains those things which are contained in Holy Scripture*, and fences them by new safeguards against those who are otherwise minded, so that nothing new is said, but only the old in a new way[2]."

[9] Trans. of Mosheim Eccl. Hist., T. vi., pp. 75—80.

[1] Art. I.—V., VII.—IX., XII., XV.—XVIII., XXIII., XXIV., XXVI., XXVII., XXX., XXXII.—XXXIV., XXXVIII., XXXIX.

[2] The original words are: "Hoc lubenter admittemus, modo non excludatur traditio, quæ articulos fidei novos non exhibet, sed confirmat et explicat ea, quæ in Sacris Literis habentur, ac adversus aliter sapientes munit eos novis cautionibus, ita ut non nova dicantur, sed antiqua nove." Macl.

He thought that the Apocryphal books would not occasion much difficulty, and allowed them to be called Deutero-canonical.

Our Homilies[3] inculcate a secondary inspiration of some, at least, of the Apocrypha, since they speak of its words as said by the Holy Ghost, and as Scripture. On the other hand the Roman Church could hardly condemn the statement of S. Jerome, which our Article quotes, received, as it was, by unquestioned authorities down to the Council of Trent[4].

The Xth he allowed, provided that by the word "power" ("we have no power to do good works") be understood what school-Divines call "Potentia proxima," or a direct and immediate power, [which plainly it does,] since without a *remote* power of doing good works sin could not be imputed.

On the XIth he says, "We do not deny that we are justified by faith only, as is set forth in the XIth Article." Maclaine paraphrases him, "we maintain that faith, charity, and good works are necessary to salvation, and this is acknowledged in the following (the XIIth) Article[5]."

[3] See the passages collected in Tract 90. The Jews agreed in speaking of the Wisdom of Sirach as Scripture. See Dr. Pusey's "Daniel the Prophet," p. 303.

[4] See, at length, in Bishop Cosins on the Canon (with notes in Ang. Cath. Lib.).

[5] The original words are: "Fide sola in Christum nos justificari, quod Articulo XImo exponitur, non inficiamur: sed

It does not seem to me clear whether Du Pin understood Article XIII. He says, "On the XIIIth Article there will be no controversy, since many divines are of the same mind. It appears somewhat harsh to say, that all those actions which are not done out of the grace of Christ are *sins* ['have the nature of sin']. Yet I would not have any discussion thereon, except among theologians [6]."

On the XIVth Article Du Pin explained away the offensive sense of the term "works of supererogation," was willing to drop the term, and only wished the distinction to be maintained between "works of strict precept," and those which were of "counsel" only. This distinction our people must, of course, admit, since our Lord says of celibacy, "All cannot receive this saying, save they to whom it *is given*. He that is able to receive it, let him receive it [7]." It is a further question whether a person's salvation may not be very seriously involved in *his* obeying a call from God, even although that to which he is called may not be in itself necessary to salvation. So that the Roman aspect may be, to look upon the act or condition

fide, charitate, et adjunctis bonis operibus, quæ omnino necessaria sunt ad salutem, ut articulo sequenti cognoscitur." Ib.

[6] "De Articulo XIIImo nulla lis erit, cum multi theologi in eadem versentur sententia. Durius videtur id dici, eas omnes actiones quæ ex gratiâ Christi non fiunt, esse peccata. Nolim tamen de hac re disceptari, nisi inter theologos."

[7] S. Matt. xix. 11, 12.

as not in itself necessary to salvation; ours, in the concrete, to look on ourselves as unprofitable servants at the best. And each must admit the statement of the other.

On Article XIX. he wished for the word "under lawful pastors," and said that "although all particular Churches, even that of Rome, may err, it is needless to say this in a Confession of Faith." So that, in principle, he agreed with us.

On Article XX. he again agreed with us in the principle, that "the Church may not ordain any thing that is contrary to God's Word written;" but said that it must be taken for granted that the Church would not do this in matters "which overthrow the substance of the faith" ["quæ fidei substantiam evertant]." This, too, our Church must hold, by virtue of our Lord's words, "The gates of hell shall not prevail against it."

On Article XXI. he made two statements, neither of which are contradicted by the Article, and both of which have often been affirmed among us. 1) That "General Councils, *received by the Universal Church*, cannot err." It would be more accurate to word it, "No General Council, received by the Universal Church, has erred;" or, "It may not be thought that the Universal Church will receive a General Council which has erred;" or, doubtless, Du Pin said, "General Councils, received by the Universal Church, cannot *have erred.*" For when they have been *received*, their whole action is a thing past, whereas "cannot err" implies a thing yet future. 2) "That, though particular Councils may err, yet every private man has not a right to reject what *he thinks* contrary to Scripture," which is self-evident on the principle of our Article, "The Church has authority in controversies of faith."

On Article XXII. he said, "*a*) as to Purgatory, that souls must be purged, i. e. purified from all defilement of sin, before they are admitted to celestial bliss; that the Church of Rome doth not affirm this to be done by fire; that *b*) indulgences are only relaxations or remissions of temporal penalties in this life; *c*) that the Roman Catholics do not worship the Cross, nor relics, nor images, nor even saints before their images, but only pay them an external respect, which is not of a religious nature; and that even this external demonstration of respect is a matter of indifference, which may be laid aside or retained without harm."

On Article XXIV. he allows that "Divine Service might be performed in the vulgar tongue, where that was customary," and, according to Maclaine, "excused" (I suppose, "defended") "the Latin and Greek Churches for preserving their ancient languages, alleging that great care had been taken that every thing should be understood by translations."

On the XXVth Article he required the acknowledgment "of the five Sacraments, whether instituted immediately by Christ or no."

As all our controversialists have said, the controversy turns not on the word, but on the meaning of the word. Even Jewell quoted Cardinal Bessarion, who, in the 15th century, A.D. 1436, distinguished, as we do, the two sacraments instituted by our Lord Himself. "This, too, seems a thing not to be disregarded, that, whereas two Sacraments were delivered to us by the Saviour, Baptism and the Eucharist, He commanded each to be effected in His own words[8]." "If, then, there we read of these two Sacraments alone as having been manifestly delivered in the Gospels, but one of them, Baptism, is effected in the words of the Lord, then we must think that the other also, the Eucharist, must be effected through these Divine and God-given words[9]." Yet Bessarion gives as the definition of other sacraments of the Church, that "they have something which is seen, something which is comprehended, not by the bodily eyes, but by the mind alone," viz. the invisible grace, which all believe to be given in Confirmation, orders, absolution[1], and in marriage also, hallowing its act. A distinction allowed in Bessarion might well be allowed to us also.

[8] De Sacr. Euch. Bibl. Patr. T. xxvi. p. 794, G. H.

[9] Ib., init.

[1] See above, pp. 20—22.

The only real difference is mainly practical, in regard to the Anointing of the sick. In this the Greek Church follows strictly the direction of S. James. The devout sick, at least, send to the physician of the soul as well as of the body, and in the "anointing of the sick," they look for benefit both to the body, if it should so please God, and to the soul. A Russian Priest informed me of a case, *which he knew*, of a man, who, by the use of anointing, with the prayer of faith by the Presbyters, had been raised up three times from dangerous illness. Had the Roman Church adhered to this practice, we could never have had the mention of "the corrupt following of the Apostles;" for that language relates to the then custom, not to anoint the sick until they were "in extremis," so that the Council of Trent had to provide, that, "if the sick should recover after receiving this unction, they *may* again be aided by the succour of this sacrament, when they should come into a like peril of life[1]." The Article plainly means, by "the corrupt

[1] Sess. xiv. de Extrem. Unct. c. 3. In the Latin Church, the bodily healing is mentioned in a homily ascribed to Cæsarius, "How much more right and healthful were it, to haste to the Church, receive the Body and Blood of Christ, faithfully anoint themselves and their's with the blessed oil, and, according to what the Apostle James says, receive not only bodily healing, but remission of sins also." Opp. S. Aug. T. v., Serm. 279, n. 5. In the Statutes of Boniface (c. 29) all the faithful sick (not those "in extremis" only) are bidden to ask for it; so also in the Excerpta of Egbert of York (A.D. 748): that "according to the definition of the holy Fathers, *if any one is sick*, let him

following of the Apostles," that what S. James directed, with a view (at least in part) to the restoration of health, was administered only, when, in man's sight, such restoration was impossible. Had they in the Roman Church retained the practice as the Greek Church retains it, we should doubtless have retained it also. As it is, the English Church, even in the unhappy time towards the close of the reign of Edward VI., virtually sanctioned it. The first Prayer Book in his reign had

be diligently anointed by the priests with hallowed oil, with prayer." Thorp, Anc. Laws, ii. 100. Egbert, in his Pœnit. (i. 15, T. ii. 179, Th.), paraphrases S. James, "that, if any be sick, he call his own priest and other servants of God, that they read over him, and the sick tell them his need, and they anoint him in the name of the Lord with holy oil, and that by the prayers of those faithful, and by the anointing, he may be preserved, and the Lord raise him up, and if he have committed sins, they may be forgiven him." In a canon under King Edgar, the priest was enjoined to give unction to the sick, *if they desire it* (Can. 65, T. ii. 259, Th.). Ælfric says, "If the sick layman *desire* to receive unction, let him then confess him and forgive every grudge, before the unction," &c. Past. Ep. n. 47, ii. 285, Th. A Council of Pavia (A.D. 850) still mentions bodily cure, "That healthful sacrament, which James recommends, 'If any man among you is sick, &c.' should, by a wise preaching, be made known to the people, truly a great and very desirable mystery, whereby, if it is asked faithfully, both sins are forgiven, and consequently bodily health restored," &c., c. 8, quoted Klee, Dogm. ii. 322. And the Capitular of Charlemagne; "That all priests should ask the Bishop for the oil of the sick, and admonish the faithful sick to seek it, that they being anointed with the same oil may be healed by the grace of God, because the prayer of faith, poured forth by the presbyters, shall save the sick," vi. 179, quoted ib.

a special prayer for "the Anointing of the sick," with this direction;

"If the sick person desire to be anointed, then shall the Priest anoint him upon the forehead or breast only, making the sign of the cross, saying thus,

"As with this visible oil thy body outwardly is anointed, so our heavenly Father, Almighty God, grant of His infinite goodness that thy soul inwardly may be anointed with the Holy Ghost, Who is the Spirit of all strength, comfort, relief, and gladness. And vouchsafe for His great mercy (if it be His blessed will) to restore unto thee thy bodily health and strength, to serve Him; and send thee release of all thy pains, troubles, and diseases, both in body and mind. And howsoever His goodness (by His Divine and unsearchable Providence) shall dispose of thee; we, His unworthy ministers and servants, humbly beseech the eternal Majesty to do with thee according to the multitude of His innumerable mercies, and to pardon thee all thy sins and offences committed by all thy bodily senses, passions, and carnal affections; Who also vouchsafe mercifully to grant unto thee ghostly strength, by His Holy Spirit, to withstand and overcome all temptations and assaults of thine adversary, that in no wise he prevail against thee, but that thou mayest have perfect victory and triumph against the devil, sin, and death: through

Christ our Lord: Who by His death hath overcome the Prince of death; and with the Father and the Holy Ghost evermore liveth and reigneth, God, world without end. Amen[3]."

This Prayer Book was declared by the Parliament to have been written "by the aid of the Holy Ghost[4]." The statement, so often quoted from the Act for substituting "the second book," that the first was a "very godly order, agreeable to the word of God and the primitive Church," and that the doubts raised about it were "rather by the curiosity of the minister and mistakers than of any other worthy cause," shows that, even in those evil times, no slur was ever cast upon the Scriptural practice of anointing the sick. The practice existed in the Scotch Church. Bishop Jolly was always prepared to anoint any sick person who should desire it. Nor do I know of any ground, except the custom of the Church, why it should not be used in England. Certainly, there is nothing herein to separate us from the Eastern Church. It is difficult to understand what its office "to remit sins" can be, which the Council of Trent sanctioned under anathema, seeing that the Church of Rome too holds that, upon confession, sins would just before have been remitted by the Abso-

[3] Two Liturgies of King Edward VI. compared, pp. 366, 367. 1838.

[4] See Collier, Eccl. Hist., vol. v. p. 296.

lution. Nor, looked upon, as the Roman Church practically does, as a mere preparation for death, (not, as the Greek does, as a means, if God so will, of restoring the sick,) does one see, what there can be lacking to our dying, whose sins, if they will, Christ absolves by the words which He gave us to pronounce with His authority and in His Name, and to whom He gives, as Food for the way, His own Body and Blood.

One statement of the Council of Trent, as to a spiritual effect of the unction of the sick, might the rather be explained to us, because Roman Catholic writers are at issue about its meaning. The Council says, "[5] The substance and effect of this sacrament is explained by those words, 'and the prayer of faith shall save the sick, and the Lord shall alleviate him, and if he be in sins, they shall be forgiven him.' For the substance is this grace of the Holy Spirit, Whose anointing wipes away offences, if any remain to be expiated, *and the remains of sin.*" And the Canon anathematizes those who deny this: "[6] If any say that the holy anointing of the sick does not confer grace, *nor remit sins*, nor alleviate the sick, but have now ceased, as though it were only formerly a grace of healing." But Bellarmine says plainly, "[7] All Theologians do not explain in the same way what

[5] Sess. xiv. de Sacr. Extr. Unct. c. 2.
[6] Can. 2.
[7] De Extr. Unct. i. 9, T. ii. p. 1198, 9.

are the remains of sin. Some would have them to be venial sins; but this is improbable, for *they* can be effaced without a Sacrament, nor is any new infusion of grace required, which is the effect of all Sacraments. So, if this were the proper and chief effect of this anointing, we could not easily prove it to be a Sacrament, nor would James say, 'If he have committed sins, they shall be forgiven him;' for all have venial sins, as he says again, 'in many things we all offend.' Lastly, it is not safe to restrain to venial sins, what James calls, generally, 'sins.' Others, by the name of 'remains;' understand the proneness or habit left from [past] sin. But this is still more improbable. For the '*if* he have committed sin' of James cannot be conveniently understood of this. Then too such habits do not appear to be taken away by this sacrament; for it often happens that they who recover feel the same proneness to sin as before."

Bellarmine then himself explains "the remains of sin" to mean "either 1) of deadly sins into which a person may have fallen through ignorance; or, 2) torpor, sadness, anxiety, which are wont to be left from sin, and which may chiefly vex a man at the point of death." But 1) deadly sins could hardly be committed in ignorance by any one of well-instructed conscience; so that this explanation would apply to very few out of the vast multitude who fall sick; viz. to those only who were truly penitent, and yet had deadly sin on their conscience contracted since their last absolution, of which they were ignorant. 2) "Torpor, sadness," &c., though they might be consequences of sin, are, of course, not sin, and so are no explanation of the Apostle's words, "if any have committed *sin*, it shall be forgiven," nor of that which the Canon of the Council of Trent affirms, under anathema, that the Unction "remits" not merely "the remains of sin," but the "sins" themselves.

The difficulty is, since sins are forgiven authoritatively upon true contrition through the Absolution, what sins there can remain afterwards to be remitted; and this the more, since the sick is to be anointed by the priests, and therefore, except *in extremis*, confession could be made, and the absolution pronounced. The earliest authority, enumerating the ways in which forgiveness of sins were given, blends the confession of sins and the anointing of the sick together. "[s] There is yet a seventh, although hard and laborious, remission of sins, through penitence, when the sinner washes his bed in tears, and his tears become his bread day and night, and when he is not ashamed to tell his sins to the priest of the Lord, and to seek the medicine, according to him who saith, 'I said, I will declare my unrighteousness against myself unto the Lord.' Wherein also is fulfilled that which the Apostle writes, 'If any is sick, let him call for the elders of the Church, and let them lay hands upon him,

[s] Origen in Lev. Hom. ii. n. 4, Opp. T. ii. p. 191.

anointing him with oil in the name of the Lord, and the prayer of faith shall save the sick, and if he be in sins, they shall be forgiven him.'" S. Chrysostome quotes the text of S. James[9], only as a proof of the power of the prayer of the priests, and so, doubtless, of the power of the keys.

Innocent I. explains that it could not be given to those who were yet doing penance, i. e. who had not yet received absolution. So far, then, from remitting deadly sin, it could not, according to Innocent I., be given to those who, having fallen into deadly sin, had not as yet, after the course of penitential discipline, been absolved from it[10]. Two sacraments alone, they say, are "given to the dead," Baptism and Penitence; Baptism, or the new birth, to give spiritual life; Penitence to restore it when

[9] De Sacerdot. iii. 6. "For not only when they regenerate us, but afterwards too, they have power to forgive sin. For he says, 'If any man be sick.'" In like way in Victor (as contained in a Catena), the efficacy is also ascribed to the prayer. "Oil remedies sufferings, and is a cause of light and cheerfulness. The oil then, wherewith one is anointed, signifies both the mercy from God, and the healing of the disease, and the illumining of the heart. For that prayer worketh all, is plain to every one; but the oil is the symbol of these things," on S. Mark vi. 13. So, still in Bede, "We read in the Gospels, that the Apostles did this, and the custom of the Church now holds, that the sick be anointed with consecrated oil, and healed by prayer accompanying," on S. James v.

[10] "It cannot be poured upon those in penitence (pœnitentibus), because it is a sort of sacrament. For they, to whom the other sacraments are refused, how can it be thought that one kind can be granted?" Ep. ad Decen. viii. 12.

lost. But neither is it given to remit venial sin. It is then not a captious question, but a reasonable request for explanation, that we ask, what that remission of sins through the anointing of the sick is, the denial of which the Roman Church has anathematized, and, as things stand, requires us, as terms of communion, to anathematize? In S. James, the forgiveness of sin is ascribed, apparently, to the whole action, including the prayer of the priest, to which alone S. Chrysostome attributes it.

In the Latin Church, too, Aquinas speaks of unction of the sick as "not being of necessity to salvation[1]."

The statement of the Russian Catechism could cause no difficulty to the English Church[2]. "Unction with oil is a mystery, in which, while the body is anointed with oil, God's grace is invoked on the sick, to heal him of spiritual and bodily infirmities." The prayer in the Enchologion expresses, so far, what we could all use, "[3]Holy Father, Healer of souls and bodies, Who didst send Thine Only-begotten Son, our Lord Jesus Christ, healing every disease and redeeming from death, heal this Thy servant also of the sickness of soul and body which encompasses him, and quicken him through the

[1] iv. dist. 23, q. 1, art. 1, fin.

[2] Orthodox Catechism, quoted by Blackmore, Harmony of Angl. Doctrine with the Doctr. of the Cath. and Ap. Church of the East, p. 124.

[3] p. 417, Par. 1647.

grace of Thy Christ—for Thou art the Fountain of healings, O Christ our God, and to Thee we send up the glory to the Father, and the Son, and the Holy Spirit."

On the XXVIIIth Du Pin was willing to omit the word "transubstantiation," and to substitute "changed." But the question remained the same, whether the "change" intended was physical or hyperphysical. He wished the statement to be adopted, "That the bread and wine are really changed into the Body and Blood of Christ, which are truly and really received by all, though none but the faithful partake of any benefit from them." The real question between the English and Roman Church is as to the nature of the change, whether it is understood in Thorndike's words, to be "a change destructive to the bodily substance of the elements, or cumulative of them [4]." Properly speaking, Scotus and others say "transubstantiation is not change [5]." Since Du Pin, as well as others, owned our Communion service to be orthodox, I should hope that the belief of the "real objective Presence" as therein contained, and so often expressed in our writers, or even the formula in the

[4] "On the Laws of the Church," c. iv. p. 33, and Pearson, On the Creed, Art. 3, note p. 288. See further, Dr. Pusey, "On the Words of the Fathers quoted in support of Transubstantiation," in "The Doctrine of the Real Presence," pp. 162—264, and "Illustrations used by the Fathers imply Sacramental Change only," ib. pp. 264—314, and above, pp. 24, 25.

[5] Ad IV. Dist. xi. Q. i. n. 20, quoted ib. p. 232.

notice at the close of our first Book of Homilies, "the due receiving of the Body and Blood of Christ under the form of bread and wine [6]," might become the basis of mutual understanding, instead of any inquiries into the meaning of the words Substance or Change. Plainly, since the meaning of the word "substance" has been changed, since the word "Transubstantiation" was adopted in the Latin Church, to express the "change" produced by consecration in the Holy Eucharist, it is not too much to ask the Roman Church to explain, what that "substance" is, which they believe to be changed. For since they require a belief in Transubstantiation, as terms of communion, and since the meaning has been changed since the times of the Schoolmen, it is but reasonable that they should explain the meaning of *that*, which they require us to express our belief in. My own conviction is, that our Articles deny Transubstantiation in one sense, and that the Roman Church, according to the explanation of the Catechism of the Council of Trent, affirms it in another.

A very eminent foreign Divine, of the Roman Communion, allows (I am informed) that "the 'materia' of bread and wine remains," and that, following Theodoret, Pope Gelasius [7], and other

[6] See on the history of that formula, Dr. Pusey's "The Real Presence the Doctrine of the English Church," pp. 4—160.

[7] See the Doctrine of the Real Presence, p. 85, sqq. The same Divine adds that "the form is changed;" but this is a

Fathers, we may say that "there are two natures in the Sacrament." But if so, the whole controversy between us is at an end. The rest is a question of the schools, not for ordinary pious Christians.

On Article XXX. he would have the reception "in both kinds," or "in one kind" only, left free to each Church.

On the XXXIst Article Du Pin maintained that "the Sacrifice of Christ is not only commemorated but *continued* in the Eucharist, and that every communicant offers Christ with the Priest." The words "we still continue and commemorate that Sacrifice, which Christ once made upon the Cross," were used by Bishop Cosins also, presupposing, of course, the fundamental truth, that that Sacrifice was finished upon the Cross, and that nothing can add to Its infinite value. We can but plead It and Its merits.

scholastic question, and cannot, of course, enter into the faith, which is to be proposed to the poor. He referred my friend to a Pastoral Letter of a Bishop of Boulogne about 1780, against the Encyclopedists, who gives with approbation the following words from Archbishop de Marca: "It may be asked, how these symbols are changed *and yet remain in their own nature.* They are changed according to the invisible [inconspicua, he suggests 'insensibilis,' 'not cognizable by the senses'] substance into the invisible Body of Christ; yet so that that invisible substance *does not cease to be,* but is attracted by the Body of Christ. But according to the visible body, which is seen and touched, they *are not changed.*" Then follows a statement in the Aristotelian terms, which could not be made intelligible to any ordinary reader.

On Article XXXII. Du Pin himself advocated the celibacy of the Clergy, but allowed of their marriage, "where not prohibited by the laws of the Church."

On the XXXVIth Article, since he allows that, in the case of an union, the English clergy might remain in their benefices, "either of right, or of the indulgence of the Church," he must have acknowledged the validity of our ordinations; since, of course, no indulgence of the Church could make that valid which is invalid. Du Pin [8] wrote to Wake, admiring the theory of our election and confirmation of bishops; he used always the tone of one writing to an Archbishop, and signed one of his letters "your son in Christ," "tuus in Christo filius;" and in his "relation" to "a very great man," (doubtless the Regent,) mentions an answer of Wake [9], "in which, without entering into any detail as to the Articles, he justified the succession of Archbishops and Bishops of England, of which M. Du Pin seems to have doubted." In Oct. 22, 1718, Beauvoir wrote to Archbishop Wake: "They [Du Pin and De Girardin] are extremely satisfied with the account of the succession of the English bishops. For before they were in error about it [1]." De Girardin himself wrote in December,

[8] Archbp. W., Ep. T. 25, n. 99, Jan. 13, 1719, three months before Du Pin's decease.

[9] l. c.

[1] Archbp. W., Ep. T. 29, n. 7.

1718,—"You can hardly think, most illustrious Prelate, with what joy it filled us, that we learnt at last from this your most learned letter, that the consecrations of the English Bishops, in due succession from the first foundation to the Reformation (as they speak), is supported by the testimony and authority of public documents; so that the enemies of ecclesiastical union have no ground, on this head at least, to disturb the communion of minds and of religion, now to be renewed among Christians[2]."

Du Pin expressed his satisfaction in these words: "I was exceedingly pleased with what you were so good as to write to me so elegantly and accurately about the election and consecration of the Bishops in England. It does not seem to me to differ much from the customs, which flourished in the time of Charlemagne, as is clear from the Capitulars of this and the following Emperors, and the formulæ of Marculfus. And I cannot sufficiently praise the precautions which you use to prevent any unworthy person from stealing into the Episcopate. Would that Bishops were proved in the same way every where, before they were consecrated[3]!" It has indeed escaped observation, that the form adopted at the consecration of Archbishop Parker was carefully framed on the old form used in the consecra-

[2] Archbp. W., T. 25, n. 111. The date appears from Wake's commenced answer, ib. n. 112.

[3] In Wake, T. 25, n. 98.

tion of Archbishop Chichele, a century before (as I found by collation of the Registers in the Archiepiscopal Library at Lambeth, now many years ago). The form used in Chichele's time, I could not trace further back. Its use was exceptional, having been resorted to at a time when the English Church did not acknowledge either of the claimants of the Papacy. The tradition of that consecration was then only a century old. It was of the Providence of God, that they had that precedent to fall back upon. But the selection of this one precedent, (amidst the number of Archbishops, consecrated in obedience to Papal Bulls, in which case the form was wholly different,) shows how careful Parker and his consecrators were to follow the ancient precedents. This fact is in itself the contradictory of the allegations of carelessness, so recklessly made by Roman Catholic controversialists. It is almost inconceivable that such an historian as Lingard (the first Roman Catholic writer who ventured to discard the Nag's Head fable) should himself have asserted that in Parker's consecration the words "Receive the Holy Ghost," were *not* used, in face of the Lambeth Register, which states that they *were*[4]. But to return.

[4] "The Record of Archbishop Parker's Confirmation and Consecration" has been carefully reprinted by the Rev. A. W. Haddan, from the Lambeth Register, in Bramhall's Works, T. iii. pp. 173—210; and the Record of his Consecration from a MS. Transcript in Corpus Christi College, Cambridge, which is believed to have been given by Archbishop Parker. Ib. pp. 210—213.

Article XXXVII. Du Pin "admitted, so far as relates to the civil power, and denied all temporal and all *immediate* spiritual jurisdiction of the Pope, and held that every Church ought to enjoy its own liberties and privileges, which the Pope has no right to infringe." It seems as if what he left to the Pope was "to see that the canons be enforced, the true faith maintained, and any violation of either be redressed, according to the Canonical laws." On this subject there is a fuller statement in a letter of Du Pin to Wake, Dec. 1, 1718,—"[5] In regard to the jurisdiction of the Roman Pontiff, as regards the State, it is restricted within narrow bounds, so that it can be of no prejudice to us. For as to temporals he has no power; and in spirituals, he is held within the rules of the ancient Canons. He can do nothing in those things which relate to the government of the Bishop in his own diocese; he cannot ordain or enact any thing pertaining to discipline; he cannot excommunicate any one, or claim any thing else to himself."

"His Primacy (i. e. that he holds the first place among Bishops, as all antiquity affirms, and the Greeks themselves, although rent from the Roman Church, confess) we acknowledge. But that Primacy does not give him a higher grade among Bishops; he is only their fellow-bishop, although first among Bishops."

Wake wrote: "The[6] honour which you give to

[5] Ib. n. 98. [6] Ib. Ep. 100.

the Roman Pontiff differs so little, I deem, from that which our sounder Theologians readily grant him, that, on this point, I think, it will not be difficult, on either side, either to agree altogether in the same opinion, or mutually to bear with a dissent of no moment."

One more extract from Du Pin will be especially interesting to you, as illustrating how earnest the good old man was in his love for peace and union, and on what terms he thought it might be effected. Indeed his whole plan seems to be an anticipation of our dear friend's Tract 90.

"[7] In these days I have read the book of William Forbes, Bishop of Edinburgh, entitled 'Considerationes Modestæ et Pacificæ Controversiarum,' &c., London, 1658. The Bishop seems to be of the same mind as you and I; for the whole subject of the work turns on this, to show that the controversies between us may easily be settled, if only the fairer Theologians are heard on both sides, if dictating is avoided, and we are led, not by party-spirit, but by love of seeking the truth. The posthumous works of Lancelot [Bishop Andrewes], published A.D. 1629, aim at the same end. I propose to transcribe from these and other works of the like sort, and from those of the more peace-loving on our side, testimonies on each Article, side by side, and to send them to you."

Many at that time shared the feeling of Du Pin.

[7] Du Pin, in Wake, T. 25, lett. 98.

"The whole town [Paris] rings of an union," reported Beauvoir to Archbishop Wake, "and many openly declare that they wish it[8]."

Du Pin's decease, the change of political relations, the ascendency of the Jesuits, quenched the hope of the restoration of union. But Du Pin's work of charity was like "bread cast upon the waters," to be found "after many days."

The reconciliation of the whole Church I used to look to as an ultimate end, which might lie, as I trusted, in the secrets of God's Providence.

With this hope I looked at the storms which have been gathering around the Roman Church, if so be she might, when imperilled, be willing to return to the relative position which she occupied in the fourth or fifth centuries. It is alleged that the Papal power has been the centre of unity. Christendom *was* united, when it was persecuted by Emperors, proscribed, and as *they* thought annihilated; when the Bishop of Rome had a precedence of dignity, not of power; and "[9] the Church was connected and joined together by the cement of Bishops mutually cleaving to each other," "[1] each Bishop ordering and directing his own proceedings, having hereafter to give account of his intentions to the Lord." One of the saddest parts of modern con-

[8] Feb. 14, 171$\frac{8}{9}$, Wake, Ep. T. 29, n. 17.

[9] S. Cypr. Ep. ad Flor. lxvi. n. 7, Oxf. Tr. p. 204.

[1] Id. Ep. lv. ad Anton. n. 17, p. 129; and Ep. lix. n. 19, p. 165 and note *u*. Præf. ad Conc. Carth. pp. 286, 287.

troversy, is the thought, how much is owing to forged writings; to what extent the prevailing system as to the B. V. came in upon the authority of writings which Roman Catholic critics now own to have been wrongly ascribed to the great Fathers whose names they bear; to what extent the present relation of Rome to the Eastern Church and to ourselves is owing to the forged Decretals.

The subject is of so much moment, as bearing on the relation both of our own and of the Greek Church to the Roman, that I will set down the changes in the discipline of the Church, which Fleury ascribes to the forged Decretals. What he draws out at length is stated in summary not by English writers, but by Divines or Canonists in the Roman Communion, as Archbishop de Marca[2], Van Espen[3], Coustant[4], &c. Fleury then writes[5]:

"Those, who have read with some attention what I have given of this history, have doubtless remarked a great difference

[2] De Concord. vii. 20. iii. 5, 6, quoted in Allies' "Church of England cleared from Schism," pp. 449, 450. 451—457. In quoting this book, I would say that his second work, after that, in despair of the English Church on the Gorham judgment, he left the Church of England, is no real answer to this, which he wrote, not as a partisan, but as the fruit of investigations, as to whose issue he was indifferent.

[3] T. iii. 478, quoted ib. 459—462.

[4] Præf. pp. 125. 127, quoted ib. 458. Comp. Pereira, Tentativa Theologica (Landon's transl.), pp. 54—57, quoted ib. p. 457.

[5] Quatrième Discours, prefixed to vol. xvi. of his Histoire Eccles., L. lxv. ed. 12mo. I have used Allies' translation, altering an expression here and there from the original.

between the discipline of the first ten and that of the three following centuries. It was in truth greatly weakened from the tenth century, but this was hardly ever but from ignorance, and by actual transgressions, which were condemned immediately that men opened their eyes to recognize them. It was ever a settled point that the Canons and ancient tradition were to be followed. It is only from the twelfth century that new foundations have been built on, and principles unknown to antiquity followed. Even then antiquity was believed to be followed, while it was departed from: the evil is come from an error of fact, and from having taken for ancient that which was not so. For in general it has always been taught in the Church, that the tradition of the first centuries was to be kept to, as well for discipline as for doctrine. I have spoken of the false Decretals attributed to the Popes of the first three centuries, which are found in the collection of Isidore Mercator, and which appeared at the end of the eighth century, and I have marked the proofs which demonstrate their falsity. Here was the source of the evil: ignorance of history and of criticism caused these Decretals to be received, and the new principles they contain to be taken for the doctrine of the purest antiquity. Bernald, Priest of Constance, writing towards the end of the eleventh century, says on the faith of these Decretals, that, according to the discipline of the Apostles and their successors, Bishops ought never or very hardly to be accused; admitting still that this discipline does not agree with the Nicene Council. And allowing that this Council has forbidden the translations of Bishops, he opposes to it, as more ancient, the Popes Euaristus, Callistus, and Anteros, who permitted them.

"After the Roman Church had groaned a hundred and fifty years under many unworthy Popes who profaned the holy See, God, casting a look of kindness on that first of Churches, gave to it Leo IX., whom his virtue has caused to be ranked in the number of the Saints, and who was followed, during the rest of the eleventh, and the whole ensuing century, by many other virtuous Popes, zealous for the restoration of discipline, as Gregory VII., Urban II., Pascal II., Eugenius III., Alexander III. But the best intentions without enlightenment cause great faults; and the faster one runs on a dark road, the more frequent and dangerous are one's falls. These great Popes, finding the authority of the false Decretals so established that nobody thought of contesting it any longer, believed themselves obliged in conscience to maintain the principles which they read there, persuaded that it was the purest discipline of the Apostolic times and of the golden age of Christianity. But they did not perceive that they contain many principles contrary to those of genuine antiquity.

1. "It is said in the false Decretals, that it is not allowable to hold a Council without the order, or at least permission, of the Pope. You, who have read this history, have you seen there any thing like it, I do not say in the first three centuries, but up to the ninth? I know that the authority of the Pope has always been necessary for General Councils, and thus is to be understood what the historian Socrates says, that there is a Canon which forbids the Churches to make any rule without the consent of the Bishop of Rome: and Sozomen says that the care of all the Churches belongs to him on account of the rank of his See. But as to Provincial and ordinary Councils, the Roman correctors of Gratian's Decretum have admitted, that the authority of the Pope is not necessary for them. In fact, is there the least trace of permission or consent of the Pope in all those Councils of which Tertullian, S. Cyprian, and Eusebius make mention, whether about Easter, the Reconciliation of penitents, or the baptism of heretics? Was there mention of the Pope in those three great Councils of Alexandria, which were held on the matter of Arius before the Nicene Council? Was there mention of him in the Council of Constantinople, convoked by the Emperor Theodosius in 381? And yet the Pope S. Damasus and all the West consented to its decisions; so that it is counted for the second Œcumenical Council. And I speak not of so many national Councils held in France, principally under the kings of the second race, and in Spain under the Gothic kings. When the Nicene Council ordered two Councils to be held yearly in each Province, did it suppose that they would send to Rome to ask permission? And how could one have sent so frequently thither from the furthest points of Asia or Africa? The holding of Provincial Councils was counted among the ordinary practices of religion, just as the celebration of the holy Sacrifice every Sunday. Nothing but the violence of persecutions interrupted the course of

it; as soon as the Bishops found themselves at liberty, they recurred to it as the most efficacious means of maintaining discipline. Yet, in consequence of that new principle, scarcely any Councils have been held from the twelfth century save those at which Papal Legates have presided, and the custom of holding Councils has insensibly gone out.

2. "It is said in the false Decretals that Bishops cannot be judged definitively save by the Pope alone, and that principle is often repeated there. Nevertheless you have seen a hundred examples of the contrary; and to take one of the most illustrious, Paul of Samosata, Bishop of Antioch, the first See of S. Peter, and the third city of the Roman Empire, was judged and deposed by the Bishops of the East and the neighbouring Provinces, without the participation of the Pope, whom they contented themselves with informing of it after it was done, as is seen by their synodal letter; and the Pope did not complain of it. Nothing is more frequent in the first nine centuries than the accusations and depositions of Bishops: but their trial took place in Provincial Councils, which were the ordinary tribunal for all Ecclesiastical causes. One must be absolutely ignorant of the history of the Church, to imagine that at any time or in any country it has ever been impossible to judge a Bishop, without sending to Rome, or causing a commission to come from the Pope.

"Without even knowing the facts, it only wants a little good sense to see that the thing was impossible.' From the fourth century there was a prodigious number of Churches in Greece, in Asia, in Syria, in Egypt, and in Africa, without speaking besides of the West: and the greater number of Bishops were poor, and unable to make great journeys: so that the Emperors defrayed their costs for the General Councils. How could one have made them come to Rome, and not them only, but their accusers and the witnesses, for the most part yet poorer? This, however, is what the author of the false Decretals must have supposed; and the absurdity of the supposition has appeared clearly, when the Popes wished to reduce it to practice. For instance, Gregory VII., sincerely persuaded that he alone was the competent judge of all Bishops, made them come daily from the end of Germany, France, or England. They had to quit their Churches for whole years, in order to go to Rome at great expense, to defend themselves against accusers who often did not appear there: delay was granted upon delay; the Pope gave commissions to take information on the spot, and after many journeys and long procedures he issued his definitive judgment, against which they came back under another pontificate. Often likewise the Bishop cited to Rome did not obey, either through incapacity to make the journey by sickness, poverty, or other impediment, or because he felt himself guilty: he despised the censures pronounced against him, and if the Pope chose to give him a successor, he defended himself by force. You have seen examples of this; and here are the inconveniences of wishing to reduce to practice what has never been practised, nor practicable.

"It is true that, on rare occasions of a manifest oppression or a crying injustice, Bishops condemned by their Councils could have recourse to the Pope, as the superior of all Bishops, and maintainer of the Canons: and this is the order of the Council of Sardica. But it directs that the Pope, whether he send a Legate or not, make the cause be reheard on the spot, because it is easy to impose on a distant judge. This is what S. Cyprian set forth in speaking of Basilides, a Spanish Bishop, who, having been deposed in his Province, had obtained from Pope S. Stephen, by concealing from him the truth, letters for his restoration, to which the Council of Africa paid no regard. And some years before, the same S. Cyprian, writing to Pope S. Cornelius respecting the schismatic Fortunatus, says these remarkable words: 'It is a rule among us that every guilty person be examined on the spot where the crime has been committed. Those then who are under us must not run hither and thither, and put disunion between the Bishops; let them plead their cause on the spot where they can have accusers and witnesses.' Thus it is that S. Cyprian speaks to the Pope himself, to whom Fortunatus had carried his complaints. After all this, recourse to the Pope, permitted by the Council of Sardica, regarded chiefly extraordinary matters, and the Bishops of the greatest Sees, as S. Athanasius, S. John Chrysostome, St. Flavian of Constantinople, who had no other superior to whom to address themselves.

3. "It is further the false Decretals, which have attributed to the Pope alone the right to translate Bishops from one See

to another. Nevertheless the Council of Sardica and the rest, which have so strictly forbidden translations, have made no exception in favour of the Pope; and when, in very rare cases, some translation has been made for the evident utility of the Church, it was made by the authority of the Metropolitan and the Council of the Province. We have an illustrious example of this in the person of Euphronius of Colonia, whom S. Basil translated to the See of Nicopolis. Far from the Pope authorizing translations, the Roman Church was the most faithful in observing the canons which forbad them: during nine hundred years we do not find any Bishop translated to the See of Rome: Formosus was the first; and this was one of the pretexts for disinterring him after his death. But since the false Decretals have been followed, translations have been frequent in the West where they were unknown; and the Popes only condemned them when they were made without their authority, as we see in the letters of Innocent III.

4. "It is the same with the erection of new Bishoprics: according to the false Decretals this belongs to the Pope alone: according to the ancient discipline it belonged to the Council of the Province, and there is an express Canon for it in the Councils of Africa. '[a]It is agreed that places, which have never had Bishops of their own, are not to receive them, save it be decreed by a plenary Council of each Province and the Primate, and with the consent of him to whose diocese the said Church belonged.' And certainly, to consider only the progress of religion and the advantage of the faithful, it was much more reasonable to refer it to the Bishops of the country, to judge of the cities which had need of new Bishops, and to choose the proper persons, than to refer the judgment to the Pope, so distant, and so little able to inform himself well of it. It is all very well to name commissioners, and take informations as to utility and inutility: these proceedings are never worth ocular inspection, and knowledge acquired by oneself. So when S. Augustine caused the new See of Fussala to be erected, he did not send to Rome, he only addressed himself to the Primate of Numidia: and if the Pope heard about it, it was only on account of the personal faults of the Bishop Antonius: but he

[a] Cod. Eccl. Afr. can. 98.

did not complain that the erection of this Bishopric had been made without his participation. Nor had S. Remi any more recourse to the Pope to found the Bishopric of Laon: but he did it, says Hincmar, by the authority of the Council of Africa, that is to say, of the Canon I have quoted. The reason is, that the Decretals, which give this right to the Pope, were not yet fabricated.

5. "As to the union or extinction of Bishoprics, I see no other reason for attributing them to the Pope alone, but certain authorities of S. Gregory alleged by Gratian. But he did not observe that Gregory only acted so in the southern part of Italy, of which Rome was the metropolis; or in Sicily and the other islands, which depended particularly on the holy See.

6. "In the first centuries Metropolitan Sees were rare in proportion to the number of Bishoprics, in order that the Councils might consist of large numbers; for the principal function of Metropolitans was to preside in them. But since the Popes have been in possession of the power to found them, they have created, principally in Italy, a great number of Metropolitans without necessity, merely to honour certain cities. The Nicene Council, which doubtless had power to assign new prerogatives to Churches, says simply that their privileges shall be preserved according to ancient custom. This shows that the distinction of Metropolitan Sees and Patriarchal Churches had already been confirmed by a long possession. The Popes since the eleventh century have not only made Metropolitans, but even Patriarchs and Primates; all on the foundation of the false Decretals, that is, of the first letter attributed to S. Clement, of the second and third of Pope Anacletus, where it is said that the Apostles and their successors established Patriarchs and Primates in the cities, where, according to the civil government, the chief magistrates lived, and where the pagans had their archflamens, a barbarous title only found in these Decretals. Now you have seen that in the first centuries even the title of Archbishop was unknown: men said, the Bishop of Rome, or of Alexandria, as of the least city, and in their letters they treated each other as brethren with a perfect equality, as is seen by the inscriptions of the letters of S. Cyprian. In proportion as charity grew cold, titles and ceremonies increased. The Bishop of Alexandria

was the first, as is believed, who took the name of Archbishop, the Bishop of Antioch took that of Patriarch, and the name of Primate was peculiar to Africa. But the author of the false Decretals did not know so much, and he makes no mention of the title of Exarch so famous in Asia.

"Nevertheless it was on the faith of this author that Gregory VII. established or rather confirmed the Primacy of Lyons, since he quotes in his Bull the words of the Decretal of Anacletus. It is on this same foundation that other Popes have pretended to found so many other Primacies, in France, in Spain, and elsewhere; supposing them ancient by an error of fact, as I have shown of each in particular. These erections being contrary to the ancient possession have produced great contests. You have seen with what vigour the Bishops of France rejected the Primacy which John VIII. had given to Ansegisus Archbishop of Sens; you have seen how they resisted afterwards the Primacy of Lyons, which a long possession has at length established: and how the Bishops of Spain opposed those of Toledo and Braga, which have never been well authorized. So it is not to be imagined that a Bull given without knowledge of the cause, as that of Calistus II. for the Primacy of Vienne, is sufficient to change at once the ancient state of Churches, in spite of the parties interested.

7. "One of the greatest wounds which the false Decretals have inflicted on the discipline of the Church is that they have extended infinitely appeals to the Pope. It appears that the forger had this point greatly at heart, by the care he has taken to diffuse through all his work the maxim, that not only every Bishop, but every Priest, and generally every person, who finds himself harassed, may on every occasion appeal directly to the Pope. He has made as many as nine Popes speak on the subject, Anacletus, the first and second Sixtus, Fabian, Cornelius, Victor, Zephyrinus, Marcellus, and Julius. But S. Cyprian, who lived in the time of S. Fabian and S. Cornelius, not only opposed appeals, he has further shown solid reasons for not yielding to them; and in the time of S. Augustine the Church of Africa did not yet receive them, as it appears by the letter of the Council held in 426 to Pope Celestine. In fine, down to the ninth century, few examples are seen of these appeals in virtue of the Council of Sardica, save, as I

have said, on the part of Bishops of the great Sees who had no other superiors beside the Pope.

"But, since the false Decretals became known, nothing but appeals were seen through all the Latin Church. Hincmar, better instructed than the rest in the ancient discipline, vigorously opposed that novelty, maintaining that this remedy ought not to be granted but to Bishops at the most, not to Priests. You have seen afterwards the complaints of Ivo of Chartres, and of S. Bernard, against this abuse, which in their times had already reached its height. They showed that this liberty of appealing to the Pope in all matters, and at every stage of the cause, utterly enervated discipline: that bad Priests, and other impenitent offenders, had thereby a sure means to elude correction, or at least to defer it: that the Pope was often ill-informed, and obliged to retract the judgments which he had given by surprise: in fine, that the Bishops, repelled by the length of the proceedings, by the expense and the fatigue of journeys, and by so many other difficulties, lost courage, and endured the disorders they could not hinder. The Popes found even themselves incommoded by that liberty of appeal on every occasion, which often retarded the execution of their orders; and hence comes the clause, 'notwithstanding appeal,' which passed into a phrase in their Bulls.

"If S. Bernard rose with such vigour against that abuse, while supposing the necessity of appeals, what would he not have said, had he known that their use was novel and founded on false documents? How much more strongly would he have spoken against that multitude of business with which the Pope was overwhelmed? He knew that, according to the maxims of the Gospel, a Bishop and a successor of the Apostles ought to be disengaged from temporal affairs, to give his time to prayer and the instruction of the people; but the authority of custom held him back, and for want of sufficient acquaintance with antiquity, and of knowing how the Popes had fallen into that embarrassment of business, he dared not speak out, and advise Eugenius to revert to the simplicity of the first centuries.

"Nevertheless the description which this holy Doctor has left us of the court of Rome, makes us see, how much this new jurisprudence of the false Decretals had injured the holy See, under pretence of extending its authority. For S. Bernard represents to us the consistory of Cardinals as a parliament, or a sovereign tribunal, occupied with judging processes from morning to evening; and the Pope who presided there so overwhelmed with business, that he had scarcely a moment to breathe: the court of Rome full of advocates, solicitors, pleaders, impassioned, artful, and interested, seeking only to surprise each other, and enrich themselves at the expense of others. We form the same notion of it by the history of the Popes of the twelfth and thirteenth centuries and by their letters, specially those of Innocent III., where we see so prodigious a detail of the affairs of all Christendom. These letters alone were a terrible occupation: for even if the Pope did not compose them himself, it was at least necessary for him to have account of them given him, and to take cognizance of the most important matters. And how could a Pope so occupied find time for prayer, for the study of the holy Scriptures, for preaching, and the other essential duties of the Episcopate? I do not speak here of the cares which his rank as a temporal prince gave him: I shall come to that in course.

"I see well that, by extending without measure the authority of the Pope, it was believed that a great advantage was gained for him, and his Primacy made to tell the more. One must have been then absolutely ignorant of the history of the Church, or have supposed that the greatest Popes, as S. Leo and S. Gregory, had neglected their rights, and suffered their dignity to be undervalued. For it is very certain in fact that they never exercised the authority marked in the Decretals of Isidore. But let us go a little deeper into things. Had not those holy Popes good reasons to act so? Had they not higher thoughts and a more perfect knowledge of religion, than Gregory VII. and Innocent III.? Vulgar men only seek their private interests: philosophers, who carry their thoughts further, see by merely natural reason that in every society the interest of each individual, even of him who governs, ought to yield to the interests of the whole society. Now we may not think that Jesus Christ established His Church on principles less pure than those of the pagan philosophers: so He has not proposed to those who govern His flock faithfully any advantage in this life, but only an eternal recompense proportioned to their charity.

"Let us then candidly admit, that the Popes of the five or six first centuries had reason to consider the advantage of the Church Universal preferably to that which might appear serviceable to their person or their See. Let us further admit, that the advantage of the Church required, that all matters should be judged on the spot by those who could do it with the greatest knowledge and facility: that the Bishops, especially their chief, should be turned aside as little as was possible from their spiritual and essential functions; and that each one of them should remain fixed in the Church where God had put him, given up continually to instruct and sanctify his people. Can one compare to such real goods the sad advantage of rendering the Pope terrible through all the earth; and of causing to come to Rome from all sides Bishops and Clergy, either through fear of censures, or for hope of favours?

"I know that that crowd of Prelates and other foreigners, whom divers interests drew to Rome, brought thither great riches, and that its people fattened at the expense of all others: but I am ashamed to mention such an advantage in a matter of religion. Was then the Pope established at Rome to make it rich, or to make it holy? And did not S. Gregory fulfil the duty of common Father better, when by his alms he spread so abundantly through all the Provinces the immense revenues of the Roman Church? Now those Popes who made Rome rich did not make it holy: it even seems that they despaired of being able to do it, according to the frightful picture which S. Bernard has given us of the Roman people in his day. Nevertheless it was the first duty of a Pope, as their Bishop, to labour for their conversion: and he was more obliged to this, than to judge so many processes between foreigners.

"Gratian's Decretum completely established and extended the authority of the false Decretals, which are found scattered every where there; for during more than three centuries no other Canons than those of this collection were known, no others were followed in the schools and tribunals. Gratian had even gone beyond these Decretals, to extend the authority of the Pope, maintaining that he was not subject to the Canons: which he says out of his own head, and without adducing any proof of authority. Thus was formed in the Latin Church a confused idea that the power of the Pope was without limits: that principle once laid down, many corollaries have been drawn from it beyond the points formally expressed in the false Decretals: and the new theologians have not sufficiently distinguished these opinions from the essential of the Catholic Faith, touching the Primacy of the Pope, and the rules of the ancient discipline.

"Besides what regards the Pope, Gratian has put into his Decretum new maxims respecting the immunity of Clerks, who cannot, as he maintains, be judged by the laity in any case; and to prove it he cites several articles of the false Decretals, and the pretended law of Theodosius adopted by Charlemagne to extend excessively the jurisdiction of Bishops. He joins to them a maimed citation from a novell of Justinian, which, when complete, asserts just the reverse. Nevertheless, this constitution so altered was the principal ground, on which S. Thomas of Canterbury resisted the king of England with a firmness, which drew upon him persecution, and at length martyrdom. The principle was false at the bottom: but it passed for true with the most skilful Canonists.

"You have just seen into what inconveniences men fell from having believed in false documents. It became a custom besides to receive without selection all sorts of narrations, for want of principles to distinguish them; and thence came so many fabulous legends, so many false miracles, so many visions and frivolous stories, as we see amongst others in the dialogues of the monk Cesarius.

"The principles cited by Gratian touching the immunity of Clerks are the foundation of the answer, which Pope Innocent III. made to the Emperor of Constantinople at the commencement of his pontificate, and from which is drawn a celebrated Decretal. In this letter the Pope gives forced explanations to the passage of S. Peter, alleged by the Emperor to show, that all Christians without exception ought to be subject to the temporal power. The Apostle, he says, spoke thus to excite the faithful to humility: the king is sovereign, but only of those who receive from him temporal things, that is to say, the laity: as if the Church had not also received her temporalities from the secular power. The Pope continues: that the prince has not received the power of the sword over all the wicked, but only over those who, using the sword, are subject to his jurisdiction. By which he understands still laymen alone, to procure for criminal Clerks exemption from temporal punishments, that is to say, impunity. He adds that no one ought to judge the servant of another, supposing that Clerks are not the servants of the prince. In fine he cites the allegory of the two great luminaries which God has placed in the heaven, to signify, says he, the two great dignities, the pontifical and the royal: as if in a serious discussion it was allowable to advance as a principle an arbitrary allegory, which one has only to deny in order to refute. It is thus that the most formal authorities of the Scriptures were eluded, in order to support prejudices drawn from the false Decretals.

"Now Pope Innocent III. could not address himself worse than to a Greek Emperor, in order to broach these principles unknown to antiquity. The Latin princes, ignorant for the most part to the degree that they could not read, believed in these matters all that the Clerks told them, of whom they took counsel; and these Clerks had all studied in the same schools, and drawn from the same source, the Decretum of Gratian. Among the Greeks all respectable persons studied, laymen as well as Clerks; and instructed themselves in the original books, Scripture, the Fathers, the ancient Canons; but they were not acquainted with the false Decretals fabricated in the West and written in Latin. So they had preserved the ancient discipline on all the points which I have here marked. You have seen that all their Bishops, and even their Patriarchs, were judged and often deposed in Councils; that permission was not asked of the Pope to assemble them, nor appeal made to him from their judgments. He was not applied to for the translations of Bishops, or the founding of Bishoprics: the Canons, comprised in the ancient code of the Greek Church, were followed. I do not say that this Church was exempt from abuses; I have marked many on different occasions, and I know that the Patriarchs of Constantinople had claimed an excessive authority by the favour of the Emperors, who had even much encroached on the Ecclesiastical power; but still the ancient formalities were always outwardly maintained, the Canons were known and respected.

"You will say, perhaps, 'one must not be astonished that the Greeks did not apply to the Pope, either for appeals, or for all the rest, since from the time of Photius they no longer recognized him as head of the Church.' But did they apply to him before? And in the times when they were most united with the Roman Church did they observe any thing of that which I call the new discipline? They were far enough from doing it, since the Latins themselves did it not, and this discipline was yet unknown to all the Church. Moreover, do not deceive yourself in that, the schism of the Greeks is not so ancient as is commonly believed: I will show it in another discourse: but in the mean time I remark to you, that it scarcely took shape before the taking of Constantinople by the Latins. Besides, I do not see that in the disputes we have had with the Greeks, from the time of Leo IX., and Michael Cerularius, we have reproached them with holding Councils without the Pope's permission, and the rest of the points in question; and I do not see any more that Gregory VII. and his successors have cited to Rome Greek Bishops, and treated them as they treated the Latin: they knew well that they would not have obeyed."

Then after two sections on the temporal power of the Pope (as being equally derived from a forgery, the donation of Constantine), and its evils, he resumes:—

11. "The spiritual power of the Pope having extended itself to such a degree by the conclusions drawn from the false Decretals, he was obliged to commit his powers to others: for it was impossible that he should go every where, or cause every body to come to him. Hence came the Legations so frequent from the eleventh century. Now the Legates were of two sorts, Bishops or Abbots of the country, or Cardinals sent from Rome. Legates taken on the spot were further different: the one established by a particular commission of the Pope, the other by the prerogative of their See, and these called themselves Legati nati, as the Archbishops of Mayence, and Canterbury. The Legates come from Rome called themselves Legates *a*

latere, to mark that the Pope had sent them from his person, and this expression was drawn from the Council of Sardica.

"The Legati nati did not willingly endure the Pope's naming others to the prejudice of their privileges, but the Pope had more confidence in those he had chosen, than in Prelates with whom he was little acquainted, or who suited him not. Now, amongst those whom he chose, the most favourable were they whom he took on the spot, because they were more capable of judging and ordering with knowledge of the cause, than foreigners come from a distance. So you have seen with what urgency Ivo of Chartres begged the Popes not to send these foreign Legates. They were not received in England, any more than in France, unless they had been asked for by the king. The Bishops hardly endured seeing themselves presided over by foreign Bishops, still less by a Cardinal Priest or Deacon, under pretext of his being Legate, for until then all Bishops took rank before Cardinals which were not so.

"But what rendered the Legates *a latere* more odious was their pride, luxury, and avarice. They travelled neither at their own expense, nor that of the Pope, but of the country whither they were sent; and they went in great pomp, that is, with a suite of at least twenty-five horses, for to this the third Council of Lateran had limited them. Wherever they passed, they caused themselves to be treated magnificently by the Bishops and Abbots, to such a degree that the monasteries were sometimes reduced to sell the sacred vessels of their Churches to provide for such expenses. You have seen complaints of this. Nor was this all: they must have presents made them besides: they received such from the princes to whom they were directed, and often from the parties to whom they rendered justice: at least the expeditions were not gratuitous. In fine, the Legations were gold mines for the Cardinals, and they returned from them generally laden with riches. You have seen what S. Bernard said of it, and with what admiration he speaks of a disinterested Legate.

"The most ordinary result of a Legation was a Council, which the Legate convoked at the place and time that he judged suitable. He presided there, and decided the affairs which came up, and published certain rules of discipline, with approbation of the Bishops, who for the most part did nothing else but applaud: for it does not appear that there was much deliberation. Thus were insensibly abolished the Provincial Councils, which each Metropolitan was bound to hold every year according to the Canons: the dignity of the Archbishops, overshadowed by that of the Legates, degenerated into titles and ceremonies, such as having a pall and causing a cross to be borne before them: but they had no longer authority over their suffragans, and Councils of Legates only were now seen. Now, to remark it in passing, I doubt not that the frequent Legations have been the source of the distinguished rank which the Cardinals of the Roman Church have since held: for each Church had its own, that is to say, Priests and Deacons attached to certain titles. But as in these Councils the Cardinal Legates were seen above not only Bishops, but Archbishops, Primates, and Patriarchs, men became accustomed to join to the title of Cardinal the idea of a dignity which only yielded to that of the Pope. The state dress of the Cardinals confirms this thought: the cape and hat were the dress on a journey, which belonged to the Legates: red was the colour of the Pope, and it was the better to represent him that the Legates wore it, according to the remark of a Greek historian.

"Here, however, is one of the greatest changes which the discipline of the Church has suffered, the cessation of Provincial Councils, and the diminution of the authority of the Metropolitans. Was, then, that beautiful order, so wisely established from the birth of the Church, and so advantageously practised during eight or ten centuries, to be overturned without deliberation, without inquiry, without cognizance of cause? But what reason could have been alleged for it? Were foreign Legates, who knew not either the manners or the language of the country, and who only sojourned there in passing, more proper than the ordinary pastors, to judge in differences, and restore discipline? And when they had published fine rules in a Council, could they be assured that these would be observed after their departure, if the Bishops did not lend their hand to it? Let us conclude upon this point as upon the rest, the ancient discipline has not been changed to establish a better. Thus we do not see that, during the frequent Legations, religion has been more flourishing.

"The Bishops and Metropolitans were so ignorant of their rights, that they sought with eagerness for the powers of Legates, not considering the advantage of a proper and independent, though less, authority, over one more extended, but borrowed and precarious. It seemed they could do nothing any longer by themselves, unless the authority of the Pope supported them: and the Pope willingly granted them these favours, which they could have done without, and which always extended his power. It is the same, in proportion, with the custom, so frequent then, of causing agreements made between Churches, and donations to their profit, to be confirmed by the Pope: as if these acts would have been less valid without the confirmation. Right is assumed by favours asked without necessity: and claims are so made to render them necessary."

Then, after a section on the evils from the large subsidies to Rome, in order to support the Court of Rome, when from the eleventh century the Popes were compelled to quit Rome, he resumes:—

13. "I well feel that it is sad to direct notice to these unedifying facts: and I fear that those who have more piety than enlightenment may derive thence occasion of offence. They will perhaps say, that these facts should have been dissembled in the history, or that, after having reported them, they ought not to have had attention drawn to them in a treatise. But truth is the foundation of history: and to suppress a part of it is not to recount it truly." . . . "If these disorders had in such sense ceased, that no vestige of them any more remained, perhaps they might have been left buried in eternal oblivion; but we see only too much their fatal consequences. The heresies which for two hundred years [1723] have been rending the Church, the ignorance and superstition which reign in some Catholic countries, the corruption of morality by new maxims, are but too sensible effects of them. And is it not useful to know whence evils so great have come?"

And after further reflections of the same sort:—

. . . "Can one still, in the light of our century, maintain

the donation of Constantine and the Decretals of Isidore? And if these documents cannot be defended, can one approve the results drawn from them? Let us then candidly admit that Gregory VII. and Innocent III., deceived by these documents, and the bad reasonings of the theologians of their times, have pushed their authority too far, and have rendered it odious by stretching it: and let us not attempt to support excesses, of which we see the causes and the fatal effects. For at last, whatever one may say, it is evident that the first centuries furnish us with a greater number of holy Popes than the last, and that the manners and discipline of the Roman Church were much purer. Now it is not credible that the Popes have begun to know their rights, and to exercise their power in its full extent, only since their life has been less edifying, and their especial flock less well regulated. This reflection supplies a disagreeable prejudice against the new maxims.

14. "Of all the changes of discipline, I see none which has brought the Church into greater disrepute, than the rigour exercised against heretics and other excommunicated persons."

He then contrasts the principles of the Ancient Church, as evinced in the case of the Priscillianists, in S. Augustine as to the Manichees and others, with the practice after the eighth century. His last head is, "The Changes in Penitences:"—

"I finish these sad reflections by the change introduced into penitences. Public penitences were turned into torments and temporal penalties." . . . 16. "It is true that the multitude of indulgences, and the facility of gaining them, were a great obstacle to the zeal of the most enlightened confessors. It was difficult to persuade a sinner to fast and discipline himself, who could buy off this by a trifling alms, or the visit of a church. For the Bishops of the twelfth and thirteenth centuries granted these indulgences to all sorts of pious works, as the building of a church, the maintenance of an hospital, in fact every public work, a bridge, a causeway, the pavement of a high road. These indulgences were indeed but a part of the penitence, but if several of them were joined, the whole might be bought off. These are the indulgences which the 4th Lateran Council calls[7] 'indiscreet and superfluous,' which render the keys of the Church contemptible, and unnerve the satisfaction of penitence. To repress this abuse, the Lateran Council directs that at the dedication of a Church the indulgence given should not exceed a year, even if several Bishops should be present; for each claimed to give his own."

Then, after some more observations on the relaxation of the ancient discipline by indulgences, he concludes:—

"Here I end by remarking to you what I think I have proved, that the changes which have taken place in the discipline of the Church since the last five or six hundred years, have not been introduced by the authority of Bishops and Councils, to correct the ancient practice: but by negligence, by ignorance, by error, founded on false documents, as the Decretals of Isidore, and on the bad reasonings of the scholastic Doctors. God grant that we may profit by the favour He has shown us of being born in a more enlightened age; and that, if we cannot bring back the ancient discipline, we may at least know how to esteem it, revere, and regret it."

Fleury says in another place, of the supposititious writings after the seventh century,

"[8] Of all these false documents the most pernicious were the Decretals attributed to the Popes of the first four centuries, which have inflicted an incurable wound on the discipline of the Church, by the new maxims which they introduced concerning the judgments of the Bishops, and the authority of the Pope."

The forgery of the Decretals after they had "passed for true during eight centuries[9]" was owned

[7] Can. 62. [8] Troisième Discours, § 2.
[9] Fleury, l. 44, § 22.

by all, even in the Church of Rome. But the system built upon the forgery abides still. The Greek Church could not be admitted to Communion with the West, without merging its whole Patriarchal or Episcopal system, such as it inherited from the times of the undivided Church, so that her Bishops should be the mere delegates of the Roman Pontiff, liable to be deposed at his mere will, as the eighty French Bishops were by Pope Pius VII. in his Concordat with Napoleon I.[10] Our Communion was rejected, because our forefathers used the same freedom, which the Church of S. Augustine enjoyed. Yet what of human authority Rome clings to in her day of power, she may exchange for the strength of union in a day of weakness. Concordats have been one step in this direction since the Reformation. The times are in God's Hands. I used to think that our office in this day was that of him who "arbores serit, quæ alteri prosint sæculo." We seemed to me in the position of the Heaven-controlled Seer, "I see Him, but not nigh; I behold Him, but not now." And meanwhile our office was within ourselves. We could not propose union, while we ourselves are so disunited. I hoped that the pressing storm of unbelief, which I

[10] See e. g. in Allies, p. 439. I have seen this lately spoken of, as it seemed to me, authoritatively, as the annihilation of the ancient Gallican Church, and the creation of a new French Church, by a single stroke of the pen of the Pope.

have seen in the distance these forty years, would drive together those who love Jesus. I hoped that, as we became united in the truth and in the characteristic principles of our Church, those other great portions of the Church, East and West, would see that "God is in us of a truth." While we said Bishop Andrewes's prayer for the Catholic Church, *Οἰκουμενικὴ, 'Ανατολικὴ, Δυτικὴ, 'Ημετέρα*, we hoped that the time was drawing on, when "Eastern, Western, our own," would melt, in visible communion too, into the one "Œcumenical."

What times may be coming on the earth, He Alone knoweth, Whose they are. Troubles are threatening our Western Christendom every where. Whether or how they shall break, or whether they shall be averted, God Alone knoweth. We only know that, before our Lord shall come, there will be "such [1] tribulation as hath never been before," and "*the* [2] apostasy," an apostasy so great that former apostasies (even that aweful apostasy through Mohammed) shall not deserve the name; and such "deceivableness of Satan [3]," that, "[4] if possible, they should deceive the very elect."

From this trouble the Roman Church has no more ground of exemption than our own. Our Lord's words, "When [5] the Son of Man cometh, shall He find *the* faith on the earth?" seem to

[1] S. Matt. xxiv. 21.
[2] 2 Thess. ii. 3, ἡ ἀποστασία.
[3] Ib. 9, 10.
[4] S. Matt. xxiv. 24.
[5] S. Luke xviii. 8.

imply that, ere He comes, the objective faith, "*the* faith,"—not only as the life of individuals, but as held by the Church,—"the Catholic faith," will be very much obscured, and may be found among few only. We have not seen such a triumph of Satan over the faith here, as that reign of his in the capital of France. Faber anticipated a new "Age of Mary," which was to be connected "with the Second Advent of her Son." Alas! who shall say what will be the cause of the falling away before that Second Advent? De Montfort speaks of those as "the free-thinkers of these [his] times," who did not believe that the Holy Trinity has made the Blessed Virgin the dispensatrix of all which They possess and will to bestow upon man. Several of the Roman Catholic Bishops wrote of the belief in the Immaculate Conception, before it was declared an Article of faith, as being so believed as "of faith," that for their people to doubt of it, would be to doubt of all. What then, as I said, if they should discover hereafter that so much, which they have been taught as certain truth in regard to the Blessed Virgin, has no Divine foundation? There must be some terrible inward cause, why so large a portion of the Church shall lose faith, as, it seems probable, will lose it before our Lord comes. The victims of Antichrist must have lost Christ out of their hearts already. Shocking as it is to think of, the collapse of an ungrounded system as to the prerogatives of her, whom God, by His wondrous condescension, has brought into a nearer relation to Himself than any other mere created being, might shake the whole faith of those whose faith was worked into one with it. People are taught that to believe in Christ involves all this vast belief in the Blessed Virgin, coextensive with the belief in Him. What if this should fail? Such an "Age of Mary," as Faber anticipates, might, not unconceivably, by the collapse of the belief, bury in the ruins the faith in Jesus also. It is very observable how the presence of the English Church keeps this belief from taking the forms which it does where it is unchecked. This may be one of her offices in God's hands. She preserves the entire faith, such as our Lord left it with the Apostles, to evangelize the world. She believes all which the undivided Church believed, as of faith. Why should not the Church again be united in that faith which she held, before a miserable quarrel first caused her disunion? Pious Roman Catholics too have felt that the Churches are mutually weakened, that faith and morals and life are alike injured in each by these mutual divisions. Apart from other evils, the strength is wasted against each other, which should be concentrated against the common foe of Jesus and of all who are His.

The organic reunion of Christendom, and of the Protestant bodies too, has been held to be possible, even by the Ultramontanes in the Roman Church. Cardinal Wiseman quoted, nearly a quarter of a century ago, the expressions of "the profound and pious Möhler." "After observing," he says[6], "that no Catholic can refuse to acknowledge with humiliation the corruptions of past ages, that this proof lies in the very existence of Protestantism which could not have existed without them; he thus concludes[7]:—'Apprenez donc une fois, ô Protestants, la grandeur des abus que vous nous reprochez sur la grandeur de vos propres égarements. Voilà le terrain, sur lequel les deux églises se rencontreront un jour, et se donneront la main. Dans le sentiment de nôtre faute commune, nous devons nous écrier, et les uns et les autres, 'Nous avons tous manqués, l'Eglise seule ne peut faillir; nous avons tous pêchés, l'Eglise seule est pure de toute souillure.'"

You will well remember the glowing words of our friend[8], who is at once a statesman and a theologian, earnest for the cause of Christ, and zealous for His truth and His Church.

"The name of the Count De Maistre has become one of European celebrity. He is one of the writers who have had the very largest share in shaping the modern tendencies of the devout and energetic portion of the Roman Catholics of Western Europe. He is, unhappily, of the 'most strictest sect' of that Church; of that Ultramontane school which

[6] Letter to the Earl of Shrewsbury on Catholic Unity, p. 33.
[7] Symbolique, T. ii. § 37.
[8] Gladstone, Remarks on the Royal Supremacy, p. 86—end.

has been from its first origin alike needful and dangerous to the Roman system; and he has defined its principles with even an augmented sharpness, and wound them up to a higher intensity than they had before attained.

"Yet listen to the words in which he writes of the Church of England:—

"'Si jamais les Chrétiens se rapprochent, comme tout les y invite, il semble que la motion doit partir de l'Eglise de l'Angleterre. Le presbytérianisme fut une œuvre Francaise, et par conséquent une œuvre exagérée. Nous sommes trop éloignés des sectateurs d'un culte trop peu substantiel; il n'y a pas moyen de nous entendre; mais l'Eglise Anglicane, qui nous touche d'une main, touche de l'autre ceux que nous ne pouvons toucher; et quoique, sous un certain point de vue, elle soit en butte aux coups des deux partis, et qu'elle présente le spectacle un peu ridicule d'un révolté qui prêche l'obéissance, cependant elle est très précieuse sous d'autres aspects, et peut être considérée comme une de ces intermèdes chimiques, capable d'approcher des élémens inassociables de leur nature[9].'

"It is now sixty years since thus a stranger and an alien, a stickler to the extremest point for the prerogatives of his Church, and nursed in every prepossession against ours, nevertheless, turning his

[9] Considérations sur la France, c. ii.

eye across the Channel, although he could then only see her in the lethargy of her organization and the dull twilight of her learning, could nevertheless discern that there was a very special work written of God for her in Heaven, and that she was VERY PRECIOUS to the Christian world. Oh! how serious a rebuke to those who, not strangers, but suckled at her breast not two generations back, but the witnesses now of her true and deep repentance and of her reviving faith and love, yet (under whatever provocation) have written concerning her even as men might write that were hired to make a case against her, and by an adverse instinct in the selection of evidence, and a severity of construction, such as no history of the deeds of man can bear, have often, too often in these last years, put her to an open shame.

"But what a word of hope and encouragement to every one who, as convinced in his heart of the glory of her providential mission, should unshrinkingly devote himself to defending within her borders the full and whole doctrine of the Cross, with that mystic symbol now as ever gleaming down on him from Heaven, now as ever showing forth its inscription—*in hoc signo vinces.*"

And now God seems again to be awakening the yearning to be visibly one, and He Who Alone, the Author of peace and the Lover of concord, must have put it into men's minds to pray for the Unity of Christendom, will, in His time, we trust, fulfil the prayer which He Himself has taught. It is not our insular self-importance; it is from beyond the seas that the voice has come, yea, it is, we trust, His Voice, "Who ruleth the seas and the noise of his waves, and the tumult of the people," Who has called to us to prepare ourselves to be such as He may employ for the reunion of Christendom. The authorities of the great Russian Church (we hear, as sounds floating on the breeze) look favourably on the wish for restored communion. Our position gives us an advantage towards her also; because, while we are wide-spread enough to be no object of contempt, there can be no dread on either side of any interference with the self-government of each, in the portion of God's heritage which, in His Providence, each occupies. We have no ground to fear in regard to her, lest she should force back upon us that vast practical system, still prevalent in the Western Church, which was one occasion, and is the justification, of our isolated condition. We had nothing to do with the great schism of the East and West. Convinced that, (as the Council of Florence states,) the Greek and Latin Fathers, though using different language, meant the same as to the Procession of God the Holy Ghost, we should have nothing to ask of her,—except Communion. With regard to her too, we may have a Providential Office, that we too have received the Filioque, not by any act of our own, but as circulated insensibly throughout the Latin Church[1]; and while we could not part with what, through so many centuries, has been the expression of our common faith, we might still reject with Anathema the heresy[2] which, since Photius, has been imputed to it, and which the Greek Church now seems, by an inveterate prejudice, to think to be involved in it. Yet it is plain that, long after the schism, her great writers and Bishops did not think so. Else they could not have proposed to the Latin Church, only to remove the word from the Creed, while continuing to teach or sing it elsewhere as they pleased[3]. For

[1] The clause does not appear to have been formally received in the West until the Council of Florence. The conjecture of Baronius seems to be most probable, that when, at the instance of Henry II. Emperor of Germany, the Nicene Creed came to be sung at all at Mass at Rome (A.D. 1014), it was sung, as it was in Spain and France and elsewhere, with the clause, "et Filio" (H. E. A.D. 447, n. 24). Baronius (A.D. 883, n. 38) expresses himself uncertain what Pope received it. He expresses his regret that the Nicene Creed came to be chanted at all at Rome (A.D. 1014, n. 5). The statement of Andr. Rhod., at the Council of Florence, that it was received by a large Western Council (Sess. 7, T. xviii. p. 124, Col.), seems a pure mistake.

[2] That there are two 'Αρχαὶ in the Godhead.

[3] Blackmore, Harm. of Eng. Doctr., &c., pp. 57—59, cites Theophylact, of the eleventh century, as quoted by John Beccus, "On other occasions, I will grant you (the Latins) the use of the expression, of the Holy Ghost 'proceeding from the Father and the Son,' as may suit your speech; in common discourses, I mean, and in Sermons in the Church, if ye please; but in the Creed, and in that alone, I will not grant it you." This was renewed by the Bishops in the time of the Emperor John Ducas, A.D. 1249, that "the interpolation should be put out of the Creed, but might be retained and used in any other form."

had they thought the formula to contain heresy, this would have involved connivance in, and assent to, heresy. But if the objection lies only to the informality or mistake of altering the common Creed, this, it seems, was unintentional on the part of the Western Church [4]; and *we* clearly had nothing to do with it; nor had we with what seems to have been a mistake [5] on the part of the Council of Florence who, laying down that the two formulæ had been used in the same sense by the great fathers, the διὰ τοῦ Υἱοῦ by the Greek, the *Filioque* by the Latin, drew the strange inference that the Greek should adopt the formula used by the Latin fathers. We had no share in this; we only ask to

Pachymeres, v. 12. This was drawn out by Michael Palæol. (A.D. 1273), quoting from the Register of the Church. He appealed to the written declarations of the Primates of that time, "bidding them notice how those Fathers had entirely abstained from taxing the Italians with impiety or heresy on account of their attempt to interpolate the Creed; leaving them free to retain and read the words as they pleased, any where else." The only complaint, then too, was as to "the scandal of innovation in changing the Creed." Tract. Zörnicav. ii. 972. In the Council of Florence too, Mark, Abp. of Ephesus, confined himself to this one question, "Expunge this clause from the Creed, and then place it where ye will, and sing it in your churches on occasion, as is sung ὁ μονογενὴς λόγος." Ib.

[4] The "Filioque" was first adopted in the Creed in Spain, after the recovery from Arianism, the Council supposing, by mistake, that such was the original Creed of Constantinople. From Spain, it passed into France.

[5] It may the rather be termed "a mistake," because the Church of Rome does not now require of the Greeks, united with her, what she then required of the whole Eastern Church.

continue to use the formula, which, without any act of our own, has been the expression of our faith immemorially. The Greeks, who value so much an inherited faith, could not, we trust, be insensible to the claim. If, on such terms and on such explanations of our belief as she may require and we could give, communion should be restored between us, a great step would have been gained towards the reunion of all Christendom.

The largeness of the hopes and longings may, we trust, draw down the more favour from Him Who "maketh men to be of one mind in one house." A plan, which should embrace the Greek Church also, would facilitate what English Catholics most desire, authoritative explanations. Cardinal Wiseman, in his memorable letter to Lord Shrewsbury, laid down as a principle, "We[6] must explain to the utmost." The Church of England and the Council of Trent have long seemed to me at cross purposes. In some cases, at least, the Council of Trent proposed the minimum, of which it would accept, but left a maximum, far beyond the letter of the Council, to be thereafter, as it was before, the practical system of the Church. The Church of England, in her Articles, protested against that maximum, the practical system which she saw around her; but, in many cases, she laid down no doctrine at all on the

[6] Letter, p. 31.

subject upon which she protested. She made negative statements to show against what she protested, but set down no positive statement to explain what, on the same subject, she accepted. Thus, in view of a Council, which was expected to be under Italian influence, and in which she did not expect to be fairly heard, she protested that "General Councils may and have erred" (which is so far true); but since she was employed only on the defensive on one side, she left it to be gathered from elsewhere that there are Councils which were "[7] allowed and received of all men," which she also accepted. And so, as to other points also.

It may be that, on any such negotiations, she might offer such explanations of the Thirty-nine Articles, as the Roman and Greek Churches would accept, such as are suggested by Bossuet[8], or by the Commonitorium of Du Pin; or, according

[7] Homilies. See above, p. 32.

[8] "A foreign Priest has pointed out to us a valuable document for our consideration, 'Bossuet's Reply to the Pope,' when consulted on the best method of reconciling the followers of the Augsburg Confession with the Holy See. The learned bishop observes, that Providence had allowed so much Catholic truth to be preserved in that Confession, that full advantage should be taken of the circumstance; that no *retractations* should be demanded, but an explanation of the Confession in accordance with Catholic doctrines. Now, for such a method as this, the way is in part prepared by the demonstration that such interpretation may be given of the most difficult [of the XXXIX] Articles, as will strip them of all contradiction to the decrees of the Tridentine Synod." Card. Wiseman, Letter, p. 38.

to the precedent of the Council of Florence, the Thirty-nine Articles and the Council of Trent (which was so largely directed against errors of Luther) might pass away and be merged in the Eighth General Council of the once-more united Christendom.

It is not, we trust, without some great purpose of His love, that God has so marvellously preserved the English Church until now. Life is the token of God's Presence in the Church; for out of Him there is no life. Dr. Manning grants, as to individuals in the English Church, that, in common with all the baptized, they, having been in Baptism made the children of God and members of Christ, are, if they have continued in that grace, members of Christ still. He admits, what he cannot deny without heresy, that they are real Christians. Even as to the number of these he casts doubts. He dwells[9] on the fact, that many of the English people are unbaptized (these are, of course, not members of any Church); he leaves out of the question all who have fallen from Baptismal grace by mortal sin, only speaking of "the[1] great difficulty and uncertainty of their restoration." And then he speaks of a small residuum whom he supposes to live on and grow in the grace which they

[9] P. 10.

[1] P. 18. He must mean, that, although God forgives, upon real contrition for past sins, it is, to any one, uncertain whether he be truly contrite.

received at their Baptism. His mode of admitting the fact implies his opinion of the rareness of such cases. Catholic[2] missionaries have known it as a fact, and he himself, too, as to *some* whom they have received into the Church. "There[3] are to be found amongst the English people *individuals* who practise in a high degree the four cardinal virtues, and, in no small degree, though with the limits and blemishes inseparable from their state, the three theological virtues of Faith, Hope, and Charity, infused into them in their Baptism." And so he comes to the result, that in England too, as well as in every other country, separate from the communion of Rome, there are indeed some few who grow up in Baptismal grace, some who have, in some imperfect degree, faith, hope, and charity, and these last chiefly among the dissenters, whose piety, he says, "is[4] more like the personal service of disciples to a personal Master, than the Anglican piety, which has *always* been more dim and distant from this central light of souls." With the exception of these few, the rest are, according to him, in a doubtful state, which he does not describe, yet which, since it is the result of a fall from grace given, and since a Christian's sins are against light, is a state worse than heathenism, except for the possibility of an uncertain and difficult recovery. To the

[2] P. 11. [3] P. 13. [4] P. 19.

Church of England he accords nothing which does not exist in any Protestant body, except something of the idea of a Church, (which, according to him, we have not,) and some probably inoperative truth, and some heathen virtues, since what piety we have, or have had, is and always has been, according to him, "more dim and distant from the central light of souls," Jesus. I say, "heathen virtues;" for the cardinal virtues, fortitude, justice, prudence, temperance, although of course they cannot be practised without the grace of God, are yet, while unanimated by the special Christian graces of Faith, Hope, and Charity, only heathen virtues, such as heathen have practised, with the grace of God. Specifically Dr. Manning denies "the validity of our Orders[5] and absolutions," and, with our Orders, whatever depends upon Orders.

[5] On our English Ordinations, it is enough to refer to the words of Mason, Courayer, Bramhall (with the important additions of the very careful editor, the Rev. A. W. Haddan, Angl. Cath. Lib.). I have examined in turn every objection made to them, and it has seemed to me that Roman Catholic controversialists took up easily any objection which might for the moment serve their turn. Cardinal Wiseman laid all aside, and took up the ground of jurisdiction. But this objection presupposes the truth of Ultramontanism. The metropolitical see in each country has inherent jurisdiction, according to the ancient canons. Parker was left in undisputed succession of the See of Canterbury, and his successors have the jurisdiction inherent in that See. Du Pin, when satisfied as to our Orders, felt, as a Gallican, no difficulty as to jurisdiction. Van Espen infers, from the very terms used in the Roman Pontifical and Ordinal, that "jurisdiction" is given in Consecration. He

The Church of England, then, according to him, teaches her children falsely, that in the Holy Eucharist "the Body and Blood of Christ preserve their bodies and souls unto eternal life;" for, according to him, the Holy Eucharist among us is but "the empty sign of an absent thing." She ordains her priests, according to him, with lying words, "Receive the Holy Ghost, for the office and work of a Priest in the Church of God, now committed unto thee by the imposition of our hands. Whose sins thou dost forgive, they are forgiven;" since he holds that the Holy Ghost is not given, and that sins remitted by them are *not* remitted. In like way he holds that she requires of

argues from the words with which the Gospel is given by the ordainer, "Receive the Gospel, and go preach to the people committed to thee," and from those in the Preface, "Give to him, Lord, the keys of the kingdom of heaven, that he may use, not boast of, the power which Thou givest to edification and not to destruction; whatsoever he shall bind on earth, &c., grant to him, O Lord, the Episcopal chair, for the ruling of Thy Church and people committed to him," that "Bishops receive their jurisdiction from God Himself, not from the Roman Pontiff." For that it would be "mocking God" so to speak and so to pray, without believing that the Bishop would have that which was prayed for. Opp. T. 5, p. 441. See further as to our orders, above, pp. 232, 233.

Bossuet says, "This holy and Apostolic doctrine of the Episcopal jurisdiction and power proceeding immediately from, and instituted by, Christ, the Gallic Church hath most zealously retained." "Therefore that very late monition, that Bishops receive their jurisdiction from the Pope, and are, as it were, Vicars of him, ought to be banished from Christian Schools, as unheard of for twelve centuries." Def. viii. 12, in Allies, p. 428.

her Priests to pronounce a material lie in the Name of the God of Truth, since we are directed to say, "By His [our Lord Jesus Christ's] authority committed unto me, I absolve thee from all thy sins in the Name of the Father and of the Son and of the Holy Ghost," whereas he denies that we have any authority committed to us, or do at all absolve.

And yet God blesseth through these Sacraments; and God blesseth through truth. If a Wesleyan minister preaches his naked Gospel, that "we are all sinners," that "Christ died to save sinners," that "He bids all sinners come to Him," and saith, "whoso cometh unto Me, I will in no wise cast out," this is, of course, fundamental Gospel-truth, and, when God blesses through it those who know no more, He blesseth them through faithful reception of His truth. So again, as to the Presbyterians. They deny, in regard to the Holy Communion, what we believe; and their account of their Communion is somewhat less than what *we* mean by a spiritual Communion. For they speak, rather, of "ascending in mind into heaven," and feeding upon Jesus there by faith, than of praying Him to come by His Spirit into the soul. I mean, that the Calvinist Confessions seem to me to speak rather of man's part than of His; of what faith, enabled by Him, *does*, than of what it *receives*. Still, be this as it may, they speak of a religious act; and although (as some of them say) there is no need, to this end, of any thing outward, and what they describe might be done in every prayer, still, doubtless, He Whom they seek, is found by them, for that which they seek. They seek a spiritual communion, and doubtless God admits them to that spiritual communion with Him which they desire. Nay, in Baptism He gives them more than they know of or believe. With the Church of England, it would, according to Dr. Manning's statement, be the very contrary of all this. We believe, when we confess our sins, that, coming in repentance and in faith, "[6] our Lord Jesus Christ, Who hath left power to His Church to absolve all sinners who truly repent and believe in Him, of His great mercy forgives" us our "offences;" and that it is "by His authority committed to" His servants, that we are "absolved from all our sins in the Name" of the All-Holy Trinity. We believe that in Holy Communion we, coming with the right dispositions, "[7] verily and indeed take and receive the Body and Blood of Christ;" that "[8] we so eat the Flesh of Christ and drink His Blood, that our sinful bodies are made clean by His Body, and our souls are washed by His most precious Blood." "According to thy faith," our gracious Lord said, "be it unto thee." I do not believe that God maintains the faith, where there is not the reality. The Lutherans set out with a belief of the Real

[6] Service for the Visitation of the Sick.
[7] Catechism.
[8] Communion Service.

Presence, clearly expressed, except that Luther degraded the Sacrament, by making it a mere sign to faith. But since they had no Orders, the belief died out. No other body, which is not admitted to have the *true* Sacrament, claims to have it. Aquinas says, in the name of the Western Church[9], "A priest consecrates validly, in heresy or schism, although he sins in so doing." Heretics, who are really cut off from the Body of Christ, receive the Sacrament, though not the grace of the Sacrament. We have the witness that we have really the true Body and Blood of Christ and the grace of the Sacrament: 1) from the knowledge of those who receive it. God would not allow His own to be deluded in such a matter as this. 2) In the supernatural lives of grace, led by persons, the life of whose souls is Christ in the Holy Eucharist. I do not mean any disparagement to any pious Presbyterians, but, believing the Holy Eucharist to be what we, in common with the whole Ancient Church, know It to be, we cannot but know that they who receive It worthily, have a much greater closeness of union with our Lord,

[9] iv. dist. 13, q. 1, art. 1, q. 3, and S. P. iii. q. lxxxii. art. vii., on the ground of S. Augustine's statement, that orders, as well as baptism, remain in those separated from the Church. (c. Ep. Parm. Ep. 2, c. 13, n. 28.) Both, however, deny the grace of the Sacraments. The grace of the Sacraments belonging to the Church alone, the undoubted presence of the grace of the Sacraments is a proof to us, that we are in the body of Christ, in which alone He gives it.

than they who do not. Presbyterians have what *they* believe; we, what *we* believe. But they who have observed pious Presbyterians and pious English Catholics, have discerned among our people a spiritual life, of a kind which was not among theirs; in a word, a sacramental life. Dr. Manning denies the validity of our absolutions. God, the Author of truth, has set His seal upon them. This enlarged use of confession, which originated in men's stirred consciences, often grew, in consequence of its visible fruits on the lives of those who had already used it. People were wont to ask, "What has so changed you?" They sought the remedy, which God had made so effectual to others. We, the English Clergy, have seen the death-beds of those, whose first confessions we had heard, and we could no longer recognize, in the ripened, humble saint, the person whom we had first known, although, then too, earnestly seeking God.

3) You remember how our dear friend J. H. Newman was impressed by God's visible and very aweful judgment upon a sacrilegious Communion. It was no insulated instance. Our Lord bore witness to His own Presence, by judging the sacrilegious communicant, and leaving him in the power of Satan, who drove him to self-murder in the precincts of the Church, where he had profaned the Body and Blood of Christ. Prejudiced as juries are, the jury, awed by the case, pronounced "felo-de-se." On the other hand, the effects of devout

communion have passed over to the body too. I have known too the evil fruit of sacrilegious confessions, very different from those of an ordinary lie.

4) It is in accordance with the truth of the Sacrament, that the enlarged life among us, has especially taken the form of increased Sacraments. The Wesleyan bodies would increase their prayer-meetings, which some of them have spoken of to me as *their* "means of grace." Protestant bodies have their revivals; the Church of England multiplied the celebration of its Sacraments.

But those who have pointed to "life" as a great note in the English Church, did not mean the life of grace in individuals. They have meant the organic operation of God the Holy Ghost upon the Church as a whole. It is the mark given by our Lord Himself. By a wonderful analogy between nature and grace, the branch, which had been severed from the True Vine, carried out with it for a time the life of the tree; but, the life-giving sap being cut off, after a time it withered. Contrariwise, as our friend observed, the Church of England has had a tough, vigorous life. Its life has been tried in every way in which it could be tried. "It has been practised upon by theorists, browbeaten by sophists, intimidated by princes, betrayed by false sons, laid waste by tyranny, corrupted by wealth, torn by schism, and persecuted by fanaticism. Revolutions have come upon it sharply and suddenly to and fro, hot and cold, as if to try what it was made of. It has been a sort of battle-field, on which opposite principles have been tried. No opinion, however extreme any way, but may be found, as the Romanists are not slow to reproach us, among its bishops and divines. Yet what has been its career upon the whole? Which way has it been moving through three hundred years? Where does it find itself at the end? Lutherans have tended to Rationalism; Calvinists have become Socinians; but what has it become[1]?"

Now, after above three centuries, it alone has a more vigorous life than ever. It seems like a tree which had been shaken for a while, yet struck its roots deep and is filling the lands. Severed in the United States from the protection of the state—nay, rather trampled in the dust by those who hated it for the loyalty of its members,—it first struck root when it was deprived of all human aid. Independent witnesses have attested some time ago, how, before this fratricidal war, it was regarded by many as the one principle of stability in the United States. It wins from all the bodies who broke off from us, and itself seldom loses to any. Long ago it quadrupled, while the population doubled only. Its clergy are very frequently the sons of the ministers of bodies not in communion with it, whom it has won. It has been recently making an

[1] Catholicity of the English Church, in British Critic, No. 53, p. 77.

impression even upon the inveterate, boastful, intellectual Socinianism.

And all this with no human aid, with no power except the Presence of God the Holy Ghost, which has been specially promised to the Church. So also in our other colonies, and in that vast heathen realm of India. If our Episcopate had not been of Divine Institution, then it would have been all one, whether those reputed to be of the second or first order, Priests or Bishops, had been sent out; for, in fact, they would have been alike laymen. On the other hand, our Episcopate being Divine, to send out Priests alone, or with a Bishop over a whole continent, as it were, was, to plant the Gospel as God willed not that it should be planted. The fact has borne witness to the truth of our Episcopate. When the Gospel was preached, even by pious men, without the Episcopate, it languished after a time; when the Church was planted according to its Divine form, it flourished.

In this restoration in which we live, very remarkable have been the organic workings of God the Holy Ghost in the Church as a whole. The last century was, by a strange harmony every where, especially "sæculum tepidum." In France, the children whom the Church had lost, aided by apostate Bishops and Priests, overthrew her. A marvellous inward decay must have prepared for the time, when the goddess of Reason could be enthroned in a Christian capital. Southern Germany became indevout; Hermesianism has, since, infested her. About thirty years ago I was, myself, asked to write against a German book, put forth in the name of Catholicism against the faith, on the ground that it had a wide, baleful influence among the German Catholics. In Italy, we have probably not yet seen the full fruits of evils long festering there. Much indifference is said to have existed during the last century in Roman Catholic Ireland. In the United States, it is commonly and confidently stated, that the Roman Church loses its hold over large proportions of the Irish immigrants[2].

And now, in this century, God has been reviving the Church every where, simultaneously. Nothing has so impressed itself upon me during all the years in which I have observed the workings of God the Holy Ghost upon the Church of England, as their organic character.

Some have all along been in the habit of looking to certain modes of revival; at the best, to the way in which God blessed the workings of one class of individuals. To these they appealed, as furnishing "tokens of life in the English Church." For myself, I always turned away, sick at heart, from this feverish watching for tokens of life. It is not

[2] The Dublin Review confirms this. "We fear that there can be little doubt that in the United States the Church loses more souls than it gains. In the second generation, the faith of the Catholic immigrant is constantly lost." July, 1865, p. 226.

in the flush of the cheek or the more brilliant eye alone, in which you would recognize the returning health of the body. These might be fever, not health-tokens. What is concentrated around individuals, even though manifoldly multiplied, is individual still. To us, the workings seemed all along far beyond any efforts of human zeal or energy or faithfulness, even as blessed by God. The dawn lay beyond our memory. Perhaps, if one might fix a time, one should say, from the French revolution, when the Voice of God spoke in such terrible warning as to the fruits of neglectful ways, and sent a coal of fire into the hearts of men. Since then, the progress has been steadily onwards. Often, as in younger years I used to hear the account of things in the generation before us, the words spoken to the Prophet and his answer shot through me, "Son of man, can these bones live? And I answered and said, O Lord God, Thou knowest." But "the bones had come together, bone to his bone; the sinews and the flesh came up upon them, and the skin covered them above, and the breath came into them, and they lived, and stood up upon their feet, an exceeding great army [s]."

Increased zeal for spreading the faith of Christ abroad returned into the bosom of the Church at home; increased zeal for the religious education of the poor won the blessing of Jesus, Whose bequest

[s] Ezek. xxxvii. 7—10.

the poor are; increased efforts to build Churches to the glory of His Name, and for the salvation of souls, were blessed by the increased Presence of Him in Whose honour they were raised. Not in one way, nor in one set of ways, but in all: not in one class of minds, but in some of every class; not in one theological section of the Church, but in all; not through one set of men, but through all; not through those only who had our full belief, but through all who loved Him; not through prosperous circumstances only, but yet more through adverse; not in England only, but throughout the whole body, has God been forming the English Church, for what purpose in His hands, He knoweth!

Even those deepest losses of all, the loss of those who "laboured most abundantly," and the suspicion which two or three sought to cast on those who remained, and most of all, the chaos into which some minds were thrown, suspecting Catholic truth, because their guides had become Roman, not English, Catholics, — these things have indeed checked, but they have not hindered the work of God among us.

It seemed, indeed, before these secessions that, with the continuance of God's gracious operation, nothing but time was needed to Catholicize England. But the waters have risen, not the less decidedly, because noiselessly. Fallow ground was broken thirty years ago; fresh seed was sown; seed time and harvest have gone on together unbroken; the seed which ripened fell again to the earth silently and yielded fresh fruit abundantly. They who wished to pluck it up, only, like the birds of the air, carried it further. Mr. Oakeley, who, when among us, seemed to watch intently the progress made within rather a narrow sphere, has lately repeated, that Tractarianism, as a movement, ended[4] with the loss of our dear friend, J. H. Newman. The tracts had been closed before: the first impulse had been given before. Had he followed his own bent, I believe that the tracts would have ended in some preceding year. The trumpet had sounded[5] steady, clear, certain; and a very great army had gathered at the call. We do not need the trumpet, when God's willing people are gathered[6]. What has had to be done since has been to build on. The building arises "without axe or hammer." Never, I am satisfied, was the work of God among us so wide and so deep as now. Far deeper and

[4] Dublin Review. Since the above has been in type, I observe a kindly mention of Mr. Keble's and my own recent exertions, in Mr. Oakeley's reprint of those Articles. As to any supposed previous "quiescence," exertion has to take a different shape, when confidence in any one has been for the time rudely destroyed.

[5] Motto of the Tracts, "If the trumpet give an uncertain sound, who shall prepare himself for battle?"

[6] I asked, contrariwise, Schleiermacher in 1826, "Why 'the Wolfenbüttel Fragments,' which had been thought so formidable an attack on Christianity at one time, were thought of no more?" He answered, "Wozu der Mist, wann die Erndte da ist?" "To what end the manure, when the harvest is there?"

wider is it than in those glad, prosperous days, because the leaven, which was hidden in the meal, has worked secretly, and has now more centres, from which it is every where working.

Dr. Manning says[7], "The known and historical evidence of Christianity is enough to convince any *prudent* man that Christianity is a Divine revelation. It is quite true that by this process he cannot entertain an explicit faith in all the doctrines of revelation, and that in rejecting Catholicism he reduces himself to human and historical evidence as the maximum of extrinsic certainty for his religion, and that this almost inevitably resolves itself in the long run into Rationalism. It is an inclined plane, on which, if individuals may stand, generations cannot." There is confusion in the statement[8]. But I fully accept as true, the result intended, that rejection of Catholicism ends in the long run in Rationalism, and that it is an inclined plane on which generations cannot stand. We have seen the

[7] Letter, pp. 26, 27.

[8] *a*) Although, in the cold phraseology of the last century, it is part of prudence to inquire into the evidence what God has revealed Himself to His creatures, prudence has no part in producing conviction. *b*) It is a truism, that "one who rejects Catholicism" cannot "attain an explicit faith in *all* the articles of the doctrines of revelation," i. e. of the Catholic faith. But this does not affect us, except on the assumption that we have rejected Catholicism or the Catholic faith, or any thing which is Divine. *c*) "*Extrinsic* certainty" must mean, I suppose, what is antecedent to the gift of faith in one who comes to the faith. For the habit of faith which God gives to Christians is internal, and we all have it from God.

truth of this in Lutheranism and Calvinism, in the length and breadth of the lands which they occupied, except where faith has been preserved by vicinity to the English Church. Why then has it not been so among us, after 300 years? The answer is plain; on those self-same principles, "because we have" *not* "rejected Catholicism." Dr. Manning refers to the downward course of the English people. The question between us is, not about the English people, but about the English Church. The Church of England is no more responsible for those of the English people who have revolted from her, than the Churches of Italy, and France, and Germany, are for those who have revolted from them. We are all responsible for any want of zeal, or faith, or self-sacrifice, or for any spirit of worldliness, which may have prevented others from seeing that "God is in us of a truth."

But the existence of all the sects in England shows the uncompromisingness of the Church of England in maintaining Catholic truth. Had she been like the Lutheran body, she would have had no Dissenters. People do not split off from that which does not hold firmly together. But, as she is not responsible for Dissenters who have rejected her authority, her teaching, her communion, neither is she responsible for their course. Nor is she more responsible for such phenomena as Dr. Colenso's heathenism [9], or Essay-

[9] The fifty answers to Dr. Colenso's first Part are much

and-Review scepticism, than the Church of France was for Talleyrand and Sieyes. Nor are we the only portion of the Catholic Church which is suffering from the attacks of Rationalism. Already in this place, Essay and Reviewism has done its worst, and is hastening to its decay. Its observant adherents own the growth of the Faith. It is but a passing storm which, desolating as it has been to the souls of individuals, yet disinfects the atmosphere. They have already done more to remove misconceptions and prejudices than twenty years of efforts of our own. They have given us a watchword, whereby the friends of Jesus may recognize one another. We have been all, in our several ways, fighting for Him and in His service, yet some of us, aloof from each other, and our fealty to our common Master suspected. Now those who love Jesus and His Word and His truth will be united, we trust, by the presence of a common foe. Now, like the battle-cry of God's chosen warrior of old, "The sword of the Lord and of Gideon," that of the English Church will be "Jesus and victory;" and the "gleaning of the grapes of Ephraim will be more than the vintage of Abiezer." For the wine-press is trodden in His Name, Who trod it alone in His bitter

greater indications of the mind of the people of England, than his solitary attack. His legal position Lord Westbury has destroyed, and declared him in fact an unattached Bishop, *his* patent also being invalid. Dr. Colenso has neither ecclesiastical position, being deposed, nor the hearts of the people of Natal. The Church in South Africa is free, and can right itself.

Passion; and the juice of the grape is His precious Blood, Which alone has healing, and life and salvation and union with Him.

May He spare you long to His Church and people, that, as in "the Christian Year" you sowed in our youth the first seeds of a rich harvest, you may help in the ingathering, of which there is such bright promise in "the year of His goodness" which God has blessed!

Your very affectionate friend,

E. B. PUSEY.

Christ Church, 1865.

POSTSCRIPT..

I HAD finished my letter, and it had been some time in type, before Dr. Manning was elevated to his present important position, or the reading of the Encyclical of last year, and the comments upon it, had shown me how advanced, above all which was known formerly, is the present theory of Papal Infallibility.

The Ultramontanes in the Roman Communion seem to be drifting off further from the principles of the early and undivided Church. Under Jesuit influence "the shores of Italy" seem ever to be "receding." We could not imagine ourselves to have lived a day out of the communion of the Church of S. Augustine. With the knowledge which we have of it, we could not imagine any, the slightest difficulty, which should have hindered our flying to it, had we been born in any sect external to it. It has been the home of our faith, our affections, our understanding, now to grey hairs. Like God's word, so that undivided Church of God satisfies our whole selves. There are no clouds there. In its faith we have been ever at rest. Even in the Gallican Church, a century and a half ago, there seemed to be a dawn of re-union; there was, if not clear day, at least a break in the clouds, such as gave token that the breath of God might disperse them. Now things seem to be taking an opposite direction. It is the boast of the English Ultramontane party, that Gallicanism is extinct; and this not as relates to any question of the relation of the Pope to the civil sovereign. *This* the successive rulers from the Restoration of 1815 did what they could to extinguish, by becoming the oppressors of the Church. But in regard to the central question, where the infallibility of the Church lies, the Ultramontanes tell us that the Gallican belief, that nothing has the seal of infallibility which has not been received by the whole Church, is extinct in France[1]. If it is to be found any where, we are, I suppose, to look to Germany, or perhaps among some of the Gallican Bishops who have not spoken. The Dublin Review would have it, that even the *tacit* reception of the Encyclical of 1864 would, even upon Gallican principles, fix as matters of faith, not only the doctrines, virtually affirmed by the Encyclical, as being the contradictories of the propositions condemned, but the main principle which Pius IX. appears to have assumed, that he is infallible in all his formal utterances, on whatever subjects, connected, in his

[1] Dublin Review, July, 1865, p. 130.

judgment, with the well-being of the Church although with no visible bearing on faith or morals, and howsoever or to whomsoever those utterances may be made. It is for those of the Roman Communion to settle this. Of twenty-four Gallican Bishops who spoke (including Algiers, and Chambéry, as now French), two only, the Bishop of Nimes and Fréjus, include the old Gallican belief of reception by the whole Episcopate in their grounds for adhesion to the late Encyclical [2]. But twenty-two are but about one-fourth of the Bishops of France. It seems also very possible that the Roman Catholic Episcopate might agree in condemning all the eighty propositions, condemned in the syllabus, and yet not intend thereby to express their belief that every enunciation of the Pope, on whatever subject, is *ipso facto* infallible. For although the writer in the Dublin Review [3] has shown that the Encyclical of 1864 does claim this, in the name of Pius IX., the doctrine does not so explicitly lie there, as to require any Bishop, who should not assent to it, to express any dissent. Least of all would it seem to be required that every one, who should dissent from it, should, in the present troubled state of the Church every where, add such an element of

[2] Dublin Review, April, 1865, p. 447.

[3] Ib. July, p. 127. The Card. Archbishop of Chambéry also notices "the condemnations having been published without exciting any protest," i. e., I suppose, having been tacitly received. Ib. p. 129.

discord to the present conflict. It would make the doctrine of "reception by the Church" a nullity, if every thing was to be held to be received, which should not be protested against, even although not formally proposed for assent.

The claim, however, now raised, goes far beyond even the school of Bellarmine. If established, it would, in Pontificates so full of activity as that of Pius IX. who has issued thirty-two authoritative documents, be adding almost yearly to the faith of those in the Roman Communion. And union with the Roman See, on the part, e. g., of the great Russian Church, would involve this,—that every one should be ready to receive whatever all past Popes had authoritatively uttered, and whatever any future Pope, though unhappily a Borgia or a Julius II., might utter upon any subject whatsoever.

To the great Gallican Divines, however respectfully they spoke of the Pope, he was but one element in the infallibility of the whole Church. Since universal reception was the test of the infallibility of any decision of the Church, nothing could have this seal of infallibility, which was not received by him who was in dignity its first Bishop. It needed not, however, that what should become infallible, should always emanate from him; nor did it. The Anti-Pelagian statements of faith, e. g., which were received by the whole Church, came from S. Augustine and Africa; the concluding parts of the Niceno-Constantinopolitan Creed came from a Council in which the East only was represented, but which became General through its reception by the West. To say, then, that the enunciations of the Pope became infallible through their reception by the whole Episcopate, would be a one-sided statement of Gallicanism; because such universal reception would equally render infallible any statement of faith which a Provincial Council should draw up against heresy: only in this case the Bishop of Rome would be an important member of those who should receive it.

From this, the doctrine set forth in Bellarmine differed, in that it ascribed infallibility to the Pope personally, but this with a limitation of its subject-matter. His two canons in this respect are:—1) "[4] The Pontiff, when he teaches the whole Church, can in no case err in those things which appertain to faith." 2) "[5] Not only in precepts of faith cannot he err, but neither can he in precepts of morals, which are prescribed to the whole Church, and *which relate to things necessary to salvation, or to such as are good or bad in themselves.*"

The doctrine, which places such an aweful power in the hands of an individual, is limited in two ways in Bellarmine's statement; 1) as to the formal way, in which the enunciation to be received as

[4] De Rom. Pont. iv. 3. [5] Ib. c. 5.

infallible is to be made. The "matters of faith" are to be such as are "taught to the whole Church;" the "precepts of morals" are to be "prescribed to the whole Church." 2) In regard to morals, mere benefit to the Church is excluded. They are to be simply things "good or bad in themselves or necessary to salvation."

Matters of fact are omitted altogether. Nothing is said of them, either that they do, or do not, fall within the scope of Papal infallibility.

It has been recently drawn out [6];

1. That Pius IX. claims infallibility in judgments which he puts forth, "which do *not* touch the dogmas of faith and morals," but "whose object is declared [by him] to regard the Church's right discipline and general good. His declarations on his civil princedom [i. e. on 'his temporal sovereignty over his temporal subjects in Italy'] may be given as instances in point." These statements of infallible truth need not, then, obviously be connected with the substance of revelation, or be supported by any thing in Holy Scripture or tradition, bearing on the subject.

2. That these statements, in order to their infallibility, need not be addressed to the whole Episcopate, or be in any way formal in their character, but may be contained in letters to this or that individual pastor [7].

[6] Dublin Review, April, 1865, p. 446.
[7] Ib., pp. 444. 448.

3. That consequently all the statements put forth in the Syllabus of 1864 are infallible truth.

4. It follows that Papal infallibility is held to extend to matters of fact, and to things unconnected with former revelation.

5. Since the claim for infallibility in these statements has been put forth, although not 'totidem verbis,' in the Encyclical of 1864, then, it is to follow, that each successive Pope is infallible on any of those or the like subjects, in whatever way or to whomsoever he may speak.

The errors condemned at the beginning of the Encyclical cannot, indeed, be said to have been condemned by any authority but that of our Lord. For Pius IX. condemned, so far, denials of God, of His Providence, and His revelations, which every peasant knows to be blasphemous. Others, again, of the propositions condemned are naked Erastianism. Some deny the first principles of morals.

I would only, in illustration of what I mean, speak of those, in regard to which the claim of infallibility is an advance apparently upon what has been hitherto taught in the Roman Communion.

1. As to matters of fact, it is claimed to be infallible truth,—that "no Pope[8] ever exceeded the

[8] Prop. xxiii., in a work of a Spanish Ecclesiastic, Lima, 1848, condemned June 10, 1851, in the *Multiplices inter*, Recueil d. Alloc. Consistor., Encycliques, &c., citées dans l'Encycl. et Syll. 1864, p. 289, "Roman Pontiffs and

limits of his power, or usurped the rights of princes, or erred in defining matters of faith or morals," in which case Bossuet would be found, in regard to the last, in opposition to infallible truth[9]. Again, it is to become infallible truth, that "[1] no too arbitrary acts of any Roman Pontiff contributed to the Church's division into east and west." Then, it is to be pronounced infallibly, that the Pope was right in the original unhappy dispute, with Photius and Ignatius alike, about Bulgaria, or in that which Fleury lamented, as finally fixing the schism, the setting up a Latin Emperor and Latin Patriarchs, or in insisting on the addition of the *Filioque* in the Nicene Creed to be recited by the Greeks, after having acknowledged that the Greek and Latin Fathers, while using different formulæ, meant the same thing; and yet subsequent Popes have abandoned this requisition in the case of the Greeks who have united themselves to the Latin Church.

Again, it is to become infallible truth, that "[2] Boniface VIII. was not the first who asserted

Œcumenical Councils have quitted the limits of their power, usurped the rights of princes, and have erred even in defining matters of faith and morals." The Dublin Review (April, 1865, p. 482) argues rightly, that each of these statements is condemned as to the Popes *or* Œcumenical Councils, not only as to both together.

[9] See above, pp. 34—36.

[1] Prop. xxxviii. of Nuytz, a Turin Professor, condemned in *Ad Apostolicas*, Aug. 22, 1851, that "'nimia arbitria' of Roman pontiffs contributed," &c. Recueil, p. 294.

[2] Prop. lxxii., also quoted from Nuytz, condemned Ib.

that the vow of chastity, made at ordination, annuls marriage,"—a point which would fall, one should have thought, under human learning, not, at this date, of Divine revelation. Again, it becomes infallible truth, that "[3] civil liberty of all worships, and full power granted to all publicly to manifest any opinions or thoughts whatsoever, conduces to the more ready corruption of the morals and minds of peoples, and to propagate the plague of indifferentism." A most thoughtful observer in the Roman Communion has said to this effect, "I had rather have to do with the open infidelity of the nineteenth century, than with the hidden infidelity of the middle ages." This is no contradiction of the statement of Pius IX., but might make an essential limitation of it, viz. that some ways of attempting to check a great evil, the open spread of unbelief, might produce a greater,—an unbelief spreading unchecked and unhealed, because hidden.

In the note there occurs, as a proposition of his, "the Emperor Justinian first annulled the marriage of priests." Ib. p. 297.

[3] Prop. lxxix. This is not opposed to any maxim *formally* maintained by any one. In the *Nunquam fore*, Dec. 15, 1856, Pius IX. stated, that this was the object of the Mexican government, "In order to corrupt more easily the minds of the people, and to propagate the detestable and most foul pest of 'indifferentism,' and to attack our most holy religion, the free exercise of all worship is admitted, and full power is given of manifesting openly and publicly any opinions or thoughts whatever."

2. In regard to matters which do not relate to the substance of the faith or of morals, we have now a formal pronouncement, that the toleration of religious worship, other than the Roman Catholic, is in itself inexpedient[4]; that immigrants, at least in some Roman Catholic countries, ought to be prohibited the use of their public worship[5]; that "[6] the Church has power to employ force against persons [vis inferendæ], and has temporal power direct or indirect." Pius IX. placed the denial of *this* power of the Church in the front of the propositions, from which, he says, "[7] It is clear

[4] Prop. lxxvii. The Proposition condemned is, "In this our age, it is no longer expedient that the Catholic religion should be held the only religion of the state, all other whatsoever being shut out." The question in the *Nemo vestrum*, to which reference is made, is not of any partial recognition or endowment of any such worship, but of its being. The convention which was broken in Spain was, "that that august religion, every other worship being shut out, continuing to be the only religion of the Spanish *nation*, was to be preserved as before," &c.

[5] Prop. lxxviii. "Hence it has been laudably provided in some Catholic countries, that immigrants should be allowed the public exercise of their several worships." Pius IX. had condemned such permission in New Grenada "most energetically" (summopere), in the *Acerbissimum*, Sept. 27, 1852. Recueil, p. 322. To admit immigrants at all, and yet forbid them their worship, would plainly be to give them over to entire godlessness. And, apart from the loss of their own souls, the presence of a godless population is more perilous than that of persons with an imperfect faith.

[6] Nuytz's proposition, denying this, is condemned in the *Ad Apostolicas*, Recueil, p. 294, and Syll., Prop. xxiv.

[7] *Ad Apost.*, Recueil, pp. 296, 7. In the Encyclical *Quantæ*

that the author [Nuytz], by such doctrine and such maxims, aims at perverting the constitution and the government of the Church, and the entire destruction of the Catholic faith, in that he deprives the Church of external judgment and corrective power, to the intent that those in error may return into the way of righteousness."

It is, then, to be infallibly certain, that this "corrective force" (such as was exercised by the Inquisition, or in the reign of Henry VIII., or Queen Mary) is essential to the maintenance of the Catholic faith; and *that*, as used not only against heresiarchs, but "in order that those in error may return to the way of justice." In fact, the only ground of not using it would be its visible inexpediency. Only such employment of force, as would exasperate, not extinguish, is unadvised.

Further, Pius IX. condemns, as by infallible authority, the denial of the *temporal* authority of the Church, or of the single Bishop [8]; of the im-

curæ, he condemns those who are "not ashamed to affirm, that the Church has not the right of correcting by temporal punishments the violators of her laws." (Recueil, p. 8.)

[8] Prop. xxv., Nuytz's, condemned. "Besides the power, inherent in the Episcopate, there is another temporal power attributed, granted either expressly or implicitly by the civil power, which may therefore be recalled by the civil power when it wills." It is involved then that the temporal power is inherent. Prop. xxvii., "The sacred ministers of the Church and the Roman Pontiff are to be excluded from all right and dominion of temporal things," is condemned in the *Maxima*

munity of Clerks from being sued or prosecuted in Civil or Criminal Courts, at least without consent of the Pope[9]; "of the sinfulness of the political principle of 'non-intervention[1],'" or the ascription

quidem, June 9, 1862, "as a saying uttered with all fallacy and guile." Recueil, p. 456.

[9] Prop. xxx., "The immunity of the Church and of Ecclesiastical persons had its origin from the civil law," was formed from one of F. de Paula G. Vigil, Lima (condemned in the *Multiplices inter*, Recueil, p. 288), who asserted that "the immunity of the Church and of persons, constituted by ordinance of God and canonical sanctions, had its origin from the civil law." Prop. xxxi. was not formally maintained as a thesis, but was acted upon. In the Allocutions referred to, Pius IX. said, "By this new constitution proposed [in the Mexican Republic], besides other things, every privilege of the Ecclesiastical forum is taken away" (*Nunquam fore*, Recueil, p. 384), and, "a law was passed (in New Grenada) whereby the Ecclesiastical forum is altogether taken away, and it is declared that all causes appertaining to the same forum, even those of the Archbishop and Bishops, whether civil or *criminal*, are for the future to be judged before lay tribunals by the magistrates of that republic" (*Acerbissimum*, Recueil, p. 322). The proposition condemned is, "The ecclesiastical forum for the temporal causes of clerks, whether civil or criminal, is to be altogether taken away, even without consulting, or against the protest of, the Apostolic see." (Recueil, p. 22.)

[1] Prop. lxii. "The principle which they term *non-intervention* is to be proclaimed and observed." The principle is condemned in the *Novos et ante* broadly. "We cannot abstain from deploring, besides other things, the destructive and pernicious principle, which they call *non-intervention*, not long ago proclaimed and acted upon by some governments, and tolerated by the rest, in the case of the unjust aggression of one government against another, so that a sort of licence and impunity of attacking and despoiling the rights, properties, and even territories of others against the laws of God and

of "the right called 'Appel comme d'Abus' to the civil power, even when exercised by an unbelieving ruler [2]," the opinion that "[3] the abrogation of the civil princedom which the Apostolic See enjoys [i. e. 'the authority which the Pope possesses as king over his imperial subjects in Italy [4]'] would conduce in the highest degree to the Church's liberty and felicity."

The two opinions on the civil princedom of the Papacy, condemned in the Syllabus, are very pronounced. The one states that its abolition would be a benefit; the other, though less strong in words, is stronger in fact: for Nuytz stated, that "[5] sons of the Christian and Catholic Church disputed among themselves as to the compatibility of the temporal kingdom with the spiritual,"—which

man, seems to be sanctioned, as we see in this sad time." (Recueil, p. 420.)

[2] Prop. xli., Nuytz's. "That the civil power, even when exercised by an infidel ruler, has an indirect negative power over sacred things, and not merely the right, called *exequatur*, but also of 'appeal from abuse'" (l'appel comme d'abus), condemned verbally in the *Ad Apost.*, Rec. p. 294.

[3] Prop. lxxvi., from the *Quibus quantisque*; 1849. "We cannot but admonish and reprove those especially, who approve that decree [of the Constituens Romana, 1849], whereby the Roman Pontiff was despoiled of all honour and dignity of his temporal princedom, and assert that that decree conduces in the highest degree to the liberty and felicity of the Church herself." (Rec., p. 224.)

[4] Dublin Rev., April, 1865, p. 441, note.

[5] Prop. lxxv. condemned in the *Ad Apost.*, Recueil, p. 294.

involves that some at least doubted whether the temporal power was not morally wrong.

Neither condemnation lays down a positive doctrine obligatory upon Roman Catholics. The Syllabus however states, that "[6] many other errors are implicitly reprobated in *the doctrine which all Catholics ought most firmly to hold on the civil princedom of the Roman Pontiff*," and that "this doctrine is clearly taught in" five Allocutions and one Apostolic letter, which it names. The doctrine is most fully stated in the earliest of 1849, that, "when [7] the Roman Empire was divided into many kingdoms and various states, it was by a very singular counsel of Divine Providence that the Roman Pontiff, to whom the government and care of the whole Church was committed by the Lord Christ, should on this ground have a civil princedom, that he might, for the government of the Church itself and for the maintenance of its unity, enjoy that full liberty which is required for discharging the supreme Apostolic ministry. For all know that the faithful people, nations, kingdoms, would never yield full confidence and observance to the Roman Pontiff, if they saw him subject to the dominion of any prince or government, and not free. For the faithful people and kingdoms would never cease vehemently to suspect

[6] Recueil, p. 33.

[7] *Quibus quantisque*, Rec., p. 224.

and fear, that the Pontiff would conform his acts to the will of the prince or government in whose dominions he lived, and therefore would not hesitate often, under that pretext, to contradict those acts. And let the enemies of the civil princedom of the Apostolic See, who now rule at Rome, themselves say with what confidence or observance they themselves would receive the exhortations, admonitions, mandates, constitutions of the supreme Pontiff, if they knew him to be subject to the empire of any prince or government, especially if he were the subject of any prince, between whom and the Roman state there should be any lasting war."

On this ground Pius IX. said, "The nature of our office requires that, in maintaining the civil princedom of the Apostolic See, we should defend with all our might the rights and possessions of the holy Roman Church, and the liberty of that See, which is conjoined with the liberty and advantage of the whole Church."

The other Allocutions add nothing to this [8],

[8] Of the Alloc., cited in the Syll., the *Si semper antea*, Rec., p. 266, *Cum Catholica*, Ib., p. 402, *Novos*, Ib., p. 420, *Maxima quidem*, Ib., p. 460, repeat, unargumentatively, the statement that the civil Princedom was given by the singular counsel of the Providence of God (the *Cum Cath.* says, "God willed that this see of S. Peter should be provided with it"), for the greater benefit of the Church, through the independent position of the Pontiff. The *Jamdudum cernimus*, Rec., p. 438, only speaks of the Civil Princedom as belonging to the R. Pontiff.

except, perhaps, that the *Cum catholica* ascribes the temporal government more directly to "the Will of God;" and the *Maxima quidem* says, "that the civil princedom was *necessary*[9]," which may be a little stronger than *required.*

I have purposely selected such statements only as do not in themselves "touch upon faith or morals." I will only instance one more, as showing that every sentence in every pronouncement of the Pope is to be held as infallible. Prop. LXI., "The injustice of a fact, being prospered, brings no detriment to the sanctity of the right," is only an incidental statement of the *jamdudum cernimus*[1], in contradiction of the claim that the Pope should yield up his right in those of the ecclesiastical states which had been rent from him. The claim, of course, was shameless on the part of those who wrested them unjustly from him. But now it is made an abstract proposition, to be condemned by all Catholics. Incidental statements then are,

[9] The Dub. Rev., April, p. 487, in stating the doctrine, says, that "*under present circumstances* it is necessary for enabling the Pope freely to govern the Church without subjection to an earthly king." I do not find that limitation in any document, unless the writer means, "The circumstances ever since the division of the Roman Empire into various kingdoms," i.e., ever since the Pope has had temporalities. The ground alleged by the Pope would apply still more strongly to earlier times, since Persia was in continual antagonism to the Roman Empire; but then there were neither the temporalities nor the rule.

[1] Recueil, p. 440.

equally with the most formal propositions, matters of faith. Yet the proposition necessarily requires limitation. For, since S. Paul commands us to submit to "[2] the powers that be," this submission must often be paid to those who are kings "de facto," and not "de jure." On this principle the early Christians yielded obedience to each successive Emperor. This principle, which justified the obedience to William and Mary, justified obedience to the first and the third Napoleon, whom Popes recognized. The proposition is equivalent to the proverb, "Might makes right," and is, in fact, a denial of justice; yet S. Paul requires us to submit, as to a Divine ordinance, to authority, whose only "right" is its "might."

In this case, however, the pronouncement did relate to a moral rule. I instance it only as evidencing the extent of the claim of infallibility. Not only the main proposition, but every argument used in all these Allocutions is held to be equally infallible truth. This illustrates the compass of the infallibility claimed. It is an infallibility equal in extent to that of the Divine Scriptures; so that each sentence, however incidental, becomes, like the Word of God, a sacred text.

The doctrine of Papal infallibility, laid down by Bellarmine, is declared in the Encyclical of last year to be inadequate. Pius IX. distinctly rejects, as "[3] contrary to the Catholic dogma of the

[2] Rom. xiii. 1. [3] Recueil, p. 10.

full power divinely given to the Roman Pontiff by the Lord Christ Himself, of feeding, ruling, and governing the Universal Church, the audacity of those who, 'not enduring sound doctrine,' contend that, without [deadly] sin, and without any loss of Catholic profession, assent and obedience may be withheld from those judgments and decrees of the Apostolic See, whose object is declared to regard the general good of the Church, its rights and discipline, provided that that object does not touch upon dogmas of faith and morals." And this "assent" to every utterance of the Pope is required to all his "judgments," which "[4] determine concerning truth and falsehood," and that, under pain of mortal sin. "Cardinal Patrizi, writing," says the Dublin Review [5], "to the Catholics of Pius IX.'s own diocese, by his express sanction, and under his very eye, claims for the Encyclical, and, consequently, for every like expression of the Pope's mind, to be *the very word of God*, to be received on pain of forfeiting heaven."

[4] Dublin Rev., April, p. 445.

[5] Ib., p. 449. Cardinal Patrizi's words there translated are, "The faithful, who show themselves such in word and act, recognize in the voice of the Church's visible head *the very word of God* [Italics of the Dub. Rev.]. That head has authority to address the whole Church; and he who listens not to him declares himself as no longer appertaining to the Church, as no longer making part of Christ's flock, and accordingly as no longer having a right to the kingdom of heaven."

But then obviously the same must apply to all past ages; and all genuine judgments and decrees of all the past Bishops of Rome, upon whatever subject, whether bearing directly upon faith or morals, or upon the general good of the Church, will be to be regarded as "the very word of God." Had this doctrine been held in times past, the very existence of General Councils appears to me perfectly unintelligible. For, if the word of the Pope was "the word of God," there was no occasion for any declaration of the hereditary faith throughout the Church, such as the General Councils affirmed. Roman-Catholic writers will perhaps explain, where was the room for the appeal to Scripture and unbroken tradition as depositories of the faith, if the word of each successive Pope was itself "the word of God."

This extension of Papal Infallibility would, I should think, embarrass the defence of the system. For those who have denied the personal infallibility of the Pope, like Bossuet, have confined themselves to pointing out those cases in which any Pope seemed to have fallen into great and obvious error. Now, since every portion of the teaching of any Pope is to be infallible, it will apparently have to be shown how any statement of any Pope which has since been abandoned, is consistent with such infallibility. To take the one subject of prohibited marriages. S. Gregory the Great declares on the ground of Leviticus, c. 18, that marriage "with a sister-in-law is forbidden, because through her former union she became the brother's flesh." In a formal answer to an inquiry of S. Augustine of Canterbury, "at what degree of consanguinity may the faithful marry, and may marriage be contracted with step-mothers or sisters-in-law?" S. Gregory states, "it is necessary that, in order to marry lawfully, they should be in the third or fourth degree," i. e. second or third cousins, and prohibits, on ground of Divine law, marriage with the sister-in-law, as well as with the mother-in-law [6]. This was directly contradicted by the unhappy Borgia, (Alexander VI.,) who gave a dispensation to marry a sister-in-law [7] and an aunt [8]. But Pope Innocent III. answered formally, that in the degrees, prohibited by the Divine law, a dispensation *cannot be given*,—"dispensari non possit." He spoke, in three Epistles [9], of degrees prohibited "by Divine law," i. e. as explained, and according to the known use of the term, "the Levitical law." Cardinal de Turrecremata, acting by command of Pope Eugenius, pronounced that "the Pope *could* not dispense" when the Dauphin asked to be allowed to marry his deceased wife's sister.

[6] Epist., lib. xi. Indict. iv. Ep. 64, Interr. 6, ed. Ben.

[7] To Emmanuel, king of Portugal.

[8] To Ferdinand, king of Sicily. See Dr. Pusey's Evidence before the commission appointed to inquire into the law of marriage, n. 464 (as reprinted with Pref., pp. 26, 27).

[9] De Restit. Spol. c. Literas; de Consang. et Aff., cap. de Infidel.; de Divort., tit. Gaudemus, quoted ib. pp. 30, 31.

Then also Pope Celestine was equally infallible, when he declared that "[1] the charge of teaching has descended [from the Apostles] *equally* upon all Bishops. We are all engaged in it *by an hereditary right;* all we, who have come in their (the Apostles') stead, preach the name of our Lord to all the countries of the world, according to what was said to them, 'Go ye, and teach all nations.' You are to observe, my brethren, that the order we have received is a general order, and that He intended that we should all execute it, when He charged them with it, as a duty devolving *equally* upon all. We ought all to enter into the labours of those *whom we have all succeeded in dignity.*" Not, as people now say, the Pope alone, but according to Pope Celestine, "[2] the assembly of priests is the visible display of the presence of the Holy Ghost. He Who cannot lie has said, 'Where two or three are gathered together in My Name, there am I in the midst of them:' much more will He be present in so large a crowd of holy men, for the

[1] Letter to the Council of Ephesus. I have adopted the translation in Allies' Church of England, from Fleury, xxv. 47, Oxf. Tr. Fleury observes, "Thus Pope Celestine acknowledged that it was Christ Himself Who established Bishops in the persons of the Apostles, as the teachers of His Church; he places himself in their rank, and declares that they ought all to concur for the preservation of the sacred deposit of Apostolic doctrine."

[2] Ib. The passage just precedes the former, which is its sequel.

Council is holy in a peculiar sense, as the representative of that most holy synod of Apostles which we read of. Their Master, Whom they were commanded to preach, never forsook them. It was He Who taught them; it was He Who instructed them what they should teach others; and He has assured the world, that, in the persons of the Apostles, they hear Him."

Then S. Leo was infallible, when he spoke of his own clear statement of doctrine having been *confirmed* by the whole Church. "[3] What God has before decreed by our ministry, He *confirmed* by the irreversible assent of the whole brotherhood, to show that what was first put forth in form by the first See of all, and then *received by the judgment of the whole Christian world*, really proceeded from Himself."

Then S. Gregory the Great was infallible, when he spoke of the See of S. Peter as existing equally in Rome, Alexandria, and Antioch. "[4] And thus, though the Apostles be many, yet the See of the chief of the Apostles, which belongs to one, though it is in three places, alone prevailed in authority, by virtue of his chiefship. For it is he who exalted the See, in which he also condescended to take his rest, and finish the present life [Rome]. It is he

[3] Ep. 120, ad Theod., quoted by Bossuet, Gall. Orthod., n. 60, 61.

[4] Ep. ad Eulog. Episc. Alex., lib. vii., quoted by Allies, Eng. Ch., &c., p. 347.

who adorned the See, to which he sent the Evangelist, his disciple [Alexandria]. It is he who established the See in which he sat for seven years, though he was to leave it [Antioch]. Inasmuch then as *the See, over which* by Divine authority *three Bishops now preside*, is one man's and one, whatever good I hear of you, I lay to mine own account."

He was infallible when he said, "[5] Himself ['the Mediator of God and man'] is the Rock from which Peter received his name, and upon which He said that He would build His Church." He was infallible when he said, "[6] It is now *said to the universal Church*, 'Whatsoever thou shalt bind on earth,'" &c.

He was infallible when he said, "[7] No one of my predecessors ever consented to use so profane a term [as Universal Bishop], because plainly, if a single Patriarch is called universal, the name of Patriarch is taken from the rest. Wherefore let your Holiness in your letters *never call any one universal*, lest in offering undue honour to another, you should deprive yourself of that which is your due." "He endeavours to claim the whole to himself, and aims by the pride of this pompous language to subjugate to himself all the *members of Christ, which are joined together to the one sole*

[5] Opp., T. iii., p. 532 A, quoted by Allies, p. 348.
[6] T. iii., 387 E, Ib. p. 349.
[7] Epp., lib. v., 43, ad Eulog., quoted Ib. p. 354.

Head, that is, Christ. If this is allowed to be said freely, the honour of all Patriarchs is denied. And when, perchance, he who is termed universal, perishes in error, presently no Bishop is found to have remained in a state of duty. Stand firm, stand fearless; *presume not ever either to give, or to receive letters with this false title of Universal.*" "[8]I exhort and advise that no one of you ever give countenance to this name, ever agree to it, ever write it, ever receive a writing wherein it is contained, or add his subscription, but, as it behoves ministers of Almighty God, keep himself clear from such poisonous infection; since this is done to the injury and disruption of the whole Church, and, as we have said, in contempt of all of you. *For if, as he thinks, one is universal,* it remains that you are not Bishops." "[9]To consent to this nefarious name, is nothing else but to lose our faith." "[1]*I confidently affirm, that whoever calls himself, or desires to be called universal Priest, in his pride goes before Antichrist,—whoever he is, who desires to be called sole Priest,* he lifts himself up above all other priests." "[2]*Far from Christian hearts be that blasphemous name, in which the honour of all the Priests* [Bishops] *is taken away, while it is madly arrogated by one to*

[8] Ad Episc. Ill., lib. ix. 68. Allies, p. 355.
[9] Ad Sabinian., lib. v. 19, Ib.
[1] Ad Imp. Maur., lib. vii. 33. Allies, p. 356.
[2] Ad Imp. Maur., v. 20, Ib.

himself. Certainly, to do honour to the blessed Peter, chief of the Apostles, this was offered to the Roman Pontiff *per*[3] the venerable Council of Chalcedon. But no one of them ever consented to use this singular appellation, that *all Priests* [Bishops] *might not be deprived of their due honour by something peculiar being given to one.* How is it, then, that we seek not the glory of this name, though offered us, yet another presumes to claim it, though not offered?" "[4]If one Bishop be called universal, the whole Church falls

[3] Allies translated "per" "during," observing that S. Gregory used *per*, or *in*, not *a*. It was in fact used, not *by* but *in*, the Council by two Alexandrian Deacons who accused Dioscorus, and probably, as Van Espen conjectured (T. v. 477, Ib.), in opposition to the like title given to Dioscorus, Archbishop of Alexandria. Allies observes, however, "The title Ecumenical has been constantly since, and is now borne by the Patriarch of Constantinople; no doubt a very innocent meaning may be given it. The remarkable thing is, that Gregory has pointed out in such plain unmistakeable language a certain power and claim, which he inferred, rightly or wrongly, would be set up on this title Ecumenical, and which he pronounces to be a corruption of the whole constitution of the Church" (Ib., p. 360), and that he and his predecessors repudiated it. Thomassin would have it, that the Council, *by its silence*, authorized the title given in "those" requests (i. 1, 11, Ib.). It is obviously unreasonable to argue any thing from the fact that the Council did not interrupt the proceedings to protest against a title occurring in a petition, and very capable of an innocent sense.

[4] Ep. ad Anastas., lib. vii. 27. Ib. 358. This, as Allies remarked, is exactly the argument used for the infallibility of the Pope; i.e. that is claimed for him, which S. Gregory the Great, being also on the same principle infallible, rejected.

to pieces if that one, being universal, falls." "[5]Your Blessedness has also taken pains to tell me that you no longer write to certain persons those proud names which have sprung from the root of vanity, and you address me, saying, '*as you commanded*,' which word '*command*' I beg you to remove from my ears, because I know who I am, and who you are. For *in rank you are my brother*, in character my father. I did not, therefore, *command*, but took pains to point out what I thought advantageous. I do not, however, find that your Blessedness was willing altogether to observe the very thing I pressed upon you. For I said that you should not write any such thing *either to me*, *or to any one else*; and, lo! in the heading of your letter, directed to me, the very person who forbad it, you set that haughty appellation, calling me *universal Pope*, which I beg your Holiness to do no more, because *whatever is given to another more than reason requires, is so much taken away from yourself. I do not consider* that *an honour, by which I acknowledge that my brethren lose their own.* For my honour is the honour of the Universal Church. My honour is the unimpaired honour of my brethren. Then am I truly honoured, when the due honour is not denied to each one in his degree. *For if your Holiness calls me universal Pope, you deny that you yourself are*

[5] Ad Euseb. viii. 30.

what you admit me to be, universal." "[6] By this rash presumption the peace of the whole Church is disturbed, and the grace, poured out upon all in common, contradicted. Surely the Apostle Paul, hearing some one say, 'I am of Paul, I of Apollos, I of Cephas,' exclaimed in exceeding horror at this rending of the Lord's body, by which His members attached themselves, as it were, to other heads, saying, 'Was Paul crucified for you, or were ye baptized in the name of Paul?' If he then rejected the members of the Lord's body being subjected to certain heads, as it were, besides Christ, and that even to Apostles themselves, as leaders of parts, what will you say to *Christ, Who is, as you know, the Head of the Universal Church, in the examination of the last judgment,—you, who endeavour to subject to yourself, under the name of Universal, all His members?* Who, I say, in this perverse name, is set forth for imitation, but he, who despised the legions of angels joined as companions to himself, and endeavoured to rise to a height unapproached by all, that he might seem to be subject to none, and be alone superior to all? (quoting Isa. xiv. 13, 14.) Surely Peter, the first of the Apostles, is a member of the holy Universal Church; Paul, Andrew, John,—what else are they but the heads of particular communities? And yet all are members under One

[6] Ep. ad Joann., Patr. Const. v. 18. Ib. p. 360.

Head. And to comprehend all under one brief expression, the saints before the law, the saints under the law, the saints under grace,—all these, making up the body of the Lord, are dispersed among the members of the Church, and no one ever wished to be called universal. No one ever chose to be called by such a name; no one claimed to himself this rash appellation; lest, should he claim to himself *the glory of singularity in the rank of the High Priesthood*, he might seem to have denied it to all his brethren. What, therefore, dearest brother, will you say in that terrible examination of the judgment to come,—you, who covet to be called *not merely father, but common father?*"

Then S. Leo IX. was infallible when he said, "[7] The humility of those venerable Pontiffs [the Bishops of Rome], worthy of all imitation, considering that the chief of the Apostles is not found called universal Apostle, utterly rejected that proud name, *by which their equality of rank seemed to be taken away from all Prelates throughout the world*, in that a claim was made for one upon the whole."

Then Leo II. was infallible, who, when the Acts of the sixth General Council were sent him, wrote back, "[8] We anathematize alike those inventors of

[7] In Mansi, xix. 640. Allies, p. 363.
[8] In Mansi, xi. 1057. Allies, p. 381.

new error, Theodore, Bp. of Pharan; Cyrus, of Alexandria, Sergius, Pyrrhus, Paul, Peter, plotters against, rather than Prelates of the Church of Constantinople; *and also Honorius, who* did not illumine this Apostolical Church with the doctrine of Apostolic tradition, but, by a foul betrayal, *attempted to subvert its spotless faith.*"

Then S. Leo I. was infallible, when he rejected the 28th Canon of the Council of Chalcedon, which placed Constantinople in the second rank, next to Rome, as being "[9] opposed to the rules of the sacred Canons established at Nicæa," in that he says, "In all Ecclesiastical causes *we obey* those laws which the Holy Spirit, by means of the 318 Prelates, appointed for the peaceable observance of all Priests," &c. And Pope Adrian was infallible, when he said, "[1] He [the Patriarch of Constantinople] never could have ranked second, save for the authority of our holy Catholic and Apostolic Church, as is plain to all" (which rank, however, Constantinople took and had on the authority of the Canon, from the time of the Council itself).

Then, again, S. Leo was infallible, when he said, "[2] The Lord Jesus, then, was *alone* born innocent among the sons of men, because He *alone*

[9] Ep. 105, ad Pulcher. c. 3.

[1] In Mansi, xii. 1073. Ib., p. 399.

[2] Serm. v. de Nativ. Dom. Opp. i. 160. Par. 1675. Comp. S. Gregory I. (Mor. in Job, l. 18), "*He alone* was truly born *holy*, Who, that He might conquer corrupt nature, was not conceived in the ordinary way."

was conceived without the pollution of carnal concupiscence;" and Pope Gelasius[3], when speaking of "saints, who have by God's abundant grace easily overcome the vices of mortality," yet "attest that they were not yet so free from them, so that it should be peculiar (proprium) to that Immaculate Lamb to have had absolutely no sin, lest this should not seem to be a thing to be ascribed to Him alone, if any other saint *whatsoever* should be believed to have been free from offence." And Innocent III., when he said, "[4]That one (Eve) was produced without fault, but produced unto fault; but this one (Mary) *was produced in fault*, but produced without fault. That one was said to be *Eva;* to this one was said *Ave;*" and that "the Holy Ghost [5]*purified her soul from original sin in her mother's womb*," which is what Gregory XV. denied by implication, when he removed the word "sanctification" from the liturgies.

[3] Epist. adv. Pelag. Hær. Conc. x. p. 181, ed. Reg.

[4] In Solemn. Assump. Glor. semper Virg. M. Serm. 2. Opp. T. i. p. 151. Colon. 1575.

[5] The whole passage is (on S. Luke i. 35, *The Holy Ghost shall come upon thee*), "But forthwith the Holy Ghost came upon her; He had indeed before come *into her*, when, in her mother's womb, He *cleansed her soul from original sin;* but now too He came upon her, to cleanse her flesh from the 'fomes' of sin, that she might be altogether without spot or wrinkle. That tyrant, then, of the flesh, the sickness of nature, the 'fomes' of sin, as I think, He altogether extinguished, that *henceforth* any motion from the law of sin should not be able to arise in her members."—In Solemn. Purif. Glor. V. M., Serm. Unic., Opp. T. i. p. 107.

I have set down no difficulty which I do not myself think insurmountable. I see absolutely no way in which, upon the forbidden degrees, Alexander VI. can be reconciled with Gregory I., or how the acceptance of the sixth General Council, which anathematized Honorius as a heretic, by Leo II., and his own individual condemnation of him, are reconcileable with the doctrine of the infallibility of both, in all which they pronounce; or how the rejection of the position of Constantinople, on the ground of the immutable decrees of Nice by Leo I., is consistent with the statement of Adrian, that that see owed its position to Rome; or how S. Gregory's denunciation, not only of the title "Universal Bishop," but of what the title contained, and *that*, in any sense in which it could be supposed to be taken by the Patriarch of Constantinople, not as taken by that Patriarch only, but as unbecoming himself also, is compatible with the Ultramontane theories about the Pope. It is a characteristic of the word of God, that it "abideth for ever." Pius IX. could not, I should think, adopt the language of Gregory I., as to the marriage of those near of kin, or in denying his own right to be called "Universal Bishop," or to what the Patriarch of Constantinople meant to assume by that name; nor could he, I conceive, use the language of S. Leo or Gelasius, of Christ "*alone* being born innocent," or having *alone* had absolutely no sin; still less that of Innocent III., that "she was produced in fault," "producta in culpa," or that "she was sanctified from original sin in her mother's womb."

These are but specimens of inextricable difficulties, in which, I fear, the Roman Church would involve itself by acceding to this doctrine of the Papal infallibility, not only as to matters of faith and doctrine, but as to matters not connected therewith, and even as to historical facts. This theory is not yet put forth for actual acceptance, although it is contained in the Encyclical of 1864. It is even remarkable that, out of nineteen propositions of Nuytz [6], all are condemned except two, which related personally to the Pope. Of these, the bearings of the one I do not understand,—"The personal law of the Pontiff cannot be the sole law." The other is in direct terms, "The Pope is not infallible." However the contrary is implied in the Encyclical, yet the marked omission of this, among the propositions condemned in the Syllabus, seems to imply that Pius IX. does not yet think the state of minds in the Roman Church ripe for a formal decision. It seems a state of things analogous to that, when the Greeks had avowed their disbelief in any material fire of Purgatory, and that belief was not affirmed [7].

Dr. (now Archbishop) Manning, however, two

[6] Printed in the Recueil, &c., pp. 294-7, from *la Croce di Savoia.*

[7] See above, p. 197.

years ago, had so made the belief in the personal Infallibility of the Pope *on matters not directly relating to faith and morals* part of his Creed, that he made the temporal princedom of the Pope also a part of that Creed, and maintained that "non-intervention in the question of the temporal power of the Pope is essentially a denial of the divine institution of the Church." He declares "that the English government[8], as proclaiming the principle of non-intervention in the Roman question, thereby denies the Divine authority of the Church," as well as of "the Holy See, and its divine mission to the nations of the world."

He forgets, apparently, the good deeds of England in restoring Pius VII., and, on the ground of a doctrine, ruled by Pius IX. fourteen years before, and not as yet formally proposed to be accepted by the Church, he declares that "the English government[8], in proclaiming this principle of non-intervention, assumes an attitude towards Christianity and the Church, and towards the Christian society, which gives it at this moment the melancholy pre-eminence of being the most Anti-Catholic, and therefore, if not in its intentions, certainly in its influences and results, the most Anti-Christian power in the world." Happy condition of the world, when mere neutrality makes a civil power the most Anti-Christian in it!

And yet, according to another Ultramontane

[8] Introd. to Sermons on Eccl. Subj., 1863, p. 65.

writer, "[9] the Church's whole doctrine on his civil princedom, as regards its methodical expression, has been commenced, matured, and perfected by Pius IX."

Before, it was an open question, whether or no the civil princedom did, or did not, contribute to strengthen the spiritual power of the Pope. Pius IX. has adopted the arguments, and nearly the words of an eminent French Bishop of the seventeenth century in maintaining that it does, amid the mutual jealousies of the Roman Catholic powers[1]. There is much to be alleged for it. Contrariwise, it has been the occasion of very grievous ill. Witness the warlike and intriguing Popedom of Julius II. Fleury balances the evil and the good,

[9] Dublin Rev., April, 1865, p. 441.

[1] "Let us return to the Bishops, and conclude that it is only ignorance and grossness which made them think these seignories, united to their sees, were useful to maintain religion. I only see the Roman Church, where one can find a special reason for uniting the two powers. While the Roman Empire lasted, it contained in its vast extent nearly all Christianity; but after Europe was divided among many princes independent of each other, if the Pope had been the subject of any one of them, there would be ground to fear that the others would have had difficulty in owning him as a common father, and that schisms would have been frequent. One may believe then, that it was by a singular effect of Providence that the Pope found himself independent and master of a state, powerful enough not to be easily oppressed by other sovereigns; in order that he might be the more free in the exercise of his spiritual power, and be able to keep more easily the other Bishops within the bounds of their duty. This was the thought of a great Bishop of our time."—Fleury, Disc. 4, sur l'Hist. Eccl., n. 10.

and of himself evidently thought the evil to preponderate. He says[2]:—

"Leo IX. and the Popes who undertook to repair the ruins of the 11th century, and to restore the Roman Church to its lustre, wished also to re-establish its temporal powers, which they founded, first on 'the donation of Constantine,' then on those of Pepin, Charlemagne, Louis le Débonnaire, and Otho. All the world knows now what is the 'donation of Constantine;' and its falsehood is more universally recognized than that of the decretals of Isidore; but, at the time of these Popes, its truth was not questioned. S. Bernard presupposed it, when he said to Pope Eugenius that he was the successor not only of Peter, but of Constantine: it was known and received as early as the 9th century, and minds hardly began to be disabused of it toward the middle of the 15th. Even the Greeks received it, as appears in Balsamon, who quotes it entire, and claims to found upon it the prerogatives of the see of Constantinople.

"Geoffrey of Viterbo, speaking of 'the donation of Constantine,' in his abridgment of history dedicated to Pope Urban III., said that 'many thought that the Church had been more holy in the three first centuries, but that afterwards it was more happy.' Whoever advanced this beautiful sentence held sentiments very low, much beneath not the Gospel only, but human philosophy. Any one, ever so little above the common herd, sees readily that the pure happiness of this life is in virtue, not in riches; but one who believes the Gospel may not doubt it. Jesus Christ showed it by His example and His words; since, being the Lord of all riches and all human greatness, He sovereignly despised them, and bequeathed to His disciples poverty and suffering as their only inheritance. I still then return to this question; did they in the 11th century discover a wisdom unknown before, and were Leo IX. and Gregory VII. more enlightened than S. Leo or S. Gregory?

"These great Popes had not yet explored their archives

---

[2] Fleuri, Disc. 4, sur l'Hist. Eccl., n. 9.

enough to find there 'the donation of Constantine;' they were neither sovereign Princes nor temporal Lords, and yet they did not complain that any thing was wanting to their power, and had no time to spare, after their spiritual occupations. They were persuaded of the distinction of the two powers so well expressed by Pope Gelasius[3], when he said that Emperors themselves are subject to Bishops in the order of religion, and that in the political order Bishops, even he of the first see, obey the laws of Emperors."

Then, after defending the lawfulness of Ecclesiastical property in itself, even that "Bishops became Counts, Dukes, and Princes, as they still are in Germany: even (which is furthest from the institution) monks, whom their humility had put below all men, found themselves with subjects and vassals, and their Abbots gained the rank of Seignors and Princes," he adds, "All these rights are legitimate; it is not lawful to dispute them with the Church more than with laymen; and, to return to the Roman Church, it would be very unjust to dispute with it the sovereignty of Rome and of great part of Italy, of which it has been in possession for so many centuries, since most sovereigns have no better title than long possession.

"Arnold of Brescia, then, was rightly condemned, who stirred up the Romans against the Pope, maintaining broadly that the Clergy ought not to have seignories, lands, or real property, but ought to be supported solely by alms and voluntary offerings. Yet I own I should have been glad to find in authors of Arnold's time the reasons whereby they refuted his errors. For the two letters of S. Bernard to the Romans thereon are only pathetic declarations, in which he enters into no proof, and presupposes the rights of the Pope indisputable[4]. Then, too, he did not, as we saw, question 'the donation of Constantine.' This document, if true, established the fact and the special right of the Pope; and for the right of the Clergy in general, it was unquestionable, as I have just shown.

"But that most wise maxim of the Apostle should have

---

[3] Ep. 8, ad Anastas.

[4] Ep. 243, 244.

been remembered, that what is lawful is not always expedient[5]; and it should have been borne in mind (as did those of old) that the human mind is too limited to be equal to exercise at once spiritual and temporal power. At least, men ought to have respected the practice of those of old, and should have thought that, had the donation of Constantine been true, S. Leo and S. Gregory would have known it, and would have had good reasons for not using it, as it is certain they did not. The experience of more than 600 years has shown the great wisdom of their conduct. Bishops who are simply Bishops give little hold to the temporal power[6]; whereas it has continually grounds of quarrel with Bishops who are Lords. The holy Bishops liked but too well to have temporal goods to manage. We see how S. Chrysostom complained of it[7], and S. Ambrose discharged the care even of his patrimony on his brother Satyrus.

"When the Church established the rule of admitting those only into the Church who had embraced a life of continence, it had not only regard to the purity befitting the frequent approach of the sacred mysteries; she also wished that her chief ministers should be disengaged from the cares which marriage necessarily brings, and which made S. Paul say that the married man is divided between God and the world[8]. But what is the care of one family compared with the care of a whole state? What is the well ordering of a wife with five or six children compared with the government of 100,000 subjects?

"We are naturally more struck with sensible objects than with spiritual. A Prince is occupied in repressing crimes, preventing seditions and conspiracies against his person and state. He labours to preserve and defend it against its enemies without, and to avail himself of occasions of aggrandizing it. To this end he has to raise and maintain troops, fortify places, amass treasures, to provide for so many expenses. He must correspond with neighbouring princes, negotiate, make treaties of commerce and alliance. To a politician these

---

[5] 1 Cor. vi. 12.
[6] Synes., Ep. 57, and 121.
[7] Hom. 85, in S. Matt.
[8] 1 Cor. vii. 33.

things seem great and serious; ecclesiastical functions seem to him little, and almost childish. To chant in a church, walk in procession, act in ceremonies, catechize, appear to him ordinary occupations, of which the first comer is capable. What in his eyes is important and solid is to maintain his power, and weaken his enemies. He regards prayer, reading, meditation on Holy Scripture as occupations more befitting a monk than a statesman, and he finds no time to give to them. You have seen what fears S. Bernard had for Pope Eugenius, lest overwhelming business should hinder him from reflecting daily on his duties and himself, and he should fall at last into a state of obduracy.

"Perhaps you will believe that a Prince-Bishop will reserve to himself his spiritual functions, and will throw the burden of the government of the state on some layman. He will take care not to do this, for fear the layman should become the real Prince. Rather he will abandon the spiritual part to others; for he fears nothing from a Priest, a Grand-Vicar, a Suffragan Bishop. He will willingly leave them the study of theology and the canons, preaching, cure of souls, of which he will at most have a general account rendered to him; but he will have detailed accounts of his troops, his fortresses, his finances. He will give charge of them to other ecclesiastics, whom he will trust more than laymen, but who will be ecclesiastics in form, and in truth men of business. If you doubt it, see how the diocese and states of those so powerful princes of Germany and Poland are governed. You will see by this experience, that those of old were very wise, and that the alliance of temporal with the spiritual power was advantageous neither to religion, nor to the state. As to religion, it is evident that it was better upheld by Bishops who were purely Bishops, and exclusively occupied with spiritual things, as S. Ambrose and S. Augustine."

I have given this long extract from Fleury, to show the freedom with which this subject of the civil princedom used to be discussed, as being entirely an open question. At the commencement of the present Pontificate it still was so, even in Rome itself. Now a declaration of Pius IX., that "it came in the Providence of God," and that (which time alone could show) it is "necessary" to the due exercise of the Pope's spiritual authority, has made, we are told, a new article of faith, so that to take no side about it is to "deny the Divine authority of the Church."

For, unless the declaration of the Pope had made it a matter of faith, it is obviously a subject of speculation of human wisdom. Fleury says, that, before the existence of this civil princedom, the Popes did not feel any thing wanting to their spiritual power,—such power as they used before the false decretals. The event only could show that the loss of that civil princedom would impair what they have now. Unless Pius IX. be directly inspired by God, like one of the old Prophets, to foretell that its abandonment would involve its injury or forfeiture, it is a question of human wisdom still.

Secular policy hangs over the relations of the Pope to Pepin[1]; and what was originally a fief,

[1] The celebrated answer, which transferred the kingdom of France to Pepin, would hardly be a precedent. "Burghard, Bishop of Wirzeburg, and Folrad, Chaplain, were sent to Zachary Pope, asking as to the kings of France, who at that time had not the royal power, if it were well or no. And Zachary Pope sent word to Pepin, that it was better that he should be called king, who had the power, than he who remained without royal power; that order might not be disturbed, he commanded that Pepin should become king by Apostolic authority."—(Annal. Lauriss., A. 749. Pertz, Mon. Germ. i. 136.) The

held of a secular monarch, became, by what all acknowledge to have been a forgery, "the donation of Constantine,"—an abdication of the temporal government in behalf of the Pope. Its loss, had human ambition had its way, would have been an event of God's Providence, Whose love is never more visible than when He chastens.

The whole turns on the inspiration of that word "necessary." Unless the Pope is so inspired, that every word of his, even in matters not bearing on faith and morals, is "the very word of God," it does not follow that "non-intervention as to the question of the temporal power of the Pope is essentially a denial of the Divine institution of the Church."

The present Ultramontanes have apparently changed the old Ultramontane doctrine of the inerrancy of the Pope, i. e. that of his preservation from error, into that of Divine perpetual inspiration. We have, according to them, a perpetual revelation from God, disclosing new truths, as infallibly as if S. Peter, or S. Paul, or S. John were yet on this earth. One recently returned

next year, "Pepin, according to the custom of the Franks, was elected king and anointed by the hand of Archbishop Boniface of holy memory, and raised by the Franks to the throne at Soissons. But Hilderic, who was falsely called king, was shorn and sent into a monastery."—(Ib. A. 750.) In return, Pepin made the Pope Patricius of the Exarchate, yet under fealty to Pepin, and for the time owning the Greek Emperor. (See authorities in Gieseler, Ser. 3, Á. 1, c. 2, § 5.) This arrangement could not be said to be by the Providence of God, in any other way, than all acts of men are overruled by Him.

from Rome, had the impression that "some of the extreme" Ultramontanes, "if they do not say so in so many words, imply a quasi-hypostatic union of the Holy Ghost with each successive Pope [2]." It is well that they should know the impression which they give to those most disposed towards them. Archbishop Manning has recently said:—

"It is surely by a disposition of the Divine Head of the Church, that, in the heart of the 19th century, when both the intellects and wills of men have reached an excess of unbelief and of licence in matters of revelation, of morals, and of politics, the Vicar of our Lord, the Teacher of all Christians (as the Council of Florence entitles him), should twice in these last years have spoken with the voice of infallible truth, thereby testifying not only to the singular prerogative, which, as the first-fruits of grace, was bestowed upon the Immaculate Mother of God, and to the great constructive principles of morality and jurisprudence, on which the Christian world is founded, but also to the perpetual assistance of the Spirit of God, by whose light the Church and its Pontiffs, in all ages, now as in the beginning, discern and declare the limits of truth and falsehood. The dogmatic Bull of the Immaculate Conception, and the Encyclical of last year will, we believe, mark an epoch in the re-constitution of the Christian order of the world [3]."

I know not why Archbishop Manning has selected two occasions only in which Pius IX. spoke with authority. For the Syllabus quotes thirty-two documents, Allocutions, or Epistles [4], all as of equal and binding authority, besides the Encyclical

[2] The accurate writer, who reported this to me, observed in answer, "This seems to me to be Llamaism."

[3] Pastoral, as published in "The Weekly Register," June 17.

[4] Recueil des Alloc. consist. encycliques, &c. Paris, 1865.

Letter and Constitution on the doctrine of the Immaculate Conception. All being of equal authority, it would follow that all are "the very Word of God[3];" and that the Pope would be the perpetual Prophet of the Church, infallible, like Isaiah or Jeremiah, or the rest of "the goodly fellowship of the Prophets," in every enunciation of his, on any matters of the Church, even if contained in a letter to a single Bishop.

This would, indeed, mark an epoch in the history of the Church. It seemed to myself, as well as to Archbishop Manning, that the declaration of the Immaculate Conception of the Blessed Virgin as revealed truth, is calculated to be full of consequences, as entailing the transmutation of other "pious opinions" about her into truths necessary to salvation. According to the principles which have been put forth in regard to the recent Encyclical, that not only the main question ruled, but expressions, however seemingly incidental, are infallible truth, very much would have been so declared already. Then it would be infallible truth (though originally a mistake of copyists), that "[4] *she* was to bruise the serpent's head;" and that "[5] as Christ, the Mediator of God and man, having taken our human nature, destroying the handwriting of the decree which was against us,

[3] See above, p. 304. The inspiration must be extended to the writers of the Bulls also.

[4] Encycl., 1849, "Ubi primum." [5] "Ineffabilis," 1854.

nailed it to His cross, triumphing, so the Most Holy Virgin, conjoined with Him, by a most strait and indissoluble bond, exerting, *together with Him*, and through Him, *eternal enmity* against the venomous serpent, and triumphing most fully over him, *bruised his head with her immaculate foot;*" then it would be matter of faith, that "[5] she slew all heresies in the whole world;" that she is "[5] the safest refuge of all in peril;" that "[5] she has in her hands the affairs of our salvation;" that the present "[5] zeal of piety, religion, love" towards her is not enough; that she "[4] is placed between Christ and the Church;" that "[4] if we have any hope, grace, salvation, all redounds from her." It would be infallible truth that "[5] the Most Blessed Virgin is a tabernacle created by God Himself, and formed by the Holy Spirit," i. e. "[6] by God, as the one only cause, without any operation of an earthly father, as was Jesus. For either she was conceived after the manner of men, in which case she was created by God in the same way in which He creates all born by human generation, and then this would have no bearing upon her immaculateness; or she was created by God directly, in which case there would be no difference so far between her conception and that of our Lord." And, if these are matters of faith, it follows that every other statement, which I have mentioned

[6] The argument of Narvaez, Exam. Bullæ Ineffabilis, p. 90.

above, is virtually matter of faith too, or may be presently made so.

Larger principles may be involved, as when the Bull Ineffabilis alleges as a ground of a doctrinal decision that "the Church had been wont, both in Ecclesiastical offices and in the most holy Liturgy, to *transfer* the words, in which the Divine Scriptures speak of uncreated Wisdom and represent Its everlasting origin, to the origin of that Virgin too; which origin was fore-established by one and the same decree with the Incarnation of the Divine Wisdom." For, in order that this should be an argument, it must be, that applied meanings of Holy Scripture, not the literal only, should be grounds of belief, whereas S. Thomas says, "[7] All the senses (of Holy Scripture) are founded on one, viz. the literal, from which alone can an argument be drawn, not from what is said allegorically, as Augustine says [8]."

Yet larger is the statement that "in the Roman Church," i. e. in the Church at Rome, "alone has religion been guarded inviolably, and from it it is requisite that all other Churches should borrow the propagation of faith[9]." "But if this were so, to what end,"

[7] P. I, q. 1, art. 10, in resp. ad arg. 1.

[8] Ep. c. Vincent. Donat. Narvaez quotes to the same end Acosta, a Jesuit, "de Christo revelato," iii. 4.

[9] The writer of the "Ineffabilis" has applied to the Church at Rome, in relation to the rest of the Catholic Church, which has the faith already, words which Tertullian uses of the Church every where, in relation to those who, being newly converted, had

asked Narvaez, "to ask from the Churches every where, what was their doctrine, or rather their devotion, as to the Immaculate Conception?" There is, indeed, an answer, which seems to be that of the writer of the "Constitution," that it was indeed superfluous, but that it was done to give greater solemnity to the proceeding, "that we might deliver our supreme judgment as solemnly as possible." But then again General Councils are declared to be superfluous.

On the principle involved in the Encyclical of 1864 and the Syllabus, that historical statements, made by the Pope, are infallible[10], it would be infallible truth, that "this doctrine was in vigour from the most ancient times, and thoroughly implanted in the minds of the faithful, and marvellously propagated through the Catholic Church by the care and zeal of its sacred Bishops;" in which way it would be difficult to see how fathers, doctors, saints, and Popes, who denied it, were not guilty of heresy; that "the distinction between the first and second moment and instant of conception" (the active and passive conception) "was

to receive the faith in the first instance. The writer of the Constitution says, "Ex qua *traducem fidei reliquæ* omnes *Ecclesiæ mutuentur* oportet." Tertullian says, "The Apostlés founded Churches in every city, from which the other Churches thenceforth borrowed the propagation of faith and seeds of doctrine (*a quibus traducem fidei* et semina doctrinæ *cæteræ* exinde *Ecclesiæ mutuatæ sunt*), and are daily borrowing them, that they may become Churches."—De Præscr. c. 20, p. 468. Oxf. Tr. 9. See notes Ib.

[10] See above, pp. 293—295.

devised, in order to *weaken* the *doctrine* of the Immaculate Conception;" whereas notoriously it was part of the philosophy of the day, and was the first stage of that doctrine, and the distinction was insisted upon, in order to admit of the law of the transmission of original sin, without admitting that it ever passed upon the *soul* of Mary. Again, it would be infallible truth, that Alexander VII. spoke of the conception of Mary as immaculate from the first moment; whereas he spoke only "of her *soul*, in the first instant of its creation and infusion into the body," in conformity with the distinction which Pius IX. rejects. Then it is infallible that his "predecessors vehemently gloried to institute by their Apostolic authority the feast of the Conception in the Roman Church;" whereas Aquinas says, that "though the Roman Church does not celebrate the Conception of the Blessed Virgin, it *tolerates* the custom of some Churches who celebrate that festival [1];" or that the celebration of the festival of the Conception in itself proves that that Conception was immaculate, whereas the Feast of the Conception of S. John Baptist was inserted in the old Martyrologies, Roman, Usuard's, Adon's [2]; and the feast of the Blessed Virgin, "de Spasmo," though since abolished as unworthy of her, would imply that this too was sacred; and

[1] P. 3, q. 29, art. 2, arg. 3.
[2] Nat. Alex. H. E. Sæc. ii. Diss. 16, § 21.

Sixtus IV. would be infallible in approving an office of the Conception, which Pius V. was infallible in suppressing, as "being made up of fictitious testimonies of fathers and ecclesiastical writers, nowhere found in their works[3]." Or if the lessons in any service authenticated the belief of what was celebrated in it, then, as Narvaez says, it might become matter of faith, which "is piously believed, that she [the Blessed Virgin] comforts the sons who are enrolled in the society of the Scapular, who have used a little abstinence and a few prayers, with a truly motherly affection, while they are expiated by the fire of purgatory, and by her intervention brings them most speedily to their heavenly home." In the same way the stigmata of S. Francis, or the piercing of the heart of S. Theresa, might be equally matter of faith[4].

Faber anticipated "an Age of Mary," in comparison to which all previous devotion to her should be slight. Archbishop Manning anticipates a new era, in which the Pope should continually be declaring new matters of faith, to be believed without authority of Scripture or tradition, on his sole authority; or to be supposed to have authority of Scrip-

[3] Nat. Al. ib.

[4] The above instances are furnished by the very remarkable work of Narvaez, "Professor of Theology in the Order of Preachers, and in the University of Complutum" [Alcara de Henares], 1858, "Examen Bullæ Ineffabilis, institutum et concinnatum juxta regulas sanioris theologiæ," Paris, 1858,—a detailed and just criticism of "the writer of the Bull."

ture or tradition, solely because he declares them. Wherein these new eras should issue, whether in the coming of Christ, as Faber thought, or through a collapse of faith, (through the amount of that, taught as "of faith," which was no part of God's revelation to the Church,) in the coming of Anti-Christ, God only knows. Turrecremata spoke of old of those who, without any solid foundation, "[5] wish by flattery to equal the Popes, as it were, to God." The unhappy marriage of Henry VIII. with his brother's wife, with the yet more unhappy scruples of one who had no other scruples, and the rent of England, was the fruit of that flattery. More perilous yet may be men's strong convictions. Yet there are still those, although slightly spoken of and depreciated [3] by the Jesuits, who look with misgiving on the rapid course with which this new state of things is hurried on [6]. It was currently said at Paris, that an Archbishop said to an English advocate of the new system, "Compared to you, Monsignor, I am not Gallican, I am Scandinavian." To such we, to whom Bossuet or De Noailles would, we believe, have listened, stretch forth our hands. The strife with unbelief stretches and strains the

[5] "Adulando eos quasi æquiparare Deo." He is speaking of those who claimed for the Pope the right to dispense with the degrees of kin prohibited by the Levitical law. He calls them "Doctorculi." See Dr. Pusey's Evidence, &c., p. 35.

[6] It could only be under such strong conviction that Card. Wiseman said of the Abp. of Paris, who died in recovering his people at the barricades, "he was a mere Gallican."

powers of the Church every where[7]; Satan's armies are united, at least in their warfare against "the truth as it is in Jesus." Are those who would maintain the faith in Him alone to be at variance? On the terms which Bossuet, we hope, would have sanctioned, we long to see the Church united; to all who, in East or West, desire to see intercommunion restored among those who hold the faith of the undivided Church, we say, "This is not our longing only; this is impressed on our Liturgy by those who were before us; for this, whenever we celebrate the Holy Eucharist, we are bound to pray, that God 'would inspire continually the Universal Church with the Spirit of truth, unity, and concord.'" For this I pray daily. For this I would gladly die. "O Lord, tarry not."

[7] See in regard to the Roman Communion too, above, pp. 188, 189; below, pp. 357—359, 361, 362, 364, 365, 366, 367, 369, 370, 372, 373, 374, 378, 380, 382, 384, 386, 387, 402, 403, 406.

NOTES.

NOTE A. on P. 22.

The Faith, according to the Fathers, is contained in Holy Scripture.

The VIth Article does not touch upon the subject of the interpretation of Holy Scripture. The questions, "Who is its interpreter? by what rules the interpretation is to be guided? what is the value of tradition or of the consent of antiquity in its interpretation?" are wholly outside of its scope. Nor again, is it the question whether any things are true or right to be observed which are grounded on tradition, without being contained in, or provable by, Holy Scripture. The Article relates only to "Articles of Faith," and lays down the duty not of individuals, but of the Church, not to require to be believed as an Article of Faith, what cannot be proved by Holy Scripture. I have put down a few passages from the fathers, stating or implying that the faith is contained in Holy Scripture, as bearing out the Article, chiefly such as are quoted by Beveridge on the Articles, in Archbishop Ussher's Answer to a Jesuit (c. 2), and in the notes on S. Athanasius against the Arians (Library of the Fathers). Some I found in an American publication, taken, without acknowledgment, from Dean Goode's laborious collection in his "Divine Rule of Faith and Practice," vol. iii. pp. 29—211. From this I have selected some few. A fuller list may be seen in the work itself, with which, although written against us, we have, thus far, no controversy; since the question between the school of Dean Goode and ourselves was not, whether Holy Scripture is the ultimate source of faith (in which we were always agreed), but whether it is its own interpreter.

The argument from tradition was pressed upon heretics by S. Irenæus and Tertullian, that the Apostles committed orally their whole doctrine to the Churches which they founded. *S. Irenæus* begins his full argument of the value of tradition by asserting that what the Apostles delivered orally, *that* they wrote. "Through no other have we known the plan of our salvation, than through them, through whom the Gospel has come to us; which Gospel they then preached, but afterwards by the will of God delivered us in the Scriptures, to be the foundation and pillar of our faith."—iii. 1. 1. In like way *Tertullian:* "What we are, *that* are the Scriptures from the beginning; *of them we are,* before that any thing existed contrary to what we are" [heresy].—De Præscr. c. 38, p. 489, Oxf. Tr. And a little before, having given the beginning and end of the Apostles' Creed, "She (the Church) joineth the law and the prophets with the writings of the Evangelists and Apostles, and thence drinketh in her faith."—Ib. § 37. And negatively, "Whether all things were made of any subject-matter, I have as yet read nowhere. Let Hermogenes' shop show that it is written. If it is not written, let them fear that woe allotted to such as add or take away."—Adv. Herm. c. 22.

S. Clement of Alexandria,—"He hath ceased to abide a man of God and faithful to the Lord, who hath kicked against the ecclesiastical tradition, and bounded off to the opinions of human heresies; but he who hath returned from this deceit, listening to the Scriptures, and turning back his life to the truth, is perfected, being in a manner deified. For we have the Lord as the source of the doctrine, guiding the true knowledge from beginning to end, 'in divers portions and in divers manners,' through the Prophets, and the Gospel, and the Holy Apostles. But if any think he needs any other first principle, that which is indeed the first principle would not be kept. But he who is trustworthy in himself may well be worthy of trust through the Scripture and voice of the Lord, which, through the Lord, worketh to the good of man. For this [Scripture and voice of the

Lord] we use as a rule of judging and discovering things. But every thing which is judged is as yet untrustworthy, before it is judged; so that what hath need of being judged cannot be a first principle. With good reason then do we, embracing by faith the first principle being undemonstrated, taking *ex abundanti* the proofs concerning the first principle from the first principle itself, are instructed by the voice of the Lord to the acknowledgment of the truth. If it suffice not simply to express what we hold, but there is need to establish what we say, we do not wait for testimony from men, but we accredit the thing to be ascertained by the voice of the Lord, which is more trustworthy than any demonstration, yea, rather is the only demonstration. In which knowledge they who have only a simple knowledge of the Scriptures are faithful.—But if those who go after heresies also venture to use prophetic Scriptures, —first, they do not use all; secondly, not perfectly; not as the body and context of the prophecy suggests, but selecting what is said doubtfully, they draw it aside to their own opinions, plucking a few sayings here and there, not attending to what is signified by them, but using the bare phrases."—Strom. vii. 16, pp. 890, 1, Pott.

S. Hippolytus,—"There is one God, Whom we do not know otherwise than from the Holy Scriptures. For as, if any one would be disciplined in the wisdom of this world, he could not obtain it without reading the doctrines of philosophers; so, whoever of us would practise piety towards God, shall not learn it except from the Divine Scriptures. Whatever, then, the Holy Scriptures set forth, let us know; and whatever they teach, let us learn; and as the Father willeth to be believed, so let us believe; and as He willeth the Son to be glorified, so let us glorify Him; and as He willeth the Holy Ghost to be given, so let us receive Him. Not according to our own will, nor according to our own sense, nor doing violence to the things given by Him, but as He willed to teach us by the Holy Scripture, so let us understand them."—c. Noet. n. 9, Opp. T. i., pp. 238, 9.

Origen,—"In the two Testaments every word appertaining to God may be sought and discussed, and from them may all knowledge be obtained. But if there be any thing, upon which Divine Scripture decideth not, no other third Scripture ought to be received as an authority for any knowledge; but what remaineth we should commit to the fire—i. e., reserve to God. For God doth not will that we should know all things in this present life."—In Lev. Hom. v. n. 9, ii. 212, ed. De la Rue.

S. Dionysius of Alexandria,—He praises the Millenarians of the Arsinoite, that "very conscientiously and guilelessly, and with childlike hearts towards God, they received the things established by proofs and teaching of the Holy Scriptures."—In Euseb., H. E. vii. 24.

S. Cyprian declares the agreement with Holy Scripture to be the test of genuine tradition. "Whence is that tradition? Whether does it descend from the authority of the Lord and the Gospel, or does it come from the injunctions and epistles of the Apostles? For that we are to do what is written, God testifieth and admonisheth, saying to Joshua, 'This book of the law shall not depart out of thy mouth,' &c. (Jos. i. 8.) Likewise the Lord, sending His Apostles, directs that the nations should be baptized and taught to observe all things whatsoever He had commanded. If, then, it is commanded in the Gospels, or contained in the Epistles or Acts of the Apostles, then be this holy and Divine tradition preserved."—Ep. 74, ad Pomp., n. 2, p. 261, Oxf. Tr.

"What presumption to prefer human tradition to Divine ordinances, and not to perceive that God is displeased and angered, as often as human tradition relaxes the Divine command" (citing Isa. xxix. 13; S. Matt. xv. 8, 9; S. Mark vii. 9; 1 Tim. vi. 3—5).

"It behoves the priests of God, who keep the Divine commandments, that, if the truth has in any respect tottered and faltered, we should go back to our Lord as our Head, and to the Evangelic and Apostolic tradition."—Ib. n. 13, p. 267.

S. Athanasius, admitted as a deacon to defend the faith at the Council of Nice, who witnesses so often that the Church there declared what it had received, states also the sufficiency of Holy Scripture:—"Vainly then do they [the Arians] run about with the pretext that they have demanded Councils for the faith's sake, for Divine Scripture is sufficient above all things; but if a Council be needed on the point, there are the proceedings of the Fathers, for the Nicene Bishops did not neglect this matter; but stated the doctrine so exactly, that persons reading their words honestly, cannot but be reminded by them of the religion towards Christ announced in Divine Scripture."—Conc. Arim. et Sel. c. i. § 8, p. 81, Oxf. Tr. See further, above, p. 43.

"Perhaps being refuted as touching the term Ingenerate also, they will say, according to their evil nature, 'it behoved, as regards our Lord and Saviour Jesus Christ also, to state from the Scriptures what is there written of Him, and not to introduce un-Scriptural expressions.' Yes, it behoved, say I too; for the tokens of truth are more exact as drawn from Scripture than from other sources; but the ill disposition and the versatile and crafty irreligion of the Eusebians, compelled the bishops, as I said before, to publish more distinctly the terms which overthrow their irreligion."—Nicene Def. c. vii. § 6, p. 57, Oxf. Tr.

"Such is their [the Arian] madness and temerity. But our faith is right, issuing from Apostolic teaching and tradition of the fathers, confirmed from both the New and Old Testament," which he proceeds to quote.—Ep. ad Adelph., § 6, T. i. p. 914, 5, Ben.

"The holy and inspired Scriptures are sufficient of themselves for the preaching of the truth, yet there are also many treatises of our blessed teachers composed for this purpose."—Cont. Gent. init.

"Since Divine Scripture is more sufficient than any thing else, I recommend persons who wish to know fully concerning these things (the doctrine of the blessed Trinity) to read the Divine oracles."—Ad Ep. Æg. 4.

"The Scriptures are sufficient for teaching; but it is good for us to exhort each other in the faith, and to refresh each other with discourses."—Vit. S. Anton. 16.

S. Cyril of Jerusalem, having given a summary of the Creed, adds, "This seal have thou ever on thy mind, which now by way of summary has been touched on in its heads, and, if the Lord grant, shall hereafter be set forth according to our power, with Scripture-proofs. For concerning the Divine and most sacred Mysteries of the Faith, we ought not to deliver even the most casual remark without the Holy Scriptures; nor be drawn aside by mere probabilities and the artifices of argument. Do not then believe me, because I tell you these things, unless thou receive from the Holy Scriptures the proof of what is set forth; for this salvation, which is of our faith, is not by ingenious reasonings, but by proof from the Holy Scriptures."—Lect. iv. 17, p. 42, Oxf. Tr.

"Take thou and hold that faith only as a learner and in profession, which is by the Church delivered to thee, and is established from all Scripture. For since all cannot read the Scriptures, but some, as being unlearned, others by business, are hindered from the knowledge of them; in order that the soul may not perish for lack of instruction, in the Articles which are few we comprehend the whole doctrine of the Faith. This I wish you to remember even in the very phrase, and to rehearse it with all diligence among yourselves, not writing it on paper, but by memory graving it on your heart as on a monument.

"This I wish you to keep all through your life as a provision for the way, and besides this to receive no other ever: whether we ourselves should change and contradict what we now teach; or some opposing Angel, transformed into an Angel of light, should aim at leading you astray. 'For though we or an Angel from heaven preach any other Gospel unto you than that ye have received, let them be accursed.' And for the present, commit to memory the Faith, merely listening to the words; and expect at the fitting season the proof of each of its parts from the Divine Scriptures. For the Articles of the Faith were not composed at the good pleasure of men; but the most important points, chosen from all Scripture, make up the one teaching of the Faith. And, as the mustard-seed in a little grain contains many branches, thus also this Faith, in a few words, hath enfolded in its bosom the whole knowledge of godliness contained both in the Old and New Testaments. Behold, therefore, brethren, and 'hold the traditions' which ye now receive, and 'write them on the table of your hearts.'"—Lect. v. § 12, p. 58, Oxf. Tr.

S. Hilary, in rejecting a statement from the Book of Enoch:— "Let us pass by this. For the things which are not contained in the book of the law, we ought not even to know" (*in Ps.* 132, n. 6), and in the context of the celebrated passage in which he speaks of the abuse of Holy Scripture by heretics, he said to Constantius, "In so far I truly admire thee, Lord Emperor

Constantius, for thy blessed and religious wish, in that thou desirest the faith *only according to that which is written*, and hastening, as is meet, to the very words of the Only-Begotten God, that your breast, which can contain an Emperor's cares, may also be filled with the Divine words. This whoso rejecteth is Anti-Christ, and whoso doth it in pretence, is anathema. But this one thing I ask—that in the presence of the Synod (of Constantinople), which is now at variance about the faith, thou wouldest vouchsafe to hear me as to the Evangelic Scriptures, that I may speak with thee in the words of my Lord Jesus Christ, whose exile or Bishop I am,—'God,' according to the prophet, 'beholdeth him who is humble and trembleth at His word.' Emperor, thou seekest the faith; hear it, not out of new writings, but out of the Books of God."—Ad Const. Aug. ii. n. 8.

S. Epiphanius,—"The children of the Church have received from their holy Fathers, that is, the holy Apostles, to guard the faith; and withal to deliver and preach it to their own children. . . . . Cease not, faithful and orthodox men, thus to speak, and to teach the like from the Divine Scriptures, and to walk, and to catechize, to the confirmation of yourselves and those who hear you; namely, that holy faith of the Catholic Church, as the holy and only Virgin of God received its custody from the holy Apostles of the Lord; and thus, in the case of each of those who are under catechizing, who are to approach the holy Laver, ye ought not only to preach faith to your children in the Lord, but also to teach them expressly, as your common mother teaches, to say, 'We believe in one God,'" &c., adding the Niceno-Constantinopolitan Creed in full.—Ancorat. 120, T. ii. p. 122.

S. Optatus,—"Why knock at heaven, when we have a Testament here in the Gospel? For here things earthly may be rightly compared with things heavenly. The case is, as when a Father, having many sons, as long as he is with them, himself directs them, a Testament is not yet necessary. So Christ, as long as He was present on earth (although now, too, He fails us not), for the time commanded the Apostles whatever was necessary. But as an earthly father, when he feels himself on the verge of death, fearing lest, after his death, the brothers should quarrel and go to law, calls witnesses, and transfers his will from his dying breast to tables which shall long endure, and, if any contention arises among the brothers, they do not go to the tomb, but ask for the Testament, and he who resteth in the tomb speaketh silently from the tables,—He Whose is the Testament is alive in heaven. So then let His Will be sought in the Gospel as in a Testament."—(*As to the re-baptizing of Heretics.*)—De Schism. Don. v. 3.

S. Basil, in his treatise on the faith, sets out with saying, "What I have learnt from the God-inspired Scripture, this would I set before you as is pleasing unto God. I have thought it suited to our common end, in the simplicity of a sound faith, to fulfil the desire of your love in Christ, saying what I have been taught from the God-inspired Scripture, being sparing as to names and words, which are not actually introduced into the Divine Scripture, yet which preserve that meaning which lieth in Scripture. But those which, besides the language being foreign to Scripture, had a meaning also foreign to it, and which cannot be found used by the saints, these I shrank from altogether, as foreign and alien to godly faith. For faith is an unhesitating assent to the things which we have heard in the fulness of the truth of the things preached by the grace of God.—But if the Lord is faithful in all His words,—it is a manifest falling from faith, and sin of pride, either to reject any thing written, or to introduce any thing unwritten, since the Lord Jesus Christ saith, 'My sheep hear My voice, and a stranger will they not follow, but will flee from him, for they know not the voice of strangers;' and the Apostle, under an example taken from men, strongly forbiddeth to add or take away any thing in the God-inspired Scriptures, in that he says, 'Now a man's covenant, when confirmed, no man annulleth or addeth thereunto.'"—De Fide, n. 1, Opp. ii. 223, 224.

"What then our Fathers said, we too say, that the Glory is common to the Father and the Son, wherefore we present our giving of glory to the Father with the Son. But this doth not suffice us, that it is the tradition of the Fathers. For they too followed the mind of the Scripture, taking as their first principle those testimonies which, a little while ago, we set before you from the Scripture."—De Spir. S. c. 7, n. 16, T. iii. p. 13.

And, though not speaking of faith, he gives it as a rule, "That every word or thing ought to be confirmed by testimony of God-inspired Scripture, to the full conviction of the good and the shaming of the evil."—Reg. 26. Ib. ii. p. 256.

"What is the character of faith? An unhesitating conviction of the truth of the God-inspired words. What is the character of the faithful? With the same conviction to embrace the meaning of what is said, and not to venture to annul or to add. For if every thing which is not of faith is sin, as the Apostle says, and faith is from hearing, and hearing through the Word, every thing which is without the God-inspired Scripture, being not of faith, is sin."—Reg. 80, c. 22. Ib. p. 317.

S. Gregory of Nyssa,—"'I think we ought to inquire, over and above what has been said, whether the God-inspired teachings agree with these things.' She said, 'And who would contradict this, that that alone is to be set down as truth, to which the seal of the teaching of the Gospel is added?'"—De Anima et Res. T. iii. p. 207.

"But since with them [the philosophers], the theory as to the soul was carried out at their own pleasure, according to what seemed to them consequential, but we have no such power of saying whatever we will, seeing that we use Holy Scripture as a canon and law of all doctrine, we, of necessity, looking to it, receive *that* alone which agreeth with the purport of what is written."—Ib. p. 201.

"Since the God-inspired testimony is the safe criterion of truth as to every doctrine, I think it well to accredit our teaching too by annexation of the Divine."—c. Eunom. L. i. T. ii. p. 346.

"That God here (Gen. xi.) addressed the ministering Angels, since it is rested on no testimony of Scripture, we have rejected as false."—De Cognit. Dei, in Euthym. Panopl. Tit. 8, B. P. T. 19, p. 49.

S. Ambrose,—"What we do not find in Holy Scripture, how can we use?" [not of doctrine.]—De Off. i. 23, § 102.

"Why labour we so much for the world—who ought to serve no other save this Lord? Here then there is no second, [as the Arians called our Lord]. I adduce this testimony. I read that He is first; I read that He is not second. Let those who say that He is second, show it by Scripture."—De Inst. Virg. c. xi. § 70, ii. 265, Ben.

"They say, that the Son is 'unlike' the Father; we deny it;

yea, rather, we are horrified at the word. But I would not have you trust my argument, sacred Emperor, or my discussion. Let us interrogate the Scriptures; let us interrogate the Apostles; let us interrogate the Prophets; let us interrogate Christ."—De Fide, i. 6, n. 41, T. ii. p. 451.

"I wish not to be myself believed; let Scripture be recited."—De Inc. Dom. Sacr. c. 3, n. 14, ii. 706.

S. Jerome,—"But as we do not deny what is written, so what is not written we reject. That God was born of a Virgin, we believe, because we read. That Mary married after that Birth we believe not, because we read not."—Adv. Helvid. § 19, Opp. ii. 222, Vall.

"The doctrine of the Church, which is the house of God, is found in the fulness of the Divine Scriptures."—Ep. 30, ad Paulam, § 6, i. 147.

"Other things, too, which they [the heretics] find and invent without the authority and testimonies of the Scriptures, as if by Apostolical tradition, the sword of God [i. e. His living Word] strikes through."—On Hagg. i. 11, T. vi. p. 749.

"The Church of Christ, which hath a goodly dwelling-place, and possesseth Churches in the whole world, is conjoined by unity of spirit, and hath the cities of the Law, the Prophets, the Gospel, the Apostles, hath not gone forth from her boundaries, i. e. the Holy Scriptures, but retains the possession which she took."—In Mic. i. 10, T. vi. pp. 444, 5.

"That treasure, in which are hidden all the treasures of wisdom and knowledge, is either God the Word, Who seemeth hidden in the flesh of Christ, or Holy Scripture, in which is laid up the knowledge of the Saviour."—In S. Matt. xiii. 44, T. vii. 97.

"It is asked how God made known to us the mystery of His will in all wisdom and knowledge. And first this is to be taken simply, that the mystery of His will is our redemption through the Blood of His Son, and remission of sins according to the riches of His grace, wherewith He hath abounded in us. Then that through His Scriptures He hath made known to us all mysteries, how He first made heaven and earth, and all things therein," &c.—In Ep. ad Eph. i. 9, p. 555.

Theophilus of Alexandria,—[Origen] "not knowing that it is the suggestion of a dæmoniacal spirit to follow the sophism of human minds, and to think any thing Divine outside of the authority of the Scriptures."—Epist. Pasch. i. (96 among S. Jerome's), § 6, T. i. p. 560, Vall.

"It is one thing, if they can teach out of the Scriptures that God the Word had His Soul before He was born of Mary, and that it was called His Soul before He took flesh. But if they are constrained by the authority of the Scriptures and reason itself, to admit that Christ had not a soul before He was born of Mary (for at the assumption of man, His Soul also was assumed), they are plainly convicted of saying that the same soul was, and was not, His. But let these madmen cease from the impiety of new dogmas. Let us, following the rule of the Scriptures, proclaim, with entire confidence of heart, that neither His Flesh nor His Soul were, before He was born of Mary."—Ep. Pasch. ii. n. 8 (Ep. 98 in S. Jer.), i. 585.

Rufinus,—After giving the catalogue of the Books of the Old and New Testament, he says: "These are they which the Fathers included within the canon, and out of which they willed the assertions of our faith to be established."—Comm. in Symb. Apost. § 37, p. 110, ed. Vallars.

"These things have been delivered unto us by the Fathers, which, as I said, it seemed opportune to set down in this place for the instruction of those who are receiving the first elements of the Church and of the faith, that they may know from what fountains they are to draw the draughts of the Word of God."—Ib. § 38, p. 101.

Perhaps *Gregory of Bætica*, anyhow before S. Augustine,—"Since, then, thou knowest this unity of substance in the Father and the Son, by authority, not only of the Prophets, but of the Gospel also, how sayest thou that the ὁμοούσιον is not found in the Divine Scriptures, as though the ὁμοούσιον were any other than what He saith, 'I came forth from the Father,' and 'I and the Father are one,' or what the Prophets plainly intimated as to the Substance of God?"—De Fide Orthod. c. 5, App. S. Ambr. ii. pp. 351, 2.

S. Augustine,—"Albeit the Lord Jesus did many things, not all are written; as this same S. John the Evangelist testifies that the Lord Christ both said and did many things which are not written: only those were selected to be written which were seen to suffice for the salvation of them that believe."—Hom. 49, in S. John, § 1, p. 649, Oxf. Tr.

And after enumerating the books of Holy Scripture, "In all these books, they who fear God and are meek through piety, seek the Will of God. Of this work and labour the first observance is, to know those books, if not so as to understand them, yet by reading either to commit them to memory, or at least not to be altogether unacquainted with them. Then those things which are set down plainly in them, whether precepts as to life, or rules of faith, are to be searched into diligently and wisely; of these any one will find the more, in proportion to his capacity and intelligence. For in those things which are set down plainly in the Scriptures, are found all things which contain faith, and the way of life, i. e., hope and charity."—De Doctr. Christ. ii. 9, § 14.

"He made the authors of the Divine Scriptures the mountains of Israel. Feed there, that ye may find safety. Whatsoever ye hear thence, let that savour well unto you; whatsoever is without, reject. Wander not in the mist; hear the voice of the Shepherd; gather yourselves to the mountains of Holy Scripture; *there* are the delights of your heart; *there* is nothing poisonous, nothing alien; it is a most rich pasture; do ye only come sound yourselves."—Serm. 46, de Past. c. 11, § 24, Opp. v. 238.

"He, having spoken first by the Prophets, then by Himself, afterwards by the Apostles, as much as He judged to be sufficient, formed also the Scripture which is called Canonical, of most eminent authority, which we trust as to those things, which it is not expedient to be ignorant of, and which yet we are not equal to know of ourselves."—De Civ. Dei, xi. 3, T. vii. p. 273.

"It [the city of God] believes the Holy Scriptures, both the Old and the New, which we call Canonical, from which the faith itself is derived whereby the just liveth, by which we walk without doubting, so long as we are absent from the Lord; which being safe and certain, we may without just blame doubt as to some things, which we have not perceived by sense or reason, and which have not become evident to us by Canonical Scriptures, nor have come to our knowledge by witnesses whom it were absurd to disbelieve."—Ib. xix. 18. Ib. p. 562.

"Being about to speak of the day of the last Judgment of God, we ought first to lay down the divine testimonies as the foundation of the building."—Ib. xx. 1. Ib. p. 562.

"Read this to us from the Law, from the Prophets, from the Psalms, from the Gospel itself, from the Apostolic Epistles; read, and we believe."—De Unit. Eccles. c. 6, ix. 345.

"Accordingly, whether as to Christ or as to His Church, or any other thing which belongs to your faith and life, I say not 'we' (seeing we are in no wise to be compared to him who said 'although we'), but I say what he added, 'if an angel from heaven preach to you any thing besides what ye have received,' in the Scriptures of the Law and the Gospel, let him be anathema."—c. litt. Petil. iii. 6, T. ix. p. 301.

S. Chrysostome,—"With good cause He calleth the Scriptures a 'door,' for they bring us to God, and open to us the knowledge of God; they make us sheep, they guard us, and suffer not wolves to come in after us. For Scripture, like some sure door, barreth the way against heretics, placing us in a state of safety as to all which we desire, and not allowing us to wander; and if we undo it not, we shall not easily be conquered by our foes. By it we can know all, both those which are, and those which are not shepherds. But what is 'into the fold?' It refers to the sheep and the care of them. For he that useth not the Scriptures, but climbeth up some other way, i. e. who cutteth out for himself another and an unusual way, 'the same is a thief.' Seest thou from this too, that Christ agreeth with the Father, in that He bringeth forward the Scriptures? On which account also He said to the Jews, 'Search the Scriptures,'" &c.—Hom. 59, on S. John x. 1, p. 513, Oxf. Tr.

"All Scripture is given by inspiration of God, and is profitable, &c. 'For doctrine.' If we ought to learn or be ignorant of any thing, thence shall we know it; if to disprove what is false, this too thence; if to be corrected and taught wisdom—that is, if any thing is lacking and hath to be added, 'that the man of God may be perfect,' he saith, to this end was the exhortation of Scripture.—Thou hast, he says, the Scriptures instead of me: if thou willest to learn any thing, thence mayest thou. But if he wrote these things to Timothy, who was filled with the Spirit, how much more to us! 'Thoroughly perfected to all good works,' he saith, not simply partaking, but thoroughly and accurately furnished."—On 2 Tim. Hom. ix. § 1, T. xi. pp. 714, 715.

S. Isidore of Pelusium,—"That these things are so, let us look into the canon of truth, I mean the Divine Scriptures. What then saith it?"—Epistt. L. iv. Ep. 114, p. 475.

"The teaching as to the fall [of souls, i. e. Origen's] not being true, I deem, yet seeming to be plausible, many other things appear to overthrow, but two especially, in my judgment: one, that it is not clearly taught in the Scriptures."—Ib. 163, against Origen, beg. p. 504.

S. Cyril of Alexandria,—"We say that the 'fountains of salvation' are the holy Prophets, Evangelists, and Apostles, who cause to gush forth on the world the saving word which is from above and from heaven, the Holy Spirit supplying them, and gladden the whole under heaven."—De Recta Fide, ad Reg. ii. init. Opp. v. 2, c. p. 128.

"Since we must needs follow the Holy Scriptures, nowhere going out of the track of what they prescribe, let us say, in what way God the Father is said to crown the Son with glory."—Ib. p. 168.

"Those who oppose must either condemn to disgrace those of old, and call those who taught the world the mysteries of the faith, false teachers, to whom Christ Himself said, 'Go, teach all nations;' or if they shudder at this, they must choose to be right-minded about Christ, and bidding farewell to their own ignorances, hold fast to the Holy Scriptures, and following the inerrant path of the saints, go straight to the Truth itself."—De Recta Fid. ad Imp. p. 6.

"A. What right-minded person can fail to see, my friend, that you bale up empty words and heap up a cold profitless multitude of ideas, unless you point out the writings of the saints as harmonizing with what you say? For we will follow, not those who will and are wont to pour out of their own ideas, but those who speak from the mouth of the Lord, as is written. B. Thou sayest right. Well, then, Divine David sang," &c.—De S. Trin. Dial. iii. T. v. 1, p. 477.

"It is best then, O Hermias, not to be flurried with the petulances of others, since they would lead us to an undistinguishing mind, but to make the words of the Divine speakers the straight and unswerving rule of faith. For it must be right to accept no others than these self-same, and to say, 'It is not ye who speak, but the Spirit of your Father which speaketh in you.'"—Ib. Dial. iv. init. p. 504.

Taken in part from *S. Cyril*, but later:—"Creation itself, and its preservation and government, proclaim the greatness of the Divine Nature. And first through the law and the prophets, then through His only-begotten Son our Lord and God and Saviour Jesus Christ, He hath made manifest the knowledge of Himself according to our capacity. All things then which are delivered to us through the law and the prophets and Apostles we receive, and know, and confess, not seeking any thing beyond them. For it is impossible to say or even conceive any thing about God, besides what has been Divinely said to us by the Divine oracles of the Old and New Testament."—De Sacrosancta Trinitate, init. Opp. T. vi. P. 3, p. 2.

Theodoret,—"From this we are taught not to quench the Spirit, but to stir up the grace which we have received, and to introduce nothing alien into Holy Scripture, but to be content with the teaching of the Spirit, and to abominate heresies, of which some have added fables to the Divine word, others have preferred their ungodly thoughts to the mind of Scripture."—Quæstt. in Lev. 9. 9.

Orth.—"Bring me not human thoughts or syllogisms. For I obey the Divine Scripture alone."—Dial. c. x. T. iv. p. 18, Sch.

Eran.—"How could one argue with those who deny the taking of the flesh, or the soul, or the mind, except by producing the proofs from the Divine Scripture? And how could one refute those who strain to lessen the Divinity of the Only-Begotten, than by showing that Holy Scripture spake some things as to His Divinity, others as to the Incarnation? *Orth.*—This saying is true. For it is ours; nay, rather that of all who have kept the Apostolic rule unbent."—Dial. ii. p. 113.

"I would not say it, persuaded by human reasonings. For I am not so rash as to say any thing on which Divine Scripture is silent."—Ib. p. 122.

S. Proclus,—"Let faith, being the head of all virtues, remain unadulterated, introducing nothing spurious from human reasonings, nor defiled by profane novelties of words, but remaining within the bounds of the Gospels and Apostles, no one venturing to discuss any thing amiss in addition to that whereby we have been saved, and which, in Baptism, we subscribed with our tongue. For the sublimity of faith repels every attack and venture of presumption, not only of man, but even if carried aloft by any spiritual nature, the blessed Paul crying aloud, 'If we or an angel from heaven preach to you any other Gospel than what ye have received, let him be anathema.' Let us guard then with vigilance what we have *received*, keeping the eye of the soul open and steadily fixed on the treasure of faith. What, then, have we *received from the* Scriptures, but altogether this, that God created the universe by the Word?"—Epist. ad Arm. App. Conc. Eph. iii. 1740, 1, Col.

S. Leo,—"Into this folly they fall, who, when they are hindered by some obscurity from knowing the truth, betake themselves, not to the voices of the Prophets, not to the writings of the Apostles, not to the authorities of the Gospels, but to themselves. And therefore they became teachers of error, because they had not been disciples of the truth. For what additional instruction did he acquire from the Divine books of the Old and New Testament, who did not grasp even the beginning of the Creed?"—Ep. 28, ad Flavian.

NOTE B. ON P. 127, sqq.

Doubts among the Roman Catholic Bishops, as to making the doctrine of the Immaculate Conception of the Blessed Virgin an Article of faith.

In giving more fully the answers of some of the Bishops, who demurred to, doubted about, or objected to, the definition of the doctrine of the Immaculate Conception of the Blessed Virgin as an Article of faith, it is right to premise two points; 1. That no one of them objected to the definition, on the ground that he did not himself believe in it. All had been educated from infancy in that belief, as much as in the belief in the Holy Trinity or the Incarnation; they had been taught it in the seminaries; they held it undoubtingly. 2. All were ready to submit their own opinion as to the expediency of making it a matter of faith to the authority of the Pope; and to receive what he decreed as "de fide." They are then opinions which have passed away, since the doubts or objections were ignored. Yet they have an historical interest, as showing how the subject was looked upon by some distinguished Bishops, how the influence of Roman decisions upon those who are not in their communion was felt by some; what principles were held by *some* as to the evidence required to establish an Article of faith, or what evidence was supposed to exist as to this, and, in part perhaps, what hopes may be entertained of meeting upon common principles.

France.—1. *The late Archbishop of Paris*, embodying the opinion of his predecessor. His full answer was written Aug. 25, 1849 (Pareri, &c., ii. 26—45), but withheld until Dec. 17, 1850 (Par. iii. 338). On July 26, 1850, he wrote, "I have consulted the gravest men, the most able theologians of my diocese. I have subsequently myself examined and weighed all things before God with the greatest care. From all this has resulted a work of which the conclusions are,

"1) In conformity with the principles of theology, the Immaculate Conception of the most holy Virgin is not a matter which can be defined as a truth of the Catholic faith, and, in no case, can be imposed as a belief obligatory under pain of eternal damnation.

"2) That any definition whatsoever, even if the Church or the Holy See believed that they could frame it, would not be opportune; for it would add nothing to the glory of the Immaculate Virgin, and it might be hurtful to the peace of the Church and the good of souls, especially in my diocese."—Par. iii. 310, 11.

His letter of Aug. 25, 1849, which was sent four months later than the above, ran,

"It was my first care (your Holiness suggested afterwards to the Venerable Cardinal of Bourges) to call into counsel the gravest men and most learned theologians of my diocese. They wrote a dissertation hereon, conspicuous for learning and wisdom, which I have judged right to transmit to you, most Blessed Father, at length. Afterwards, I weighed diligently the matter before God, and will humbly explain my opinion to the supreme judgment of the Vicar of Christ. The Encyclical letter of your Blessedness, most Holy Father, raised two questions, the first whereof must be solved by learning, the other by prudence;

"1st. As the theologians, my counsellors, observe, it must be inquired whether, according to the principles of sound theology, the doctrine of the Immaculate Conception of the Most Holy Virgin can be solved by a decree of the Church or of the Holy See, whereby the faithful should be bound to embrace this doctrine:

"2ndly. Whether it is opportune to publish such a decree *now*.

"As to the dogmatic question, the authors of the Dissertation lay down, 1) that the doctrine of the Immaculate Conception can be enacted by a decree of the Church or of the Holy See, so as to be declared certain, yet not so as to be accounted among articles of faith; 2) that the Immaculate Conception of the Most Holy Virgin cannot, as they think, be placed among articles of faith or truths of the Catholic faith, by a decree of the Church or the Holy See.

"As to prudence, having weighed the advantages and disadvantages of a solemn decree, whereby all the faithful should be bound to embrace the doctrine of the Immaculate Conception, they think such a promulgation altogether inopportune. And I myself, most Holy Father, as well as the theologians, my counsellors, think that from the promulgation of such a decree the most grave disadvantages, and perhaps great calamities, will arise to the Church. And I myself think with them, that *it is not lawful, either for the Church or for the Holy See* to count the doctrine of the Immaculate Conception in any case among the articles of faith, or verities of the Catholic faith. Yea, most Holy Father, I go further than the said theologians, and doubt whether the Church or the Holy See can enact by a solemn decree, that this doctrine is *certain* and must be embraced by all under pain of eternal damnation. The Advisers think that their judgment can be easily demonstrated by those grounds which theologians are wont to employ to establish the doctrine as to the Immaculate Conception of the Most Holy Virgin. For, as these say, setting aside the testimonies of the Holy Fathers, who flourished in the first ages of the Church, whose explanation lies under no slight difficulties, the truth of the Immaculate Conception is demonstrated by most grave Theological reasons, which rest especially on the glorious privilege of the Divine maternity, and the constant practice of the Church for the last five centuries.

"I will presently, most Blessed Father, set forth several doubts as to the force of these reasons, which, moreover, are reducible to the single ground of convenience. But for the time, admitting the gravity of this argument, I would explain modestly, and not without some fear, the following doubts."—[The original contains answers, enforcing these doubts. These I have omitted, when they seemed to be involved in the terms of the doubt itself, or were nearly identical in terms with it:—]

"Doubt 1. Can the Church make a definition as to a doctrine, which rests neither on Holy Scripture nor Tradition?

"D. 2. Can any thing else be inferred from the passages adduced from the Fathers of the earlier centuries, besides the sanctification of Mary from her mother's womb? [He instanced such expressions as "Immaculate," "Most pure," "Free from stain of sin," which, he says, were used by S. Bernard, or S. Thomas Aquinas too, who denied the Immaculate Conception.]

"D. 3. Can the Church, when it exceeds the limits of her authority, declare any truth as *certain*, on the sole ground of intrinsic suitableness?

"D. 4. Is the Church bound by no limit of lawfulness in the exercise of her authority, so that she can make a definition in all possible cases, in all circumstances, at her own will?

"D. 5. Did the Church, without evident necessity, ever define a question of doctrine, as to which, here and now, no controversy is raised? Would not the practice of Councils and the Holy See be contradicted by so doing?

"D. 6. Are the wishes of the faithful a sufficient motive that the Church should, by a solemn decision, settle a question of doctrine in their sense? ["One of the most learned Bishops of Belgium, who extremely desires the doctrinal decision, confessed to me, that this practice of the Church seemed to him of so much moment, that on this ground alone he somewhat hesitated."]

"D. 7. Can the Church propose as obligatory an opinion as to doctrine, which is not necessarily connected with any revealed dogma?

"D. 8. Can the Church define, either as "de Fide," or as infallibly certain, a proposition which cannot be brought under theological conclusions? [He explains, "Among the truths which the Church teaches with infallible authority, the last place is held by those which are contained in theological conclusions, i. e., such as are deduced from a major proposition, not revealed, and a minor, revealed. Such conclusions then must be connected by some necessary and evident link with some verity of faith. But the Immaculate Conception is not so connected."]

"D. 9. Can the Church define, as certainly to be believed, a truth which does not touch upon the economy of religion?

"D. 10. Can the Church propose, under pain of eternal damnation, a doctrine which is altogether indifferent, in respect of dogma or rule of life?

"D. 11. Was it not always the mind of the Council of Trent to maintain liberty of opinions which do not injure dogma or morals?

"D. 12. As to the Immaculate Conception itself, did not the Holy Council of Trent and the Holy See decree that opinions were free, and so, in themselves, indifferent?

"D. 13. After the Church has declared, at least implicitly, that neither of these opinions affects dogma or rules of life, would it not, by defining that the one was necessarily to be believed and anathematizing the other, seem to confess that it had erred, in tolerating error in its bosom?

"D. 14. Would not a new decision presuppose fresh grounds? But whence have these arisen? ["From the 'pious wishes' of the faithful perchance?"]

"D. 15. Failing testimonies of Scripture or tradition, can a doctrinal decision rest on pious wishes of the faithful?

"D. 16. Failing texts of Scripture, or Apostolic tradition, what else will the testimonies of Bishops be, save a new weighing of theological grounds in favour of the Immaculate Conception?

"D. 17. Can a new judgment, as to the value of theological

grounds, be prudently passed without a new controversy, which however has not been raised?

"D. 18. But why this new controversy, if the question has been solved by the Council of Trent and the Holy See?

"D. 19. After a decree, declaring that opinions as to the Immaculate Conception are free, who will dare to assert the contrary?

"D. 20. Can a more vivid sense of some reason of theological congruity, even if it affected the mind of all the Bishops of the Catholic world unanimously, be a sufficient ground for a doctrinal decision?

"D. 21. What weight is there in the ground of congruity, whereon alone the doctrine of the Immaculate Conception rests?

"D. 22. Does not God destroy all those reasons of congruity by the mystery of the Incarnation?

"D. 23. Why, in such a mystery of the self-emptying of the Word, should there be any dispute as to the one or other degree of humility?

"D. 24. Might not perhaps the ground of congruence be brought forward more truly to prove that the Virgin Mary was sanctified in her mother's womb?

"D. 25. If some Theologians hold that the dogma of the Divine maternity is connected by a bond of *mere* congruence with the Immaculate Conception of the Virgin, do not others contrariwise teach that it contradicts several revealed dogmas?

"D. 26. In matter of revealed religion, before the authority of the Church pronounces decisively, must it not first be examined, whether the difficulties both of sacred and profane knowledge can be solved? [Dismissing the difficulties of modern physiology, he asks,]

"D. 27. If, by a special grace, the fruit of human generation can be holy, immaculate, free from all fault, why was not Christ so born? [He says, "The learned Bishop whom I mentioned, when urged by this argument, did not hesitate to assert that the Fathers only hinted a certain necessity of propriety, when they speak of the Virginity of the Mother of God being necessary, and that in truth the Son of God might have taken flesh in the ordinary way of generation. I doubt not that that pious Bishop, on weighing the matter more maturely, would acknowledge that such a concession was altogether contrary to the doctrine of the Church. All testimonies of tradition, I deem, contradict it."]

"D. 28. Would not Christ have been united with us by a closer bond of brotherhood, if born of man and woman, had this been possible, as is supposed in the opinion of the Immaculate Conception?

"D. 29. Is any special teaching for the forming of life derivable from that mystery, so that a definition could be judged, if not necessary, at least useful?

"D. 30. Do they not do wrong to the Blessed Virgin, who expect singular and illustrious graces from the decree as to the Immaculate Conception? ["Such as, that there should hereafter be no foreign wars, no civil discord, the empire of error be destroyed; every where truth, peace, and charity." "When they exhibit to us the Blessed Virgin rejoicing in such honour, and therefore exulting, that we acknowledge her singular privilege, and, as a reward, taking care to pour most copious treasures of her gifts into the Church, do they not clothe the Queen of the heavenly Court with the failings of our infirmities? Do they not represent her as a woman, desirous of vain glory, to whose feet each makes his way by flattery and blandishments? These things, if not vain phrenzies, are invented to the reproach of the Virgin."]

"D. 31. Will not the doctrinal decision, contrary to the mind of the Church, diminish the cultus and glory of the Blessed Virgin?

"D. 32. The doctrinal decision will profit neither the faithful nor the Church, nor the glory of the holy Mother of God.

"D. 33. Will not Dissenters mock the Church for such a solemn decision, and be repelled further from it?

"D. 34. Perils, which will arise thence, in respect to the unbelievers and politicians of this time.

"D. 35. Perils, which will arise thence in respect to some faithful, especially in the Diocese of Paris. ["These, though they neglect the precepts of religion, yet profess to reverence its doctrines. Their faith, philosophic (so to speak) rather than Christian, will be too weak to bear such a trial. We fear, lest they should reject what they have hitherto venerated, or at least remove further from the Church. These perils are especially to be feared in the diocese" of Paris. "There are to be found in Paris, more than any where else, men eminent for civil dignity, or science, or wealth, or authority, who by their example affect others, and whom we are constrained to count in this class. Moved thereby, my predecessor of glorious memory" (the Archbishop who died as a martyr) "gave the same opinion as myself to the Holy See, asserting that the definition as to the Immaculate Conception would be rather a scandal than to edification among those of his Diocese."]

"D. 36. Perils, which will arise as to some Catholic Theologians. ["These will endure anxiously this new head of controversy, this new definition which can be confirmed by no tradition, nay, which, as many learned among them think, is at variance with the belief of former centuries of the Church. Which peril, if it be lighter on the part of those who listen tractably to the Church, will appear much graver, if we consider those who profess to reject the heretics condemned in modern times, yet tread closely in their footsteps. Such perchance may be found among us."]

"D. 37. Will not new heresies arise out of a doctrinal decision? ["Probably 'Anti-conceptionists' will arise, and some of them will not hesitate to assert that the assistance of the Holy Spirit was not promised to the Church, to settle at pleasure mere theoretical questions. What marvel, if among the adherents of the new dogma, some, of more rigid minds, resting on the grounds I have hinted at [Doubts 27, 28], should come to deny the Virginity of Mary, and the operation of the Holy Ghost in the Incarnation?"]

"D. 38. Will not the decision of the question turn to the ruin of a great number of souls without any compensation?

"The wishes of the faithful, that the pious opinion of the Immaculate Conception should be counted among dogmas of faith, or at least among truths defined as certain, are incessantly produced to us as a decisive ground. They who so boast, most Blessed Father, exceed the limits of truth. To us the faithful seem to have no wish as to this definition. They are contented to pour forth devout prayers to the Immaculate Virgin. If any pious souls, more inclined to that faith, have uttered such a wish, they are, beyond question, very few. But be they, in respect to the unbelieving, heretics, or indifferent, as one, I do not say, to a thousand, but to a hundred, the piety or faith of this faithful soul will profit nothing by that definition, if it turn to the destruction of those hundred unbelievers, heretics, indifferentists. Why, without reasonable or sufficient motive, without evident necessity, or any benefit, at the good pleasure alone of some pious faithful, should we imperil so many souls? I conclude,

"1. It is at least doubtful whether the Church *can* declare the doctrine of the Immaculate Conception to be certain and obligatory. If its power is doubtful, it ought to be silent, since there is no necessity of speaking at this time. Your Holiness is not unaware, that many of the theologians who have written about the definability of this question, even such as have grave weight with the Holy See, went further than we; they do not say that the authority of the Church in defining such questions is doubtful, they deny it altogether. But we, most Blessed Father, believe the matter to be doubtful, and that in matters of doubt there ought to be no action. 2. Since the Immaculate Conception cannot be demonstrated to the unbelieving or to heretics, either by Holy Scripture or by tradition; since, moreover, both reason and science raise difficulties, either in themselves insoluble or at least inextricable, against this opinion, if the Church were by a solemn decree to declare it obligatory, the Catholic controversy would in this point become weak and powerless. But thereby the authority of the Church becomes cheaper, the gravity of her decrees becomes questioned, and the truth of her doctrinal decisions is denied with increased temerity. Again then, most Blessed Father, moved by this most grave argument, we will say, the Church ought to abstain from any decree whereby the opinion as to the Immaculate Conception would become obligatory. 3. Although by such a decree the Church should neither weaken her own sacred and infallible authority, nor the deposit of revealed doctrines which have been already defined, in the sight of the unbelieving and of heretics, she ought to abstain from passing it, on account of the inutility of the decree itself. For as we have tried to show, the decree in question would be useless, if not hurtful,—useless to the faithful, useless to the Church, useless in respect to the glory of the Blessed Virgin. This threefold inutility, even apart from the perils to souls, abundantly suffices to make the course, which some expect the Supreme Pontiff to attempt, to appear illegitimate."—ii. 26.

2. *Louis, Archbishop of Rouen.*—"I consider that this belief is not clearly contained in the deposit of the Holy Scriptures. I consider that tradition in this respect is wanting in precision and unanimity. Had the tradition been clear, could S. Anselm, S. Bonaventura, S. Bernard, S. Thomas, Bellarmine, and so many others, have been ignorant of it? I consider that the belief in the Immaculate Conception does not reach, in a way at all explicit or imposing, above the eleventh century; and that if new beliefs or devotions, favourable to piety and nowise contrary to order, may be wisely tolerated and even encouraged, it is still advisable to leave them as free beliefs and simple devotions. I consider that a dogmatic definition, under present circumstances, would be both superfluous and perilous. Superfluous, because no one now disputes the Blessed Virgin the privilege of her most pure Conception, *and it is not the custom of the Church to erect into an article of faith what is disputed by no one.* Perilous, because, considering the state of minds at this moment, it is to be feared that such a definition will only be a signal for the most lively discussions, the most wounding imputations. What, for instance, will the English Theologians, so well versed in the study of Ecclesiastical Antiquity, do or say, when they shall see the Holy See define, as a point of faith, a matter which so many ages have scarcely had a glimpse of (entrevue), which so many holy persons and great doctors have either denied or been ignorant of? *Will they not think that the Church, at this day, holds cheap that principle of S. Vincent of Lerins,* so certain and venerable, *quod ubique, quod semper, quod ab omnibus?* And will not the Catholic doctrine itself suffer much, as a whole, if, as has been recently the case, certain imprudent champions of the most Holy Virgin, in order the better to support the privilege of her Immaculate Conception, maintain publicly, that many of our sacred doctrines do not rest on any more solid foundation, on any more certain tradition? Instead of the doctrine of the Immaculate Conception being fortified, will not other much more important doctrines be shaken? And, most Holy Father, I fear much that in this case the wish to make good

better will injure the good. I fear for the peace of the Church, which, on occasion of this new dogma, may witness destructive passions roused against her and within her own bosom. I fear for the honour of the Popes, who will be represented as having been, for 300 years, occupied in stifling free discussion on the subject; forbidding on the one side, under grave penalties, any sort of attack upon the privilege of the Immaculate Conception, and, on the other, favouring, by all possible means, the expansion of this pious belief. I fear even for yourself.—Will it not be said that Pius IX. exposed the bark of Peter to frightful tempests, for a matter in which the faith is not concerned, and which is incapable of any application to human conduct? On all these grounds, I opine that there is no room for erecting into a dogma of faith the pious belief in the Immaculate Conception of the Holy Virgin. Far from desiring such a decree, I should regard it as a dangerous thing, as a two-edged sword, capable of wounding the hand which should use it. I should rejoice certainly, in the interest of the mother of God, but I should be disquieted, in the interest of the Church and her glorious head; and I would not purchase so dear the consolations of piety."—i. 357—9.

3. *The Bishop of Coutançes.*—"Having been taught that pious opinion from boyhood, we, for ourselves and as the interpreters of the whole Clergy, all profess that Mary was conceived without stain. Yet we are persuaded, that there is no necessity or advantage in deciding or teaching, as an Article of faith, that Mary was conceived without stain of original sin; nay, we all unanimously think it inopportune and full of peril. For whence should that necessity or advantage be derived? No question is raised about it; no adversary of the Immaculate Conception, not the very least, appears; Catechists teach it to boys, Divinity Professors to seminarists, Preachers of the Divine word to the faithful. Every where piously preached, it is every where piously received.

"Moreover, neither the Church nor the Holy See ever, as far as we know, erected any opinion piously believed into the dignity of a dogma, unless some controversy of greater moment were raised about it.

"We think then, positively, that there is absolutely no

fitting occasion for it; but there appears to us grave peril, if the matter be touched in the very least.

"Every one knows with what efforts Rationalists and Protestants are assailing the bark of Peter, the authority of the Roman Pontiff, nay, the Church herself. Every one knows how many blasphemies the enemies of the Christian name pour out to weaken the Divine Monarchy. Every one knows with what calumnies those same inexorable enemies impugn daily the articles of faith.

"If what was hitherto a mere opinion is to-morrow, at the good pleasure of certain Bishops, to be believed *de Fide*, under pain of damnation; if, what the S. Council of Trent itself (as Pallavicini attests) would not decree, although *then* controverted and strongly impugned; if, what Pope Pius V., of holy memory, Gregory XV., and Alexander VII. declared to be, not a dogma, but a mere pious opinion, what might be contradicted without note of heresy, should be delivered as a doctrine by decree of the present supreme Pontiff, would not the aforesaid Rationalists and all uncatholics take occasion for assailing anew and more fiercely all our doctrines with their impious speeches? Nay, doubtless, a handle would be given them causelessly for so doing.

"But what is to be more feared, than to raise up these waves of passions and opinions, especially at this time, when the whole world is shaken with unwonted commotions, in which Peter (alas!) is ejected from his See, &c.? In these storms of tribulations, in this whirlpool of great crimes, in these perils and straits of all sorts, all faithful Christians turn their eyes to Mary, think of Mary, and call on her, piously and most inwardly believing that she was conceived without stain.

"Moved by these reasons of graver moment, we judge that a dogmatic decree as to the Immaculate Conception of the Blessed Virgin Mary, *which could with the greatest difficulty be derived from Holy Scripture or tradition*, should, at least for a time, be abstained from."—i. 362, 363.

4. *The Bishop of Evreux.*—"In obedience to the commands of your Holiness, I have convened the most able Theologians of my diocese; I joined them to my Episcopal Council, and, after having interrogated and heard them, after having long studied and meditated in presence of our Lord Jesus

Christ in the most Holy Sacrament of the Altar, after having humbly entreated the Holy Spirit to have pity upon my misery and profound ignorance, this is my answer to the questions put by your Blessedness in your admirable letter.

"1. I do not think it well-timed to agitate at this moment the question of the Immaculate Conception; (1) because it is attacked by no Catholic, and has never been more generally admitted than in our century; (2) because many Protestants, reconciled by our most loved and holy Pope Pius IX. with the Papacy, are in the way to return, and that nothing would be more calculated to alienate them, than the obligation which would be laid upon them to cease to regard the belief in the Immaculate Conception as a matter of opinion.

"2. I do not believe that the passages of Holy Scripture are precise enough, nor the language of tradition explicit enough, or certain enough in all Centuries, that this opinion (certain as it seems to me) should be advanced to be a dogma of faith.

"The rules laid down by all Theologians seem to contradict this.

"Our great strength, when we discuss with heretics, is this maxim of S. Vincent of Lerins,—*Quod semper, quod ubique, quod ab omnibus traditum est, &c.*

"On these grounds, which it would seem to me unsuitable and perfectly useless to develope to your Holiness, I would conjure you to abide by the examples of your Venerable Predecessors in the Apostolic See, and to leave amid oppositions this holy opinion, which Bossuet called the most certain of truths."—i. 100, 101.

5. *The Bishop of Chartres.*—"Never in my flock, and, I assert confidently, in all the Dioceses of France, did faithful Catholics burn with greater devotion and love towards Mary, never did they place fuller confidence in her; never in tribulations did they with more fervent impetus seek protection at her feet. Nothing can be added to the most lively significations of cultus towards Mary, which burst forth on all sides from the hearts of the faithful. It follows, that the pronouncing of this dogma 'of faith' will add nothing to this full, complete, and (so to speak) exuberant devotion. Nay, so far from kindling, it would burden, hinder, disturb it. For what confusion! what tumults! what protestations of rebellious

men! The Jansenists and other Catholics of weak or less proved faith would cry out against the insertion of this dogma among articles of faith; they would rise up most boldly against it, try to draw Augustine, Bernard, Thomas, on their side; excite discord, assail with doubts and cavils the cultus of the Deipara which already includes the Immaculate Conception, and, so far from procuring any relaxation or comfort, would further accumulate the most vehement affliction of the Church.

"2. The Protestants, who incline to the Catholic faith, which the numerous conversions of very learned men, especially in England, attest most gloriously, would be deterred by the newness of this dogma from completing what they have begun. They would think, that all the articles of faith were declared in the Council of Trent, and that that most learned synod completed the Catholic doctrine. The impious Rationalists, Socialists, who are busy in entrapping the ignorance of the people by false interpretations of Evangelic doctrine, would try to accommodate this novelty to their ends, exclaiming that the Apostolic See, by sanctioning things hitherto unknown and unheard of, plainly favours their detestable comments. So then this plague, which no tears can expiate, would exult with fouler and more abominable licence.

"3. The faithful spontaneously, without constraint, without terror of Apostolic fulmination, believe, admire, venerate most profoundly the Immaculate Conception: devotion towards Mary seems thence the sweeter; for voluntariness is the condiment of love, the sweet aspiration of piety, the seal of filial affection, &c.

"To condense my meaning in few words, I declare it as represented with wonderful clearness and absolute precision in the following clause of the most learned Pétau: 'To bring to a close the discussion of this question, I think that the most holy Virgin Mother of God was free, not only from all actual sin of her own, but from original also. But I am so far persuaded of this, that I would not have it counted *of faith*, nor would I believe that any one was to be condemned, or speak hardly of one who thinks otherwise; nor am I prepared to maintain it in any other way than that now prescribed by the Roman Pontiffs and the Council of Trent, i. e. by the Catholic Church' (de Incarn. xiv. 2. 10). This tempered zeal circumstances seem to me especially to recommend, as also Apostolic moderation, and the very necessary counsel not to add sharpest strifes about matters of faith to horrible civil tumults. I think that nothing ought to be added to the causes of division and heat of mind, whose fury and rage is unexampled from the beginning of the world. For the glory of the Virgin and the good of the Church, what, as Pétau says, has been already decreed by supreme Pontiffs and the Council of Trent suffices. If, in a short time, as I most firmly believe, the most splendid benefits of the Virgin, who is terrible as an armed host, require other attestations of gratitude, your Holiness has other honours at hand to discharge this debt, and declare throughout the world your piety and grateful remembrance."—i. 175, 176.

6. *The Bishop of Anneçy.*—"We readily own to your Blessedness, that to us it would appear better, if a solemn sentence, whereby the Immaculate Conception of the Virgin should be proposed to be believed as an article of faith and true dogma, should be abstained from. For, in our opinion, such a judgment could not easily escape the note of novelty, as being contrary to the practice of the Church, which has not been wont to define Christian truths, resting on Scripture or transmitted by tradition, as to be held as dogmas under pain of anathema, unless they were impugned by some."—i. 445, 446.

7. *The Bishop of Meaux.*—"We confess that we do not think that, in the circumstances of these times, it is opportune that a matter, about which Doctors and Theologians, most distinguished for piety and knowledge, have so long controverted among themselves, should be defined by a solemn judgment. We confess too, that we fear lest the cultus of the most Holy Virgin, conceived without stain, should suffer detriment; and the piety which now of its own accord pays her distinguished honours should be chilled, when, by force of a dogmatic definition, they shall seem less voluntary. It is to be feared too, lest the authority of Mother Church should perchance be diminished by the clamours of the pseudo-reformed and unbelieving philosophers of these times, on all sides, that the faith is changed in the lapse of time, and that new doctrines are daily coined by the Church."—ii. 363.

8. *The Bishop of Carcassonne.*—"In these most miserable and sorrowful times, very many, who have been baptized in the

faith of our Lord Jesus Christ, desert this faith, or, retaining its elements, have entangled it with so many false doctrines, that their mind, ever struggling against the truth, is most ready for every sort of scandal. Wherefore we fear lest, things being so, a solemn dogmatic definition of the Immaculate Conception of the Most Holy Virgin Mary would give occasion to the ungodly and to heretics to sadden the Church by disputations, and to assail with contumelies and blasphemies the Mother of the Saviour, whom we venerate singularly with the inmost affections of the heart. Whence we think that there is ground to doubt, whether the promulgation of such a decree, which in other times would fill our heart with joy, would be opportune at present."—iii. 333.

9. *The Bishop of Amiens.*—"But although, by that definition, the most pious opinion as to the Immaculate Conception of the Mother of God is set forth, as founded in the doctrine of the Universal Church, nor can it be called in question without condemnable temerity, or contradicted without note of error, there lack not among us such as think that, if that doctrine should be assimilated to an express article of faith, there would be ground to fear, lest controversies should arise in the schools as to the conditions required for an express article of faith. Thence, they say, perhaps would be scandal to the weak, discussions and strifes of words among the learned; and to the heretics and unbelieving occasion would be given of speaking things wrong and injurious to religion." —i. 135.

10, 11. *The Archbishop of Rheims*, and the *Bishop of Soissons* said the same, more concisely, but with the same leading words, as the wish of themselves, the Canons, Directors of Seminaries, Professors of Divinity, Parish Priests, and pious Laity. —i. 121, 122. iii. 290.

12. *The Bishop of Beauvais.*—"In order to proceed with due prudence in a matter of such moment, we did not neglect to consult the Canons of our Church and some presbyters conspicuous for piety and learning. Some of them, (although all believe from the heart that Mary was free from original taint, yet having maturely weighed the question,) had some doubts whether the testimonies of Holy Scripture and tradition were so clear and unshaken that it might be settled

by a dogmatic decree. They thought also that perhaps it was not necessary, since the most pious opinion as to the Immaculate Conception is, at this time, not impugned, and is not connected with the defence of other dogma or rules of life; nay, that it was not opportune, since there was ground to fear that heretics and unbelievers would say, that tradition was corrupted by the Church, or that new dogmas gradually crept in or were invented at will, and that thus, on account of a new decree on controverted doctrine, the weak might be turned away from embracing the ancient faith. We should be glad that the words of the decree should be so softened, that they who do not assent to this privilege [of the Blessed Virgin] should remain free from the note of heresy, in that it should be declared that the Church does not err when it teaches, that the Blessed Virgin, the Mother of God, was wholly free from all taint of original fault. By a decree thus tempered, the end intended would be gained, the Catholic truth would be asserted, the piety of the faithful fostered, and heretics or unbelievers would have no place of crying out against the Church."—i. 320, 321.

13. *The Bishop of Blois.*—"In publishing such a definition, there is need of very great caution and indulgence for the salvation of many, since, in our times, the sense of Catholic truths is much diminished. Every one sees this, who considers things attentively and judges from experience, that there are men now, some indifferent to religion, others wholly intent on politics, many fevered with the licence of thinking what they will, and so that the truths of Christian faith and piety are obscured among the people; and, accordingly, that the dogmatic definition of our most pious opinion, whereas at first it would be entertained with joy and gratulation by the pious and learned, would be received by most other Catholics with a dull carelessness, not to say, worse. For perchance (and this is not improbable on account of the age, the feverishness of men and the pride of the insolent) an opinion which seems to them new will cause hindrance or delay to some sinners in returning to the Father's house. Nay, manifoldly as the pastors may instruct the people, it is to be feared that many pious faithful will, with difficulty or not at all, understand how the Church, after eighteen centuries, should now employ

itself in proposing to all Christians, as an article of faith necessary to salvation, that which before it had left to the free and pious choice of each; especially since, in these our times, there is scarcely any one who disputes the truth of the Immaculate Conception, but every learned and religious Catholic accounts it a duty and merit to believe and profess it."—i. 211, 212.

On the other hand, the Bishop of Blois set the need of consolation which the Church had from the Blessed Virgin, which rendered the definition timely; and so, in due regard to the charity needed by so many, weak and ignorant, blind and unbelieving, asked the Pope not to define it so directly and expressly, that they who should not believe it, should thereby be separated from the Church, and incur the note and penalty of heresy.

14. *The Archbishop of Bourges* gave the opinion of ecclesiastics very distinguished for theological science, whom he had consulted, and who had given him their mature judgment. "It seems that, in these troubled and stormy times, the publication of this definition would perhaps give a handle to the enemies of God's Holy Church to raise new calumnies, and vomit forth blasphemies, whence no light scandal might arise, especially to the unlearned and weak; they too, who are frequently engaged in controversy with un-Catholics, fear lest the very greatest hindrance should thus be put to the return of heretics on the point of coming back to the bosom of Mother Church, since there is nothing which they more abhor, nothing which turns them more from the Catholic faith. Moreover, some, who piously believe and profess the Immaculate Conception of the Blessed Virgin, think that this question, although clear, *is not such that that well-known rule of Vincent of Lerins*, 'quod semper, quod ubique, quod ab omnibus traditum est,' *could be applied to it.* Whence *they think that, according to the ancient custom of the Church, it ought not to be defined.* But I, most Holy Father, although I exceedingly desire whatever would be to the honour of the glorious Virgin, cannot but acknowledge, on the aforesaid grounds, that a definition thereon from the Apostolic See perhaps would be inopportune, and would not make for peace and unity, especially amid these present storms, fearing that greater evils would come from it than good."—i. 497, 498.

15. *The Bishop of Versailles.*—"Although I was myself among those who, out of a feeling of filial piety toward Mary, humbly prayed his Holiness, Gregory XVI. of glorious memory, to declare the Conception of Mary Immaculate by a solemn decree, I think it due to my conscience to set before your Holiness a thought of fear, perhaps exaggerated, which takes hold of me.

"In the bosom of France there still live unbelieving children whom heresy keeps far from their home. In their deplorable blindness, they still reproach us with the worship we render to Mary. It is not without difficulty that we can bring them to believe about the Mother of God, what is already of faith. Shall we not find more obstacles to their return, when, to reconcile them to the Church, we shall have to require of them explicit faith in the Immaculate Conception? Perhaps, to anticipate this difficulty, there would be ground for not giving the character of a Catholic dogma to the truth of the Immaculate Conception, especially seeing that, even if the Immaculate Conception should not be a necessary object of faith, the glorious Virgin would not be less honoured by all the pious faithful under this title."—ii. 101. 103.

16. *The Bishop of Angers.*—"A doubt arises, first, because minds are at rest, as I said, not only in my Diocese, but in every part of France, yea, in the whole Catholic Church. Would it not be to be wished, that this peace and rest of souls should be maintained? Would there not be peril of disturbing minds by passing a decree on that subject, the minds not of the pious, but of those, no few, who contradict the truth, and subject all things to the examination of reason? I confess that there is, as far as I know, no such peril for my diocese; but, in our times, there are many who love liberty, impatient of a yoke, who superextol reason and its discoveries. In France, there is great liberty, not to say, great licence of thinking, writing, printing, which writers, and those of no mean sort, use and abuse, to bring all things, even religious and sacred, into mockery and contempt; and so they impel others and are impelled themselves to evil and blasphemy. In this condition, then, of things and minds, it is to be feared that a dogmatic decision may perhaps cherish evil passions and open a door to dangerous discussions.

"A doubt arises, secondly, not now from the clamours of impious men, but from the novelty of the definition itself. For among those who are less audacious, among those too who seem fairly good, not a few may be found, who will wonder that this definition has been so long delayed, the thing being so evident and clear; and who will venture to say, although undeservedly, that new dogmas are fabricated and devised by the Church. Many things have indeed been defined, in the lapse of time, which before were not counted among articles of faith. They were often impugned, whence it became necessary in a manner to define them. Here the case is different. The fact of the Immaculate Conception is admitted, and securely believed, in the whole Catholic Church; nor does it appear, that piety toward the Blessed Virgin would be much increased by the supervention of such a decree."—i. 257.

17. *Savoy. The Archbishop of Chambéry.*—"The Clergy and people of this diocese burn with the most sincere devotion towards the Blessed Virgin; they profess her Immaculate Conception as a pious and most probable opinion, but not as a doctrine to be held of necessity and 'de fide,' i. e. in much the same way in which they profess the Assumption of the Virgin to heaven, and her preservation from all, even venial sin; and this, because the tradition of former ages of the Church does not seem clear enough to constitute an article of faith, and a true dogma to be believed by all under pain of mortal sin. It would seem then to us better to imitate the prudent line of the Council of Trent, by abstaining from any definition, as did that same Council (sess. 24, can. 7 and 8), by asserting, e. g. that the cultus which 'the Catholic Church uses towards the Conception of the Blessed Virgin Mother is pious and holy.'"—i. 411, 412.

18. *Switzerland. The Bishop of S. Gall.*—"From all this, I and my Councillors are persuaded that the veneration of the Blessed Virgin Mary, whom, with the Holy Father and Holy Church, we firmly believe to have been conceived without stain and exempt from original sin, cannot be increased by any dogmatic decision or definition that she was so conceived, and that such a dogmatic decision is for this time superfluous.

"But what, in our disturbed times, every where seduced by a false worldly light, seems to advise, not to enact, at present, the dogma of the Immaculate Conception, but rather to defer it to a new era, as is hoped, more friendly to the Catholic religion and obedient to the Vicar of Christ and Bishops of the Holy Church, is as follows,—

"Such a superfluous dogmatic decree being delivered and published in Switzerland and Germany, infected by un-Catholics and innovators, various disputations would be caused, pamphlets full of hatred and calumnies would be published, the dogma would be impugned and wickedly deformed in public papers, which find entrance every where; and so the seduction of many would be to be feared, the obstinacy of un-Catholics would be strengthened, and they be turned further away from the truth. Public papers and pamphlets written against religion would be published in far greater numbers than those in defence of the Catholic faith.

"It does not seem advisable to bring forward a matter so delicate as that of the Conception, or any treatise about it, without necessity. The temptation to wicked and carnal authors, of casting forth foul things after the manner of the wretched Voltaire and his followers, would be too great."—iii. 302, 303.

19. *Bavaria. The Archbishop of Munich.*—"But whether, in the present circumstances of the Church, a definition is advisable or no, I scarce venture to decide, since it may be said, not without some appearance of truth, that such a definition will provoke fresh discussions in countries where Catholics live mixed with heretics."—ii. 417.

20. *Archbishop of Bamberg.*—"By far the greatest part of the Clergy is persuaded that this is not the time to decide what remained so long undecided, and which so many of your Predecessors, and those so great, and the fathers of the Tridentine Council itself, hesitated to decide. They think that such a decision will be of no benefit to the faithful people, in that it adheres to the pious opinion of the Immaculate Conception of the Blessed Virgin spread far and wide; and to the body of the more erudite and learned in our Germany the matter does not seem so clear that (whatever the very learned and illustrious Tramontanes may say, who have very recently written in behalf of the Immaculate Conception of the Blessed Virgin) they can think that this opinion, which has been hitherto cherished

as pious, should be enrolled among dogmas, about which no one may doubt. They think that account should be had of the state of the times, most troubled both as to the ecclesiastical and civil polity; that it does not belong to these times to revive inveterate disputes; that there is peril, lest new rents should take place in the Church; lastly, that it is no derogation from the cultus of the Blessed Virgin, if *that* should be left longer undecided, which has so long seemed matter of most difficult discussion. In this opinion of far the greatest part of my Clergy, which I have learned from the report of the Deans, the Chapter of the Cathedral Church of Bamberg joined unanimously, to which I cannot but unite myself. Be the dogmatic definition of this question left, most Holy Father, to other times. Be the decision of this matter reserved to a General Council to be celebrated hereafter. We have that sacred deposit of dogmas decided by the most holy fathers in General Councils, to defend which against the very frequent attacks of the heresies of this time, and to establish it in the minds of our faithful people, will suffice for our most arduous office."—ii. 59.

21. *Archbishop of Gorizia and Gradisca.*—"The peasantry, and other of the lower orders of the Diocese committed to my care, worships [*colit*] most devotedly the most Blessed Virgin Mary, and frequents in great numbers the shrines in my diocese dedicated to her; but it does not desire that the pious belief of her Immaculate Conception should be turned into a Catholic dogma, an Article of faith; nor is the least wish for any such decision manifested among the people, as far as has become known to myself and other neighbouring Bishops. As for persons of the upper, and, as they are called, more cultivated classes, they do indeed still retain the devotion and cultus of the Virgin Mary, although not in that fervour and number observable in the peasantry and poorer artisans; but so far from desiring that the most pious opinion of the Immaculate Conception of the Virgin Mary should be raised to the rank of Catholic dogmas or articles of the Holy Faith, they (at least the larger part of the aforesaid classes) are of directly the opposite mind.

"The fratres minores of S. Francis, called Observants in the Convent of Castagnavira, are most devoted to the cultus of the Blessed Virgin Mary, and have an office of their own of the Immaculate Conception, but they have never manifested the least wish that the most pious belief of the Immaculate Conception should be changed into an article of faith, nay, rather, though most observant of the discipline of their rule, they fear the effect of such a decision in regard to the heterodox and to lukewarm Catholics, the number of whom is at this time immense.

"I must say the same of the secular Clergy, which, with few exceptions, is pious and studious of sacerdotal discipline. [Then follows, "If the present state—full of peril," given above, pp. 188, 189.] "For in past years there were heard, and still are heard, the assertions of Protestants and indifferent Catholics, 'that Rome puts an unbearable yoke on the faithful, by coining new dogmas, and forming articles of faith from the rhetorical expressions of one or two fathers, and enjoining that *that* should be held with firm faith as a dogma, which a few centuries, nay, a few decennia before, might be questioned, and the assertors of the contrary whereof Roman Pontiffs had forbidden to condemn.' What then would happen, if the most pious faith (yea, 'the pious opinion,' as it still stands in Catechisms) of the Immaculate Conception of the Blessed Virgin Mary, should be declared as a dogma of sacred faith? Will it be an increase of faith? Will it be a happier condition of the Catholic Church? Is a restoration of affairs at Rome to be hoped therefrom? I, as far as it is given me by God to see, fear exceedingly the contrary. It is a matter, I must repeat, full of peril. When some years ago, under Gregory XVI., the same question was proposed to the Bishops, there came to me letters of Catholic Bishops from countries very remote from this, the writers whereof exclaimed in amazement, 'Does Rome mean to form new articles of faith?' Should we have a more beneficial result now? I doubt most exceedingly." [Then follows, "Under these circumstances—the Son of God." Above, p. 189.] He sums up, "This is what, after instituting a mature examination in the sight of God in this most grave matter, I thought I ought to explain to your Holiness, and I do explain it with all befitting submission of mind and reverence," &c.—i. 178, 179.

22. *The Archbishop of Salzburg.*—"This pious faith being now nowhere controverted, nay, every one being free, undisturbed by any, to indulge this cultus in his own way, all gladly acquiesce in the most wise constitution of the Council of Trent published thereon, so that I do not know that any one wishes for a new decree of the Apostolic See. Moreover, history attests, that the Church *then* chiefly intervened by a peremptory decision, when the wrongful zeal of men attempted either to question, or to corrupt by sinister interpretation the faith given by God, neither of which is done (it is known) in the present case. Added to this, the opinion is fixed in the minds of very many, that there exists not such authority of Apostolic tradition, that the Immaculate Conception of the most Blessed Virgin *can* be established by a decree divinely certain. Wherefore I think that it is much to be feared, that, whereas formerly most grave and lasting controversies were lulled by Apostolic decrees, issued on matters of faith, the declaration of the Holy See would this time rather furnish fresh matter for doubts and discords about that question which are now quite hushed or unknown, and the enemies of the Church, ever ready to censure, would take occasion thence of impiously calumniating her, as though she delivered new dogmas without the suffrage of Divine tradition. Being then commanded by your Holiness to explain candidly my mind in this matter, considering the adjuncts of the times, I cannot bring myself to think that the counsel to declare that pious belief as a Catholic dogma is opportune, or that it will really advance that cultus. In that ferment of minds which now prevails, very inimical to religion and piety, I fear that such a public and solemn declaration is a matter full of peril, such as the other many and great difficulties with which the Church now struggles, seem to dissuade from voluntarily provoking."—i. 326, 327.

23. *The Bishop of Trieste.*—"The people of the united Diocese of Trieste and Capo d'Istria are animated with such devotion to the Immaculate Conception of the Blessed Virgin Mary, that any doubt which might be newly raised as to this doctrine would excite the greatest disturbance of mind, and give useless, nay, very perilous occasion to theological questions among the laity themselves. For this cause I omitted express

mention of the wish that it should at last be decided by a solemn judgment that the Blessed Virgin was conceived without original taint, in order to maintain the laudable and firm opinion of the faithful people herein; and also I did not venture to express openly the consideration of the topic, to guard against discussions among some of the clergy themselves, who keep silence as to the opposite opinion, not out of any conviction of their own, but rather out of obedience.

"For myself, I own plainly, that it is extremely to be desired that the intention of the most Holy Council of Trent (Sess. v.), according to which the Blessed and Immaculate Virgin Mary was not comprised in the decree as to original sin, should be explained more clearly, and the Catholic doctrine of her Immaculate Conception should be defined in unambiguous terms; yet, having weighed the aforesaid considerations, I should wish to follow the counsel of *many brethren* ('confratrum,' other Bishops), who in the present circumstances and at this time hold that it is better that any direct definition should be deferred, and wish only for a tacit definition, decreeing the sanctity of the ecclesiastical rite now used in the cultus of the Conception of the Blessed Virgin." — i. 435, 436.

24, 25. *Moravia. The Archbishop of Olmütz, and the Bishop of Brünn.*—" Nevertheless, the most humbly subscribed cannot adopt the opinion that now at present this pious assertion should be placed by a Pontifical decree among dogmas of faith. The gravest reason, whereby, after mature deliberation and fervid imploring of light from above, they feel themselves moved so to judge, is taken from the most difficult circumstances of the countries over whose Churches they are set. A most cunning heresy spreads with impunity in these parts, which has been wont most greedily to seize every handle for criminating the Catholic Church. Among divers protests, whereby it attempts to entice the faithful to its side, is this also, that they blatter, (certainly, without any solid foundation,) that the Catholic Church forms new dogmas at will. But if, by a solemn judgment of the Holy Apostolic See, the Immaculate Conception of the Blessed Virgin should be defined at this time as a dogmatic doctrine of the Catholic Church, doubtless that most false incrimination would shake many, less firm in the Catholic faith, with great peril of souls. This peril ought the more to be considered, because hitherto, through an erroneous statement of the subject, the Immaculate Conception of the Blessed Virgin Mary has been considered by many faithful of the Catholic Church as only a pious opinion; accordingly, it could not be without disturbance of minds, that what (although persuaded of its truth, and not doubting) they seemed until now only to opine, they should be obliged to revere as a Catholic dogma.

"Our counsel, therefore, tends to this, that, until circumstances be changed, things should remain as they are. The faithful do not doubt the Immaculate Conception to the Virgin Deipara; the cultus of that mystery increases daily; souls then are not imperilled on the head of truth's not being acknowledged; but contrariwise no slight perils are avoided, which come reasonably to be feared from the dogmatic pronouncement of the truth by the Apostolic See.

"This state of things was the ground why the most humbly subscribed hesitated to execute the exhortation of your Holiness, prudently accounting that the appointment of public prayers in their dioceses for the obtaining of light from above for counsel to be taken in this matter, could not be without detriment to religion and the Holy Apostolic See."—iii. 232, 233.

25. *b*) *The four Bishops of Bohemia.*—They thank the Pope, for "the most precious letter, wherein in sweetest words the feelings of our mind towards the most Blessed Virgin are expressed;" and they state that they had assiduously endeavoured to promote among the people "the Catholic cultus of her."

"Full of the same faith as your Holiness, that the most Blessed Virgin was conceived without any stain of original fault, we gave public testimony of this faith in the prayer addressed to the Predecessor of your Holiness, of most pious memory, Gregory XVI., that we might be allowed publicly to enunciate and add the word Immaculate in the Preface and Litanies of the Blessed Virgin Mary.

"So then, unanimous and joyous, we report to your Holiness that this faith, that the Blessed Virgin Mary was conceived without any stain of original fault, is held both by the clergy and the faithful people as a doctrine of our Holy Church from most ancient tradition.

"Nevertheless, since the question is, that this faith be decreed by the solemn judgment of the Apostolic See, we, following the most venerable example of your Holiness, thought that we ought to consult some persons proved by piety and theological discipline. Having heard their judgment, and weighed it maturely in the Lord, we thought that we ought to signify to your Holiness that this faith, as we have set forth, is vivid, and is taught of old in our Christian people and clergy, but that because in these last times there has been no controversy about this belief, and no heretical doctrines, opposed to it, seem to urge such a decision; the modern adjuncts of time, place, and men do not recommend that this most ancient belief should be decreed as a doctrine by the solemn judgment of our holy Roman Catholic Church. For the multitude of unbelievers, heretics, and adversaries of our holy Church in our neighbourhood, and living among the faithful in our regions, would abuse such a decision most foully to their own perverse ends by their diabolic calumnies; so that we have good grounds to fear, lest many of the weak, the number whereof hath very greatly increased through the machinations of false prophets, be seduced, and make shipwreck of their faith, and, with their faith, of their everlasting salvation.

"This our judgment, besought from the Lord with assiduous prayers, which we signify to your Holiness," &c.—ii. 403.

26. *Archbishop of Breslau, to the Apostolic Nuncio at Vienna.*—"According to the opinion of the most zealous and enlightened Catholics such a disturbance would infallibly arise, if the dogmatic decree [on the Immaculate Conception] should be passed by the Holy See. The Protestant writers contending, *pro aris et focis*, would seize it as a welcome prey, to deafen anew their poor people by their cries against the papacy and the manufacture of dogmas discovered after eighteen centuries; unbelievers would join in chorus with the pietists, and would discharge fresh floods of sarcasms and blasphemies against this holy mystery; the literary Jewish youth would especially excel therein. So much for those

without. Within, the secular war in the schools of theology, appeased with so much difficulty, would be kindled anew; that very delicate point of the infallibility of the Pope would give it an accession of combustible matter; the opposition of a part of the clergy imbued with Neologism, in the Rhine provinces, in Baden, and in Bohemia, would also find food therein; and as the result, instead of edification and a new spring of piety and devotion in the Catholic people, there would be nothing but troubles, divisions, scandals, disturbances without and within,—*things a thousand times more dangerous now than they were in past centuries.*

"I have re-read before I decided on writing this letter to you, my Lord, the chapters of Pallavicini (Hist. of the Council of Trent), and of Pétau (Theol. Dogm. T. vi. L. xiv. c. 2) on this subject; and this study has encouraged me to do so. History proves that hitherto the Holy See has only given dogmatic decrees to appease polemic and scandalous strifes, or to repress dangerous errors. In the present case neither of these grounds is apparent; the ground for acting would be a pure motive of piety, of devotion,—a motive very beautiful, very precious in the eyes of God and of every faithful soul,—a motive, which for certain countries and certain people might also be founded on the fruits to be looked for, but which for our country (as I have had the honour to explain to you, my Lord) is counterbalanced by greater considerations, which discover the greatest dangers to the Church in the pronouncing of such a decree. I have allayed my Episcopal conscience, my Lord, in communicating to you my thoughts and apprehensions in this matter. I have spoken to you as the organ of the sovereign Pontiff. I repeat once more, that, in what I have just set forth, I find myself of one mind with all the most zealous and enlightened Catholics in our country. Make what use of this letter you please. 'Dixi et salvavi animam meam.'"—ii. 466. 477.

27. *The Bishop of Warmia.*—"The Clergy of this diocese—entertain a singular devotion to the most glorious Virgin;—but as to her conception, many (and among them the Chapter of Warmia) have given their judgment, that in these turbulent times, ill-disposed as to ecclesiastical as well as civil matters, for the guarding against heresies and avoidance of schisms, it

is not expedient to decree any thing new in this matter by Apostolic authority, but that it is more suitable, that this faith should, until a more fitting time, be left under the terms which the holy Tridentine Synod laid down (Sess. v.), on original sin. Yet after deducting these, there is still a great number of those who have openly professed the Immaculate Conception, with the most ardent desire that this faith should be decreed and confirmed by Apostolic authority." "Among the people of the diocese of Warmia, which is, with inmost devotion, addicted to the worship of the most Holy Virgin, —the faith of the Immaculate Conception obtains universally, although there are those, who, being less instructed in the faith, under the term 'Immaculate Conception,' apprehend and believe not the origin of the Virgin herself, but the Conception of God-Man in the Virgin's womb, by the operation of the Holy Ghost. The faith in the Immaculate Conception is cherished and fed among the people of Warmia by the diligence of the parish priests, especially in sermons; and, as I am persuaded, none of the clergy, *although he hold an opposite opinion*, would venture to teach or say any thing to injure the pious faith in the Immaculate Conception among the people, or whereby that faith might be imperilled or made matter of doubt. But there are some among the people of Warmia, who fear lest, if any thing new be decreed by Apostolic authority about the Conception of the Blessed Virgin, the uninstructed people, who cannot distinguish between dogma and that which is only to be piously believed, may bring into some peril the faith as to the Immaculate Conception too, which now exists universally."

28. *The Bishop of Munster.*—"As to the longing that this opinion should now be defined by the Apostolic See as a doctrine of the Catholic Church, no wishes of this sort have reached me hitherto, except of some men whose opinion was especially sought. Nay, there are not wanting those who think that a dogmatic decision will not be without peril for these times and for Germany. Nor would I deny that, according to the character of the times, and in the provinces of our German fatherland, in which so many adherents of un-Catholic dogmas live mostly mixed with Catholics, controversies might arise on occasion of this definition, injurious to Catholicism, and perilous

to those Catholics who are less deeply acquainted with Catholic doctrine, and so are more easily moved by the objections of unbelievers and heretics."—vii. pp. cxxxviii, ix.

29. *The Bishop of Paderborn.*—"But even though I am persuaded that the dogmatic definition of the Immaculate Conception rests on a firm foundation of truth, yet about the other question, whether this our time is opportune and fitted for the emanation of the aforesaid dogmatic declaration, I can scarce remove all doubt. At least, considering the circumstances of my diocese, which is manifoldly extended amid regions altogether Protestant, and weighing especially the character of this restless time, very much inclined to dissensions and disputations, religious as well as political, it is to be feared that the adversaries of the Church would from that dogmatic definition get a handle for disputations and revilings against our holy religion; and lest to such of the faithful as are inadequately instructed in Divine things, or who cleave but lukewarmly to the Holy Mother Church, scandals should arise thence and perils of discord and alienation from the orthodox faith. When I weigh these things, and at the same time revolve that the greater part of the faithful people are already heartily devoted to the pious opinion of the Immaculate Conception of the Most Blessed Virgin Mary, and so, that there is no urgent necessity for the dogmatic declaration of the same; after having long and much weighed in my mind the bearings of this most grave matter, it seems to me most expedient, to the benefit of the Church, and to the praise of our most loving Mother Mary, if that dogmatic definition should be 'not abandoned altogether,' but deferred for a time, until more quiet and peaceful times be restored to our Germany, and until the Church shall enjoy a firmer and consolidated fruition of the liberties granted to her in these last times by kings and princes.

"This my sentence, whereto all the members of the Chapter of this Cathedral Church and other learned and good priests agree, I, explaining to your Holiness with the greatest devotion and all fitting confidence, leave the whole matter to your prudence and wisdom; and whatever you, under the inspiration of God, shall think it conducive to His honour to determine or define thereon, that I will, with readiest heart and due submission, receive as the utterance of God, will ratify and profess by word and deed throughout the diocese entrusted to my pastoral care."—iii. 181.

30. *The Bishop of Trèves.*—"I confess that, for some little time, I, with some other Ecclesiastics, hesitated whether, having regard to un-Catholics, with whom, in most dioceses in Germany, we live intermixed, an opportune time has arrived for such a solemn declaration, in that I fear therefrom new cavils and incriminations against holy Mother Church, and against the holy Apostolic See.

"But, having weighed the matter more maturely, I have laid aside all doubt, and firmly trust in the Lord, that the Conception of the Immaculate Virgin, defined as a doctrine of the Catholic Church, will contribute most exceedingly to confound the adversaries of the faith, inasmuch as it is she who alone slew all heresies in the whole world."—vii. p. clvii.

31. *The Bishop of Hildesheim.*—"1. In celebrating this [feast of the Immaculate Conception] the most Blessed Virgin is considered by the people all beautiful and without stain, so that they could not think that it would come into controversy; hence they do not desire any decision.

"2. There is scarce any hope that the devotion of the people should be increased by such decision; rather, it is to be feared lest they should marvel at such a decree in a matter certain to them, and lest the younger should by its publication be incited 'ad cogitationes minus puras.' But as to the rest, who are alien from the Catholic Church, there is danger lest it should be made a handle of assailing the cultus of the Blessed Virgin with new calumnies.

"Wherefore the greater part thought that a dogmatic decree was neither necessary, at least in these regions, nor desirable.

"As to the Clergy, their opinions differed. The greater part professes the doctrine of the Immaculate Conception of the Virgin; others consider it only a 'pious opinion,' supporting themselves by the decree of the Council of Trent. (Sess. v., of Original Sin.)

"For myself, I profess that the Immaculate Conception of the Virgin seems to me inseparable from the dignity of the Mother of God, and, on the ground of the consent of the Church at this time, certain. But whether or no its dogmatic definition is desirable, at least for our regions, and is for the good of the Church and the greater honour of the Blessed Virgin, this, for the reasons set forth above by the Clergy, and which are not to be altogether thought lightly of, I would not dare to affirm."—iii. 346.

32. *Bishop of Fulda.*—"Yet neither among the Clergy are there wanting men, who, distinguished for knowledge, full of piety towards Mother Church, have indeed the same faith as others as to the Immaculate Conception of the Virgin Mary, and who, should any thing be enacted by the Apostolic See thereon, would embrace it most humbly; yet do not advise or wish that it should be done in our turbulent times, wherein impiety rages with such impunity, and neither Church nor State enjoy peace. They regard the greater part of the faithful people, who, even without any declaration of the Church that the most Blessed Virgin enjoys this prerogative, venerate the undefiled Mother: they regard the tepid, living chiefly in cities with un-Catholics, who, not being *stable in faith,* nor *well grounded in charity* towards the most pious Virgin, if a controversy should perchance arise between them and the adversaries of the Catholic faith, may easily be worsted: they regard the countless host of enemies, to whom, as they fear, an opportune occasion and handle would be given by the doctrine decided by the judgment of the Apostolic See, of calumniating the spouse of our Lord, the Catholic Church, and of inveighing most bitterly against the undefiled Virgin, especially since, at this time, all things are disturbed in Germany, all are confused, and that ancient serpent aims at the heel more vehemently than ever. Although I do not deny that these anxieties are not to be held cheap or despised, and would not conceal them from your Holiness, yet, after having poured forth copious prayers to God the Father of Light, I cannot subscribe to their opinion, which, approaching the throne of your Holiness, I candidly confess. For the greater the number of adversaries, the more insolently they persecute the Lord Christ in His Church, the more the secular arm is shortened, the more impotent have become the kings who protect her, the more ought the Church, who has to contend with the powers of darkness, to pray for *her* aid and help, who *bruised the serpent's head,* to extol with praises and venerate with prayers her, who, praying her Son, alone slew all heresies in the whole world."—ii. 439.

33. *J. A. Paredis, Apostolic Administrator of Limburg.*—Alleged against the decision: "1. The question was too much agitated formerly without any fruit to souls. 2. Both sides have been defended by persons above all exception, nay, saints. 3. Those who denied or opposed it were as devoted to the Blessed Virgin Mary, and venerated her as much as those who defended it. 4. The question is at this time extinct altogether, at least in this country. 5. The faithful are either ignorant of, or misunderstand the question."

"But, on the other side, 1. According to the mind of the most Holy Lord, the mind of all Bishops, &c. in this matter has been sought. 2. The faithful were instructed of this, and exhorted to pour out prayer to this end. 3. The question then has in some measure revived, and if a definition do not follow, its issue is unknown. 4. For the affirmative, there are motives founded on theological reason, and on practice pretty general at this day; therefore on this side I think the contrary, and judge that a dogmatic definition may be published.

"Meanwhile, our most Holy Lord, Pope Pius IX., will judge in his prudence and infallibility, and his judgment is ours."—iii. 308.

33. *b*) *The Bishop of Spire.*—Himself desired its promulgation as an article of faith, but added, "The matter being of so great moment I cannot but observe, that there are some theologians and ecclesiastics who do not at all think that a doctrine hitherto left to the disputations of the schools should be defined by an immutable sentence, whereby free judgment on the matter should be cut off, and pertinacious spirits might be harassed and irritated."—ii. 442.

34. *Engelbert, Card. Archbishop of Malines.*—"I thought, however, that I ought to add, that in these regions (and especially in the neighbouring kingdoms of France and Holland) there are ecclesiastics, conspicuous for piety, knowledge, and prudence, who, although they acknowledge that great advantage would arise from an Apostolic decree, whereby it should be enacted, that all must believe of Divine faith, that the most Blessed Virgin was preserved from original stain, since thereby larger honour would accrue to the most Holy Deipara, and the faithful would conceive yet greater reverence towards her, and would be kindled more and more to worship

her, fear lest very great inconveniences should arise from it. They fear especially lest heretics and unbelievers, who, in journals and other writings dispersed every where, do not cease to attack the faith, should derive thence fresh ground for calumniating the Catholic Church, as though it were devising new doctrines, and paying undue cultus to the most Holy Mother of God. Whence also it might follow that many, who now seem ready to embrace the faith, might start back from their purpose. If, then, having heard the report of the most eminent Divines, Doctors, Cardinals, and other distinguished men, to whom the examination of that most grave matter has been committed, your Holiness should judge that the Immaculate Conception of the Mother of God is to be defined as a Catholic dogma, perhaps it will be better to explain the Divine tradition clearly and luminously in the Apostolic decree, that it may be plain that nothing new is enacted, but that the ancient faith of the Church is alone declared and confirmed. For thus it may be hoped that the mouth of the malicious may be stopped, or at least the defenders of the faith may more readily refute their calumnies.

"Then, seeing that in these times those who have care of souls are compelled in moral matters to interpret the laws favourably [to men's wishes], and to use great indulgence, because the faith of many is languid and charity is cold, those same men doubt whether it is expedient at this day to bring in a new obligation in a matter of doctrine, as to which not only there is no controversy, but it is extended more and more with a marvellous consent of all Catholics. For they fear lest perchance in countries in which there are theologians, who groundlessly deny the infallibility of the Roman See in defining dogmas of faith, some may arise even out of the Clergy themselves, who, out of the itch of writing which there prevails, may with rash boldness openly impugn the Apostolic decree, and so raise public scandal. These doubts and these fears I report, most Blessed Father, simply that your Holiness may clearly know the state of things, and provide by a fitting remedy for any inconveniences, if it should seem that any are to be apprehended."—pp. 447, 448.

35. *Italy. The Bishop of Adria.*—"I know that the gates of hell cannot prevail against this rock founded by Christ; yet

we must beware lest we give occasion to our enemies, that it should be assailed with new wars, which will, I am horribly afraid, be the case, if the Church after so many centuries exhibit to the faithful to be believed a new mystery, of which we find no testimony in the Scriptures or holy fathers, if we except many allegories spoken of the Eternal Wisdom.

"But what if very many faithful, who, while the world rages, persevere still in the faith? I fear lest they too suffer scandal, rather than be built up. For faith in the Immaculate Conception of the Blessed Virgin Mother is so deeply settled in their minds, that they do not allow themselves even to doubt its truth. Where is room for suspicion? The Bishops continually discourse thereon in their homilies, the Parish Priests in their catechizings, Preachers in their sermons. What, when they know by the new decree of this holy See, that that was for so many ages uncertain which they held for certain, and which was every where announced as so certain? 'If we were deceived in this,' they will say, 'perhaps we are mistaken and deceived about other mysteries of faith too,' or perhaps they will allow themselves to doubt of the truth of the same."—i. 317.

36. *The Bishop of Mondovi.*—"But whether the arguments, which they who at this day uphold this pious opinion, derived whether from Scripture or tradition and the almost universal zeal of the Church of the present time, suffice to prove that it ought to be transferred to a dogma of faith, if they be compared with what the fathers of the Councils of Florence, Lateran, and Trent, have uttered on this subject, and very chief theologians have discussed, I should fear to affirm. Nor, now that prayers have been poured out to God through the whole diocese, is it given to me to dare to do so. And I own that I am withheld by the same doubt, when I consider the fitting season of the aforesaid definition, which, since it is not of necessity to salvation, it seems to some may with greater advantage be put off to happier times of the Church. None of these difficulties, however, would perhaps arise, if it were only defined that the Church rightly promotes the cultus of the Immaculate Conception of Mary, yet so that the contrary opinion cannot be ever accounted heretical."—iii. 144.

37. *The Cardinal Bishop of Viterbo and Toscanella.*—"Two classes of the faithful are to be distinguished, the learned and

unlearned. The unlearned, speaking of the Conception of the Blessed Virgin Mary, suppose and believe *de fide* that it was most exempt from all stain, and therefore do not think it a matter liable to be disputed, and so neither to be defined by the Apostolic See; wherefore, from ignorance, they neither have, nor can have any wish about it. The learned have not all the same mind or wish. Although all now hold most firmly that the most Blessed Virgin was conceived without any stain whatever, they are not unanimous that it is necessary or convenient to define it by a dogmatic judgment of the Holy See. Some wish such decision; others think it ought not to be proceeded to, especially considering the circumstances of the times.

"For myself, I own ingenuously, that on the one side, from my observance and devotion to the most Holy Virgin, I wish that your Holiness should number the mystery of the Immaculate Conception too among the articles of faith; yet, on the other, weighing the reasons adduced by many most grave theologians, and especially by the most Eminent Cardinal Gotti, in his discourse on this controversy, exhibited to Clement XII., and recently published at Rome, I feel myself vehemently urged to judge that, in the present state of things, and especially in the coldness and infirmity of faith and religion at this day, it is more useful not to proceed further in so weighty a matter."—iii. 33, 34.

38. *The Archbishop of Urbino.*—"As to the necessity of publishing any definition, I do not think that there is any. For the Immaculate Conception of the most Blessed Virgin has no such close connexion with the other articles of faith (at least as far as I know), that, if this privilege were denied, it would follow that any of those articles should be impugned. But this being removed, I see not from what other head this real necessity should be extracted.

"Whether this definition should be held to be opportune, I confess that I still doubt. I have again and again weighed the ending of all contentions, the dissipating of doubt, maintenance of truth, greater glory of God, praise of the Virgin, hope most sweet of new benefits to the good of the Church militant, and other grounds, which seem to support such opportuneness, and I have always owned them to be most excellent. But the peril of perdition which may come to some from the definition, makes me doubt, now as ever, whether it is opportune. For although, as seems to me, it is now sounder to hold the Immaculate Conception of the most Blessed Virgin, and less sound to doubt it, and altogether folly openly to deny it, yet since, in these most unhappy times, the number of those is very great, who do not hesitate to question, or altogether to impugn, all the dogmas of the Church, yea, and the existence of God too, with the ruin of many, there seems to be a probable peril that they will the more easily impugn this doctrine too; and that thence will follow the perdition of those, who, lightly esteeming the definition of the Church, seduced by perverse discourses, will either not embrace the pious opinion, or, having embraced, will desert it, or at least be unable to lay aside their doubts. Nor does it seem difficult for the malice of the ungodly to pervert in this the understandings of the simple, since we see it done in more evident truths; and since the example of those, who, in past time, though distinguished for learning and holiness, are thought to have denied this privilege, may be very moving; and because, apart from the authority of the Church, the theological grounds do not seem to be so consequent, as to leave no room for the possibility of the contrary, nor so transparent, that at the first glance this truth should be clear to any one. Since, then, there seems to be this evident, or at least probable peril of perdition, which would be imminent to some, though perhaps few, even of those who are now counted among such as have been gained to Christ, I should not fully believe it opportune to add dogmatic certainty to this truth.

"I say this, most Holy Father, with inmost grief of heart; but the necessity of charity seems to require it of me to consult alike for the salvation of *the wise and the unwise;* and the example of the Apostolic See itself moves me thereto, which hitherto seemed to have '*been made weak to the weak, that it may gain the weak,*' wishing that those who hold the contrary should neither sin, nor be heretics."

The Archbishop of Urbino appended to this response a letter to the same effect, which he had written Nov. 10, 1847, to the Bishop of Fano, who had urged him to ask for the decree.

He used there the same topics, and quoted the maxim of Sixtus III., that treating of dogmas, "nihil addi convenit vetustati."—iii. 43—45.

39. *The Bishop of Ancona and Umana.*—"Having asked aid of God, I venture to opine that it is best to adopt that mode of defining, which should be free from all asperity, viz. by deciding directly that the Church is not deceived as to the truth of the object proposed by this cultus, whereby the immunity of the Blessed Virgin from all stain in the first moment of her Conception is celebrated; and that the Church does not err, when, according to the pious true opinion to be held by all, she proposes that the immunity of the Holy Mother of God from all fault in the first instant of her Conception should be celebrated.

"But since the sanction of this opinion necessarily involves the disapproval and proscription of the contrary, which no few eminent and learned men held determinedly, men of eminent deserts towards the Christian religion, some account ought, it seems, to be had of them, that the words of the decree should be softened, and no note be branded on the advocates of the contrary opinion; and that it should be so concluded, that the authors of the opposite opinion should be said to have expressed the contrary out of love of truth; and the more, because they were destitute of those supports which came in afterwards, and which, burning as they were with piety to Mary, would have inclined them to the opinion which now prevails."—ii. 153.

40. *The Bishop of Cervia.*—"If I turn to weigh what is the rigorous import of a solemn, and *that* a direct declaration of any dogma, as *de fide*, no slight difficulties float as clouds over my mind, and I do not in any way ascertain which opinion I ought to prefer. That saying of Vincent of Lerins must move me, received as a rule by all theologians, and constantly observed, whenever it was the question of distinguishing or defining dogmas of faith, *what was always, every where, by all, received as a dogma of faith, and has been believed till now.* Every Catholic dogma, being a fact manifest to us by Divine revelation, can neither be known or proved, save by the word of God, written or handed down; and, since God could, either expressly or implicitly, by Scripture or tradition, reveal a truth

unattainable by human intellect or reason, the Church never proposes any truth as a dogma to be received and believed by all, under pain of anathema or heresy, unless it be contained explicitly, or at least implicitly, in the Word of God, written or handed down. But some theologians contend, that this could scarcely be affirmed as to the proposed truth. For, had it been expressly or implicitly revealed in Scripture or tradition, how should older Fathers, and Doctors, Theologians, and the whole order of Dominicans, and the whole school of the Thomists, not only be ignorant of it, but venture, with all their might and vehement abundance of argument [assail it], the Supreme Pontiffs conniving, or at least not condemning as heretics those who for many ages opposed with their whole strength the Conception, 'immaculate at the first instant?' On what ground was that most wise, and, above all the Œcumenical Councils held in the Church, most learned Council of Trent, unwilling to define this truth expressly, but left it 'in its own possession' and *statu quo*, yet with that prudence and precision of words, that a grave and reverent weight should be added to establish and strengthen so pious and Catholic a truth, yet not to advance it to the sublimity of a dogma by a judgment and unalterable decree? There was a deep silence as to this truth in the first centuries; in subsequent centuries it was controverted, which would not have been, if in any of the above ways the Church had owned it as either expressly or implicitly revealed. Else we should fall into the heresy of Lutherans and un-Catholics, who, no less absurdly than impiously, tattle that the Church was obscured after the Apostolic times, the light of faith being almost extinguished, and that true dogmas were involved in the darkness of ignorance, &c.

"It must be confessed that all dogmas were not always believed in the Church with a solemn and open faith, which now, errors having been defeated, we profess with a noble and universal belief. Yet scarce did error dare to raise its venomous head, but the Church too did not keep silence: it took arms, and gained an entire triumph over the rash attempt.

"The question, which now occupies minds, does not relate to the truth of the Immaculate Conception, as is clear. For it is so supported by most solid arguments, and engraven on the minds of all, that the opposite opinion is rejected by the faithful as a manifest error. This truth, so sweet, so sublime, and to be cherished, remains unconquered, and now very near to faith; yet so, that the doubt is not lost out of sight or mind, 'whether it be dogmatically definable *de fide*, as mysteries, which are proposed to all by the Church, to be believed by an act of faith under pain of heresy.' For although all dogma is truth, yet not conversely is all truth dogma. God willed not to reveal to us all truths, as of the end of the world and the time of His Second Advent, and many others, which John confesses to be unwritten, and so many, that if they had been written, they would fill the world. Many of the most profound theologians of the first rank, whom P. Perrone mentions, have impugned its definability, chiefly on the ground that it cannot be plainly extracted either from Scripture or tradition as *de fide*. The Church, taught by the Holy Spirit, cannot deceive the faithful in teaching; but it does not frame new and impervious dogmas, but either explains or proposes to be believed what occur, as expressly or implicitly revealed. But all do not agree as to this express or implicit revelation: the divine revelation then remains as yet doubtful, or at least inevident, and consequently the foundation necessary for directly promulging a dogmatic definition fails altogether."—ii. 217—219.

41. *The Archbishop of Otranto.*—"As to my own opinion, I should think ('*I speak as one unwise*') that such a declaration is not at all necessary, both because there are not, as in past ages, any disagreements among Catholics as to this privilege of the Blessed Virgin, no enemy, no controversy in the schools; and they who once supported the opposite opinion, panegyrize this privilege in the preaching of the Word of God; and all Churches, during Mass, gladly praise God for the Immaculate Conception of the Blessed Virgin Mary, as also because the chief end of any decree or dogmatic declaration is already obtained, such a cultus throughout the world as should seem to need no new accession of piety. Yet I am constrained to confess that the grounds, whereon this privilege of the Blessed Virgin rests, are of such weight, that they ought to induce any Catholic to believe it *de fide*. In my opinion then there are all the grounds of probability to induce me to assert

that this privilege of the Immaculate Conception of the Blessed Virgin Mary may be declared as a dogma of faith.

"Yet I should think that, if the Church should judge that it should come to this declaration, out of many forms which she has at times used in defining a dogma of faith, it would be most prudent to use that, whereby the dogma of the privilege should be defined indirectly as the subject-matter, but directly the infallibility of the Church which teaches it, which formula the Tridentine Fathers at times used, Sess. xxiv. c. 7, 'If any say that the Church errs when it teaches,'" &c.—ii. 365, 366.

42. *The Archbishop of Perugia.*—"I should think that, before any definition is published, some account should be had of that difficulty which the adversaries cease not to proclaim loudly, that not without wrong would so many most wise men, who, either with the assent or at least the permission of the Church, adopted with impunity the opposite opinion, be proscribed at one blow, and punished with the note of heresy, and so, (unless your Blessedness should think of any other mode of satisfying as far as possible this specious difficulty,) the words of the decree should be so tempered for the former Theologians, that all, even the slightest, occasion of new complaints should be removed."—ii. 290.

Three weeks afterwards he united with the Archbishop of Spoleto, two other Archbishops and fifteen Bishops, in earnestly imploring the issue of the decree, on account of "the increased devotion to the Blessed Virgin which it would occasion, and the help and defence which she, so honoured and invoked under this title, would give to the whole Christian people and the Holy Roman Church." He did not, however, withdraw the above wish.—ii. 379—81.

42. *b*) *The Bishop of Santorino*—"Although most devoted to the Immaculate Conception of the most Holy Mother, they [his Chapter and Clergy] did not deem it suitable, in these calamitous times of general confusion, to decide the question of the Conception. The speaker, moreover, who stood forward in the name of the rest, said that he thought it more advisable that the question of the Immaculate Conception should continue undecided, because the devotion of the people was deeply rooted; and that to bring it to a decision and make it an article

of faith would perhaps be an obstacle in the case of attempting union with the Greek schismatics, it not being possible to prove it by clear arguments from Scripture and the Fathers, but merely by the argument of congruity. Thus far this Canon. Had he, however, said that in the case of the Protestants it would have given rise to new disputes, all very good; but as for the Greeks, I do not see either that union with them is a likely thing to happen immediately, or that they have any rights: and, besides, the Greeks believe in and celebrate the festival of the Conception of the Blessed Virgin by S. Anne, which is what the Catholics also say and believe." He himself held, as decisive, the texts "full of grace," "the power of the Highest shall overshadow thee," "*she* shall bruise thy head;" "nondum erant abyssi, et ego jam concepta eram" (Prov. viii.), "Fecit potentiam in brachio suo," and this, "ab initio creaturæ." —i. 201.

43. *The Bishop of Majorca.*—"To these most pious wishes, longings, feelings, the Bishop of Majorca, (to express at length his own mind) knowing well how much (in things which in any way appertain to faith) that criterion is to be accounted of, which is not unfitly called an instinct of piety, infused into the hearts of the faithful by inspiration of God, viz., the unanimous feeling of Pastors and faithful, or of the whole Catholic Church, especially when Holy Scripture and the holy Fathers, the chief witnesses of tradition, are either altogether silent, or speak somewhat obscurely, or do not so agree together in attesting it, that their opinion can be certainly known, nor can any certainty be arrived at, through their aid, *what* was handed down from the beginning of the Catholic Church.

"No testimony is, in truth, found in Scripture which any so clear tradition has explained, as to be equal to the passing of a dogmatic judgment and to be a stable foundation thereof, although in some one, perhaps, the meaning may perhaps lie hid, as the germ in the seed. Some Fathers seem to oppose the 'pious opinion,' especially S. Bernard and the Angelic Doctor, whose words S. Antoninus, Abp. of Florence, asserted to be twisted by the defenders of the Immaculate Conception against their intention; others, as S. Bonaventura, seem at one time to support the one opinion, at another the opposite. But it is marvellous and worthy of consideration, that the sayings of the Holy Fathers, whereby the Immaculate Conception is impugned, at least in appearance, are found to have been for the most part written or spoken, when, as Doctors and Theologians, they were discussing the doctrine of faith by the light of the Divine word, written or handed down; contrariwise, what has been wont to be adduced in behalf of the singular privilege of the Virgin, whether in plain or equivalent terms, is taken almost entirely from sermons, prayers, hymns, and praises, when they expressed the affection of the heart towards the most benignant Mother rather than the judgment of the mind, the feelings of piety rather than the opinion of the understanding. Nay, the words of certain Fathers, which seem self-contradictory, may perhaps be reconciled in this way, that some attest the obscurity of Scripture and tradition in their eyes, some explain their inmost feelings, which led the Fathers and orthodox writers from the very birth of the Church to extol the integrity of the Virgin Mother from all spot with so many distinguished and elegant praises, yet so as sometimes to enunciate explicitly the mystery of the Conception. For the vehicles of tradition cannot be said to be clear, viz., sayings of Fathers, practice of the Church, sacred liturgies, and consent or persuasion of the faithful as to so excellent a privilege, since those most clear-sighted Bernard and Aquinas, Orators of the Blessed Virgin, did not see it. There lurked in the heart, and sometimes there burst forth in flames, as it were, that divine ardour and inmost feeling whereby the whole Church was borne to extol and celebrate the dignity and excellence of the Mother of God, than which no greater can be conceived under God. The opinion as to the Immaculate Conception had its germ, was cherished, grew, through the implanted warmth of piety, seizing step by step on the sacred rites of outward worship, the universities, and the minds of the faithful. Yet not so rapidly did it pervade the minds of the learned, who, in scholastic method, especially under the guidance of Aquinas and the Master of the Sentences, evolved the testimonies of the Bible and the ancient Fathers as to original sin (among whom are Card. Caietan, Melchior Cano, and other most excellent Theologians), until silence being imposed by the supreme Pontiffs on the opposite party, and the Feast of the Conception being sanctioned, there now remains no country, city, college, or community which does not, from the inmost heart, venerate that mystery. Although then, perhaps, some are not wanting, who, sincerely using the cultus of the Immaculate Conception in heart and external practice in order to obey the Pontifical decrees, yet in the inner judgment of the mind do not assent to it as a dogma of revelation (of which number were the most illustrious P. de Herrera and Master Vincent Ferré, whose MS. elucubrations are certainly extant at Salamanca, perhaps elsewhere); yet at present there is doubtless a common feeling of the faithful, a consent of the living instruction of Pastors with their wishes; there is in the Church a wondrous conspiracy of minds who profess the privilege of Mary, to which our safest criterion of the mystery which lurked obscurely under the veil of Scripture and the folds of primitive tradition, it pleased the Holy Spirit to reserve a clearer revelation in process of time.

"The aim of all this, most Blessed Father, is, that while the Bishop of Majorca, giving his judgment, so subscribes to the truth of the Immaculate Conception, that else the Holy Spirit would seem to him to have deserted the Catholic Church, he at the same time estimates the difficulties which might arise out of the dogmatic definition, on account of the number and authority of distinguished Doctors who dissent, of the odium cast on the opposite opinion; and lastly (unless it seem otherwise to the prudence of the Supreme Pastor, led by the hand, as it were, by the Holy Spirit), the Bishop does not, on reflection, see any reason why that most safe way, trodden by the Council of Trent and your Predecessors, should be deserted, who thought good not to decide or define any thing dogmatically which had not been decided before, although Bishops, Congregations of religious, flourishing Universities, most powerful Kings and Princes who had deserved well of the Church, urged it. Of a truth, the cultus of this great mystery has so prevailed throughout the whole world, that it could hardly be carried further by a dogmatic definition, as other mysteries also of the Nativity and Assumption of the Virgin Mary, which have most solid foundation in ancient tradition, are celebrated throughout the world, without the faithful any where being anxious about their dogmatic definition, not from any carelessness about sacred things, but being content with the reverence which they entertain and manifest towards the Divine Mother.

"But, most Blessed Father, your Holiness, placed in the highest watch-tower of the Church, and approaching nearer to the light from above, by the office of the Apostolate and singular piety towards the Mother of God, will, by the Divine inspiration, understand and certainly know in what way the opinion of the Immaculate Conception ought to be confirmed, or more or less directly defined by a solemn judgment, which judgment of your Holiness, whatsoever it may be," &c.—ii. 157—160.

44. *The Bishop of Lugo.*—"But as our humble opinion also is asked, not only upon the ground of the doctrine, but also on the convenience and utility of the authoritative declaration of it, perhaps our agreement in this particular may not be so general or comprehensive. In Spain already no Academical Degrees are received in the Schools, nor is any Collation to Prebends or Ecclesiastical Benefices allowed, whether the Benefice be with or without cure of souls . . . . without the previous requirement of an oath expressly made, to defend the mystery of the Immaculate Conception. . . . . I do not therefore understand,—and some of our first-rate Theologians are of the same judgment with me,—that there is any necessity or expediency in now proceeding to the declaration, which certain persons, carried along by their tender devotion towards the most Holy Virgin, are soliciting from your Holiness: for there would be no augmentation made by this means to the devotion and unbounded confidence in the protection of the Queen of Angels; on the contrary, it would in some measure go to impair that confidence by depriving the pious opinion of its voluntary character, adopted, without being made a dogma of faith; in that it holds it as a duty to our Lady to attribute to her the gift of original purity: for we thus understand the honour, rather than that she was set free from the guilt of the children of Adam after having contracted it. Notwithstanding, it is possible that in this opinion we may deceive ourselves, as we should deceive ourselves if we believed it was a greater honour to Jesus Christ and His holy Mother to descend only from holy women, and not to reckon in this genealogy Thamar, Rahab, Ruth, and Bathsheba, the four

specially marked with dishonourable stains among the people of Judah. Wherein is seen how different the judgment of men is wont to be from the judgment of God, which we can only know by the revelation made of it in Holy Scripture and constant tradition of the old Fathers, as the Universal Church has understood and understands them.

"My opinion therefore is, most Holy Father, keeping in view these reasons which I have slightly intimated, that there is no express mention in Holy Scripture, nor in consistent Tradition, of the exclusion of the most Holy Virgin from the general mass of mankind which sinned in Adam; and that it is not expedient, even supposing that I deceive myself in the opinion which I have formed, to declare as a point of doctrine that which is only a pious persuasion. Nevertheless, if your Holiness should judge and define otherwise, I, for my part, as a faithful and obedient son of the Holy Roman Catholic Church, will submit my heart and mind to the decisions of its supreme Chief. Yet I venture to entreat your Holiness, that, supposing you decide the pious persuasion to be a point of Faith, you will condescend to adopt such modification of it as you may judge to be most suitable, that the great defender of the Church, S. Thomas Aquinas, may continue to hold the distinguished and honourable place which the Church itself on very solemn occasions has granted him."—ij. 98.

45. *The Bishop of Zamora.*—"But as regards the mode of defining, your excellent prudence and wisdom will judge what is most right, and the same as to formulas of words; and this only he [the Bishop] suppliantly desires, that no note be branded upon the supporters of the opposite judgment, who flourished before and after the aforesaid Council of Trent."—i. 415.

46. *The Bishop of Iaca.*—"I cannot dissemble, that the Church has not been wont to publish her dogmatic decisions, except when compelled by a sort of necessity, especially the impugning of heretics, and that in our days they wage no special war against the Immaculate Conception of the Virgin, which perhaps would burst out anew if a definition were asked for. But I am fully persuaded that no account is to be had of heretics in this matter, since their learned and instructed teachers have passed over in great measure into rationalism, and have

sunk in the deep, despising these and all other controversies of this sort. The same judgment is not to be passed as to Catholics, who, if in any numbers they impugned the Immaculate Conception, might cause some trouble. But since those who, in our time, do not acquiesce in 'the pious opinion,' seem to be few, I trust that they will not (out of a sort of reverence to the Doctors who hitherto thought otherwise) resist the votes of the Church every where, when weighed and solemnly pronounced by your Holiness. . . . .

"I have explained my own opinion as to this most grave controversy. But I think it not unadvisable to inform your Holiness that there are, in the very celebrated University of Salamanca, where I long taught Greek, some Doctors of Divinity, of no low rank, who, so far from holding that the Word of God written or handed down favours the pious opinion, contend determinedly that it is contrary thereto; and who hold most firmly that the definition ought to be abstained from altogether, as not at all necessary, they say, to the life of the Church, and as likely, perhaps, to occasion division and tumult. I had lately a great discussion hereon, by letter, with my master, F. P. Sanchez, a Doctor in Theology of Salamanca, of the Dominicans, whom I thought that I ought to consult, as being eminent in all sorts of learning, extremely well versed in Theology, and thoroughly acquainted with the whole history and turns of this question. Moreover he took with him two MSS. in folio from the library of the Convent of S. Stephen in Salamanca (when, the tempest raging, all the Spanish families of religious were expelled from their convents); the one, a copy of which is said to be in the Vatican, elaborated by M. Herrera, the most wise moderator of the first class of Theology at Salamanca, afterwards a Bishop: the other, elaborated by M. Ferré[1] with unwearied toil, to prove the assertion of Maracci to be false, who affirms that both Greek and Latin

[1] Narvaez (l. c. p. 56) mentions another learned Spanish writer on the same side: "A Dominican father, Vincentius de Bandelis of New Castille, who, as that most wise Pontiff, Lord Benedict XIV., says (de festo V. M., c. xv., de festo Conceptionis, n. 8), maintained the opinion contrary to the Immaculate Conception, printed and published a treatise on the subject, whose title is, 'On the singular purity and prerogative of the Conception of our Saviour Jesus Christ, on the authorities of 260 most illustrious Doctors.'"

Fathers are on the side of the pious opinion. He weighs them all one by one, cites editions, chapters, pages, and at last concludes that that saying of S. Antoninus of the defenders of the Immaculate Conception is most true, 'that they twist the sayings of the ancients against the intention of the speakers.' I own that I have not read these MSS., which, it is said, ought to be highly accounted of, nor can I give any judgment of my own about them; but I have no doubt that that saying of my master is most true, that there is nothing missing in them, which can avail to throw great light on all this question, nothing which has not been examined and weighed; so that they should be waited for, as master-works, treating the controversy thoroughly and most copiously, and as magazines, from which the adversaries may draw their arguments, both to impugn the Immaculate Conception and to throw discredit on the object of the definition. I wish then, most Blessed Father, that these two MSS. should be examined by the Theological body, with the aid of your Holiness, before any thing be decreed on this most grave question, lest we should incur that censure, 'Whoso decrees any thing, one side unheard, though he decree what is just, is himself not just.' "—i. 480.

46. *b*) *The Bishop of Santander.*—" I say, '*if it be ripe for a definition,*' because there are some here, who, although they shrink from imagining that Mary was conceived in original sin, yet think that her immunity from this stain was not revealed by God through Scripture or the tradition of the Church, but was left only to the piety and reverence of the faithful. For since there are many truths, which are not certainly to be revealed to men, except in their heavenly home, such as are, perhaps, those which maintain that S. John Baptist was ever free from any even light fault of speech, and S. Joseph, the spouse of the most pure Virgin, from any stain concerning chastity; these think that of the number of these truths is this also, which maintains the immunity of the most Blessed Mother of God from original guilt. For sought out, say those who thus think, and too far-fetched are those arguments, whereby some celebrated writers contend that they demonstrate that this pious opinion is proximately definable. Too twisted are the interpretations whereby they endeavour to draw over to their side others, who are even openly opposed

to it; so that one may now, too, say of them, what S. Antoninus said formerly of their leaders (Summ. part. v. lib. 8, c. 2), 'They twist their sayings (those of ancient and modern doctors) against the intention of the speakers.' And they say that they have found a notable instance of such forced interpretation in a celebrated dissertation on this subject, published a few years ago by a most eminent man. For in it (at least as it was published in Spanish in 1847) Melchior Cano is counted among writers who supported the pious opinion, whereas neither did he utter the words adduced in confirmation thereof in his own person, but in the person of those who impugn the authority of the Holy Fathers; nor do those words signify other than that the opinion of the immunity of the most Holy Virgin from original sin is pious and praiseworthy, which any one who estimates things fairly would in such questions, not defined by the Church, doubt not readily to confess of the opinion adverse to his own.

"So these think, more freely perchance than is meet."—i. 424, 425.

47. *The Bishop of Chiapo in Mexico.*—"Omitting what all know, that the adapted or allegorical meaning, unless inspired writers themselves have in other places so employed it, does not yield any firm argument in Theological matters, I wish to use the words of a Theologian of the first rank, and one of the chief maintainers of the Immaculate Conception of the Blessed Virgin, F. F. Suarez, who says when writing thereon, 'You must not ask for any clear passage from Scripture, where this should be asserted, for it would be rash to require this, when other privileges of the Virgin, which the Church holds for certain, do not require such testimony of Scripture.' And in respect to tradition, he says, that 'it is worthy of consideration that the ancient Fathers have said little of this privilege of the Virgin,' having said before, as to the sanctification of the Blessed Virgin in the womb, 'This truth is not expressly defined, nor handed down as of faith.' And S. Thomas, who had read the writings of the Fathers better, perhaps, than any, did not find it, I say not 'handed down as of faith,' but not in any way; else, doubtless, he would never have maintained the contrary. I am aware how many have strained with all their might to detach this most eminent

Saint therefrom; but in vain, as I think; since in so many places of his works, especially the Summa, in which, last of all and expressly, he treated this question, he taught it most openly, on account of the reverence due to the general sayings of Holy Scripture, and because there was as yet no leaning of the Church towards the pious opinion. Pétau again, another of the more eminent Theologians, and most versed in the Fathers, although he contended for the Immaculate Conception of the most Holy Virgin, did not find it clearly handed down in them. If then, as is evident, the truth of the Immaculate Conception is not found so expressed in the Holy Scriptures that it can be proposed to the people as a dogma of faith; if it is not clear in the writings of the holy Fathers that it was 'always, every where, and by all' handed down, and much more handed down as of faith, since neither was her sanctification in the womb, (which was easier,) as Suarez asserts, so handed down; since I have no qualifications which enable me to decide better than S. Thomas, or at least Pétau, what is contained in tradition thereon; since neither did the Fathers, who remained at Basle, and who left nothing untried to settle this matter, define it in this sense; and since those words, whereby the most Blessed Virgin is called 'Immaculate,' may be understood, like those in 2 Pet. iii. 12, 'Wherefore, most dearly beloved, considering these things, be diligent, that ye may be found of Him *immaculate* in peace,' not without great grief of heart, most Blessed Father, I dare not give a suffrage for the declaration of the aforesaid truth as a dogma of faith. Let, then, that most firm truth abide among all, yet with that certainty, wherewith the Assumption of the most Blessed Virgin into heaven, with body and soul at once, is believed, although it is not held as a dogma of faith. I have been not a little delayed, because a 'religious' man, who had done good service in literature, with others whom I called that I might have the more light, only on the 16th of April last, showed me a work of some magnitude, elaborated with great care, and chiefly derived from the Seraphic treasure-house, without examining which, from the desire I had of embracing a different opinion, I did not think it at all reasonable to deliver my judgment.

"Although this has not happened [that his opinion had been changed], and what I have said notwithstanding, if the

Immaculate Conception of the most Holy Virgin be defined by your Holiness, or by any successor of yours, should I not myself be departed, I will receive it with the greatest exultation, and with my whole heart, and will defend it with all my power."—T. ix., App. i. 19, 20.

48. *Vicar Apostolic of Mysore.*—"Although we are all by nature children of wrath, even although all perished in the first Adam, yet it is not repugnant either to my faith or reason to admit a marvellous and free exception as to the most Blessed Virgin in fact; nay, it seems to me in the highest degree congruous, that there should have been such an exception; whence I believe, by a faith of nature ('naturaliter credo'), that God gave such a privilege with many other gifts of His free mercy to the Blessed Virgin Mary. But because neither Holy Scripture nor ancient tradition prove sufficiently clearly that such exemption from the stain of original sin was granted to the Blessed Virgin Mary, I cannot believe it with a Divine faith. On the other side, considering that the Word of God had no repugnance to many other indignities in the life of His ancestors according to the flesh, both men and women, by parity of reason, it might have been absolutely, that He should have taken a Mother who had the stain of a fault strictly not her own, at least in the original moment [of her being]; whence my opinion, therefore, stands only in the natural sense of fittingness towards my Redeemer, and in the pious desire of glory and veneration towards His most beloved Mother.

"Fearing, lest Protestants and philosophers, objecting that such a decision, as *de fide*, is contrary to the Catholic axiom, '*quod ubique, quod semper, quod ab omnibus*,' and muttering that the Roman Church imposes mere opinions under pain of damnation, should also refuse most certain dogmas; and, moreover, not clearly seeing that the confidence of Christians as to the most pure Mary, or their fervour in the cultus of Mary, the refuge of sinners, can be increased by such a decision; especially being unwilling at t[illegible] time to impose, as *de fide*, and under pain of damnation, an opinion which was free for eighteen centuries, and which, although thoroughly examined by many most pious and most learned Pontiffs, has yet always been undecided, with the most profound submission to the future judgment of your Holiness, I can in no way desire such a definition, and am compelled by my conscience so to confess."—iii. 353.

49. *The Vicar Apostolic of Coimbatoor.*—"Although, I repeat, I have no doubt as to the Immaculate Conception of the Blessed Virgin, I cannot but fear that from the definition of that doctrine as an article of faith some evils would arise to the Church; I cannot but fear that such a definition (saving the reverence due to the many and most pious theologians who urge it) bears on its front a certain appearance of novelty, and diminishes the force and majesty of tradition, the firmness whereof will hereafter be more and more to be desired.

"Doubtless, if the Holy See shall declare the Immaculate Conception of the Blessed Virgin Mary an article of revealed faith, it will thereby define that the tradition was always such (for I think that this revelation will never be rested on Scripture alone, which seems to me yet more perilous). This will suffice for one who is firm and constant in the faith. But as to those weaker in the faith, whose weakness will always be to be indulged, the grounds of this tradition, resting on which the Church delivers the definition, are to be weighed. No easy task. Notwithstanding the pious attempts and industry of more recent theologians, must we not confess that their demonstrations, though rigorous, are not mostly easy to the conception of the faithful? But it seems to me of great moment that tradition, on other grounds most precious (which will be an anchor of safety in the storms whereby Mother Church will still be tossed), should be found clear and conspicuous to the minds of all.

"Perhaps, most Blessed Father, *I fear where no fear is.* But I own I fear the thick falsehood, which seems about to involve the human mind more and more. Aided thereby, the prince of darkness will seduce many, unless we reverence tradition most scrupulously. Let others boast the vain science of this world, and assert that the world day by day makes progress. I grieve to see mankind casting itself headlong into an inevitable gulf of darkness. The portentous abuses of printing, the venom of journals, which creeps even into uncivilized nations, corrupt the minds, and turn them from the right path: licence in writing, printing, and circulating every where all sorts of books, good or bad, on any subject, with an unworthy mixture of sacred with profane, maintaining error with a bold iron forehead; and under the appearance of sound philosophy or theology propagating false doctrine, enveloped in artfully contrived subtleties, so that the most wise laws of the Church hereon cannot be effectually maintained even in empires wholly Catholic; these things, with many other causes, seem likely to bring so great a disturbance on the intellect of men, that hereafter, more perhaps than before, Catholics, mistrusting reasoning, but cleaving to the documents of sacred tradition, will be compelled to acknowledge *that* only with the certainty of faith, '*which has been believed, every where, always, and by all.*'

"To return; notwithstanding the pious industry of more recent theologians, and their diligence in scrutinizing the works of the Fathers, and adducing every thing which, directly or indirectly, evidently or inferentially, supports our opinion, it remains difficult to prove, in my opinion, that the Immaculate Conception of the Blessed Virgin Mary was believed *always*, and especially that it was believed *every where*. But will not minds, weak in the faith, be by that difficulty put in danger of doubting not only the articles defined, but moreover tradition itself, which was the shrine of this revelation? But hence what perils are not to be feared for weak faith, to whose infirmity it is our office to be indulgent?

"So then, most Blessed Father, I should prefer that the truth of the Immaculate Conception of Mary should remain among truths which are generally admitted to be 'piously believed.'"—iii. 354, 355.

50. *The Roman Catholic Archbishop of Dublin.*—"It must be confessed, that there are some among us, (I believe, very few,) who are otherwise minded, and who think that it has not been revealed with sufficient clearness, that the Holy Virgin Mary had no ground to cry out like the other daughters of Adam, *In sin did my mother conceive me.*—[S. Bernard, Ep. 174, n. 8.] Although they most readily acknowledge that, through the foreseen merits of her future most Holy Son, He who is mighty freed her immediately from original fault, and made her full of richest graces. Now as to that, on which your

Holiness vouchsafed chiefly to inquire, whether or no it seems expedient for the advance of the glory of God, that the Holy See should declare by a dogmatical decision, that it is to be believed, *de fide*, that the most Holy Virgin never, even in the first instant of her Conception, bore the very slightest spot of sin, herein too the opinions are different. For the greater part of the priests of this diocese think that the time is come, when the doctrine of the Immaculate Conception of the most Holy Ever-Virgin Mary is known to be so universal, that it may and ought to be promulgated as an article of faith. But no contemptible part of grave, pious, and learned priests and laymen think otherwise; and although they believe undoubtingly, that the Mother of the most Holy Saviour was always free from all spot of original sin, they do not at all think it expedient, that such a doctrine, however true, should be proposed to the faithful, to be believed as of Divine faith; and that chiefly for these reasons: 1. A dogmatic decision of this matter, on which there is no dissension, would seem to them contrary to the practice of the Church, since hitherto such decisions have only been promulged at such time as heretics dared to assail sound doctrine; and they are not aware of any ground sufficiently grave for departing, in the present case, from the ancient custom, and incurring the note of novelty. 2. The Immaculate Conception of the Blessed Ever-Virgin Mary is believed peacefully almost every where, and is assailed publicly by no one; and they think it much safer for the peace of religion 'quieta non movere,' than, under no pressure of necessity, to agitate the question as to a new article of faith in the present state of minds, when men, even Catholics, both in foreign parts and in Italy itself, are, alas! too much inclined to examine, without due reverence, the limits of Ecclesiastical power. 3. They would hardly dare to hope that the devotion towards the most Blessed Virgin, which already every where is lively in the hearts of the faithful, could be much increased by the solemn decision that she was always Immaculate, since, on the one side, the Church, which is already extensively attacked, would be exposed to new assaults by embittered and ever-vigilant enemies, who would doubtless seize occasion thence of chattering, 'Lo! the Church of the Catholics has devised a new Article of faith after ages, which, as is evident, was *not believed every where, nor always, nor by all.* What new light then dawns now upon that Church, which was denied to its Council of Trent?' Such fallacies the well-instructed Catholic will easily dissipate; but they think that it is to be feared that the minds of the simple may be disturbed thereby, and their faith also perchance shaken. 4. Lastly, they fear, lest many Protestants who, as they hope, are now verging towards the Catholic Church, seeking a refuge there from their ever-varying errors, may be driven further from us on account of this new Article of faith, recently, as they will perhaps think, devised. These are some of the reasons which move those whose minds I have explained, to desire vehemently, unless the Holy Lord shall think differently, that nothing further should be done therein at present.

"Among those who thus think are the Jesuit fathers at Dublin, almost all the Professors of our national College at Maynooth, and many others, both priests and laymen, conspicuous for zeal for religion. And knowing their most pious feelings towards the Blessed Mother of God, and their desire that she should be honoured and worshipped every where with most ardent devotion, I cannot hold their opinion cheap; and therefore do not venture to advise that a dogmatic decision should go forth from the Holy See, declaring that it is to be believed, *de fide*, 'that the most Holy Virgin Mary was conceived without stain of original sin,' however certain it be that that doctrine is true."—ii. 142—144.

He subsequently joined the other Roman Catholic Archbishops and Bishops in praying the Pope to define it.—iii. 376—378.

The Archbishop of Tarragona left the question of expediency to the judgment of the Pope (ii. 126). *The Bishop of Oviedo* said, "*Perhaps* the fulness of time has come to declare this article" (ii. 229). *The Archbishop of Braga* desired it, "*if* there was no reason to fear for other realms, as in this most religious nation nothing is to be feared" (i. 126). *The Bishop of Lamego* evidently leant to think it inopportune: "Whether in the actual state of things the passing of such a decision is more opportune than it was in the time of some supreme Pontiffs of venerable memory, and of the most learned fathers of the Council of Trent, I dare not give an opinion" (iii. 73).

So, I think, did *the Cardinal Patriarch of Lisbon*: "Whether for this longed-for definition a more opportune time has now come; and those things are no longer to be feared, which were a hindrance to the Tridentine fathers, and the supreme Pontiffs; whether the present state of many nations, most turbulent and most hostile to all authority, and the impious and most insidious efforts of Protestants and of all enemies of the Catholic Church, who do not cease to censure as new dogmas what are defined in the Catholic Church, and who endeavour with their whole might to impugn the infallibility of that Church, the existence of Divine tradition, and the authority of the Apostolic See, ought to cause some delay to that longed-for and implored decree;—this, I think, to be left to thy most wise and prudent judgment."—iii. 56, 57.

Narvaez (p. 48), counting the Bishops in Communion with Rome at 748, and those who answered the Encyclical at 576, leaves 172 who did not answer, of whom, allowing for vacancies, letters not reaching, &c., many, like the Austrian Bishops, must have been silent, because they did not wish to express their dissent.

Narvaez gives, in strange contrast with 1864, this statement as to Cardinal Bona: "Alexander VII., when asked by the ambassador of Philip IV. of Spain to decide the Conception of the Blessed Virgin to be a dogma of faith, asked the wise and pious Cardinal Bona, whether he could decide the question by himself? The Cardinal answered, that 'neither the Holy See, nor the Church herself can form new articles of faith; that it can only declare what God has revealed to His Church, after having examined the matter according to the rules of the traditions transmitted by the Apostles.' The Pontiff replied, 'Can I decide what is to be believed on this matter under inspiration of the Holy Ghost?' Cardinal Bona said, 'Most Holy Father, if any thing should be revealed to you by God, this will profit yourself alone; but it will not be lawful for you, nor can you bind the faithful to adhere to your decision, as neither can you bind me.'"—pp. 91, 92.

One of the earliest fruits of the decision fell upon Spain, where the last sacraments were refused to "Father Mr. Pascual, who, until A.D. 1855, was the oracle of Salamanca, and was held by learned men a fountain of religious wisdom, gushing forth on all sides," because, "when interrogated by certain Bishops, he wrote that the Immaculate Conception of the Blessed Virgin never could come to be an article of faith, and never acknowledged the dogma, after the Lord Pope Pius IX. pronounced it a dogma of faith, and did not recant." And yet "inconsistently," Narvaez says, "the divine office was said for his soul."—p. 54.

NOTE C.

The Greek Church believes the Blessed Virgin to have been conceived in original sin.

On this subject too, we are one with the Greek Church, and it is even strange, that of all the Bishops who returned answers, one only mentioned the Greeks as likely to be kept away by this decision of the Latin Church apart, and he only, summarily to overrule the objection as of less account than if it had been the Protestants.

In regard to the belief of the Russian Church, my friend the Rev. G. Williams has furnished me with the following references. No exception is made, as though the Blessed Virgin had been exempt from the transmission of original sin to "all who are naturally engendered of the offspring of Adam."

"1. Confessio orthodoxa of 1642, 3, which has very great authority in the Church."

"The sin from our first parents is the transgression of Divine law given in Paradise to our forefather Adam, when it was said to him, 'Of the tree of knowledge of good and evil ye shall not eat; but in the day that ye eat thereof ye shall surely die.' This original (προπατορικὸν) sin passed from Adam to the whole human race, since we were all contained at that time in Adam. And thus through the one Adam sin passed to us all. Therefore we are all conceived and born with this sin, as the Holy Scripture teaches, 'By one man sin entered into the world, and death by sin; and so death passed unto all men, because in him all sinned.' This original sin can be done away by no repentance, but only by the grace of God. But it is abolished by the dispensation of our Lord Jesus Christ in the Flesh, and the shedding of His precious Blood. And this takes place through the mystery of holy Baptism; for whoso is not baptized, he is not free from sin, but is a child of wrath and of everlasting punishment, according to what is said (John iii. 5), 'Verily I say unto you, unless a man be born of water and the Spirit, he cannot enter into the kingdom of God.'"—P. iii., qu. xx., Kimmel, Libri Symb. Eccl. Orient., pp. 272, 273.

In the Acts of the Synod at Giasion, in condemning Cyril Lucar for holding that "all had been guilty of actual *mortal* sin," it professed that the teaching of the Church was that none was exempt from original sin.

"The sixth, that he includeth all human nature under sin, not only original (*as our Church confesseth*), but also under that which springeth from it, being of free choice and deadly (*προαιρετικὴν καὶ θανάσιμον*), which he calls the fruits of that, and exempting none from *this*, (the deadly sin which maketh him who doeth it condemned,) neither him who is the greatest among those born of women, nor her, the 'blessed among women,' the spotless and Ever-Virgin Mary, or certain Patriarchs or Prophets and Apostles, is condemned as alien from our faith."—§ 6. Ib. pp. 410, 411.

"The Confession of Dositheus, Patriarch of Jerusalem: 'We believe that the first man, created by God, fell in Paradise, neglecting the Divine command: he obeyed the deceitful counsel of the serpent; and that thence, by succession, flowed original sin; so that no one is born according to the flesh who does not bear this burden, and who does not feel its fruits in this present hour. *The fruits,* we say, *and burden,* not sin, such as ungodliness, blasphemy, murder, adultery, fornication, hatred, and whatever else is gendered by wicked choice, not by nature, contrary to the Divine will. For many, both of the Patriarchs and Prophets, and very many others, both under the shadow [the Law], and the truth [the Gospel], the divine forerunner (S. John Baptist), and especially the Mother of the Divine Word, the Ever-Virgin Mary, were not tempted by such and the like offences, but only [suffered] those things which the Divine righteousness assigned as punishment to men for the transgression, as the weariness of toil, afflictions, bodily weaknesses, pangs of childbirth, laborious life in our pilgrimage, and lastly, bodily death.' "—Decr. vi. pp. 432, 433.

A Russian layman, in vindicating the Greek Church on occasion of a "mandement" of the Archbishop of Paris, says remarkably:—

"This last time has seen an obligatory decree on a dogmatic question emanate from the Pontifical throne. It is then an act completely ecclesiastic in the highest sense of the word; and, as being the only one for many years, it deserves special attention. This decree announces to all Christendom, and to ages to come, that the Blessed Mother of the Saviour was exempt from all, even original sin. But the Holy Virgin, did she not undergo death, like the rest of mankind? She did. And death, is it not (as the Spirit of God said by the Apostle) the penalty of sin? (lit. the wages of sin?) It is so no longer: by a Papal decree it has become independent of sin; it has become a simple accident of nature, and all Christendom is convicted of falsehood. Or the Blessed Virgin, has she undergone death like Christ, making herself sin for others? We should have two Saviours; and Christendom would again be convicted of falsehood. Lo, how Divine mysteries manifest themselves to the Roman Communion; lo, the heritage which she bequeathed to futurity!"—Quelques Mots sur les Communions occidentales (Leipz., 1855), pp. 83, 84.

THE END.

CPSIA information can be obtained
at www.ICGtesting.com
Printed in the USA
LVHW100511130422
716029LV00002B/59

9 783752 590715